CLAUDIA RIESS

Knight Light

An Art History Mystery

First published by Level Best Books 2021

Copyright © 2021 by Claudia Riess

This novel is entirely a work of fiction. The names, characters and incidents portrayed in it are the work of the author's imagination. Any resemblance to actual persons, living or dead, events or localities is entirely coincidental.

Claudia Riess asserts the moral right to be identified as the author of this work.

First edition

ISBN: 9781947915312

Cover art by Level Best Designs

This book was professionally typeset on Reedsy.
Find out more at reedsy.com

For my parents, Chester and Marion

Praise for the Art History Mystery Series

"Real-life art history made more interesting by the endearing romance of its two main characters." — S.R. Cronin (Becoming Extraordinary)

"...admirable research, sympathy for professional women wanting a family, the plight of LGBT couples, and an overall good heart for those who still believe in love in a cynical world." — Joan Baum (Easthampton newspaper: The Independent)

"Mystery. Passion. Crime. All in one. What more could a book-lover want?" — Elizabeth Cooke (The Hotel Marcel Series)

"...a painting itself, rich with art and the artists who create masterpieces." — Jillian (Goodreads)

"Riess uses words as an artist uses a paintbrush. The words come to life." — J. Epstein, Ph.D.

"Complex and intriguing." — Kirkus Reviews

"Shifting an attack from one wing to the other is a strategy originally developed to a fine science by Alexander Alekhine. That feinting back and forth not only forced his opponents to spread their defenses thin, but also confused them as to what direction the attack was really coming from." —Robert Byrne, "He Kept Them Coming," CHESS column The New York Times, April 3, 1977

Prologue

Praia do Tamariz

Estoril, Portugal

March 24, 1946

As he strolled along the beach promenade, Alexander Alekhine felt a dull pain on his right side just below his ribs, his diseased liver reminding him of his approaching demise. Not that he needed reminding. A doctor had recently delivered the odds—"I give it one month, possibly two"—with all the concern of a jaded bookie.

He tugged at the cuffs of his worn overcoat in a gesture of defiance. As world chess champion for the past decade, he had outwitted countless opponents far cleverer than the Grim Reaper. Surely, he could forestall the inevitable endgame longer than some run-of-the-mill mortal.

It was off season here in the resort town of Estoril, where Alex had lately won a tournament, one of the few he hadn't been blackballed from. Although the sheltered beachfront wasn't bustling with tourists, a number of residents were out and about taking in the view, some stopping to refuel in one of the cafes or bars along the promenade. It depressed him that his dwindling funds could not be frittered away at one of these charming oases, and he began to regret having given in to one of his rare fits of restlessness to venture forth from the refuge of his hotel room, paid for by the grudging magnanimity of the Portuguese Chess Foundation.

A couple walking arm-in-arm skirted around him without acknowledging him, either failing to notice that they'd come close to brushing shoulders with the world champion or else purposely snubbing him. Fuming, he realized anew how imperative it was that his reputation and financial stability be reestablished as soon as possible. He thought of the letter he'd mailed to that end—how arduously he had struggled to perfect its wording!—and fretted, once again, over not yet having heard back from its recipient, by all rights a person of influence. *Maybe today*, he suddenly thought, hope rising. *Maybe a letter has been delivered today, slipped under the door and waiting for me to snatch it up!* He could almost see his name on the envelope in bold script, and he turned on his heels to head back to the hotel to live out his vision.

Winded from his effort to maintain a rapid pace, he arrived at the door to his room without an ounce of energy to spare. No sooner had he shut the door and removed his coat than he heard a double rap muted by thick wood.

"Your dinner, Dr. Alekhine!" piped a voice on the other side of the door.

"Have you been lying in wait?" Alex joked as he opened the door.

"This will calm you," the woman said, raising a hand just within his left visual field. It held a syringe, awkwardly, like a child clutching a fork handle. No insights on the meaning of life streaked through his brain, no memories of childhood, no reflections on his brilliant chess moves or on the sun breaking through the clouds. The only fragment of ordered thought he experienced as the needle pierced his neck was that tonight there would be no dinner for him.

Chapter 1

Madison Avenue at 78th Street

New York City

Present day

Erika bent to remove the last item from the laundry basket: a pair of stretchy blue and white striped pull-on pants, size 0-3 months. So tiny, yet still plenty of room for her three-week old son to grow into. She folded the pants and placed them on the lower shelf of the changing table next to the one-piece outfits and T-shirts with side snaps. She picked up the empty basket and turned to deliver it to the room's walk-in closet. "Hi!" she said, lighting up at the sight of her husband framed in the doorway. "You're home early."

Harrison set his briefcase at his feet. "First day of spring and my students of Renaissance Painting were antsy. I cut them loose." He cocked his head. "My dear Mrs. Shawn-Wheatley, how the hell do you do it?"

"You mean my labors?" she asked with a chuckle directed at the laundry basket. "I get a lot more help than I need. It's embarrassing, really."

"No, I mean how did you get back your slender figure in three weeks?"

She dropped the basket and patted her tummy, still a bit poofy but getting there. "They say it's all in the eyes of the beholder. I'm counting on it." She strutted toward him.

He folded her in his arms, and they luxuriated in full body contact. "Don't get me wrong," he said. "I did love the baby bump, but *this*—oh." He pressed her closer and their lips merged in a brief but spellbinding kiss. Then, without a word they walked in synchronized step to the beckoning white-skirted bassinet, as if the movement were choreographed.

"He's beautiful, isn't he?" Erika said, gazing in ever-renewed wonder at their sleeping son, arms flung open at his sides in total vulnerability. *Lucas*, she crooned inwardly, smiling at the origin of his name: Renaissance painter, da Lucca, whose mystery had brought her and Harrison together over two years ago. She brushed the baby's cheek with the tips of her fingers. Harrison did the same. "We won't wake him up, will we?" he asked in a near whisper.

"No, darling, I nursed him only a half hour ago. He'll be sleeping soundly for at least another hour or so. Sing away."

He sighed. "I hope I'm half as confident during *my* parental leave."

"You have fifteen more weeks to watch and learn," she reassured, wrapping her arms around his waist and gazing up at the face she would never tire of.

He held her face in his hands. "And you'll freeze enough milk for Lucas?"

"Gallons."

"By the way, where's the nanny? In her room?"

"I sent her home. If you insist, we'll have her stay twenty-four-seven when we're both back at work. Right now, staying over a night here and there is more than sufficient. Grace is doing just fine helping out."

Their housekeeper, Grace Jones, had joined the Wheatley family over fifty years ago, living with Harrison's grandparents in this very home. She'd known Harrison since his birth and her affection for him was of a highly protective nature, especially since he'd been badly mistreated by his first wife. It had taken many months for Grace to entrust Erika with her adored "Mr. Harry," but now that her guardedness had relaxed, the women were good friends.

"I love Grace, but she's almost ninety years old," Harrison objected.

"Don't be an ageist," Erika countered. "Grace is as spry as a gazelle. In fact, being around Lucas has put an extra spring to her step, if that's even possible." She snuggled him a kiss on his mouth. "I think Lucas reminds Grace of you as a baby."

"It took us long enough to find this nanny," Harrison replied, unwavering. "We don't want to lose her to greener pastures."

Indeed, it had taken countless interviews to settle on Kate Mendelsohn, a twenty-four-year-old math whiz working toward an online master's degree from Fordham University. "Kate assured me she's not going anywhere," Erika said, feeling a twinge of suspicion from out of the blue: *Why's he so worried about losing her?* "She appreciates the time off. It gives her more time to study. Besides, she adores Lucas."

Harrison rested his eyes on their sleeping angel. "Who wouldn't?" he said, losing himself in the study.

"Come," she urged, his absorption in Lucas banishing her aberrant thought. "Let's have a cup of tea, and you can tell me about your day. I crave news of the world."

"Ah yes," he said, looking up while bearing the remnants of a goofy smile. "I'd like your take on something I received today."

"I'm already intrigued."

Foregoing their plushy elevator—one mark of privilege Erika still found it hard to accept—they trotted down two flights of stairs to the second floor. Minutes later they were sitting side by side at the dining room table and catching sight of Grace darting about in the adjoining kitchen as she prepared dinner. The earlier Grace got started, the more extravagant the fare. It was only 3:00 p.m. They were in for a feast. "You want a cookie or something?" Erika asked Harrison before taking a sip of her tea.

"No, sweetie. I want to show you this." He had taken a paper from his briefcase before leaving the master bedroom. He laid it on the table. The paper was folded, concealing its contents. She reached for it. "Wait," he said, placing his hand on hers. "Let me explain."

"You have my attention, sir," she yielded, mugging the misty-eyed student. She sensed one of his professorial lectures coming on and reveled in the mischievous intimacy of role-playing, however unilaterally.

He laced his fingers through hers. "Let me tell you about the source of this document. About five years ago, there was a student in my 19th-Century European Art class, Charles—Chuck, he liked to be called—Bloom. He was a good, solid student; nothing remarkable, but lively as hell, with a quirky sense of humor. Everybody liked him. His father was an art historian, an authority on Pre-Columbian art at U Penn, and Chuck was following in his wake. One day he met me in my office to discuss his term paper. He opened his notebook, in which he was always scribbling." Harrison grinned. "I had actually thought he was recording my every word. What I saw, as he flipped through the pages to find the notes he was after, were dozens of cartoon characters—whimsical, original, full of movement and energy just like Chuck himself. Jokingly—no, half-jokingly—I suggested he should consider animation as his field. I recommended he talk to a friend of mine in administration at NYU Tisch School of the Arts."

"You gave him the green light to follow his dreams," Erika suggested, irresistibly slipping from the role of rapt student. "Am I right?"

"You are!" he said, beaming at her as if she'd discovered the unifying theory of the universe. "Within a year, his animated short film had won an entry at the Tribeca Film Festival. Now he's being courted by Pixar and Walt Disney. He calls me from time to time, so I know he's into other pursuits. No surprise, given his energy level. His wife's a real estate agent, and over the last year or so he's taken an interest in flipping houses."

"With his artistic talent, he must be great at staging homes for resale," Erika said, increasingly curious about where Chuck's back story was leading.

Harrison tapped the folded paper, a good indication he was getting there. "Anyway, while Chuck was cleaning out his recent flip, a foreclosure in Westchester County, he came across a box of archival material in a beaten-up cardboard box. Luckily, he opened it up before consigning it to the trash heap. What he found were photos, documents, letters dating from the nineteen-thirties and forties, the War World II era."

"Enough suspense. Who owned the box?"

"Maria and Carlos Martins," Harrison declared.

"Oh," Erika replied, anticipating a luminary like Eleanor Roosevelt or Dwight David Eisenhower. "Who are the Martins?"

"Carlos Martins was Brazil's ambassador to the United States from 1939 to 1948. His wife Maria Alves was an avant-garde sculptress and the painter Marcel Duchamp's mistress from 1946 to 1951."

"While married to Carlos?"

"Yes." He flashed her a bemused smile.

"Well, it might be relevant." She took another sip of her tea, wishing it was coffee.

His smile turned self-recriminatory. "Of course, you're right. And how could you know, since we might be turning gray before I get to the point?"

"True," she said, reaching for his hand. "So, what prompted Chuck to call you about his find?"

"It opens up a mystery of art confiscated during the Holocaust. He thought you and I might want to dig into it." He took her hand. "Looks like we've acquired the reputation of sleuths," he said, referring to their previous forays into the criminal world.

"Not the second career I had in mind," she said soberly, thinking of the tragedies they'd witnessed.

"But still," he said. "You put your all into it. Your aim has always been to right the wrongs in the art world."

"I sound like a Marvel comic." She slipped her hand from his and unfolded the paper. She shot him a questioning look.

"Yes, now," he said.

They read the letter in silence. Its author's name was written above the letterhead:

Alexander Alekhine, World Chess Champion
 Parque Hotel
 Esteril, Portugal

The Honorable Carlos Martins
 Brazil's Ambassador to the United States of America

Washington, D.C., U.S.A.

February 17, 1946

Dear Ambassador Martins,

Several weeks ago, at an art exhibition and in the attendance of a mutual acquaintance, I had the good fortune to meet your charming wife, Maria. In the course of conversation I felt sufficiently at ease to divulge my present circumstances, and your wife was gracious enough to suggest that I reach out to you for help.

I am aware that Your Excellency is a busy man, so I will get straight to the point. As you must know, my reputation has been sullied by rumors of my collaboration with the Nazis. This is supported by a number of articles with my byline that appeared in Der Zeitgeist, in which it is argued that the chess mentality of the Jews is inferior to that of the Aryans. I have sworn that the articles were not written by me, but my protest has, by and large, fallen on deaf ears.

For reasons to be discussed at a later date, I am in possession of information that, if revealed, will clear my name and redeem my deserved reputation in the chess world. In short, if you put me in touch with the appropriate American authorities, I will release to them the names and critical facts leading to a significant collection of art works seized by the Nazis from the Jules Eisenberg Gallery in Paris. Works by such artists as Hans Arp ("Fool's Bells") and Max Ernst ("Sigmund's Dream") are among the items in question, none of which can be traced without my input. My disclosing the name of a certain German individual who fled to your country will prove relevant.

In exchange for my cooperation, I would expect to secure a visa to the United States, funds to provide passage to that country and a reasonable stipend, to be determined, to cover living expenses for a finite period of time.

Please be assured that I am not asking you to plead my case, only that you submit my petition.

I anticipate your reply with much hope for both the restoration of lost art as well as my good name. In the interim, I remain,

Respectfully yours,

Alexander Alekhine

"This is fascinating!" Erika remarked, wide-eyed. "Was the loot ultimately recovered?"

"No, actually, it wasn't," Harrison said.

"Could the 'mutual acquaintance' Alekhine refers to at the beginning of the letter be Marcel Duchamp? Wasn't Duchamp an avid chess player?"

"Yes, and yes. In fact, they both played on the French team at the 1933 Chess Olympiad in the Netherlands. I'm betting that Duchamp is the third party out of discretion, unnamed."

"What else did Chuck find in the carton?" Erika asked, already pumped from the excitement of the chase. "Did Ambassador Martins or the Americans respond to the letter?"

"Apparently nothing in the carton answers that question, and even if Alekhine did receive a response, the fact that he was found dead in his hotel room about a month after he drafted his letter, I doubt whether he ever got to arrange a settlement with anyone in authority."

"We can look into that," Erika said, wishing she had a note pad at her elbow. "How did Alekhine die?" she asked, before lifting her cup for another sip of tea, if only to busy her hands.

"The cause of death remains controversial to this day," Harrison said. "Some say he asphyxiated on a piece of ham stuck in his throat. Others are sure he was murdered by members of the French Resistance in retaliation for his alleged collaboration with the Nazis. Still others believe the Russians killed him for the same reason. Since he was wearing a coat at the time of his death, and the arrangement on the chess board at his side was perfectly intact, the picture of a man in the throes of choking on a piece of dinner meat does not exactly fit the bill."

"Maybe there's another explanation altogether," Erika mused.

Harrison cupped his hand to his ear. "I hear it," he said.

Erika shot him a questioning glance.

"Your wheels spinning," he said, patting her head.

"Funny," she said. "I thought the sound was coming from you."

He smiled. "In concert, then."

"Is Chuck going to share his stash with us?" Erika asked, pressing on. "Let us borrow it, I mean?"

"Yes, but first he wants to publicize it in the form of a lecture and slide show. I suggested he give his presentation at the Grant Gallery," Harrison went on, referring to the West Chelsea art gallery he had purchased, virtually anonymously, last year. "After that he can put the material on display there for however many weeks the curator, Fiona Clark, sees fit. After *that*, we'll have it to ourselves."

"Great. I assume we won't have to wait until the artifacts are in our hands. We can put on our track shoes starting now."

Harrison gave her bare feet, hooked on the rung of her chair, a loving look. "Of course."

"When do you predict Chuck's presentation will be ready?"

"He's put in a request with Fiona to reserve the meeting room 6:00 to 8:00 p.m. Thursday, April ninth, three weeks from today. I hear she's given her approval. Chuck's ready to roll, but he wants some time to get the word out—to the local papers, the university bulletins, that sort of thing."

"Of course, we'll invite the usual subjects—Greg Smith and John Mitchell, for starters."

With a nod, Harrison acknowledged their friends and sleuthing allies: Greg, board member of Art Loss Register and John, Big Apple detective turned private eye. "We will not be nosing around on our own," he cautioned. "The big guns will be out in force to find this alleged cache of art works."

"I know that the art theft division of the FBI and various international organizations will be seeking restitution," Erika granted. "But does that preclude our getting involved? No way!" The prospect of digging into this project was making her hungry. "It smells delicious!" she called to Grace, whom she spied flitting from counter to stove.

Grace appeared at the door. "It's beef bourguignon," she offered, wiping her hands on the dishtowel looped onto the belt of her starched white apron.

Erika breathed in the aroma, nostrils flaring. "I knew it!"

"Give it an hour," Grace said, with a modest smile. "Make that an hour and a half."

"I'll try," Erika replied, as the scent of the chase and Grace's divine stew curled into one longing.

Harrison rested an arm around her shoulders, his eyes conveying another longing altogether. "Come on," he whispered in her ear. "We have time, don't we?"

His look was wired to her groin. She smiled, suddenly dreamy. "I don't need much time, darling." They rose in unison and headed to the third floor.

At the foot of the staircase, Jake, their aging Chocolate Lab, appeared from out of nowhere to lumber up the stairs behind them. When they arrived at the room that had recently become the couple's hideaway, Jake plopped down on his belly in the hallway, knowing by experience that this was as far as he would be allowed to go. Guarding his loved ones was not as good as cuddling with them, but it would do. He sighed and lay his head on his folded paws.

Erika closed the door behind them. This was the first room she'd slept in as a guest at the Wheatley mansion and it would always have a special spot in her heart, which is probably why this had been her first choice when they were deciding which room to convert into a nursery. It was called the Blue Room, named after the color of the dress worn by the girl in the Mary Cassatt painting that had hung above the headboard of the twin bed, newly replaced by a crib. Erika considered herself relatively free of gender hang-ups, but an impressionist painting of a young girl knitting did not seem like an appropriate fit for a boy's room. Maybe one day Lucas would demand it be put back on his wall, at which time Erika would happily oblige, but in the meantime, it would reside in the master bedroom.

The wall art had not yet been chosen, but other than that, the room was all set for its tenant, Master Lucas, who would be moving into his new digs in five months' time. Aside from the assorted baby furniture, the room contained a floor lamp in polished nickel and an inviting cream-colored convertible sofa, which neither visitor sought to open up.

Erika flung herself on her back across the cushions and opened her arms to Harrison. He kicked off his shoes and undid his belt buckle and zipper. Not quite acclimated to the fact that Erika's womb no longer harbored a living creature, he was cautious when he descended on her.

"Open my blouse," she ordered, beginning to undo the buttons on his shirt. He obeyed, lifting his torso so she could get to his lower buttons and release the shirttails. When he had finished parting the sides of her blouse, he snapped open the front closure of her nursing bra and revealed her luminous breasts. He gently stroked between them before cupping them in his hands ever so lightly. "Are they sore?" he whispered, as if his natural voice might bruise them.

"Not when you touch them," she said, closing her eyes. "Or kiss them."

He took the hint, brushing his lips across their taut surfaces, pausing everywhere.

"Help me," she said at last, writhing beneath him in an effort to tug down her sweatpants and underpants. Her body was glutted with desire. "Please. I can't bear it."

He rose to help free her legs. When he was done, she slid one leg off the edge of the couch to open herself to him as much as possible. He let his trousers fall to the floor and stepped out of them along with his jockey shorts. Looking down at her, he froze in lustful awe and knew he would remember this image forever.

As he sank onto her, he pulled apart the sides of his shirt so that when their bodies made contact there would be nothing between them.

"Hurry," she implored, her hips rising to meet him.

One thrust, then another, and she exploded in a torrent of pulsations. "Oh," he grunted, feeling her pleasure as his own, prompting his own climactic release.

"More," she pleaded, clutching his buttocks as another flurry of contractions overtook her. Breathing against him was all that was needed to stimulate yet another helpless flutter.

He was giddy with both her pleasure and—*be honest*—a tingle of boyish bravado for having caused it. "My love," he whispered with an irrepressible giggle.

"Show off," she teased in an easing of desire.

A whimper, not Harrison's, answered her.

"Good timing," Harrison declared, glancing at Lucas's chest of drawers, where one of their many strategically placed baby monitors sat. A more animated yawp answered Harrison, as if in rebuke.

"I'm coming, sweetie!" Erika called, as she wriggled out from under Harrison, who was lagging in reaction time. Lucas had begun wailing in earnest.

Erika was fully dressed and squirting a parting gob of Purell on her hands before Harrison had pulled up his pants. "Nice meeting you; call me some time!" she merrily tossed as she headed for the door.

She almost tripped over Jake as she sprang from the room. "Come, boy, come keep us company," she beckoned as she hurried down the hall to her hungry infant.

The old Lab, whose love was as boundless as the sky, needed no urging. He struggled to his feet and with a vigorous wag of his tail, trotted after his mistress like the puppy he truly was.

Chapter 2

At 5:00 p.m., an hour before Chuck Bloom was scheduled to give his presentation in the second-floor lecture room at the Owen Grant Gallery, a handful of early birds were touring the display area on the ground floor. Erika was one of them. Smitten by the work of one of the artists on display, she stood before a painting from the group: a slender figure sheathed in a white unitard who seemed to be staring back at her in puzzled curiosity. The background in muted colors depicted a dance studio that resembled a desert, vast and silent. Erika had read the leaflet accompanying the display. It described Terri Ford's work as "a collection of enigmatic and meticulously rendered portraits of gender-neutral beings sizing up the visible world."

"What do you think?" a woman's voice sounded from behind.

The assured voice of Fiona Clark, the gallery's curator, fresh out of grad school, was unmistakable. It was clear *Fiona* certainly knew what to think! She stepped alongside Erika.

"Ford's works are captivating," Erika said, smiling inwardly. It was refreshing how Fiona's delicately petite frame contrasted with her leadership skills, which were pure alpha. "I love the unbroken line of their silhouettes, the bare scalps contributing to the effect. Beyond that, I'm drawn into their thoughts without being able to capture them. You know what I mean?"

Fiona nodded vigorously. "I see them as profoundly human extra-terrestrials," she declared. "What do you make of the other artist on exhibit, the sculptor, Hans Lindermann?" She gestured toward the additional section of the spacious display area, separated by a high archway where Lindermann's creations were thoughtfully arranged, allowing for viewers to circle them with ease. "His work is reminiscent of Brancusi without being derivative. Each piece appears bent on defying gravity. Inevitably one's glance skims upward along the graceful form, overshooting the pinnacle." Fiona grinned. "Do you love them?" she asked, lighting up, revealing, at last, her underlying enthusiasm not only for the particular artist, but for the field of art in general.

"I do," Erika replied, checking the alignment of the fitted bodice of her pantsuit jacket to verify that her bra strap was not showing. It had been weeks since she'd worn anything but sweatpants and expendable shirts, and it took some getting used to. "In fact," she added, "I think you've done a remarkable job putting together all the gallery exhibits and event schedules. You're new at it, but it seems to come naturally to you."

"Thank you. I do my best."

A young man in chinos and white starched shirt approached. He was holding a lined pad. "I hate to interrupt, but may I let in someone who's not on the attendance list? It's the wife of a guy who did sign up."

"Sure, David," Fiona said. "We do have a few spare seats, and even so, we can always make room. Are you remembering to keep the door locked?"

"Oh, yes," David assured her before running off to admit the couple.

"My intern cum security guard," Fiona explained. "The gallery closes at four-thirty, so we have to check who gains entry. By the way, I didn't have a chance to thank Professor Wheatley for helping our volunteers set up the lecture room tonight. Don't let me forget!"

"I won't. He's up there now, slaving away."

Fiona blanched.

"I'm joking, Fiona. You know he loves helping out. Even if it's unfolding bridge chairs." She lay a hand on Fiona's shoulder. At twenty-eight, she was Fiona's senior by no more than four years, but she suddenly felt like her mother. Maybe because she had so recently become one.

Fiona looked relieved. "He should be impressed by our new state-of-the-art audio-video equipment. Have you seen it yet? It was given to us by an anonymous donor. A very generous one!"

"How nice," Erika replied, putting on her best poker face. The equipment had of course been donated by Harrison, whose amalgam of modesty and guilt kept him securely behind the scenes. This state of affairs had been created by his grandmother. Knowing him well and foreseeing his discomfit at becoming the beneficiary of unearned bounty, she had taken steps to prevent him from disencumbering himself of it by stipulating in her will a yearly cap on charitable giving. The clause could be challenged, but Harrison would never consider breaking his grandmother's heart, even posthumously. He did, however, make sure to disburse the charitable allowance to its limit. The art gallery itself was itself an example of this practice. He had purchased the real estate, but the deeded owner was PAPNEA (Partnership to Aid and Promote New and Emerging Artists). Harrison was on the organization's board of directors, but only two of its members were in on the details of the transaction, and he had sworn them to secrecy.

"I'm going to pop upstairs, see how things are going," Fiona said, looking at her watch. "Frankly, I was expecting Mr. Bloom to be here by now." She started for the staircase.

"Don't worry," Erika said, falling into step beside her. "I've never met Chuck, but Harrison says no matter how many projects he's got going at once, he manages to complete every one on schedule, even if by the skin of his teeth."

"Erika!" a rich baritone sounded from the gallery's entryway.

Erika recognized the voice at once. The two women turned toward it. "Come, let me introduce you," Erika said, taking Fiona's arm. "Fiona Clark, Greg Smith," she said, as the three came together. "Fiona is the gallery's curator; Greg is on the board of Art Loss Register." As the two shook hands, she added, "Greg shuttles back and forth between the organization's offices in New York and London. So glad we nabbed him on the New York hop."

Erika and Greg peremptorily kissed cheeks, European style. "Amazing space," Greg commented, looking around, his gaze terminating on Fiona's face, causing it to flush.

"That's because Fiona makes use of it so wonderfully," Erika said, delighting in the figure the twosome cut—Greg, big and burly, an art sleuth who looked more like a downhill skier and Fiona, tiny and delicate and smart as a whip. "Fiona, why don't you give Greg a tour of the exhibits? I'll run upstairs and check things out."

The couple seemed all too willing, Fiona even more so as she looped her arm in Greg's, Erika headed for the staircase, an extra spring in her step.

The lecture room held a smattering of guests that had taken over the center sections of the first and second rows of unreserved seats, directly opposite the podium and squarely facing the spectacular paneled video wall. Harrison was standing at the back of the room by a table set with light refreshments and non-alcoholic drinks. He was chatting with a woman in a pin-striped business suit and a man in a flannel shirt and jeans. He excused himself when he spotted Erika enter the room. As he approached her, he caught the glint in her eye. "Merry or smug, I can't tell which," he pondered, hamming it up with a chin stroke.

"Fiona and Greg," she said. "There may be a spark there."

Harrison ginned. "I think you need to get out more." He put his arm around her waist. "Come, let me introduce you to a couple of interesting people who've come to hear Chuck's talk. The guy is from a local chess club. The woman's deputy-head of revenue management at the office of the Consulate General of Brazil over on Sixth Avenue."

Erika raised a brow. "Did Chuck send out notifications to them?"

Harrison nodded. "I told you he was resourceful."

"By the way, the video wall is amazing," Erika said, as they proceeded to the snack table.

"Isn't it? Most important, the projector meets the highest standards in resolution and brightness." Arriving at the table, he declared, "My wife, Erika. Maria Lopez, of the Brazilian embassy; Jerry Weiss of the Manhattan Chess Club."

Jerry raised his cracker and cheese in the gesture of a toast. "Hi."

Maria and Erika were about to shake hands, when a percussive pounding came from the floor below—vibratory, like a fist striking impenetrable glass. Erika started for the staircase, Harrison jumping ahead of her. Maria and

Jerry followed in their footsteps. The seated guests turned their heads but held fast their claimed territory.

"Don't fucking stand there, let him in!" a shrill voice ordered, before the scene came into view for the foursome. "Now!" the woman detonated, as the field became visible; Fiona, the source of the command.

For an instant, Fiona's intern, David, stood frozen in place as the man outside the door fell to his knees, his fist opening against the glass as if in surrender.

David lunged at the door and unlatched it, seemingly in one movement, while Fiona raced from across the room to drop beside the man and take hold of his shoulders to prevent his head from striking the floor. David held open the door with his foot as he helped Fiona pull the man past the entry into the gallery, then let it swing shut.

The early arrivals who had been touring the exhibits stood in wait, but when there was no longer a plate of glass separating them from the action like a television screen, they moved in on it. A few whipped out their cell phones to record the event. "Did anyone call 9-1-1?" someone shouted.

"I did!" Fiona yelled back. Struggling for calmness, she braced the man against her chest and soothed, her voice cracking, "You'll be okay. Help is coming."

"Out of the way!" Harrison bellowed, almost knocking down an onlooker as he rushed to the fallen man's side, folding to his knees and gently wresting him from Fiona in order to cradle him in his arms. "Chuck, my man, what happened?" he cried, unable to disguise his alarm. His hand was on Chuck's back and he felt a sticky fluid against his palm. He noticed smears of blood on the floor, and Fiona was looking down at her hand like a startled Lady Macbeth. "Oh my God," Harrison uttered without meaning to. He rocked Chuck in his arms. "Stay back!" he seethed at the visitors drawing near.

Erika knelt behind her husband and leaned up against him, her cheek coming to rest against the back of his head. "I'm here."

"Bonnie," Chuck groaned—the first sound from him. His eyes were focusing everywhere and nowhere. "Bonnie, where's Bonnie?"

"Stay with me," Harrison pleaded to Erika as much as Chuck. "Stay awake."

He'd never met her, but he knew Bonnie was his wife's name. Where the hell was she? *Asshole, apply pressure to the wound!* He dug the heel of his palm as hard as he could against the site of the blood loss. A gun shot—*knife*—wound? He felt the blood leak past his palm and snake under his shirt cuff. "Is there a doctor—a nurse?" he cried out to the gawking bystanders. *Useless bastards!* Erika's presence was the only thing keeping him from exploding. "Who did this to you?" he asked Chuck, wincing from the effort to sound calm.

"Where's Bonnie?" Chuck repeated, barely audible, his eyes closing. He smiled, as if he'd located her elsewhere.

"She's coming, buddy," Harrison assured him without knowing if it were true. "She's coming." A wisp of hair strayed from Chuck's combed-back style and fell against an eyelid. When he opened his eyes, Harrison thought, the hair would abrade his cornea. He wanted to brush it away, but both his hands were occupied. "Erika, would you brush the hair out of his eyes?"

Curving around Harrison, Erika swept the hair back from Chuck's forehead and continued to stroke his head as if he were a child recovering from a nightmare. She worried that Chuck might be going into shock, but kept quiet about it, fearing Harrison would lose it altogether.

A cell phone rang its generic alert from the pocket of Chuck's blazer. Erika carefully reached for it. "Bonnie," she whispered to Harrison. She pressed the "accept" display and held the phone to Harrison's ear.

"Chuck, honey?" Bonnie began unprompted, loud enough for Erika to hear. "I couldn't find a spot nearby. I parked in a lot. I'm on my way. Be there in a minute...Chuck?"

Erika handed the cell to Harrison. "Hello, Bonnie," he said, feeling inescapably foolish. "This is Harrison Wheatley." The ominous ring in his voice frightened him; what must it sound like to *Bonnie*? "We've never met, but I know Chuck from—"

"Yes, I know—where is he?" Bonnie cried, as audibly as if she were on speakerphone.

A wail of sirens came into hearing range, the decibel level quickly rising.

"Bonnie," Harrison re-started. "I'm afraid there's been an accident." *An accident?*

"What do you mean, an accident? What are those sirens?"

"An *incident*," Harrison corrected himself, awkwardness mounting. "Chuck has been injured. Hurry, okay? Be careful. Don't run."

Bonnie didn't answer, but neither did she disconnect. Harrison and Erika could hear the street sounds behind her strenuous panting as she disregarded the useless warning not to run. Throughout, Chuck failed to react.

There was a clamor at the gallery entrance as a pair of Emergency Medical Technicians maneuvered through the passageway with their gurney. The wiry one was in the lead, guiding it; his cohort, a burly woman at least twice his age, was in the rear, refining its path. A bulging canvas bag hung from her right shoulder.

Harrison and Erika were expecting a barrage of questions and spoke at once in anticipation of them. "The injury is to his back," Harrison said, reluctantly giving up his protective hold on the patient. "His name is Charles Bloom." Erika pitched in, slipping Chuck's cell phone back in his pocket. "Be careful," she added, as the team wordlessly hauled Chuck onto the gurney, laying him on his side to examine his wound.

"Knife?" the young man presupposed, his teammate nodding in return, before opening up her bag to retrieve a pair of scissors to cut away the patient's bloody jacket and shirt, then gauze to bind his wound and a device to assist his breathing. "Mr. Bloom—Charles?" the female attendant said, her face right up against Chuck's as she and her fellow EMT began wheeling him to the exit. "Do you hear me? Can you open your eyes for us, Charles?"

"Chuck, call him Chuck!" Harrison scolded, following after them.

Erika grabbed Harrison's hand to accompany him. "They've got him," she said. "It's all right."

While all attention had been focused on preparing the patient for transport, two police cars had pulled up in front of the gallery. Two officers were removing crime scene tape and metal posts from the trunk of one of the cars, and another two were backing out of a huddle with John Mitchell, cop turned private detective, and friend of the Wheatleys since what Erika had dubbed their "Cuban caper." Erika guessed that John had been badgering them with questions. He was still talking at them as they turned away to head for the gurney, which was rolling toward the parked ambulance. He tagged after them, all parties converging at the receiving end of the ambulance.

Erika and John exchanged a peremptory cheek-to-cheek greeting, ludicrous under the circumstances. John gave Harrison a wide-eyed stare, and Harrison realized his jacket sleeve was soaked in blood. "Jesus, man!" John commented, before nudging up behind the EMTs to catch a glimpse of their charge as the gurney slowly rose to meet the floor of the ambulance.

"Detective Tim Riley," one of the officers announced, directing himself to John and the Wheatleys. "Is there a rear exit, do you know? We're going to be sealing off the immediate area, and I'd like to keep it as pristine as possible. I can see there are folks inside the building. After we interview them, I'd prefer they don't trample out the front door."

"There's a rear exit," Harrison said. "Fiona—the curator—has the key. She's inside."

Riley turned to the officer beside him. "Go post yourself at the door. See that no one leaves." He gave the man a paternal slap on the back as he moved off. One of the officers setting up the barrier tape was encouraging a small party of arrivals to move on. "No admissions!" Riley called to the group, backing up his colleague.

"I just got here," John informed his friends in an aside. "I know the bare essentials, but did Bloom manage to say anything to either of you?"

Harrison's face fell, and Erika was about to answer John, when a woman sprinted into view, nearly losing her balance as the toe of one of her stilettos caught a crack in the pavement. "Stop!" she cried, as the ambulance doors were being pulled shut from inside the vehicle. "My husband, is that my husband?" she demanded, throwing herself against Riley, who stood in her way. "I'm Bonnie Bloom! Let me get in!"

The doors stopped mid-arc. "Officer?" the female EMT asked, appearing at the opening.

Bonnie, wild-eyed and frazzled, but in equal measure determined, held her ground, pushing against Riley as if he were a jammed door. Riley yielded, and after giving Bonnie's driver's license a quick glance to verify her identity, hoisted her, with the helping hand of the EMT, into the compartment. Harrison pressed forward in an attempt to accompany the Blooms and was visibly crushed when Detective Riley, along with Bonnie, denied him access in no uncertain terms.

"You can go visit him on your own," Riley said, as the ambulance pulled away. "He's being taken to Mount Sinai Beth Israel at First Avenue at 16th Street." To the officer guarding the door five yards away, he directed, "Kev, start taking statements from the folks inside. They must be restless as hell. You know how to transmit smartphone images and audio to our official government email account?"

"I do, yes sir."

"You must register permission from each individual and maintain a strong chain of custody. You got that?"

The officer nodded his understanding.

"I'll be right behind you. I just have to check that the barrier is set up to specification." Addressing Erika, Harrison and John, he ordered, "Follow the sergeant inside. We're wasting time."

John led the way. Erika, threading her arm through Harrison's, drew him along. "Don't worry," she softly urged. "We'll be able to visit Chuck very soon." She wished she could slip off Harrison's bloody jacket, but knew he would not want to be distracted. She was desperate to ease his despair, but felt powerless to do so.

Stepping into the gallery was like setting foot on another planet, she thought; barely distinguishable from Earth, except here the art enthusiasts were news hounds, abuzz with morbid curiosity. Greg and Fiona, standing at opposite ends of the gathering, seemed never to have met. In reality, she supposed, the violence of the event must have ended their fragile romance, or one that she had imagined for them. She recognized two of the visitors being corralled for questioning as occupants of front and center seats in the lecture room above. She wondered if they'd left any of their belongings on the seats to reserve them, just in case. "Oh!" she suddenly remarked, loud enough for heads to snap in her direction.

"What?" Harrison and Riley asked in unison. The detective, about to take down the statement of David the intern, hopped to her side.

"Did you find a parcel of some sort?" she asked him, bewildered almost.

"What are you saying?" Riley asked curtly.

Harrison lasered him a narrow-eyed look.

"Mr. Bloom would have been carrying materials with him," Erika answered.

Harrison shot to attention. "Of course, for his presentation!" he declared. "Did you recover anything like a briefcase—or any contents that may have fallen out of it?"

Riley scribbled something in his pad. "We haven't, no, not yet," he said. "Good point," he added with some reluctance.

"Which means chances are, whoever attacked Bloom was after that item," John offered. "If he needed to eliminate Bloom, he would have been more efficient about it. Off the top of my head, he meant to disable him and make his getaway with no one on his tail."

Riley shook his head; hard to determine if out of respect or chagrin. "I'll consider that," he said. He flipped a page in his pad. "Now, let's get back to business." He turned to Erika. With pen poised: "Your name, ma'am?"

Riley was at the point of jotting down Erika's cell phone number, when one of the officers who had been stationed outside the building burst through the entrance. "Sir!" he called as he approached on a run. "We just got a radio alert!"

"What is it?" Riley asked with pointed composure, as the officer skidded up alongside him.

"A witness to the stabbing," the officer began. "He called central station. Saw it happen and was freaked out. He thought the assailant might have seen him, so—"

"He took off," Riley finished. "Did he describe the guy?"

"Average height, wearing a jogging suit, hood covering his head." The officer shrugged. "His, her. He couldn't say for sure. May have been a female."

"Hard to put out an APB with that description," Riley scoffed. He waved off his annoyance. "No problem. I take it Central's got a complete ID on the caller. There'll be a follow-up. How's it going out there?"

"Good—I mean nothing unusual, sir."

Riley sent the flustered officer back to his post and got on with his questioning of Erika; then on to Harrison and John and whatever individuals were not being interrogated by his subordinate, "Kev."

The debriefing took over an hour, after which the exhausted and over-stimulated participants were ushered out the rear exit of the building by Curator Fiona, who had turned officious by the end of the proceedings.

Harrison bolted out of the door like a freed hostage. The original plan had been that the Wheatleys' driver, Bill, would pick them up at the end of the evening's event. They were supposed to text him fifteen, twenty minutes ahead of time. Given the circumstances, neither had thought to contact him.

"Wait!" Erika called, running after Harrison as he headed for the front of the building and to the street. She tried to snag her cell phone from the tote bag bouncing on her hip, but caught up with Harrison at the curb before she was able to retrieve it.

Harrison jumped off the curb, waving for a cab not yet in sight. "Shit" he cried into the void.

Erika ran up beside him. "Let's go to the next block," she urged, giving up the idea of calling Bill. "It's more of a main thoroughfare." She grabbed his arm and pressed him forward. He offered no resistance, and together they hightailed it to the busier street, where Harrison finally broke away from her to throw himself into the middle of it to hail a cab. Erika scurried after him, tossing her arms about like a traffic cop to ward off disaster.

A cab, its roof light a beacon of hope, pulled up alongside them. Harrison threw open the rear door. "Mount Sinai, First Avenue at 16th Street!" he ordered as Erika hopped past him to slide across the beat-up leather seat.

"Hold up!" a voice shouted from behind as Harrison shoved up beside Erika, at the same time grabbing the inner door handle.

Erika craned her neck to see. "It's John!" she cried. "Wait!"

Harrison slammed shut the door. "No time!"

The driver inched forward, unclear about whose directive to follow. A horn sounded. He picked up speed.

John, catching up to the vehicle, yanked on the door handle. The driver slowed down to near zero miles an hour.

"Unlock the door!" Erika demanded. She heard the click of the lock being released.

In quick succession, John leapt in beside Harrison, pulled shut the door, and the cab shot forward like the last helicopter leaving a war zone.

"So glad I spotted you!" John exhaled, settling in. "Where are we going?"

* * *

Harrison hovered over the Intensive Care Unit's reception desk. "Tell me exactly what's happening!"

The nurse, a no-nonsense matron, refused to be nettled. "I told you the patient's condition is critical and he is in surgery. I have no additional information at this time. Again, please have a seat in the waiting room."

Reluctantly, Harrison submitted, and he, Erika and John proceeded to the designated area, where they set themselves down in sculpted plastic chairs, Harrison between his two escorts. They were the only ones in the room.

John patted Harrison's knee. "You looked like hell back there at the gallery and I didn't want you two to be alone—*wherever* the hell you were headed."

"Thanks," Harrison muttered. "Go grab a cup of coffee or something. I'm sorry to have dragged you into this."

"You didn't drag me anywhere, but that's an idea: anyone want anything? Coffee? A sandwich?" His offer was declined. "Okay, just say the word." He leaned back in his chair.

They had been sitting alone and in silence for no more than ten minutes, when a plaintive cry rose from a place hard to pinpoint—a corridor, a room. Harrison jumped to his feet, as if the cry had been directed at him. He made a dash for the reception desk, his companions following at his heels. "Was that Mrs. Bloom?" he called out, on the run.

The nurse waited for the group to arrive at the desk before responding.

"Sir, please keep your voice down. I know you're anxious and upset, but we don't want to disturb the patients."

"Did I just hear Mrs. Bloom's cry out?" Harrison rephrased in a voice just above a whisper.

The nurse swallowed hard. "I'm afraid so, yes." Erika thought she seemed genuinely upset. Harrison heard only the words. "Unfortunately, her husband has just passed."

Harrison cringed at the euphemism. "He's *dead?*" he asked, knees buckling at the sound of it. He clung to Erika. *Don't fucking move*, he inwardly pleaded.

She didn't, not an inch.

"Why couldn't you save him?" Harrison asked. Simple as a child's question: why do we die?

"Mr. Bloom suffered a stab wound to the upper torso. There was a massive amount of internal bleeding. He succumbed on the operating table. I'm sorry." Harrison's hand was resting on the countertop. She squeezed it and withdrew. "You were a close friend, I think."

"A *friend*," Erika answered for him, as if putting the relationship into perspective would reduce the keenness of his grief.

Harrison was not attending to nuance. "I want to see his wife."

"I can appreciate that," the nurse said, looking down at her hands, "but Mrs. Bloom does not want to see anyone right now, outside the doctors and hospital staff. I think you can understand."

He understood. He did not accept.

* * *

Lucas lay asleep in his bassinet, sedated by his mother's milk. Harrison, showered and in fresh clothes, sat motionless at the edge of the bed. He had watched Erika nurse the baby in their private universe: the rocking chair. He usually felt like he belonged in their world. Tonight he felt excluded from it, unworthy.

Erika stood by the bassinet, watching Lucas sleep and basking in the serenity it inspired, even while knowing Harrison was in despair. The bond she felt with Lucas was overwhelming. In a moment she would turn to the man she had grown accustomed to adoring, but first she must submit to this newer love.

"Erika," Harrison pronounced.

It sounded declarative, but Erika knew it was an entreaty. "Yes, darling," she said, turning away from Lucas before she'd had her fill of him. She sat beside Harrison on the bed. "Please stop blaming yourself. You must know it's unreasonable."

"Because I'm a reasonable man?" he quipped.

"Yes, exactly." She remembered how unequivocally she had blamed herself for the miscarriage she had suffered the year before, and how determinedly he had rebutted her flawed arguments. She wanted to remind him of this, but she could not bring herself to say the words in Lucas's presence, however illogical.

Harrison covered his face in his hands. "I told Chuck to give his talk at the gallery. Even further back—I encouraged him to pursue his interest in animation. He changed the course of his life because of me."

"No." She stroked the back of his neck. "Remember? You agreed with me when I said he switched out of Art History in order to follow his dreams?"

"How romantic. The truth is he changed plans because he looked up to me. He wanted to please me."

"There's an equally cogent argument he was rebelling against his father in order to set his own path." *What are we doing?* She fluttered her hand as if to shoo off their exchange; start over. "This is crazy. You might as well blame the cat Chuck tripped over at the age of two for the glitch in time that altered all that followed. What happened today is nobody's fault but the killer's!" She heard the rise in her voice; panicked that she'd awaken Lucas. "Let's go down and get a glass of wine or something." She rose from the bed.

"Bonnie blames me."

She sank back down beside him. "Bonnie wanted to be by herself." She took his hands from his face and held them. She wished she could make his distress go away as easily as she could Lucas's. "Come on, let's go get a glass of wine."

He shook his head.

"For me, then."

"Okay, but only if we're alone. Do you know if Kate and Grace are lurking about?"

She shook her head. "I saw them go off to their rooms a while ago. Kate said she was planning to study for an exam and Grace was going to watch a movie on Netflix." The women each had a bedroom suite on the second floor. Kate's had once been the butler's quarters, although never referred to as such by Harrison's grandparents, who had been, in Harrison's words, "conflicted liberals." Grace's slightly larger suite was down the hall from Kate's. It had always been known as "Grace Place," according to Harrison. "I'll double check if you want me to."

He rose to his feet. "No, it's okay, I trust we'll be alone."

Jake, their loving appendage and exception to the rule, appeared out of nowhere to accompany them downstairs.

When they arrived at the dining room, Erika ordered Harrison to take a seat. He obeyed, and Jake planted himself at his feet. Erika retrieved a bottle of red wine, a corkscrew and two stemmed glasses from the credenza and placed them on the table. To Harrison's head-shake, she said, "You may change your mind." She continued on to the kitchen.

It was 9:30 p.m. and neither of them had eaten in over eight hours. Erika opened the refrigerator. "There's tuna salad and egg salad," she announced. How routine it sounded. Could she spirit him into normalcy? "Which do you want?"

"Neither," he answered. "But you have something."

She pulled open the freezer door. "Let's see what else we've got. How about we nuke a couple of chicken dinners?"

"Honey, please!"

Despite his protests, she piled a tray with salads, breads, utensils, plates and napkins and carried it into the dining room. "You may change your mind." She lay the tray on the table within his reach and sat down beside him.

He stared hard at her, tears welling up.

She froze. "What?"

"Don't ever leave me."

She threw her arms around him. "Where did *that* come from?" She realized where before she uttered the words: "I'm not going anywhere. Ever."

The tacit, although impossible, reassurance that she would never die soothed him, enough for him to acknowledge his hunger and even take the edge off it with a couple of forkfuls of tuna salad. He let her persuade him to take a few sips of the red wine, too, and the miniscule dose had the effect of a binge—or so he thought.

He was bending in his seat to stroke Jake, whose head was resting on his bare left foot, when his cell phone rang. He dug it from the pocket of his sweatpants, but only as he swiped to connect with the caller did he notice the word BONNIE on the top of the screen. His heart stopped like a sprinter poised at the starting block, only to race ahead at the sound of the gunshot—her voice: "Harrison?"

Erika saw his face go pale. She stiffened. *"Who?"*

He activated the speakerphone. "Yes, Bonnie," he said, trying so hard to be even-toned he sounded like a pastor. "Are you all right? We wanted to stay with you, but the nurse said you wanted to be alone. What can we do?"

"I'm home now," Bonnie said, a tremor in her voice. "There was nothing I could do. They kept me away from him. They're going to perform an autopsy. I had no say in the matter."

"I wish we had stayed with you. Are you with a relative—a friend?"

"The police just left," she said abruptly. "I shot my mouth off. I shouldn't have."

"Why do you say that?"

"Because I was pushed. Because I wasn't thinking."

Erika wanted to speak, but as a stranger she was afraid her words would be taken as pointless tongue-clucking.

Harrison sat forward. "What can we do, Bonnie?"

Silence.

"Anything," he encouraged.

Bonnie made a quiet throat-clearing sound. "I don't really know you, but

I feel as though I do. Chuck thought very highly of you as his professor, and then, more recently, of you and your wife—as a team, I mean." After another hesitation: "I know it would be an imposition, but…" Her voice drifted off.

"Would you like us to come see you now?" Erika asked.

Harrison, beaming with relief, grabbed Erika's hand as if he'd never let go.

"I would, yes, oh yes," Bonnie said, her voice breaking. "You'll need directions and—oh God, thank you!"

* * *

Bill pulled up in front of the Blooms' apartment building, a modern high-rise on the Upper West Side that basked in the aura of Lincoln Center. He turned to make eye contact. "Text when you're ready to be picked up, whatever the hour."

Erika felt a delayed pang of separation as she slid from the back seat of the limo after Harrison. It was the first time she was out of hearing range of Lucas's cries. Sure, she had aroused Kate from her studies to review every telephone number and instruction that might be required in any imaginable circumstance, but had she confused Kate with too much information?

"Lucas will be okay," Harrison reassured, taking her hand as she stepped onto the pavement.

"Am I that transparent?"

"Only to me." He kissed her hand. "Thanks for coming. You didn't have to."

"Yes, I did." She leaned into him, their brush with intimacy easing the tension of their walk to the building's entrance.

The concierge, properly somber for the occasion, called Bonnie on the intercom to announce the Wheatleys' presence in the lobby. "Mrs. Bloom will see you," he informed them, with a touch of camaraderie. "Twenty-eighth floor." He shook his head slowly, connoting their mutual sadness. "Apartment B."

Bonnie was waiting for them at her open door. She'd changed into a pair of black jeans, sweatshirt, and sneakers. Her urban up-do was still in place or had been redone and her lips were bright orange. The only giveaways were her red-rimmed eyes and swollen lids. "Come in," she whispered hoarsely, suddenly frantic, glancing about as if someone was about to spring at them from out of nowhere.

"I'm sorry," she said, closing the door behind them. "I'm all nerves. Everything is suddenly—*different!*" She closed her eyes, then opened them, as if expecting the world to have changed back. "I don't know how to behave. Shall I offer you coffee and cake?"

"Maybe later, if it'll make you feel better," Erika said, putting her hand on Bonnie's shoulder. "Now let's just sit and talk."

"We were broken into," Bonnie said flatly.

"What?" Harrison asked, uttering his first word.

The apartment, generically modern, its character enhanced by Chuck's mounted artwork, looked totally undisturbed. Not an item out of place. Had something about today's tragic event awakened a memory from the couple's past? Erika wondered.

"We were broken into," Bonnie repeated. "It had to have been between the time we left for the gallery and the time I returned home."

Harrison took in the living room with a sweep of his hand. "I don't understand."

Bonnie emitted a fragment of a laugh. "No, I didn't clean up the mess in record time. There was no mess. The lock was picked and our computers were taken along with the material that was in the carton Chuck had turned up. End of story. The carton was sitting alongside Chuck's desk in plain sight. Please, sit down." She gestured toward the sleek black leather sofa, then settled into its matching chair, only to jump up as her guests took their assigned places. "Can't I offer you...?"

"Really, no," Harrison said, removing the throw pillow jamming his back and propping it against the arm rest. "We only want to keep you company; hear what you want to say." He lay his hand on Erika's knee, making a point of including her.

Bonnie sat back down and folded her hands in her lap. Not like a schoolgirl, Erika thought, but like she was holding herself together, fingers entwined so tightly, her knuckles were white. "I called the detective who was at the gallery and later showed up at the hospital. I was sure the break-in, like the assault, was related to the material Chuck had found." She looked down at the knot that lay in her lap as if she wasn't sure where it had come from.

"Didn't Detective Riley agree with you?" Erika gently prodded.

Bonnie shook her head before looking up. "He had an agenda of his own. By the time he and his crew left, it was a done deal, thanks to me."

Harrison frowned. "What do you mean?"

"They found Chuck's cell phone."

"I put the phone back in his pocket after your call," Erika confirmed.

"Yes. Well, they hacked into it and found a nasty exchange of texts between Chuck and Gary Kessler. From two days ago, in fact." Bonnie hammered her welded fists against her thigh. "They asked me a lot of questions about their relationship, and I gave them a lot more than they bargained for. Gary can be a hostile son-of-a-bitch, but he's not a killer."

Erika waited for her to go on. Harrison did not. "Who's Gary Kessler?" he asked. "A fellow artist?"

Bonnie flinched, as if he'd hurled an insult at her. "Not at all. Gary's a veteran in the world of house-flipping. He hates Chuck because Chuck trespassed on what he considers his territory. A couple of months ago Chuck sweet-talked a deal in Westchester County right out from under him and ended up making a profit of half a million on the flip. The contract was signed only a week ago."

"Is that what the exchange of texts was all about?" Harrison pressed on.

Bonnie closed her eyes, as if to keep from seeing what she was about to reveal. "Yes, that's what it was all about." Her nostrils flared. "But I took it one step further. I told Riley that there was another issue of contention between the two men. I told him Gary had accused Chuck of having an affair with his wife, Jodie." Her eyes popped open like a doll's.

The question blared in the silence: *Was* he?

Bonnie blinked and her eyes came back to life. "I didn't leave it there. I told Riley that at a party last month, Gary lost it when he caught Chuck and Jodie talking and laughing off in a corner. He accused them of inappropriate touching. He'd had too much to drink. He was aggressive. He asked them why they had to flaunt their affair in public, couldn't they have kept it behind closed doors. I tried to calm him down. He called me a naïve bitch and came at Chuck. He had to be forcibly pulled off, but not before landing a punch. It was mortifying."

The unspoken question remained unanswered.

Bonnie unlocked her hands and lay them palms down on her knees. "When Riley started bombarding me with questions about the texts, I felt more and more resentful toward Gary. How could he have been so jealous of Chuck's success? So vengeful? I thought of how he had assaulted Chuck at the party, and I became more furious still. I described the event in detail. I may have elaborated on it, I don't know. I was not myself."

Erika wondered if Bonnie's anger with Gary had been a stand-in for her anger with Chuck. Had she muddled Chuck's ultimate act of abandonment with his possible unfaithfulness, a lesser act of desertion, but more dreaded—for Bonnie herself: annihilating? For whatever reason, Bonnie was clearly feeling guilty about her damning characterization.

"I feel an awful bitterness," Bonnie said, trespassing Erika's thoughts. "For myself, mostly. I don't understand it."

"What's to understand?" Erika gently posed. "In the state you're in, your emotions must be all over the place."

Bonnie's features relaxed, as if she'd just been acquitted of a crime. "I suppose that's true."

Harrison was fixated on Chuck's murder; on Bonnie's state of mind only as it applied to solving it. "Given the tidy state of the apartment," he said rather forcefully, "I don't see how Riley could have pinned the break-in on a man presumably in a state of rage. Not to mention his going after the contents of a beat-up carton. Why would Kessler be interested in this particular heap of documents at the exclusion of all others? How did Riley square *that* circle?"

Bonnie was noticeably taken aback by the pitch of Harrison's delivery. She rallied. "As far as Riley's concerned, there's no circle to square. He believes the break-in had nothing to do with the assault. He said that lately there's been an uptick—that's the word he used—in the number of such occurrences in the neighborhood, where electronic devices are the only objects of interest."

"Then how does Riley explain the culprit's interest in a pile of old papers?" Harrison persisted.

"He doesn't believe they were stolen. He believes Chuck moved them somewhere without feeling obliged to notify me, or he stuffed them into his briefcase before we drove to the gallery. It doesn't matter what I said. His mind was made up." Bonnie's eyes suddenly filled with tears.

Thrust into a good cop, bad cop routine of Harrison's making, Erika reached across the seating divide to take hold of Bonnie's hand. "It's okay," she soothed. *Say something nice!* she silently bade him.

Harrison needed no cue to realize his aggressive approach had been taken personally. "I'm sorry, Bonnie, the last thing you need is for me to be sounding off in your face." He shook his head slowly. "I just want them to get it right. I want them to be *smart*."

Bonnie slipped her hand from Erika's and sat up straight. "I know, Harrison. And in fact, that's what I admire about you. Both of you. Your passion, your fervor. I'm the one who should apologize."

Harrison frowned. "Whatever for?"

"For being soft. For wanting sympathy." She looked directly at Erika. "I don't want to be coddled, my dear. I don't want to be considered at all, in fact. It's inefficient."

Bonnie appeared to have made a complete turnaround. Through sheer willpower, Erika suspected. The abrupt shift in demeanor made her appear sterner, more matronly. It suddenly struck Erika that Bonnie was Chuck's senior by at least ten years. Curious, not for the fact, but for the delayed observation.

"Will you help me?" Bonnie asked. "I realize that's a broad question. You can interpret it any way you like."

Harrison took the lead. "I think we all agree that whoever attacked your husband was after the documents he had unearthed—either to learn their secrets or to keep them from being revealed. Our primary resource is a letter

Chuck found in the carton. It's dated February 17, 1946, and was written by chess master Alexander Alekhine and addressed to Carlos Martins, Brazil's Ambassador to the United States. Chuck faxed me a copy of the letter, so whoever stole your laptops won't find evidence of that transmission. Moreover, although he made it known to the public that he was in possession of a letter from Alekhine to Martins concerning looted art, he made a point of telling me that I was the only person with whom he shared the actual letter."

Bonnie hinted at a smile. "That includes me—which should give you added assurance he meant what he said."

Erika was anxious to see where Harrison was going with this. She hoped not to risk-taking.

Harrison spotted her tentativeness and made a go at putting her at her ease. "The chess player's letter would be our jumping off point," he said, as if he was talking about a turn on the trampoline. "It contains a number of very specific references. Tackling them can have an impact in the search and recovery of stolen art."

Research that expanded the horizons of the art world was irresistible. In this case there was an added moral imperative. Erika was hooked. With qualifications. "We have a new baby," she said. "We can't be putting ourselves in harm's way."

Bonnie threw up her hands, the gesture unconvincingly histrionic. "God forbid!" she declared. "What I believe is that you have the passion, the curiosity and not least of all, the creativity, to track down people and events of interest. Your vantage point will be academic—that is, remote. It will be up to officers of the law to confront individuals of interest head-on. At your recommendation, not presence!"

Erika sensed that Bonnie was on a mission; empathy, not on her list of priorities.

"We can take care of ourselves, Bonnie." Harrison briskly affirmed.

Erika sighed. What irony. Usually it was Harrison who was more risk-averse than she. Guilt was the determining factor, she figured.

"Erika?" Bonnie queried with burrowing gaze.

"Sure. I agree with Harrison." She felt a frisson of fear as an image of her sleeping son swept into focus and held fast. She turned to Harrison. "I think we should text Bill and tell him to come get us." To Bonnie, as a tactful afterthought: "We should leave you in peace. This has been very demanding on you." She dove for her cell phone.

Bonnie rose to her feet. "Can't I persuade you to stay for a cup of coffee or tea?"

Erika was texting Bill. Harrison answered for both of them. "Another time, Bonnie. Erika's right. You need to get some rest."

"I don't want to rest. I need to do something. Give me something to do."

Harrison nodded his understanding. "Well, for a start, do you know the provenance of that critical carton of documents?"

"No. The owner of the house was eager to make a quick sale and wanted to leave the property basically as is. Chuck offered to clean out the place after the closing, and the owner removed only those belongings he valued. The carton was not among them."

"I see. Do you happen to know how old the house is?"

"I took a look at it before Chuck put down a deposit, and I can tell you from some of the hand-crafted details, like the way the outer bricks of the fireplace were cut at an angle, that it dates back to at least the mid-1850's."

Erika rose to leave. Harrison rose in compliance. "Interesting," he said to Bonnie. "Do you think you can come up with a list of previous owners, along with as much personal data as is available?"

"Yes, although I can't promise you there won't be gaps. There are many sources—a town's property tax records, historical societies, area maps, genealogical internet sites. I know where to go."

"You might want to keep in mind that an owner vacating the house before 1946, the date of the chess master's letter, could not have had anything to do with the carton that ended up in the attic."

Erika picked up her bag from the floor and hooked the strap on her shoulder. "What about renters?" she asked. "Shouldn't they be taken into account?" To offset her abruptness, she moved toward Bonnie for a parting embrace.

"Of course!" Harrison declared. "Bonnie, would it be too much to ask if you could check for any rentals on record?"

"I'll do what I can." She opened her arms to Erika. They held each other briefly, but with a sisterly warmth that blossomed between them as they touched, taking Erika, with Lucas presently dominating her thoughts, quite by surprise.

* * *

"Bonnie kept it together pretty well," Harrison commented later, as they sat in bed; he, hugging Erika's side, Lucas at her breast, she, exquisitely whole again.

"So did you," she said.

"I found a cause. It distracts me."

"We'll begin tomorrow. I'll think about it while you're in class. I'll make a list—an agenda."

"I owe it to Chuck."

"There are no debts. You're just a good man." She stroked the top of Lucas's head. "He's something, isn't he?"

His gaze encompassed them both. "Yes."

Chapter 3

Mid-afternoon Harrison was back from his lecture class on Baroque painting. He found Erika holed up in her third-floor study, absorbed in whatever she was scribbling in her notepad. He pulled out the chair from what had once been his grandmother's vanity and sat beside her. Displayed on the computer screen was a series of lines structured like a poem; at a glance, unintelligible. He planted a kiss on her cheek. "What the hell is it?"

She put down her pen and turned to him. "It's a translated excerpt from Jean Arp's poem *'Der Vogel Selbdritt.'*"

"That explains why it's inscrutable. It's Dada. Why is it of interest to you?"

"To us," she corrected. "I've been trying to get a handle on our proposed investigation. Let me start from the beginning."

"Will Lucas be joining us?"

"Not for a while. He's sleeping."

"He does a lot of that."

She smiled and flipped back the pages of her pad. "First question: What's the main subject of interest—the MacGuffin, so to speak? Answer: Alekhine's letter. Why? Because Alekhine died under murky circumstances shortly after he wrote it. Because it contains leads to recovering art lost during the war, which is of great interest on all fronts honorable and evil. Because it's the only document Chuck conveyed to you, so he must have thought it was the most important one of the collection. And last, because it's the only tangible item we've got." She took a breath. "Next. Who would benefit from getting their hands on this letter, either to gain information from it or to make sure the information remains hidden? We have to exclude anyone with honorable intentions, since violence was employed to secure the document. The agency of evil comes from the dark side of the art world. From blackmail to black market." She stared hard at him. "We can voice our suspicions, but we cannot actually *go* there. You do understand, right?"

Harrison nodded. "I do."

"I'm not convinced."

"I will never put you at risk."

She shook her head. "You left yourself out of the equation. Not good enough."

It will have to be, sweetheart. "We will both stay safe," he said aloud. "Behind the line of scrimmage. Go on with your report."

"Just so you know, I don't quite believe you. But for now, let's not lose our train of thought. So. What are the lines of inquiry generated by Alekhine's letter to Ambassador Martins? One. Learn anything we can about the fate of the Jules Eisenberg Gallery in Paris. This includes its owners, their living relatives, if any, and its wartime art inventory. Two. Try to trace the provenance of the paintings specified in the letter. Three. Contact organizations that might help identify the German referred to in the letter—the one who Alekhine says fled to Brazil." She skewered him with another look. "The operative word here is *identify*. We identify. The guys in bullet-proof vests *track down*."

"Got it."

"Do you?" She glanced down at her notes to check if she'd missed anything. She hadn't. "Anyway, the hope is that down the road these lines of inquiry will intersect, and we'll be able to contribute a couple of leads to pass on to the authorities."

"Who are fixated on another line of reasoning altogether," Harrison reminded her.

"We'll have enough evidence to convince them otherwise."

"You're an optimist."

"Realistic, not wide-eyed."

"And it's contagious," he said, laying his hand on hers. "Now, tell me why you've got Jean Arp's poetry on display."

"I thought I'd get a head start. First thing, I Googled the Jules Eisenberg Gallery in Paris. This led to a notice giving the address of the establishment with the word 'closed' in capital letters and the year, 1940. I'm sure there's a French bureau we can contact for more information. Next, I looked up the two paintings identified in Alekhine's letter: Max Ernst's *Sigmund's Dream* and Jean Arp's *Fools' Bells*. No mention anywhere of either. However, my search turned up the poem you see on the screen. See line four, where 'black eggs and fools' bells fall from the trees'?"

Harrison scanned it. "Ah, yes. Interesting you found no reference to the painting whose title is derived from the poem. You think it's possible that these particular works by Ernst and Arp never made it to auction, or for that matter, to any legitimate sale?"

Erika nodded. "Which is why I emailed Greg Smith. Not only does he have access to the Art Loss Registry database, but as a board member, he can connect to the databases of the world's major auction houses. Plus he had information on successful black market stings, both past and on the horizon."

"He hasn't gotten back to you yet, has he?"

"No. He predicts two to three days—longer, if he runs into a roadblock." At Harrison's crestfallen look, she added, "Be patient. We'll get there."

"Can't help it," he said. "I'm getting impatient as hell. The case gets colder with every passing minute."

She turned her hand palm up under his and interlaced her fingers with his. "What do you want to do?"

He shrugged. "I don't know. Go to Paris."

She sat back. "And what? Scour the city for centenarians who remember the Eisenberg Gallery and what became of it?"

"It's a start. What was its address?"

She thumbed through her notes. "Number 110 rue La Boetie. I checked it out. It's in the eighth administrative district, or arrondissement."

Harrison gave a nod of recognition. "Right off the Champs-Élysées. I can scout out the area, talk to the locals, maybe run into someone who maybe didn't *know* Jules Eisenberg, but knows *of* him. Or who can direct me to someone who does."

"What are the odds?"

"Six degrees of separation. Not unsurmountable." He smiled at her eye-roll. "Besides, I can kill two birds with one stone."

She guessed where this was going. "Your research," she said, referring to the monograph on Eugene Delacroix he was working on for Phaidon Press, as part of the publisher's series on painters of the Romantic Era.

"Right. The Louvre did the first-ever comprehensive retrospective of Delacroix in 2018, and I'd like to meet with the curator who put it together."

"The exhibit was on loan to the Metropolitan Museum in 2019," Erika replied, knowing he'd have a comeback.

"I'd like to hear any substantive or anecdotal stories associated with the show straight from the horse's mouth." He waited a beat. "I may even stop by Gericault's tomb at the Père Lachaise Cemetery while I'm in Paris."

"To pay homage?" Erika good-naturedly teased. For a scholarly work, Harrison's study of Theodore Gericault, published the year before by Princeton University Press, continued to engender a surprising amount of interest from the general public, mostly due to Harrison's lively commentary on the transformation of art, politics and mores from the Industrial Revolution to the Romantic Era.

Harrison smiled, getting it. "But seriously," he said, turning deadly so, "I want to go—*must* go—to Paris to investigate the Jules Eisenberg Gallery." His nostrils flared. "The details of its *pillage*," he fairly spat.

His ferocity unnerved her. "I'm worried you'll venture down dark alleys, chasing after clues. I should go with you, see that you don't."

"The 8th arrondissement is a posh part of town," he said. "No dark alleys."

"Not even figurative?" She winced at her forced cleverness.

"Not even those," he said.

"Still, I should go. I mean, I want to go, but I can't leave Lucas. Not yet. Not across an ocean."

Harrison breathed a sigh of relief—*figurative;* any other and she would have observed his equivocation. "Of course you can't. I knew that." His nosing around Paris was pretty much going to be a scattershot affair. He didn't know where it would take him, and he was planning to let it take him anywhere. He did not want to be hampered by what was far and away his main concern: Erika's well-being. "I'll only be gone a few days," he said. "Not long enough to get into trouble."

Erika's raised brow said it all.

The generic ring from Harrison's pants pocket saved him from further evasiveness. He retrieved his cell phone and glanced at the caller ID. "Bonnie," he announced, before swiping to connect. "How are you, Bonnie?" he greeted, sounding overly solicitous to his own ears. He tapped on the speakerphone.

"Leaden," Bonnie said.

He and Erika waited a beat for her to say more.

"Understandable," Erika encouraged.

"I haven't done anything about the flipped house," Bonnie said. "Tracing its provenance and all that."

Erika looked at Harrison and gave a sad shrug. "It's the second day, Bonnie. You shouldn't be doing anything but taking care of yourself." *What did* that *mean? Getting a manicure? Going to the spa?* "Dumb," she mouthed to herself.

"I was pumped yesterday," Bonnie said. "I guess from adrenaline. Chuck's body will be released to me tomorrow and I have to make arrangements with a funeral home and a cemetery. I have to see his parents. I feel overwhelmed—no, numb."

"Do you want us to help in some way?" Harrison asked, the question itself exaggerating his helplessness.

"No, Harrison, but thank you."

"Paris?" Erika mouthed to Harrison.

He shook his head, reluctant to divulge his plans to Bonnie. He wanted no interference, direct or indirect. From anyone.

"Oh, and another thing," Bonnie said, with unconvincing off-handedness. "I found Chuck's second"—she cleared her throat—"*auxiliary* cell phone. It was in a pocket of his Windbreaker. Not that I was looking for it."

"Did you find anything on it that would help in the investigation?" Erika asked coolly, detouring any hints of impropriety.

"I don't know the password. I called Detective Riley. He came and picked it up. I seem to remember the real estate agency Chuck was associated with issuing him a work-related phone. I'm sure there's nothing of interest on it, but to be on the safe side…"

"Good idea," Harrison commented too airily, when it was apparent Bonnie's sentence would remain unfinished. "You never know."

"No stone left unturned," Bonnie said, hitching her cliché to his. "I'm glad I called you. I feel a bit more…awake."

Erika and Harrison overlapped words of thanks, and the three agreed to talk soon, or whenever Bonnie felt the need.

"What do you think?" Erika asked after the call ended.

Harrison responded to her narrow-eyed look. "I think we should reserve judgment until the phone's been analyzed. Although I'm not going to pass judgment on him, *whatever* the results."

Erika felt the stirrings of old insecurities. "Are you being macho defensive?"

He stared at her in disbelief. "Erika!"

She tapped her forehead. "A hormonal glitch," she half-joked. She needed a hug, badly.

Reading her, he obliged. "Do you know how much?"

She could read him, too. "As much as I love you," she said.

The moment was in danger of turning maudlin. A call from the baby monitor stopped it cold. "Mrs. Wheatley—Erika?"

Such a smart woman, why couldn't Kate remember Erika had asked to be addressed by her first name? There was barely a five-year gap between them, for God's sake. She clicked on the monitor's talk-back feature. "Yes, Kate?"

"I just looked in on Lucas and he's wide awake. Not a peep out of him. Do you want to come nurse him here or shall I bring him to you?"

"I'll come."

"He's got a diaper-full. Give me a minute to change him—or would you like to?"

Harrison leaned in to speak, although with their top-of-the-line monitor he would have been heard from across a ballroom. "I'll do it. I need to practice my skills before I'm on full-time paternity watch."

"I'll be right with you," Erika informed Kate. "I'm just going to shut down my computer. See that Doctor Wheatley doesn't mess up," she added, her divergent use of the surname not escaping her notice.

* * *

The door to the master bedroom was wide open, yet seeing the tableau of nanny and infant locked in a look he read as mutual devotion, Harrison felt obliged to rap on the door before disturbing the scene.

Kate was standing in profile, cradling Lucas in her arms. She had on a form-fitting tank top and tights, and her mop of flaxen hair was reined into a high pony tail. When she broke gaze with Lucas to look toward Harrison, her expression bore the remnants of affection. "Ready, Daddy?" she asked, looping him into their orbit.

"Absolutely," he said, striding toward them.

As Kate handed Lucas to him, Harrison was moved by the tenderness of her movements, the glimmer of regret in her relinquishment. Unlike Kate, he held Lucas at arm's length, wary of the soiled diaper. Carrying him to the changing table—the infant surprisingly unperturbed by the awkward means of transport—it suddenly occurred to Harrison that a woman like Kate would make an agreeable match for his son. Beautiful, intelligent, caring, what more could a father wish for? It was not until Lucas had been placed on the changing table and began wriggling in protest did Harrison realize the hilarious prematurity of the notion, along with his own libidinous detachment from it. Equally amusing.

He could not help but grin as he un-Velcroed Lucas's diaper. Kate, meanwhile, rushed to his side to hand him a baby wipe from the shelf under the table. "Let me do it," he said, as their hands brushed against each other's at the wipe's retrieval. Kate whisked away her hand, with a smile inadequately masking unease.

What was she thinking? That he was about to make an Arnold Schwarzenegger move on her? Think again. He admired her body the way he admired Renoir's *Bather*. Skin deep. He wiped down Lucas's bottom and deposited the soiled items into the bin designed for that purpose. With one hand on Lucas's belly to stabilize him, he reached with the other for a fresh diaper on the lowest shelf of the changing table. Kate stood right next to him, her hands poised above Lucas like a priest about to deliver a benediction, in case she had to come to the infant's rescue.

Erika stepped into the room. "How's it going?" she asked evenly, not quite as impressed by the tableau before her as Harrison had been of his.

"Going great," Kate answered. On such a fair complexion, even the tiniest blush was visible. "Your husband's doing just fine," she said, stepping away from her charge, considering the critical stage of Mission Diaper had passed.

"When expectations are low, every minor advance is a major victory," Harrison said, struggling with the diaper alignment.

"Let me help you," Erika said, coming near.

"He doesn't want to be helped," Kate said with a little laugh. "Take it from me."

Take it from you? Erika sniped within. "You're right," she said, straining to be her better self.

"There we are!" Harrison declared, as he stuck closed the second pair of diaper flaps. "A little awry, but good as new."

Lucas, who had been intermittently releasing grunted complaints, suddenly launched a full-throated protest.

Kate started for the bedroom door. "You'll want your privacy," she said. "I'll be in my room studying. Call me whenever, okay?" Without asking, she knew to shut the door on her way out.

Erika lifted Lucas from the changing table and immediately his cries became anticipatory. She sat down in the rocking chair and raised her shirt, then snapped open one of the panels of her nursing bra and held Lucas to her breast. "Kate's a wonder, isn't she?" she tested.

Harrison assumed the question was rhetorical and didn't respond to it.

Besides, looking at her prompted a response to a thought he had had earlier, about certain forms of admiration being only skin deep. He approached the rocking chair and dropped to one knee before her.

She was nonplussed. "Are you going to propose again?"

He didn't answer that question either. He slid his hands along her outer thighs, stopping when he reached her hips. He held her there, just like that, saying nothing for a moment, just looking. "To the bone," he said finally.

She knew it was a declaration of love, but it seemed to have come from out of the blue. No matter. Its sincerity put her needling questions to rest.

* * *

Harrison might have lingered in the bedroom with them, mesmerized by Lucas's tiny fingers fanned against Erika's breast, as well as her loving gaze focused on their son, but billowing out to include him, too, just because he wished it to be so. But another part of him, where guilt festers, convinced him he would be disrespecting Chuck's memory by indulging himself.

And so he tore himself away from the reverie and headed for his study on the first floor, where the task at hand, or rather his commitment to it, breached the surface the instant he caught sight of his computer.

First thing he did was check his calendar for the approaching week's appointments: a meeting with a student about mentoring her senior thesis; a curriculum review scheduled by the department head; a working lunch with an editor from Phaidon Press. He shot off apologetic emails to all three and made a beeline to the computer's homepage, where he punched in preferred flight dates. He figured he'd book a three-day trip. If it looked like he needed to extend his stay, he'd edit his plans.

Air France offered a non-stop flight from JFK to Charles de Gaulle (CDG) Airport leaving 9:55 p.m. the coming Monday and arriving seven and a half hours later, Tuesday, 11:20 a.m., Paris time. He selected a return flight leaving CDG early Friday morning and booked the round trip without a second thought. Next, he made a quick survey of available accommodations in and around the 8th arrondissement and decided on a small apartment at the Rodin Inn on rue La Boetie, steps away from the premises of what had once been the Jules Eisenberg Gallery. From the photos on its site, the living quarters looked quite comfortable, elegant even, and the accompanying notes indicated that each unit came with a refrigerator, oven and microwave, which meant that he wouldn't have to dine out every evening and feel that he was on vacation without Erika. There was only one unit at the venue available for the time span he selected, and he booked it on the spot before it was grabbed out from under him by one of the many tourists he imagined were at his heels.

Once he had nailed down his basic itinerary, he set out on a course of online research, first to learn as much as he could about Alekhine—family, friends, pastimes—and then to broaden his knowledge of the German occupation of Paris, from the events that led to it, to its aftermath. One link led to another. An article on the Vichy Regime cited a reference to the *Kunstschutz,* the Nazi "art preservation" mission, a cover for the systematic plunder of art. This awakened his interest in the "ratlines," escape routes for the Nazi war criminals. A brief summary caused him to dig deeper into their origins, rooted in pre-WWII Vatican-Argentine relations. The site-surfing continued. Time passed. His shoulders stiffened. He leaned back in his chair to take a breather. Jake, who had been lounging under the desk, suddenly stirred, as if he sensed Harrison's availability, and pawed at his calf. Harrison reached down to rub the old dog's back. Jake rolled over: Belly, please.

Jake's desire for affection was insatiable, but the dog knew there were limits to its fulfillment. When Harrison's stroking began to peter out, Jake rolled over and resumed his customary position of repose.

Harrison reawakened his email. Having had occasion to communicate with various personnel at the Louvre in the past, he was able to tap on the administration's general email without having to look it up. He was in the middle of framing a request to meet with the curator of the Delacroix retrospective, when there was light rap on the door followed by Erika's entrance.

"I thought you'd be packed by now," she opened, with forced levity, concealing her twinge of abandonment.

"Not 'til Monday, my love."

The endearment boosting her morale, she asked, "Then you can join me for dinner?"

He looked at his watch. Seven forty-five; later than he thought. "I should finish an email to the Delacroix curator, and before I forget, get off a one-liner to Phaidon, reminding them to add my insert to the Acknowledgments section. Can you give me a couple of minutes to wrap up?"

"Sure. Kate and Grace have already eaten, and Grace has left the Crock Pot on warm for us."

"Let me guess. Texas chili?"

"Good guess. You have five minutes before I dig in. Shall I take Jake out for a quick pee?"

Jake popped up at the suggestion.

"I take that as a 'yes,'" Erika said, as the old pup trotted to her side. She looked back at Harrison as they exited the room. "Five minutes," she warned with mock severity. "Not a second more."

Chapter 4

Harrison's jet touched down on the Charles de Gaulle runway in terminal 2 at noon, forty minutes later than the time listed on the published itinerary. Passengers with connecting flights were beside themselves, considering the complicated routes they had to navigate to get to their departure gates. There were three terminals at the airport. Terminal 2 alone had seven sub-terminals to maneuver. The directionally challenged were in for a punishing experience.

On one hand, the airport was an architectural marvel, futuristically domed with a seemingly impossible expanse of steel-girded glass. On the other, a puzzling maze of walkways and conveyer belts containing two basic categories of travelers: old hands plowing confidently to their endpoints and those—the majority—intermittently freezing in place like deer in the headlights.

Harrison, without being an old hand, was one step ahead of most. With only a carry-on in tow, he was able to skip the bi-level race to Baggage Claim and head straight to Customs, thus beating the crowds.

After breezing through Customs, he proceeded to the Public Arrival Area. Two days prior, he had booked a driver through the airport's Private Transfer Service, and he hoped to locate him or her before the area become congested. He scanned the area. There, by one of the airport's many information kiosks, he spotted a tall, dark-skinned gentleman wearing a maroon turban and carrying a sign that read, in slender lower case letters, "h. wheatley." He waved to the man, who acknowledged him with a peremptory nod, as if the exchange was either intimidating or beneath him. The latter, Harrison concluded, as he approached the man and the proud bearing became more apparent. For all he knew, the gentleman had been a nuclear scientist before his luck had run out in whatever troubled country he had fled from.

"Hi, I'm Harrison Wheatley," Harrison said collegially, hoping to bridge whatever cultural or ideological gap separated them. He extended his hand.

"Khalid Nadim," the driver said, taking the proffered hand and giving it a vigorous pump, as if he were unjamming a lever. "I'm parked in the lot, not far from here." He reached for the handle of the carry-on. "Please follow me."

* * *

According to travel websites, the fifteen-or-so-mile drive from the airport to the center of Paris should take about forty-five minutes, but due to either the time of day or blind luck, the trip on the A5 motorway took no more than a half hour. Harrison's watch, re-set to Paris time the moment he was seated on the plane, read 1:07 as Khalid pulled up in front of the Rodin Inn on rue La Boetie.

The gentleman standing behind the reception desk stiffened at Harrison's approach, as if to brace himself for a stressful encounter. "You must be Professor Wheatley," he said, his tight-lipped smile straining to be genial, his eyes registering something closer to fear.

The man must be at least in his sixties. Was this his first day on the job? "Yes, I'm Harrison Wheatley. Thank you for speaking English. May I have a word with the manager?"

"I am the manager, sir. Louis Corsair." He extended his hand as if someone had dared him to pet a crocodile. "Welcome to Paris."

Harrison shook the reluctantly offered hand. "You need to see my credit card?"

Louis did indeed. In fact, he wanted to examine Harrison's driver's license as well. "Routine procedure," he said, placing the license and card beneath the lid of the copying machine on the wall-shelf behind him. When the printed copy emerged, he turned over the items and repeated the process. "Here you are," he said, his voice rising to jittery falsetto.

Harrison reached for the items, restraining himself from snapping them out of Louis's grasp.

Discharged from further engagement with Louis, Harrison was about to be ushered to his suite by the manager's assistant, Justine, a wide-eyed young woman who spoke only French. He turned to follow her, but suddenly felt the impulse to glance back at Louis, as if he might catch him cheating on an exam like one of his students. Louis was punching in a number on his mobile phone. When his eyes met Harrison's, his hand froze. *Don't go imagining things*, Harrison warned himself, not quite convincingly.

The disquiet followed him up to his suite, and well into its tour, when he decided he'd had enough. "*Merci*, Justine," he said, cutting short her instructions on how to use the microwave. "*Tout est bien.*" It was work following her mile-a-minute speech. Although he'd become relatively fluent in the language years ago, during a semester interning at Kent University's School of Arts and Culture in Paris, his speaking ability had always lagged behind his facility with the written word, namely scholarly works on French painters of the Romantic Era.

He gestured toward the main door, stopping himself from taking hold of Justine's elbow and actively propelling her there. After she took the hint and hurried off, blushing from ear to ear, Harrison reached into his jacket pocket for his cell phone.

He punched Erika's number. She answered after one ring. Her voice sounded like it was coming from a foot away. "You've arrived," she said. "How was the trip?"

The sound of her voice instantly downgraded his disquiet. "Uneventful. I miss you already."

"I bet. Have you checked in?"

"Just now, yes." He heard Lucas's coo. "I hear Lucas."

"He's had his *petit dejeuner*. He's happy. So, I looked up the weather conditions in Paris. Seventy-eight degrees and balmy. What a day to stroll the Champs-Elysee Élysées, you lucky *chien*."

"I'm on a totally different vibe," he said. "The rue La Boetie is right off the Champs- Élysées, which did nothing for me this time around. It's a wide street, that's it. I haven't even opened the blinds."

"I see," she said. "You're on a mission."

"Yes."

"Possessed."

"Truly."

"I'm holding you up, then."

Did he detect resentment in her voice? He wished he could see her. "Not at all, Erika. I wish the hell you were here. Why didn't we FaceTime? Let's do it later tonight."

"You can tell me what you've accomplished."

"That's what I want to do. How late can I call?"

"One a.m., two? Anytime."

It killed him to break the connection with her. On the other hand, it killed him to be languishing in the damn suite.

* * *

He left the unpacking for later; who cared if his suit retained its wrinkles? He peed, grabbed a notepad and a ballpoint and headed to the street.

Erika was right. The weather was indeed "balmy." The elegant rue La Boetie was bustling with natives and tourists exploring the range of gustatory and visual pleasures, from aromatic *boulangeries* to trend-setting *maisons de couture*. In contrast to Harrison's single-minded focus—finding the connection between the murder of a friend and the looting of art in the time of the Holocaust—the lively city scene appeared to be an exhibition of vanity and denial. Even the diversity of its milling crowd—multi-ethnic, multi-lingual—taunted the souls ripped from their homes and places of business on this very street; their forgotten footprints trampled beneath the flashy Jimmy Choos and Michael Jordans. And wasn't he himself, most days, part of the terminally unaware? It made his blood boil.

He strode past a series of upscale storefronts—an *esthetique*, a *charcuterie*,

50

a *pharmacie*—before coming upon a high-fashion boutique, *Chez Aristede,* displaying the number he was after: 110, address of the defunct Jules Eisenberg Gallery. A melodic tinkle—mockery of a mournful knell—sounded as he pulled open the brass-framed door.

"*Bonjour, monsieur!*" chimed a voice, equally tuneful, coming from the rear of the shop and just preceding its source: a willowy gentleman in his late thirties or, judging from his collagen-sculpted features, aspiring to be so. "*Puis-je vous aider?*"

"*Je suis un Americain,*" Harrison began. "*Un professeur d'universite.*" The man's accent seemed as forced as his own, but to promote the guy's feeling of leadership, he thought he'd let him decide whether or not to suggest the language switch. "*Plus precisement,* New York University." *Feel free to break in anytime*, he telepathed.

"Would you feel more comfortable in English?"

"How did you guess?"

"I don't know, something in the air," the man replied, garnishing his wit with a grand hand flourish. "By the by, my name is Francois de la Louvre."

Harrison's brow shot up before he had a chance to stop it.

"One adapts," Francois confessed, with a naughty grin. "How can I help you? I take it you're not here to recruit students for whatever it is you teach."

Harrison laughed. "Hardly. And it's art history—my field, that is. Which is what brings me here. I'm working on a magazine piece on the history of art galleries in Paris."

"Its rise and fall?"

"We'll see. Hopefully not so dire. To get to the point, your boutique—"

"Not mine, dear boy."

"Well, yes, I understand." Francois was looking fidgety, switching his weight from one patent-leathered foot to another; so why was he drawing out the process? "Nevertheless, you may be able to answer a question or two, or you can direct me to the proprietor himself."

"*Her*self."

"Oh, sorry. You see, this site is where the Jules Eisenberg art gallery once stood. All I'm asking for is any information you may have on its closure—who bought the property, what became of its contents, and, for that matter, Monsieur Eisenberg and his family."

Francois shook his head. "All you're asking, you say? That's quite a request! But seriously, I myself can't help you. All I know is the boutique is one of the site's multiple iterations. I've been the manager since it opened four years ago. It replaced a yoga gym."

"That's of some help," Harrison exaggerated. He reached into his pocket for one of the business cards he'd brought along for just such an occasion. "Let me give you my card in case something else comes to mind." He handed the card to Francois. "Or you can pass it on to the owner. In fact, perhaps you can give me her card?"

"Of course." Francois stepped over to a shelved display cabinet. From a small easel sitting on the unit's glass countertop, he peeled off a business card and sauntered back to Harrison. The card was shell pink and embossed with lower-case black print. He was about to hand it over. "One moment. I'll give you her personal mobile number. Let me fetch a pen."

"Here, I have one." Harrison grabbed his ballpoint from the breast pocket of his blazer.

Francois scribbled a number on the card and passed it and the pen to Harrison.

"Celeste Marin," Harrison noted on examination.

"Lovely woman."

Harrison returned the pen to his pocket, along with the card. "With lovely taste, apparently," he said, his comment sincere and politically motivated in equal measure. Each of the sleek bronze mannequins strategically placed around the room was clad in a monochromatic garment, simple, but meticulously designed to flatter the female figure. On one, a fitted suit in cobalt blue; on another, a long-sleeved shimmery gray gown with a plunging V-neck. "I think my wife would like this designer a lot."

"Excellent," Francois said, with mounting enthusiasm. "Aristede is a rising star. How would you characterize your wife's style?"

In rapid sequence Harrison pictured Erika in sweat pants and T-shirt, then in black strapless cocktail dress. "Casual elegance," he said, straddling both worlds.

"A jeans and stilettos girl," Francois said. "I love her already. Is there anything here that would capture her fancy?"

Harrison was by no means a conniving individual, but a critical situation may demand a modicum of guile. A purchase would keep him in Francois's and Celeste's sights. He surveyed the options, his attention coming to rest on a mannequin donned in a black silk jumpsuit with halter top and palazzo pant legs. "That jumpsuit. Does it come in size eight?"

Credit card sale and shipment arrangements were made on the spot. As Harrison was signing the merchant's copy of his receipt, an additional tie to the establishment came to mind. "Let me give you our email address," he said. "That way you can notify us of new arrivals." In his effort to prompt Francois and Celeste to want to please him, that is, to supply him with information about the Jules Eisenberg gallery, even if they had to dig for it, Harrison was, he discovered, shameless.

He was about to exit the shop to begin his catch-as-catch-can fact-gathering tour of art galleries in the neighborhood, when Francois called out to him, "Wait! There's someone who might be able to help you."

What? Was his ploy working already? Harrison spun on his heels. "Yes?" he asked eagerly.

"Madame Denise Fontaine is her name," Francois divulged, beaming with self-importance, "but people refer to her as Madame D. She's well into her nineties and, according to Celeste, a virtual Wikipedia of local lore. I don't know her personally, but I hear she's a bit of an eccentric." He flicked the lapel of his mauve silk jacket. "Aren't we all?"

Harrison flashed the smile of assent he presumed was expected of him. "Where can I find this woman?"

"She owns a shop, *Rouge Tatuage*, on rue de Ponthieu," Francois said, waving toward his left. "Just around the corner, mid-block. She keeps pretty much to herself, which adds to the allure."

Harrison, edging toward the door, was about to respond when the melodic door chime sounded, and a woman dressed to the nines stepped into the shop, providing the perfect excuse for him to opt for a polite but succinct leave-taking.

* * *

Walking at a moderate pace, he arrived in front of the *Rouge Tatuage* less than two minutes later. The shop, like its neighbors, made up the ground level of a six-story residential building. In contrast to the building's stark white stone façade, the shop-fronts were as varied as a patchwork quilt, the *Rouge Tatuage* one of the more colorful. One glance at the contents of its window case confirmed his provisional translation of the word *"tatuage."* Madame Denise Fontaine was the proprietor of a tattoo parlor. The case displayed a number of tasteful photographs of various limbs and torsos inked with images ranging from interlocking hearts to detailed portraiture. The photographs were framed in antiqued gold and either mounted on easels or propped against one of the vases of fresh flowers that adorned the space.

When he entered the shop, Harrison's untested stereotype of a tattoo parlor was instantly shattered. Covering the buff-painted walls were framed photographs similar, but larger than the ones showcased. Not only was the artistic quality of the photographs up to museum standards, but the exhibition itself seemed to have been mounted by a museum curator, or a layperson who'd missed his calling.

A sleek wood table desk stood at the near side of the parquet-tiled room. A dark-haired young woman with a colorful headband and a rose tattoo on the apple of her cheek sat at the desk. She was in the process of setting up an appointment with a couple dressed in business clothes—another departure from Harrison's stereotype—who were deciding between early-morning *jeudi* or mid-afternoon *samedi.* He waited at a distance for them to make up their minds. From beyond the closed red curtain at the far side of the room floated the muffled voices of what he assumed were patrons and their tattooists—*taloueuses, tatiueurs?*—discussing the works in progress or passing the time of day.

As the couple at the reception desk were pocketing a sampling of leaflets lined up on the tabletop, the receptionist addressed Harrison. *"Desole de vous avait attentre. Etes-vous ici pour un rendez-vous?"*

In French Harrison assured her that waiting had been no problem and that no, he wasn't here for an appointment, not scheduled, at any rate. He handed her his card. "I'm an art history professor, and I'm here to have a word with Madame D, if she's available."

The couple, on their way to the door, unabashedly turned to check him out.

The receptionist sat up straight, her features registering mild alarm. *"Un instant s'il vous plait,"* she said. She picked up the phone at her elbow and punched in a button, which Harrison hoped connected her to Madame D and not a security guard. To the respondent, thankfully the Madame herself, she reported Harrison's request for *"une visite"* and reeled off the information on his business card. She nodded as she listened to the reply. *"Oui Madame,"* she acknowledged. She held the phone away from her ear and asked Harrison for the reason for his requested meeting.

He gave her the same doctored version of the truth he'd given Francois.

Apparently it was good enough to gain him an audience. After concluding her call, the receptionist stepped from behind her desk and asked him to follow her.

She led him to the far side of the room, pulled aside the red curtain and beckoned him to walk past her. When he did so, she let the curtain drop closed.

There were two cubicles on either side of the narrow hallway into which they'd entered. Harrison heard voices and the stuttered buzz of what he assumed were tools of the trade coming from behind at least two of the white accordion doors as he was ushered passed them. At the end of the hallway a red-painted wood door blocked further passage. The receptionist drew a key from her pocket and after rapping what sounded like a Morse code signal on the door, carefully unlocked it. She opened the door a crack; waited a moment, as if to determine that no alarms or bombs had been activated, then opened it all the way. *"Vous pouvez entrer, Monsier,"* she said, granting him a token smile. She waited for him to enter the area revealed then shut the door behind him.

He heard the key turn in the lock.

He found himself standing in a vestibule that opened into a small windowless living room modestly furnished with a couch and armchair upholstered in unmatched but harmonious floral prints and several useful accessories such as a coffee table and floor lamp. At the far end of the couch, a wheelchair stood in place of what might have been a companion armchair. Seated in the wheelchair was an elderly woman dressed entirely in black. A long flowing skirt covered all but the tips of her shoes; a lightweight wool cape, all but the pale hands folded in her lap. She was staring straight ahead at a flat-screen TV mounted on the wall opposite. It was tuned to a news program, the sound on mute, the captioned message streaming below the incident being reported.

The vision of the woman in profile instantly recalled the portrait of Whistler's Mother. Even the white cotton day cap worn by the archetypal Mother was represented by Madame D's white hair drawn into a bun, loose strands of it falling to her shoulders, like the loose ties of the painted cap. Incredible, Harrison thought, just as the portrait before him came to life.

"Ah, *bonjour Professeur* Harrison Wheatley," Madame D cheerfully greeted, turning her face toward her visitor before angling her wheelchair in his direction. "I'm told you're a professor of art history at New York University School of Fine Arts. Are you an American in Paris or an expat in America?"

Harrison smiled, immediately at ease. "The former, Madame."

"I suspected so. May I call you Harry? I'm ninety-three. I may not live long enough to utter your name in full."

"Of course you may, although I'm sure you can handle a lot more syllables than you admit to. Your English is impeccable, by the way."

"I should hope so. I received my degree at King's College London." She gestured toward the couch. "Here, sit beside me. Would you care for a coffee or tea? A sandwich, perhaps?" From the folds of her skirt she plucked a remote control. She aimed the device at the TV screen as if she were about to Taser it and the screen went black. "Enough of that." With a decided clack she placed the device on the circular ledge of the table lamp alongside the wheelchair. "Well?" she asked, focusing again on Harrison as he took his assigned place on the couch.

"What?—oh, no thanks. Nothing for me, Madame."

"Please call me Denise," she admonished light-heartedly. "It puts us on equal footing. Are you sure about declining the offer of a snack? I am prepared, you know. My living quarters are modest, but fully equipped to sustain life."

Harrison again declined.

"Perhaps later," his hostess declared. She swiveled her chair further around to face Harrison more squarely. "Now, then, tell me more explicitly the nature of your visit. My secretary, Gretchen, said you're looking for material for an article you're writing on the history of art galleries in Paris."

"That's correct," Harrison said, almost imperceptibly shifting his position on the couch cushion.

She eyed him closely. "Why me?"

"Pardon?"

"Why come to *me* for help?"

"Well, I was told that on the subject of Parisian history your memory is encyclopedic."

"And who is the source of this information?"

Harrison emitted an almost inaudible throat-clearing sound. "Francois, over at *Chez Aristede*. Actually, Francois was quoting the shop's owner, Celeste Marin. Maybe you know her?"

Madame D blanched. "No, I don't know Celeste Marin, but I *am* familiar with the study of body language."

Harrison reflexively squirmed, giving Madame D more material to work with. "Pardon?" he uttered for the second time. It was a response he found pompous, hence never used. Until now.

"*Chez Aristede* is a fashion boutique," Madame D said quietly. "But you went there not to buy a designer dress, but to inquire about the Jules Eisenberg Art Gallery. Am I right, Harry?"

"Yes, I was going to mention that." In fact, Harrison had prepared quite a plausible-sounding account to explain his interest in the Jules Eisenberg

Art Gallery by characterizing it as one of the many such institutions he hoped to include in his scholarly submission to *Art News* magazine. He planned to say that his intention was to explore the current and historic sites of art galleries throughout Paris, but since he'd just checked into a hotel in the 8th arrondissement, he'd chosen to begin his research in the immediate neighborhood; quite by happenstance, with the site of the former Jules Eisenberg Gallery.

He could not get the words out. Madame D reminded him too much of his grandmother: wise, stern, loveable and all-knowing.

"Harry?"

"Yes, Denise."

"You're withholding something from me. I think you want to come clean."

She was irresistible. "I haven't lied to you yet."

"Proactively, then."

"I've been hesitating to reveal my true intentions because they have to do with sensitive matters." He was about to open up to her, after all, when she threw up her hands in frustration.

"Mon Dieu, sauvez-nous!" she cried, extending her arms heavenward, her cape falling from her shoulders. She let her arms drop to the armrests of her wheelchair, where they lay motionless, her hands, palms up, still in a posture of supplication. "Spit it out, Harry!"

Harrison was silent, his gaze locked on Madame D's bared forearm, the one closest to him, the left. Running down its side a row of five numbers were tattooed in black: 97438. He knew the numbers would be recorded in his memory as indelibly as they had been on her flesh.

She noticed. "No, don't waste your pity on me," she said, pulling her cape back over her shoulders and burying her arms under the cloth. "I was not an Auschwitz inmate. My childhood friend, Gloria Feinman was."

"I'm sorry for your loss," Harrison said, stricken into banality.

Madame D's lips curled into a smile so bitter Harrison could almost taste it. "Gloria survived the camp, all right. However, she did die a year later from ailments caused by the prolonged period of malnutrition she'd suffered. So I suppose condolences are in order, after all." She shook her head. "I had her number tattooed on my arm many years ago. It now seems to have been a shamefully pretentious act."

"It wasn't," Harrison said, forsaking another, more innocuous remark on the tip of his tongue: *Don't be so hard on yourself.* Irony was, after what he'd just been privy to, he felt more sanguine about being upfront about his trip to Paris. His motivation for having altered the truth by eliminating its Jewish component stemmed from his fear of encountering anti-Semitic interviewees who might either hamper his mission or outright sabotage it. He was not cynical enough to believe that anti-Semitism was ubiquitous in France, but neither was he naïve enough to think it had lost its foothold altogether. He explained this to Madame D, who commended his caution, adamantly so.

"This used to be my family's Antique Prints and Maps establishment," she declared without segue, although judging from her mental acuity, Harrison knew a relevant point was about to be disclosed. She continued. "This apartment had been, in fact, its storage area. Our researchers and brokers were mostly Jewish, and you know what became of *them.* Our sources basically dried up and in 1955 we threw in the towel and became the business you see today. However, we were merely inconvenienced compared to the horrors that millions experienced. But I know for a fact—from experience!—that your trepidations are not unfounded. At least three of our Jewish associates in the antique business were delivered to the Nazis by their *amis francais.* And still today, there are people in my country, old and young alike, who feel not a drop of sorrow or remorse with what went on in those dark days. And they are not alone in the world!"

"But neither are you," Harrison reminded her.

"I'm aware of that," she said, waving off the remark. "It's discouraging nonetheless." She nodded toward the wall opposite. "Have you noticed the prints—remnants of my previous life? They're in the shadows. Have a look. There's a light switch next to the television screen."

He did as he was told. When illuminated, the prints could be fully appreciated. An 1842 etching by Frederick Christian Lewis of a country cottage nested in a densely wooded area and a rendition of the Western

Hemisphere drawn and engraved by J. Rapkin in 1853 particularly struck his fancy. "The details are amazing," he commented. "I see now why the tattoo work produced here is so meticulous. You set very high standards."

"My father did," Madame D corrected. He set the precedent for all that followed. He died fifty years ago, but his influence is still felt—oh, dear!" She delivered a genteel little stomp on the footrest of her wheelchair. "There I was, cracking the whip and commanding that you tell me the unadulterated story of what brought you here, and here am I rambling on and detaining you. Shall we chalk it up to old age?"

"Not at all," he declared. "You're not rambling and I'm enjoying your company immensely."

"Good of you to humor me. Now, shall we get on with it?"

"I meant what I said, Denise, but yes, let's discuss the reason for my trip." He paused before going on. "I know that you might take this as an affront, but I must have your word that you will not divulge what I'm about to tell you."

"You never know whom I might encounter, yes?"

The disquieting attitude of Louis Corsair popped into mind. "Yes."

"I assure you, I have no intention of sharing our conversation with anyone. Despite my present loquacity, I am able to keep my mouth shut. You must believe me. Shall I fetch a bible?"

Harrison smiled. "No need." He switched off the wall light and returned to his seat beside her, where he explained his interest in the Jules Eisenberg gallery and, indeed, the Eisenbergs themselves. His mission was two-fold, he said. First, to help track down the individual who had murdered a former student of his, and second, to do his part in recovering the Eisenberg art collection and restoring it to its rightful owners or, at this point at least, to the public domain. As to the question of how these two goals were linked, he refused to divulge, both for the sake of Madame D's protection and the integrity of the investigation. He simply told her that documents containing clues interconnecting the seemingly divergent quests had recently been unearthed. Madame D was content with the scanty report, at least outwardly. He then launched what he anticipated to be his interview proper with what he thought was a neutral question: "Denise, did you personally know Jules and Eva Eisenberg?"

"Stop!" Madame D suddenly demanded, thrusting forward her palm like a traffic cop.

Harrison froze. "What's wrong?"

Madame D grabbed hold of the wheels of her chair and started to maneuver herself out of her parking spot between the couch and the table lamp. "I'm not proud, Harry. Give me a hand."

Harrison sprang to her side. "Are you ill? Shall I call someone?"

"Do I *look* ill? We're going out. All I want is for you to expedite our departure." She lifted her hands from the tire rims and lay them back in her lap.

Harrison grabbed the handles of the wheelchair and guided the chair to the center of the room. "I don't understand."

"I realized if I'm to talk about the Eisenberg family I must go out, breathe in the fresh air. Stay in and I'll dry up and crumble into bits like the pages of an old book. I must bring them into the light. It doesn't matter if you don't understand, but it would be a comfort if you do."

"I think I do, Denise," he said, more out of expedience than comprehension.

"Good," she said, as he proceeded to push her toward the door to her apartment. "I'm rather unsteady on my legs, otherwise I'd hop along beside you."

Arriving at the door, Madame D half-rose to her feet and, while holding onto an armrest with one hand, with the other she released the deadbolt.

When they burst through the red curtains and approached the reception desk, Gretchen's jaw dropped, exposing her tongue- piercing.

"As you can see, I don't get out much," Madame D said, addressing Harrison. To Gretchen, she beamed, "*A plus tard, ma cherie!*" She drew in a deep breath, as if she were already outdoors.

"Where to?" Harrison asked, once they were in fact positioned outside the shop. "The Parc Monceau?" Many times during his year of internship he had studied and idled in the twenty-acre bucolic wonderland situated right off the Champs- Élysées.

"But of course," Madame D heartily agreed. "Wherever *else?*"

He waited while she tucked the folds of her skirt under her to prevent them from getting caught up in the spokes. When she felt sufficiently secure, she gave the go-ahead, and Harrison angled the wheelchair in the direction of the Boulevard de Courcelles, one of the three streets at the junction of which lay the Parc Monceau.

After he had established a steady pace, Harrison thought he'd test the waters. "Did you know the Eisenberg family really well?" he asked.

She paused as he waited on tenterhooks.

"Did I ever!" she declared at last.

Walking behind her, he was unable to read the expression on her face, and so it was impossible to pinpoint her emotion.

Chapter 5

"That was Daddy," Erika informed Lucas, gently patting his back to encourage a burp. Five minutes had gone by since her long-distance connection with Harrison had terminated, and already she was anticipating their FaceTime reunion. She hoped Lucas would be awake at one or two in the morning so she could see his reaction to Harrison's screen image. "There you go!" she praised, hearing his little expulsion of air.

After putting Lucas down for one of his hour-and-a-half interludes of sleep, Erika took Jake out for his evening walk, then went off to her study to work on the *Art News* article she'd set aside when she'd gone into labor. The topic, the spike in interest in performance art, was rather timely, and although Sara was perfectly sanguine with a possible delay in issue placement, Erika felt remiss in having taken three full weeks to get back to the piece. Truth is, she felt at a loss if she was not engaged in a challenging project. Taking care of Lucas was a heaven-sent exercise in nurturing; it did not qualify as a goal-oriented task.

She was slowly scrolling down the text to get back into the rhythm of her writing, when her mobile phone sounded from the back pocket of her jeans.

John Mitchell's number registered on the screen. "John?" she answered.

"An awkward hour?" John replied.

"For you? Never. What's up?"

"You know how my detective brain shifts into automatic when you two are involved in one of your risky projects, right? Well, I pressed one of my former colleagues for information on the Bloom case, and he's let me in on a police action before it becomes breaking news. You want to get Harrison to the phone for a three-way?"

"He's in Paris, John."

"What's he doing in Paris? I'm guessing not for the guided tour."

"No."

John groaned. "He's sleuthing, isn't he?"

"Yes, but please keep it to yourself. What's the news? I'll be talking to Harrison soon and I can share it with him."

"Gary Kessler has been arrested," John bluntly delivered.

Erika was taken aback. "So *soon*? On what evidence? Harrison and I are sure there's a more sinister motive behind Bloom's murder than jealousy over a flipped house!"

"Or a wife," John amended. "Actually, the police made a felony arrest for assault and battery perpetrated on his wife, Jodie. Since the Fourth Amendment precludes an arrest without probable cause, most of the time the cops suggest the wife-beater go cool off somewhere off premises. But in this case, the offender is already a prime murder suspect, so they were less forgiving. Especially since Kessler took a crack at his wife in front of their eyes: probable cause with a vengeance. Jodie's in the hospital, pretty messed up; broken nose, a couple of ribs, swollen eye." After a pause, "Erika? You there?"

Erika was stunned. "I'm here. What happened? What set him off?" She suddenly remembered the last conversation with Bonnie and anticipated what was coming.

"The top honcho on the case, Detective Tim Riley, had Bloom's secret cell phone hacked," John began. "I got the general gist of the texts—*illustrated* texts—that passed between Bloom and Jodie Kessler. The story is, Gary got a look at his wife's phone before she had the sense to delete the correspondence, and he exploded."

"Will Jodie be okay?" Erika asked, at the same time wondering how Harrison would take this news. "There'll be no permanent damage, I hope."

"I can't say for certain, but they're predicting a full recovery. How will

Harrison react to this turn of events? You think Bloom's sordid behavior will dampen his commitment to tracking down his killer?"

"I was just asking myself that. I don't know. Becoming Chuck's sole advocate might in fact *strengthen* his commitment." She was surprised to hear herself say that. Even more surprised to feel an accompanying twinge of resentment. She told herself that Harrison's loyalty to Chuck did not mean that he condoned Chuck's behavior, but her dormant distrust in men stirred in its sleep. *Damn it.*

As if hearing her thoughts, John suggested, "You know, Bloom is unable to defend himself. Who knows what prompted his affair with Jodie Kessler?"

"Perhaps Bonnie overcooked his eggs."

"Erika, really," John amicably chided, drawing out the syllables.

His paternal sing-song was irksome, but she knew she was being supersensitive. "Just joking, John. Thanks for getting this information to us."

"No problem. I look after my friends. Especially the daredevils. You'll tell Harrison I called?"

"Of course."

"I'll let you know if I hear anything else about the case—anything out of public earshot, that is."

"Thanks. I'll—we'll—keep you up-to-date, too." She was getting restless. After the call ended, she wondered if it had shown in her voice.

She thought about calling Bonnie. Were auxiliary condolences in order? She ran through a couple of opening lines, the most innocuous: *How are you doing?* They all sounded disingenuous, especially since her primary objective was to learn if Bonnie had made any headway in her background check of the flipped house. No, it was too early. She must give Bonnie time to thrash out what must be wildly conflicting emotions.

Instead, she chose to work off her growing anxiety, ominous as a darkening sky, by pedaling her way to exhaustion on her stationary bike parked in the corner of the room.

An hour-and-a-half later, after an invigorating shower and mood-elevating session of nursing and chatting away at Lucas, mostly in untranslatable coos and chirps, she put him down for his post-prandial nap and headed back to her study to get on with her abandoned magazine article. It was 10:00 p.m. when, at the sound of Lucas's wake-up rustle amplified by the monitor at her elbow, she realized that she'd skipped her usual sit-down dinner and that she desperately had to pee.

By the time she'd taken care of her immediate need and arrived at the master bedroom to feed Lucas, Kate was already there, about to change his diaper.

"This might be a good time to try out the formula," Kate said on Erika's entrance. "What do you think?"

"We'll wait for the next feeding," Erika replied, if only to be the one to decide the timing. Early on, she and Harrison had decided that they would try to acclimate Lucas to a combination of breast and formula milk in order to ensure a schedule easily adaptable to their outside commitments. Experts' consensus was that the optimum age an infant was ready to be introduced to the milk formula without the likelihood of rejection was three weeks. "Anyway, thanks for reminding me," Erika added, backing off her self-righteous tone. To further compensate, she demonstrated her interest in Kate by detaining her with a flurry of questions about the progress of her online degree. Erika's interest became more authentic as the discussion progressed, and Kate ended up sitting on the edge of the bed and opening up to Erika about the man whom she had recently met and who was pressing her into a serious relationship, which she was not ready for. The lively tell-all went on through the entire breastfeeding period, at the end of which Erika handed off Lucas to Kate for the burping, clean-up and play rituals and headed down to the kitchen to drum up a meal for herself.

When she returned, Lucas was lying on his back in the bassinet and staring up at his colorful mobile as Kate tapped at one of its dangling forest animals, making it bobble to the computer-generated tune of Debussy's "Clair de Lune." Erika knew the repertoire: if left to run its course, a Chopin waltz and a Brahms lullaby would follow before the device shut itself off. She left Kate to bond with Lucas and returned to her study to polish up her article.

Three-quarters of an hour later, its rough draft was ready to be fine-tuned. She generally liked to allow a piece to settle for a day or two before coming back to it with fresh eyes, so she closed the document, put away her notes and retired to the master bedroom.

Kate had left the room and Lucas, freshly clad in a onesie adorned with plump yellow bunnies, was asleep on his back. Erika reached in and brushed her palm over the gentle rise of his belly. An unburdening peace rippled through her like a drug. She bent to kiss his cheek, deliciously close to a corner of his lips, and breathed in his delicate scent.

A high-pitched sound, plaintive yet unobtrusive, came from behind. Erika turned to respond to Jake's request, delivered from just outside the doorway. "It's okay, boy," she urged, waving him in. With one swish of his tail, he complied, halting by the foot of the bed. "Go on, hop to it," she decreed, with another wave of encouragement, enjoying his response of disbelief and delight. He climbed onto the bed, splaying himself in as broad an expanse as his limbs would allow, as if to make himself as difficult to dislodge as possible.

Erika pulled her cell phone from her back pocket, set it on vibrate, and attached it to the charger on her night table. She propped her pillows against the headboard and got into bed, arranging herself in a cross-legged position on top of the bedclothes. She planned to perform her nighttime ablutions after she'd spoken to Harrison. There was no way she would take the chance of missing his call by drowning out its incoming signal with the rush of running water.

Poised at last to receive the much-awaited call, she felt her heart hiccup into high speed. A couple of deep breaths lowered its pace to near normal, but still, she was too jumpy to open the book she had planned to start reading that night: a study of cultural life in Paris, 1940-1945. Too intense for her present state of mind. Instead, she clicked on the television. It awakened to the late night news. She switched the audio output to closed captions and sat back to absorb the just-left-of-the-center version of current events and environmental alerts. Jake, deciding to chance it, crawled on his belly, like a soldier on a battlefield, to her side. She welcomed him with a luxurious pet from his neck to his tailbone, then, in shorter strokes, continued the caress until he fell asleep.

She was just beginning to lose herself in the soundless flow of history in the making when her cell phone vibrated against the surface of her night table. She grabbed for it, assuming it was Harrison. "Hi!" she sang without checking the caller's number, realizing her error belatedly. "Bonnie, hello!" she added in the same tone, only forced.

"I hope I didn't wake you," Bonnie clipped, equally insincere.

"Not at all. What's up?" The elephant in the room was tapping his hoof.

"Nothing good. I'm sorry, but I can't continue with the research into the flipped house. I'll give you what I've got and that's it. You can do what you want with it."

"Are you okay?" Erika asked, neutral enough to give Bonnie the option to talk or pass.

"Not okay, but I'd rather not discuss it. Watch the news, you'll find out why soon enough. I was afraid if I didn't call now, I wouldn't call at all. Do you have a pen?"

Erika scrounged for one in the night table drawer, along with a note pad. "Yes. Go ahead."

"I didn't look for owners who vacated prior to 1946 because, as you pointed out, they of course couldn't have left behind a letter dated that year. I have three owners who qualify. First, Edward Ainsworth." She spelled the last name. "Ainsworth purchased the house in 1940 and sold it in 1952 to Patrick and Susan Crowley." Her tone becoming more frigid, she reported, "The Crowleys sold it to Abraham and Rose Jacobsen in 1973, who held onto it until"—cold as ice—"*Charles* bought it. I didn't check if there had been renters over the years. You might want to pursue that."

"Thanks, Bonnie. I know Harrison will find this information useful."

"Is he in? I'd like to thank him for his interest and apologize for my—I suppose *withdrawal* is the right word."

"He's not available right now," Erika hedged, "but I'll be sure to give him the message."

There was a pause on the line. "Thank you, Erika," Bonnie finally said. There was a distinct tremor in her voice, impossible to conceal. It was clear her brave front had collapsed.

Erika felt a sudden connection with her, as if she herself had exposed her vulnerability along with Bonnie's. She would have liked to have prolonged the conversation a bit, if only to provide some sisterly comfort, but Bonnie cut it short, leaving her with a sense of incompletion. It was impossible, after that, to recapture the sense of unalloyed eagerness with which she awaited Harrison's call.

Chapter 6

Harrison pushed the wheelchair transporting Madame D through the arched wrought-iron gate of the Parc Monceau, and instantly they were in another world, or rather a distillation of beauty from the known world; of landscaped gardens and lily ponds, temples and pyramids, antique statuary and monuments dedicated to icons of the arts: de Maupassant, Proust, Chopin, Gounod.

"A harmonious hodgepodge," Madame D declared, sarcasm interlacing admiration. "Representing the best of us, without a hint of our intractable bent for violence." She shifted in her seat to try and get a glimpse of Harrison, and he came round to face her. "Ironic, isn't it," she went on, "that the Duke of Orleans, who planned this beautiful rendering of humanity, was, in the end, guillotined?"

"It is ironic," he agreed. "Like most of our endeavors, I suppose."

She nodded. "Like what we've come here to talk about—a story of innocence and depravity." She readjusted her position so that she was facing straight ahead. "Take us to the Roman colonnade," she said. "Do you remember where it is?"

He did. He brought her to the spot, so often depicted in postcards, and found an ideally situated bench by the pond and across from the monument, its strict verticality both enhanced and offset by an ancient weeping willow. There are some things, he thought, as he maneuvered the wheelchair into position, that resist trivialization, no matter how often their images are mass-produced. The Statue of Liberty, Michelangelo's *David*, the Eiffel

Tower. *This.* "Are you comfortable?" he asked, straightening out the cape that had slipped off one of her shoulders.

"Perfect. Stop fussing about and sit down."

He did so, at the end of the bench. He had angled the wheelchair alongside it so that they would be in tête-à-tête contact.

"I've been thinking about how to approach the subject," Madame D said, looking directly into his eyes and thereby demanding his undivided attention. "Like a stage play, I've decided." She leaned forward in her seat, as if she were about to hear, not relate, a story. "Let us set the scene," she began. "It is early October 1940. Paris. 8th arrondissement."

"And do you have a starring role?" Harrison asked, if only to acknowledge her tactic. He whipped out his pad and pen from his breast pocket.

"Hardly. In your playbill I shall be listed as 'Witness.'" She flicked her fingers at his writing materials. "Put them away. Since when do you take notes in the theater? You must be thoroughly involved." She gave him a sidewise look. "Especially since you'll be composing the denouement." She folded her hands in her lap; waited for him to stow the pad and pen. "It is early October 1940," she repeated, after the items were out of sight. "The Germans have been occupying Paris for almost four months. Their persecution of the Jews has not yet reached peak efficiency. At 110 rue La Boetie, site of the Jules Eisenberg Gallery and residence, Jules and his wife, Ava, are worried about the fate of their precious collection of artworks, but more so, about the future of their thirteen-year-old son, Benjamin. Benny is a mercurial boy, a bit on the wild side and full of himself, a boy who can't imagine that anyone, once they got to know him, would want to exclude him from their society. His bravado has rubbed off on his parents, and while they're far from complacent, they're not as frightened as they should be.

"Ten, twelve minutes away on foot, at 21 rue La Boetie, the location of the art gallery owned by partners Georges Wildenstein and Paul Rosenberg, the outlook is grimmer. Emigration plans are in the works." Madame D paused to question Harrison: "You're familiar with the Wildenstein art dealership empire, yes?"

"I am," Harrison said, "but probably not as familiar as you. "I do know that after the war Georges was accused of dealing art with the Nazis, but fought and won the suit brought against him by Andre Malraux. I myself am not sure what to think."

"You're not to think ill of Georges, at least not in regard to *that* issue!" Madame D declared. "I was present on many an occasion when Georges and his wife, Jeanne, ranted on about their hatred for the Nazis. These people shunned the Nazis more than they themselves were shunned, if you can imagine such a thing. You may know more than I about the present-day Wildenstein crowd—the Cat Lady and the like—but as for prior generations of the clan, I appoint myself as authority."

Harrison smiled. "Here, here!"

"Forgive my presumptiveness."

Harrison touched her cape-enshrouded forearm. "Not a bit. I want to learn everything I can from you, Denise."

Madame D sighed. "You say that to be kind. A few names and references are all you're after, and here I go, elaborating on all things extraneous. It's for my own benefit, this recitation, and it's most selfish. Moreover, I predicted as much."

"Do you think I'm being disingenuous?" Harrison asked.

"How so?"

"When I say I'm interested in learning all I can about your recollections of that time. Really, Denise, you are being too"—he hesitated to use the word, but could think of none better—"demure!"

Madame D's cheeks reddened. "*Bien.* I'm convinced. I'll continue, then, without a care to either the time or your forbearance. We may be here until midnight."

Harrison grinned. "Fine with me, but I thought the park closes at five-thirty."

"Ah, *mais oui.* Then I must talk twice as fast." She leaned back in her chair in a relaxed manner, clearly with no intention of quickening the pace. "Georges and Jeanne Wildenstein," she began, picking up the thread. "They had a son, Daniel. He was twenty-three in 1940. Here's a note of interest, possibly useful to you: Daniel was the director of the *Gazette des Beaux-*

Arts, a most prestigious art review magazine headquartered in Paris, from the early 1960s to his death in 2001. His father, Georges, had bought the magazine back in the late 1920s, and was its director from the mid-1930s on, until he passed the baton to Daniel."

"Yes, this might very well be useful," Harrison agreed, not yet knowing in what capacity.

"Especially since the Eisenbergs and the Wildensteins were good friends," Madame D went on. "They had a kind of working relationship, occasionally trading paintings or brokering sales for each other. It was a two-way street."

Harrison sat up as neural pathways of investigation fired into being. "Would you mind if I break the rules by jotting these facts in my notepad?" he asked, totally without guile.

"Oh my dear, how imperious I've been!" Madame D pronounced. "This is what comes from sitting alone in my apartment, with no one to critique my thoughts but myself, and you know how loath one is to admit one's shortcomings. Of *course* you may take notes!"

"Thanks—discounting your self-recrimination." He scribbled the pertinent names and dates in his pad and returned his attention to her.

"I haven't as yet mentioned my own family, the Fontaines," she went on. "In 1940 I was thirteen years old, bookish and sadly unsophisticated. My parents and I lived and conducted business on rue de Ponthieu. We were in close proximity to the Eisenbergs and Wildensteins, both geographically and in regard to our sensibilities. Only one thing set us apart. By a fluke of fate, our forefathers had not chosen to call themselves Jews.

"I want you to picture a particular day back then. I've told you it was early October. I remember it was a Saturday, but I don't remember the exact date, and given its significance, I should. After what seemed like a lifetime of rain, the sky had cleared, and just seeing the sun from my bedroom window had tricked me into dressing for a day in June. I left the house with only a light sweater over my cotton print dress.

"I was more excited than I'd ever been. By some miracle, Daniel Wildenstein—handsome, clever, *twenty-three-year-old* Daniel Wildenstein—had offered—perhaps not of his own accord, but who cared?—to take me and

Ben Eisenberg to the cinema that afternoon

"The three o'clock feature was a rollicking comedy. I sat between Daniel and Benny. I hardly laughed because I was afraid Daniel would think I was loud and foolish, and Daniel himself wasn't making a sound. Benny, on the other hand, wasn't holding back, and why should he? I smiled to think that after the show he would announce that he was going to be a movie director or an actor. Without fail, whatever field of endeavor captured his interest at any given moment, Benny would plan to excel in it. I don't know if he was aware that the Jews had been banned from the movie business even before the Germans arrived, but it wouldn't have stopped him. He'd vow to single-handedly reverse the rule or be the exception to it.

"Somewhere about the middle of the film, as I was directing a scene inside my head starring Daniel and me, I felt something briefly touch my right hand, the hand near Benny. I looked at him and he looked back at me and smiled sheepishly, possibly for the first time in his life. He took my hand in his then, and I pulled mine away. It was a small movement, but deliberate. He didn't laugh again, not once, for the rest of the film. I felt a twinge of pity, but not an ounce of remorse.

"After the show Daniel invited us over to his father's gallery for a bite to eat. I knew there was a tiny kitchen area in the back that was set apart from the display rooms. 'I'll make you sandwiches,' he said. 'Fat ones. Besides,' he added, 'my father's acquired a couple of Picasso oils on commission, and I think you two might like to see them before they're snatched up by one of Pablo's avid fans.' I needed no excuse to trail after him like a puppy, and Benny tagged along, pretending to be jolly.

"More than treating us to a look at his father's prized Picassos, Daniel escorted us on a leisurely tour of the crowded showrooms, lecturing us on style and subject matter as we stood before each painting. I don't know what his motivation was. Perhaps he foresaw the lot of them being confiscated by the Germans and needed to memorialize them. Perhaps he was simply growing bored with Ben and me.

"By the end of the tour, my stomach was growling. Food was rationed in those days, and I was never fully sated. Daniel's utterance of the word 'fat,' as in sandwich, had become as enticing as Daniel himself. The sandwich he ultimately made for each of us—a sliver of brisket between two stale slices of rye—was hardly what one could call substantial, but I was in heaven.

"We were cleaning up after our meal, when we heard footsteps in the gallery proper. 'My parents are back,' Daniel informed us. We dropped everything and went back out front to greet them, only to discover that they were in the company of Madeline Paquard, the French girl—well, she was barely twenty—and her Nazi lover, Hans, a brawny young man of few words, especially around this crowd. I had seen the couple at the Wildenstein's gallery on one other occasion, when Madeline had come to pick up a painting her parents had purchased. I never could figure out why she'd bring along her lover when she knew the Wildensteins hated him so, but when I thought about it years later, I realized that it must have been at the direction of her parents, whose art collection—amassed at quite a bargain, I heard—depended in large part on the gallery's continued existence. A certain bonding, however forced, between the German and the gallery owners, would surely help keep them safe, right? Hah!

"Well, I did wonder why these mismatched couples had been gallivanting around town together that day, but as it turned out they hadn't been. The Wildensteins had been visiting friends that afternoon, and they and Madeline and her beau had simply arrived on the gallery's doorstep at the same moment. Madeline was there to pick up her parents' latest purchase: a lovely still life by Chardin. I remember thinking the peaches looked good enough to eat.

"'What are *you* two doing here?' little Miss Paquard asked Ben and me in the above-it-all manner she'd adopted since the German had taken a fancy to her. She lived in the area and I'd seen her around before the occupation, and she'd impressed me as a normal sort of girl, with fine features and light blond hair. Now, with her Wagnerian god beside her, her self-image seemed to have hooked onto his. Even her hair, which she'd taken to conspicuously tossing back, appeared to have become a symbol of her newly acquired superiority. 'Don't you know there's an eight o'clock curfew?' she went on, as if she'd personally imposed it. 'You ought to have gone home by now. It's nearly seven-fifty!'

"Apparently the curfew had been announced on loudspeakers and on the radio. We told her we hadn't heard it at the cinema. There had been an attack on a group of German officers the night before, the Wildensteins explained, and that was the reason for the curfew. It was to last four days, at least. They gave the German an accusatory look, but, as was their policy, did not address him. Hans, on the other hand, was clearly making an effort to be cordial that night, praising the art on display, asking after our health, even requesting that I give him a summary of the movie we had seen. He suggested that my friend and I stay the night at the Wildensteins', if they'd be so kind, and in that way avoid being accosted by the police. He was going to accompany Madeline home to ensure her safety, and I remember wondering why he didn't offer to escort Ben and me home, too. Maybe the suggestion was about to be posed by another of our party, but at that moment a warning to clear the streets blared over a truck's loudspeaker, and the next thing I knew, the Wildensteins were insisting Ben and I join them in their apartment above the gallery, a duplex accessible via an interior staircase.

"My parents were beside themselves with relief and anger when I called to tell them the news. They berated me for not reporting in earlier, but of course gave me permission to stay over. Ben called his parents, who reacted in kind. That night I slept in the Wildenstein's spare bedroom in a pair of Jeanne's silk pajamas, and Ben slept in Daniel's room. The next morning Ben and I..."

Madame D had been talking steadily. She suddenly went silent. Harrison, who had been engrossed all the while, wondered if the curtain had fallen on the play's intermission or if the theater had gone dark. He waited to find out.

"Something just came to me. Why now, after all these years?" Madame D finally asked, directing her question to the distant horizon. She turned to Harrison. "Do you suppose it's because this is the first time since childhood that I'm reliving the experience? I mean visually and in detail—minute by minute, it feels like?"

"Yes," he said. "I think that when we're reexamining a particular time in our remote past, a recollection can appear to materialize out of nowhere." He had no idea what sight or utterance had erupted from Madame D's memory, but he could see its impact. She was struggling to restrain her tears. "Deep breaths," she told herself, the corners of her mouth twitching downward. She pursed her lips and drew in her breath, then slowly let it out. She repeated the exercise several times without altering its rhythm. "I'm sorry," she said at last. "Please don't think I'm trying to create a dramatic effect. Although it must look that way." She smiled—so fleetingly, Harrison thought he might have imagined it.

Taking the bull by the horns, he asked bluntly, "What suddenly came to mind, Denise?"

"He never looked at him, not once," she said, dovetailing the question.

"Who, Denise?"

"The German," she said, more to herself than Harrison, as if she, not he, had posed the question. "He made eye contact with Daniel, with me, even tried to with Jeanne and George—unsuccessfully, of course. But never with Ben."

"Was he angry with Ben for some particular reason, do you think?"

"That's just it," she said. "There was no animosity in his demeanor, only a kind of...*unease*. It was as if the boy reminded him of something perilous in his past"—she drew in her breath sharply—"or in his future." With her eyes she implored Harrison to answer a question she had not yet articulated.

Harrison was at a loss. "Denise, what is so disturbing to you about this?"

She opened her mouth to answer, then changed her mind. After a beat, she said, "I'll tell you what happened next, and you will know for yourself."

He had no choice. He nodded and waited for her to continue.

She smoothed her skirt and refolded her hands, as if this would bring order to what was to come. "The next morning after breakfast—dry rolls and tea without sugar, it was—Ben and I set out for our respective homes." Her voice had cracked a bit, and she cleared her throat. "Ever since the incident at the cinema, Benny was keeping his distance from me. It was clear he was unsure how to act in my presence. I wanted us to go back to the way we were, so I turned around and caught up with him. 'I'll walk you home,' I said. 'I'm perfectly capable of walking by myself,' he said. I walked with him anyway. I hardly knew what to say next, and he was of no help, giving me the cold shoulder, so we walked down the street in silence for the entire ten minutes it took us to get to number 110, the address of the Eisenberg gallery and residence. You should know that the Eisenberg's apartment, like the Wildenstein's, was accessible from inside the building. The apartment was not as grand as theirs, though. Three rooms, three flights up." Madame D paused to take another of her curative deep breaths.

"I will get right to the point," she said evenly, although Harrison saw her hands briefly unclasp to take up a patch of skirt material and clutch it between her palms. "The door to the gallery was wide open, but we didn't need that clue to realize that something terrible had happened. We could see it through the gallery window. Ben let out a low grunt, like an animal that had just been wounded, and ran into the building. I followed after him.

"The floor was strewn with empty frames, like a heap of firewood. Not a single canvas had been left behind. I stood dumbly in the center of it as Ben tore around in circles screaming '*Maman? Papa? Maman? Papa?*' before shooting out of orbit to head for the back office. I followed behind in a kind of wide-awake daze, and when I reached the room, I saw first a neat pile of paperwork on a small desk, and then, beside it on the floor, the bodies of two German officers piled together like discarded rag dolls. Ben was crammed in a corner as if pinned there by an invisible force, his mouth open, screaming without making a sound. And then, as if suddenly released, he sprang out the door, brushing by me without seeing me, running and stumbling toward the stairwell that led up to the apartment. I followed him like a sleepwalker, alert to every detail, but viewing it from another dimension of time and space.

"I was standing behind him as he pushed open the door to the apartment, and so my first view of the scene was obstructed. His was not. Both his parents were lying face-up on the hardwood floor. Each had been shot in the middle of the forehead. Except for the neat bullet holes, their faces were remarkably intact. The pools of blood, like crimson pillows beneath their heads, were proof enough their wounds had been fatal, but Ben, dropping to his knees beside his mother's inert form, refused to believe it, whispering and howling that she wake up. And still, not a word had passed between us. What happened next was so unearthly, even more so than the murders, that I did not truly believe it was happening until it was done."

Madame D paused a moment before going on, and Harrison felt that if he said a word it would be considered an act of transgression. "The window in the living room—we were in the living room, you see—went nearly from the floor to the ceiling. The window was open and the long white curtains—cotton batiste they must have been—were fluttering in the breeze. Maybe Ben saw them as angel wings, I don't know. Maybe he thought he could fly—remember, he believed he could become anything he wanted to be—and that the curtains were heavenly portals or something of the sort. It's so painful not to know what he was thinking when he rose to his feet and without a word, without a cry, ran to the window and flew off. In my mind I hear myself shouting 'Ben, no!' just as he is about to jump, so I *must* have shouted, don't you think?" She looked at Harrison, actually wanting him to answer.

Harrison felt keenly aware of what he had just been hearing, yet stunned speechless by it. Like the young Denise, he reflected.

"Harry?" she urged. "Don't you think I shouted that?"

He must choose his words carefully—*no! say what you think!* "Yes, I believe you did," he said, faltering. "Probably you did." Counter punching in the forefront of consciousness: *What? Two German officers and two Jews killed by the same person?*

"In the end I know it doesn't matter," she said, "but I want to believe I said *something.*"

"How can anyone know how to react in such a situation?" he asked, as the question in his head refused to be gaveled into silence. "I hardly know how to react in *this* situation, and I'm a grown-up!"

She granted him a smile, but her thoughts were elsewhere: "I blame myself, you know," she said quietly. "If I had let Ben hold my hand in the theater, or if I had pulled my hand away less forcefully, he might have rushed to me, if even for a parting embrace, and I would have held onto him until that dreadful impulse had melted into a river of tears."

The image struck a nerve, and empathy overrode his internal inquiry. He covered Madame D's clasped hands with one of his. "Denise, if you had allowed Ben to hold your hand in the theater, you would have been leading him on. You also would have been betraying your feelings for Daniel—sitting right beside you! As for calibrating the stratagem of your hand's withdrawal—who does that? One reacts to an amorous advance instinctively, and that's that. Besides, you're only scripting one of an infinite number of scenarios that might have been. Ben might have carried you along with him out that window, for one."

Madame D studied the pond that lay before them, her features as still as its surface. After a time, she said, "Logic is one thing, but the heart has a mind of its own. My own heart bonded with guilt that day and there's nothing's to be done about it. My sorrow only deepened when the Wildenstein-Rosenberg gallery was aryanized less than a week later, and the Wildensteins left the country to start a new life in America." She aimed a sardonic smile at the uncontested beauty glistening in the sunlight. "I guess their connection with the Paquards and, by association, with Madeline's beau, didn't stop the Gestapo from seizing their property. I never thought I'd ever meet a man I loved as much as Daniel, and after the part I'd played in Benny's death, I didn't think I deserved to. I never married." She turned to Harrison. "Well, there you have it. My story. I think we should go now." She slipped her hands from beneath his palm to unlock the brakes of her wheelchair.

There were not many people milling about, and those who were had begun to gravitate toward the exit gates. Harrison looked at his watch. It read *5:17*. Madame D's narration seemed to have been calculated to close at roughly the same time as the Parc Monceau. There were questions he'd printed in boldface in his pad, including the one that had been temporarily stifled, and he'd been waiting for this moment to ask them. They were key in the investigation he'd taken upon himself to begin, and he was bent on having them answered before the day was out. It was therefore not solely because he enjoyed Madame D's company that he invited her out to dinner on the spot. "It's early, I know, but I suspect neither of us have had lunch, am I right?"

"You're right, but we're going to have dinner at my place, not out on the town. I thank you for the invitation, but it's where I'll feel most comfortable answering your questions." He had risen to his feet and was standing beside the wheelchair, about to position himself at its rear. "And I can guess every one of them," she added, with a friendly jab at his arm.

Chapter 7

After her phone call with Bonnie, Erika added a note to the realty information Bonnie had given her: *call John Mitchell*. She was sure that with his many connections in the law-and-order hierarchy, John would find a way to expand on Bonnie's limited input. If he was lucky, he'd come up with the most likely candidate to have stowed that critical box of documents—including Alekhine's letter—under the attic boards of Chuck Bloom's flipped house in Westchester County. She felt a degree of self-recrimination for not having been able to ease Bonnie's unexpressed pain, but even more so for feeling more passionate about solving the crime than dwelling on the well-being of the person who'd suffered most by it.

Acting as her own shrink, she rebuked herself for feeling guilty, then changed into a fresh pair of sweatpants and nursing bra and traded her buttoned shirt for one of Harrison's roomier ones, more comfortable to sleep in, should she ever recover the skill. The hell with her nighttime ablutions. She'd perform them in the morning. Instead, she climbed back into bed with the intention of having another go at the book on French cultural life in the 1940s while she waited for Harrison's call.

She had just settled herself into her default lotus position on top of the bedcovers and was reaching for the book, when her cell phone vibrated alongside it. The ID was Greg Smith's.

"Too late?" he responded to her "Hi, Greg." He sounded breathless, as if he had run to catch the call rather than initiate it.

"No problem." She sat back against the propped pillows. "Where are you, in London or New York?" Greg shuttled back and forth between the two Art Loss Register offices on an irregular basis. It was impossible to guess where he'd be on any given day.

"New York. You're sure it's not too late? My sleep patterns are forever in flux. I'll call tomorrow if it's a bad time."

"It's okay. Are you calling about the Hans Arp and Max Ernst paintings mentioned in Alekhine's letter to Ambassador Martins?"

"Yes, but not with good news. I said I'd get back to you sooner, but a sting operation in Munich uncovered a dozen or so paintings auctioned on the black market, and I thought I'd wait to see the inventory. No sign of transference of either of the two paintings in question, legitimate or underworld. Sorry."

She could hear his rapid breathing. She'd always envisioned him as the stereotypical Olympic athlete, confident and fearless. Flustering did not fit the picture. She wondered if he was okay, but thought it would be too forward of her to inquire. "Don't be sorry. One of these days I'm hoping we'll hit pay dirt," she declared, heading for a wrap-up.

"What?—oh, yes," Greg replied. "Is Harrison there?"

"Not yet," she shot back, off-balance. "Shall I have him call you?"

"No, I was just wondering if you were alone."

Erika sat forward. "Why?"

"No reason."

"I'm not alone. I'm here with Lucas, Kate and Grace," she enumerated, fortifying her space. *It's time*, she decided. "Are you okay, Greg?"

"Not really. I guess I thought it would bolster my ego to talk to a smart beautiful woman."

"In lieu of talking to your mother?" she asked, disabling his compliment as if it were a time bomb.

"My mother's dead."

"I'm sorry."

"It's been years, but thanks." After a pause, he added, "She walked out on me."

"Your mother?"

"My partner. Ex-partner. After three years, moved out, just like that. No trace of her when I flew in from London."

"There was no warning?" she asked, with pointed objectivity. "No explanation?" She flashed back on the introductory exchange of glances between Greg and Fiona, or on her version of it. She would never have guessed he'd had a serious partner. It felt prurient, this private musing.

"She left me a letter. She said my scuttling back and forth to and from London was equivalent to a lack of commitment. Does that sound like a valid reason to you, or a cover-up?"

"Greg, I don't know the dynamic of your relationship. Is it possible she's simply been hoping for a marriage proposal?"

"No—at least I don't think so. Maybe I'm a damn fool. Do you think a woman like *you* could put up with the likes of me, Erika?"

In her previous, unencumbered life, when men were definitively untrustworthy and the concept of sex and commitment were incompatible, her retort would have been a breezy putdown. However, in her new life of restored trust, only lately challenged by bouts of insecurity, her inner reply was a regrettable mix of gratitude and nostalgia. She was flattered that she was admired, even subliminally sought after, in the world of sweatpants and leaky breasts—a world that glittered, if only briefly, in her place of seclusion, tucked against the bed pillows.

Aiming at neutrality and kindness, she said, "I don't know you well enough to know what sort of man you are, Greg, never mind what sort of life you lead. How can I give you an honest answer?"

"You can't, of course. I guess I just wanted to talk to you. You have a soothing voice."

"Glad you think so." In fact, Greg seemed to have calmed down considerably.

"So, you'll let me know if you come across any other art works you'd like me to research," Greg said, phrasing the question as a statement. "You'll get in touch, one way or the other?" he added, more tentatively.

"Yes, of course." Her recollection of total freedom—no longer desired but momentarily gratifying—had left her with a billowing ache just below her ribs. She'd never known guilt to have taken that form. She needed to end the call.

When it was done, she sat on the edge of the bed and softly chanted, she didn't know to whom, nor did it matter, "I'm sorry, I'm sorry, I'm sorry, I'm sorry."

Chapter 8

Madame D retrieved a large plastic container from her refrigerator and set it on the countertop beside the gas stove. She had exchanged her wheelchair for her aluminum walker to allow her greater mobility in the kitchen. She had assigned Harrison to a captain's chair at her round cherry-wood kitchen table, from which he was not permitted to move. "I never have guests for dinner, so I am not going to allow my first one to lift a finger." As with his grandmother, there was no arguing with her.

"I have a natural inclination to reclusiveness," she remarked, as she transferred the contents of the plastic container into a large iron frying pan waiting on one of the front burners of the stove. She covered the pan and set the flame on low. "My withdrawal has become more entrenched with old age and the passing of most of my friends. I should add that my fifteen minutes of fame back in 2013 further encouraged this predisposition. You're going to love this—*coq au vin* with *choux de bruxelles.* Gretchen is a cook extraordinaire, and twice a week she brings me a variety of dishes fit for a family of four. Would you care for a beer? I don't drink wine, but the beer is excellent—Pelforth Blonde—or Brune, if you prefer."

"The Brune would be great, thanks." Upon delivery of bottle and mug, he filled the mug and took a hearty swig, then reminded Madame D about her reference to 2013.

"Ah, yes," she said, back to tending to her chicken and Brussel sprouts. "A local journalist spotted me among the group of onlookers at the dedication of a war monument on the site of the Rosenberg Gallery. Did you know that the gallery was opened in 1910 by Paul Rosenberg, and that it was not until 1928 that George Wildenstein's father bought Paul a share in the enterprise? Well, the journalist decided that this old woman might be able to help flesh out her article on the war years. As it turned out, she wrote a feature article on my recollections. It did not include any part of what I've related to you, Harry. I revealed my private life to you, as I've never done. What I told her was as cut and dry as a chapter in a schoolbook. Oddly enough, the article vaulted me to local fame. I became a curiosity, a village pet. I did not enjoy it." She touched a chicken breast with the crook of her pinky. "Ready," she concluded.

With more than a modicum of difficulty, Madame D fetched a pair of dinner plates from the pantry above the sink and two sets of utensils from the drawer below it and, in two trips, carried the items to the table as Harrison writhed in captive passivity. Finally, and with great reluctance, she requested that he transport the heavy iron pan to the trivet in the center of the table. He leaped at the opportunity, not only to be of service, but to hasten the proceedings. He needed to broach the questions that were uppermost in his mind, and the most opportune time, he had decided, would be when they were settled at the table, face to face; Madame D distracted no longer by the calisthenics of preparing a meal.

Thus, he had discreetly placed his pad and pen at his elbow well before the plates had been put on the table.

"Would you be good enough to fetch me a beer?" Madame D asked, before he had a chance to raise his fork. "I confess, the spring in my step needs a moment to recharge. The Blonde, *s'il vous plait*. Grab another bottle for yourself as well."

Harrison happily did her bidding, minus helping himself to another beer. When they were at last settled in earnest, he cut himself a bite-size wedge of chicken thigh and lifted it to his lips, while Madame D waited for his reaction. "Delicious!" he declared with genuine enthusiasm, as the savory morsel graced his taste buds. He continued the sampling with a pair of skewered green buds, slightly seared, and was rewarded with a delightfully pungent combination of crispness and succulence. "Excellent!"

"I believe it's the quality of the Cognac; I'm glad you approve," she said, before bringing a forkful of chicken breast to her own lips.

He waited until she had consumed her first mouthful. "So," he began, ready to reboot the conversation terminated in the Parc Monceau.

"I wish you had allowed me to serve the *salade d'Auvergne,*" Madame D suddenly complained, with a furtive glance at the note pad at his elbow. "The arugula will have gone limp by tomorrow and the apples-and-walnut vinaigrette is to die for. Well, at least you won't deny me the pleasure of watching you enjoy Gretchen's *mousse au chocolat.* That I simply won't allow!"

"I wouldn't miss it for the world," Harrison assured her, puzzled by what he could only characterize as her growing coyness.

"Do you think I'm trying to divert you from your final Q and A?" she asked, as if divining his thoughts. "Heaven forbid. Fire away."

He pretended not to hear the sudden petulance in her tone. If he responded to it, it would put a damper on any meaningful discourse; at the least, slow it down. "I was wondering if you could describe the aftermath of that tragic night at the Eisenbergs'. How did the authorities interpret it?"

She snickered. "You mean what story did they feed the public? I knew that would be your first order of business, Harry." She scraped the food around in her plate as if she were scribbling a message to herself. "First, let me finish telling you what happened that night. After Ben performed that impossible act, for a moment I couldn't move and then I moved so fast I had no concept of going from where I stood to the street, kneeling beside him. There were three or four people standing close to him, and I must have pushed them aside to get to Ben, but I don't remember that. I was just *there,* beside his lifeless form. Then, out of the blue—except it couldn't have been out of the blue, could it?—a German officer was barking orders for us to disperse. I wanted to tell him what had happened, but he pushed me so hard I fell down and he pulled me up by my hair and ordered me to go home. I wanted to report the incident to the local police—the French police, I mean—but my parents forbid it, afraid I'd be punished—they along with me—for sympathizing with the Jews. It wouldn't matter, anyway, they said. The Gestapo would invent a story that suited their needs. And, of course they were right. There was no investigation. The Gestapo didn't give a damn about the three Jews who died that night. They cared about the art that went missing and about the two officers who were killed. The story they chose to report was that the theft had been committed by common criminals taking advantage of the deserted streets, a result of the curfew in effect that night. They concluded that when the officers on patrol noticed something suspicious going on and entered the place, they were ambushed by the thugs. The boy, they said—another witness—was thrown out the window."

Harrison studied the stripped chicken bone that lay on his plate. "Why did they go upstairs?" he wondered aloud. He looked across the table at Madame D, intending to explain his wayward thought.

There was no need to. "When we were in the park and I told you what happened, I was carried away by the unthinkable horror," she said. "I'm sorry, but I failed to mention that the apartment, like the gallery, was stripped of its artwork—all the paintings that were especially dear to the Eisenbergs; the works they couldn't part with. That's why they went upstairs. Can there be any other explanation?"

"I can't think of one," he said aloud, while inwardly countering: *But Erika will.* "Were there any suspects taken into custody?" he asked, impatient to connect with his wife.

"Hardly. They rounded up ten random citizens and executed them on the spot. Who knows, they may have done some follow-up detective work behind the scenes, but we townsfolk had to learn a lesson while the news was still fresh in our minds." She took a sip of her beer and looked pensively at her mug. "Why did they choose ten citizens to slaughter? Why not twelve? Did they pat themselves on the back for their restraint? I wonder about such matters every now and then." She shook her head. "Why not *eight?*"

Harrison was about to take a crack at the psychodynamics of brutality, but instead gave a collaborative nod and plowed ahead. "When you were describing the German's odd behavior toward Ben Eisenberg—his uneasy avoidance of the boy—I felt that you were experiencing a revelation of sorts."

"Yes. I said you would figure it out, remember?"

"Yes, I do. I believe you suddenly realized that Hans might very well have known, or at least suspect, that something nefarious was going to take place at the Eisenberg's that night. And because he was familiar with the boy, it made him uncomfortable."

Madame D slowly shook her head. "Don't let his touch of humanity sway you, Harry. When you and your buddies are brainstorming the last act of my play, don't let the bastard off the hook."

"I'll keep that in mind, Denise. I trust your instincts."

For a moment or two, they picked at what remained in their plates, Madame D reviewing every morsel as if it were a lab specimen she'd been assigned to analyze.

Harrison set down his fork. "What became of them—Hans and Madeline Paquard?" he asked.

"Hans got himself billeted in a charming little cottage in the village of Auvers-sur-Oise," Madame D replied, laying down her fork as well. "A quaint suburb of Paris immortalized by van Gogh, as you must know."

"Yes, the painter lived the last months of his life in the garret of the Ravoux Inn. He created some of his best '*degenerate*' art in Auvers-sur-Oise," he added with a bitter smile. "Did his relationship with Madeline survive the move?"

"It more than survived. It thrived. Hans kicked the owners out of the house and the girl moved in with him. A year later, she bore him a son. For all I know their progeny is still living in that house. It's his now. After the war its owner sold the property to Madeline, with the help of her parents, and moved in with his relatives. Madeline herself died about twenty-five years ago. As for the Paquards senior, they pulled up roots in the late 1940s and moved elsewhere to start a new life—to Spain, I believe. I hear they sold their art collection in the process. I do know that they were killed in a car accident barely a year after they emigrated."

Harrison expressed his perfunctory regrets, then asked the most critical question of the day, "What became of Hans?"

"Hans?" she repeated. "Hans vanished. Just before the German occupation came to an end, in 1944."

To Brazil, perhaps? In the absence of proof, instinct cast Hans as the anonymous quid pro quo offered by Alekhine in his letter to Brazil's Ambassador Martins. "How did Madeline take his departure? Was she devastated?"

Madame D shrugged. "One would think."

Harrison fought for a foothold in the scant groundwork of facts. "Did the couple ever marry?" he posed, the question itself giving rise to hope, as he imagined himself, inveterate researcher that he was, poring over musty library files, a town registry, a local church's unwieldy tomes containing birth, marriage, death records penned in black ink, fading, but still legible. When Madame D answered his question, he was already planning his trip to Auvers-sur-Oise. *Do I rent a car? Hire a driver?*

"I have no idea if they married. In fact, I couldn't tell you Hans's last name. They kept that to themselves."

Harrison had expected that to be the case, but he was not to be deterred. "There are areas to be explored," he assured her.

"Yes, we can work on that later." Madame D struggled to her feet and grabbed hold of the handles of her walker. "Right now, we will enjoy Gretchen's *piece de resistance,* her *mousse au chocolat!*" She stabilized herself before taking hold of her dinner plate and starting out for the sink, as precarious a journey as a tightrope walk.

Harrison leaped to his feet and gently wrested Madame D's plate from her grip. He placed the utensils they'd used onto his own dinner plate and deposited the collection onto the sink counter, all the while processing Madame D's last remark. *We can work on that later.* Did she envision herself as his newly-acquired partner? Had he led her on in some way? He hurried back to the table to fetch the iron pan containing the leftovers; then back again to the sink. "Denise, please sit down!"

"Sit yourself down, Harry!" She set two white ramekins filled to the brim with chocolate mousse and two dessert spoons onto the countertop and reached for a small serving tray in the overhead cabinet.

"You'll let me clean up afterward," he said, back in his chair. Meanwhile, his thoughts were hung up on her collaborative expectations: *We can work on that later.* He was looking forward to continuing his research in the comfort of his little apartment at the Rodin Inn, sharing his efforts only with Erika, with whom he was becoming more anxious to speak to with each passing minute.

"Yes, I'll allow you to help with the dishes," Madame D conceded. "Now dig in." She raised her spoon, but waited for him to take the first mouthful.

He did. His eyes widened.

"I didn't exaggerate, did I?" she said.

"No, you didn't. This is heavenly." It was an honest answer, but still, he felt like a damn fraud, keeping his proprietorial thoughts about his investigation to himself. She was a marvelous woman, but she was not about to become his sleuthing mate.

Madame D leaned forward, as if to avoid being overheard. "I tell you, Harry, Gretchen may be a master at engaging the taste buds," she confided, "but truth be told, her taste in men is hardly as refined. I've seen several of what may be loosely defined as her boyfriends—they drop by every now and then—and they are a sorry crew. Boorish and controlling, the lot of them. I want to tell her that she ought not to be selling herself short, but I don't want to be seen as meddling." She sat back. "What do you think, Harry? Do you think I should initiate a heart-to-heart with the girl?" Without losing a beat, she added, "You've scarfed down the mousse. I'm so glad. You must have another. And tea—or coffee. I insist." She started to rise. With a "No, no, please!" from him, she sank back down, crestfallen.

He suddenly realized—how stupid of him not to have seen it sooner!—that Madame D's goal was not to become part of his research team or hear his advice on any of a variety of subjects, it was to prolong his visit! By her own admission, he had been the first person she had opened herself up to regarding the event that had had such a profound impact on her life. Her catharsis had connected them, and as a recluse, the connection must have been especially significant for her. His lack of insight filled him with remorse. He hardly knew what to say. "I think your advice to Gretchen might be useful to her," he heard come out of his mouth. "The very act of your expressing interest in her may boost her ego, don't you agree?"

She seemed not to hear him. "I shall never see you again," she said with such ponderous certainty that he thought she was about to confess to suffering a terminal disease.

"Of course you'll see me!" he objected, with a vigor that startled her out of her despondence; at least caused her to meet his gaze. "My wife and I will come to Paris to visit you," he added, making a spur-of-the-moment commitment he meant to keep. "I know that you and Erika will discover that you're kindred spirits—just like you and I!"

"Don't make rash promises. I'll be happy if you keep in touch, let me know how your investigation is going, and if I can be of further help."

"Without you I would be nowhere," he said. Of course, I'll keep in touch; and I *do* look forward to visiting you with Erika in the very near future." He rose from the table. "And now you must live up to your promise that I be allowed to help with the dishes!"

When, twenty minutes later, Harrison at last stood at the back door of Madame D's apartment and was about take his leave, the mood had been stabilized into a realistic mix of gratitude and projected nostalgia. He reached for her hand then, and she held it as if she would never let it go; and he wondered, in that passing moment of undocumented history, if he was acting as surrogate for a boy long gone.

Chapter 9

Erika sat in the rocker with her cell phone on her lap. She could neither sleep nor read, only wait. It was almost two in the morning, nearing the outer limit of the call-time span she'd stipulated—*suggested* more accurate, to be fair. She was just about to call Harrison, but decided to give him another fifteen minutes. After all, he might be in the middle of some critical investigation. She did the math: eight o'clock in Paris; what could he be investigating at this hour? There they go again, those disruptive hormones, teasing up the old issues of mistrust she thought had been put to rest by her beloved soul-mate.

Her cell phone vibrated against her thigh, stemming the surge of doubt before it got out of hand. "Hey!" she responded to the smiling face on her screen. She could see he was sitting on the edge of a bed, which, she could not help noticing, looked perfectly unruffled. She smiled back, hoping she looked as good to him as he did to her. "How did it go?"

"I miss you," he said. "Am I calling too late?"

"No. Except Lucas has been asleep fifteen minutes; not likely to wake up for a while. You'll have to postpone your conversation with him." She rose from the chair. "Let me take this to the bathroom, so I won't worry about disturbing him." On arrival, she closed the door and sat down on the lid of the toilet seat. "Tell me everything."

"What about you, darling? How was your day?"

"The high point was experimenting with formula milk at Lucas's last feeding. It went without a hitch." Less lightheartedly, she announced, "I spoke to Bonnie and John."

His face fell. "What did they have to say?"

"Please, you first. I've been waiting on tenterhooks."

He nodded his acquiescence, then shifted his position so that he was further from the edge of the bed and half reclined, resting his weight on his left forearm and leaving the cell phone to lie face-up on the bedcover. "How's this? Can you see me?" She confirmed that she did. Without further ado, he launched into his narrative of his encounter with Madame Denise Fontaine: nonagenarian proprietor of *Rouge Tatuage* and source of the most significant information to date regarding their investigation.

Erika remained virtually silent and in awe during his recitation, much like he had during its original telling. At the end of his account, the questions tumbled from her as they formed. He had thought she would bring new ideas to the table and in so doing, further clarify where they were headed, and he had not been wrong. "Is there any other person of interest besides Hans that the authorities, Denise, and even you, for that matter, have come up with?" she asked. "No? Then Hans is the person we must wholeheartedly assume is guilty of the three murders. If we don't, our pursuit will be half-assed, uninspired." She went on. "Didn't you say the Wildensteins emigrated to the United States despite the seizure of their art collection? The Gestapo officers that commandeered their art gallery weren't afraid of being ratted on, were they? Stealing from Jews for the benefit of the Reich was permissible. Then why would Hans find it necessary to kill the Eisenbergs? The most logical answer is that he was appropriating their property for himself, not for the Fuhrer. I mean, Hermann Goering was known to have taken a painting or two here and there for his own private use, but, then, Hans was not Hitler's second in command! He would have been punished! To save his skin, Hans needed to kill the witnesses to his crime, that is the Eisenbergs and the two patrolling officers that walked in on him. This is the simplest explanation, Harrison, requiring the least amount of speculation. Think Occam's razor."

She asked if he planned to search the archives of the *Beaux-Arts Gazette* for any reviews or ads referring to the Eisenberg Gallery, suggesting that 1928 to 1940 would be the optimum time slot to concentrate on; that is, when Georges Wildenstein was the periodical's director. When Harrison replied that he planned to do just that, Erika did an instant search on Google and found that the Robarts Library at the University of Toronto was the *Gazette's* digital sponsor. "If they seem to be dragging their heels, you can always check to see if a used book dealer can come up with the relevant issues. In fact, why don't I get the ball rolling on this while you're gallivanting around Paris and environs? What do you say?"

Harrison was impressed with her resourcefulness, especially at two in the morning. "I say yes—God, I wish you were here!"

"I do, too, darling."

He let that echo in the space between them, then asked, "So, what have *you* been up to?"

She hesitated a microsecond too long.

"Erika?"

"Well," she began, "I heard from Greg earlier. He searched the Art Loss Register database and those of the major international auction houses for a sign of either of the two paintings mentioned in Alekhine's letter. He also probed the underworld for past and present breakthroughs. He came up empty." She was about to inform him of Greg's and her more personal exchange, but, maybe because sharing a secret with Greg shored up her skittish self-confidence, she went instead with, "I'm hoping we'll get lucky when I review the *Gazettes,* and the name of some individual or organization will bring us closer to the elusive Hans."

"Yes, let's hope," Harrison said, a quizzical frown forming. "What else?"

Between her reticence about Greg and her uneasiness about what she was about to reveal, she worried that she was showing her nerves by speaking too fast. She took a deep breath and dove in. "John found out that Gary Kessler was arrested for the assault and battery of his wife, Jodie. The cops called to the scene had no choice but to charge him with a felony, since they witnessed him land a blow. Jodie was hurt pretty badly and was hospitalized, but John says she's expected to make a full recovery."

There was a pause while Harrison processed this. "I'm happy to hear she'll be alright," he said slowly, as if to delay what was coming. "Do you know what provoked the attack?" he asked, features tensing.

"The detective assigned to Chuck's case had his auxiliary phone hacked and discovered he and Jodie had been carrying on an affair. Kessler found proof of this on his wife's cell phone before she had a chance to delete the evidence. He reacted badly." She omitted the lurid details of the lovers' exchange to keep Harrison's discomfort to a minimum.

"I see," he said, returning to his straight-backed position, sitting on the edge of the bed. "Did John learn anything—I mean actually relevant to the homicide?" he inquired, slipping to his professorial tone.

"No, he didn't. You do realize, don't you, that the authorities will be even more entrenched in their belief that Kessler murdered Bloom and will crowbar into their scenario any scrap of evidence they find?"

"I do realize that, which is why we have to use every possible resource available to us to try and track down his real killer, and in so doing, unravel an art theft crime that took place eighty years prior, but to which this person is—*must* be—in some way linked."

"Exactly!" Erika emphatically agreed, glad they'd veered from the touchy subject. "I'm thinking it would be great if we could find some concrete evidence connecting Alekhine and Hans. It would solidify our working theory that Hans is the anonymous German in the chess master's letter, and it would narrow down our field of inquiry considerably."

"It would indeed," Harrison replied, back to his calmer state, now that the question of Chuck's morality was no longer hovering over their conversation like a drone. He yawned, more out of relief than fatigue. "Sorry."

"You must be exhausted!" Erika declared, rising to her feet. "You should get some rest. I'm sure you have a busy day ahead of you."

He followed her example and rose from the bed. He toyed with the idea that they were standing face-to-face. "Shall we dance?" he asked, perhaps a bit giddy with fatigue, after all. "Yes, I do have a busy day planned. Starting with my trip to Auvers-sur-Oise. I did include the Auvers-sur-Oise chapter of Madeline Paquard and Hans's life together in my lengthy account, didn't

I?"

Erika nodded. "You said the couple moved into a commandeered house in the town, where Madeline later gave birth to their son. It's the town from which Hans eventually vanished. You can be sure that I'll be reading whatever I can get my hands on about Auvers-sur-Oise."

Harrison smiled. "Of course, you will. And, of course you'll text me any information you think may be useful to me. In fact, I'm counting on it."

"Oh, I'll be doing a lot of sedentary research while you're gadding about," she assured him.

"That's what I like to hear," he said. "I worry when your research turns ambulatory. You have a habit of wandering into harm's way." He suddenly lowered his gaze. "You said you spoke to Bonnie. Anything I need to know?" His demeanor said *Be quick about it!*

Erika was glad she had neutral information with which to reply. "She gave me the names of previous owners of the house where the carton was found." Short and sweet. It would do.

He looked up; his shoulders relaxed. "I wish you were coming with me tomorrow," he said, clearly relieved the sordid details of Chuck's affair had been elided.

"I do, too, but I can't leave Lucas; not yet."

"When is Luc due to wake up, by the way?"

"Not anytime soon. You'll have to put off his first lesson in French until tomorrow—that is, for us, later today."

"How about late afternoon, then? Will that be good?"

"Wait, I'll check my schedule—you're in luck, I'm free. Goodnight. I love you, sweetheart."

"I love you, too, goodnight," he said.

His words had sounded clipped. It worried her.

Chapter 10

After FaceTiming with Erika, Harrison checked his watch: 8:45 p.m. Paris time, or 3:45 a.m. somatic time. No way was he about to tuck himself in. Every moment of research counted. He would work his way through jet lag.

First thing, he searched the net for instructions on how to locate France's vital records of births, marriages and deaths. He came up with the French Civil Registration offices, where he discovered that for reasons of privacy and security, online genealogy records were released only if over one-hundred years old. It was suggested that for more recent records the mayor of the town in question be contacted. That turned out to be Isabelle Mezieres, and after many dead ends, he finally found her contact information. He jotted down her office's physical address and phone number, which would be of use the next day, Wednesday, and shot an email to her at cabinetdumaire@ville-auverssuroise.fr, summarizing his project—or rather the faux version he'd given Francois—and listing his credentials. At the last minute he decided not to mention the real objective of his visit, namely to learn about Madeline Paquard, her son and his birth father. He was probably more susceptible to paranoia when he was fatigued, but be that as it may, the mayor's address on Rue du General de Gaulle was the same given for the town's tourist office, and he preferred, at least for the time being, that the mayor assume the information he sought could be found within that unprovocative domain. He requested a Wednesday meeting, any time at her convenience and apologized for the short notice.

He added his cell phone number for good measure.

Next, he had Google pinpoint a top-rated private car service in the area and booked a driver for the day, pickup at 7:30 a.m. Auvers-sur-Oise was about an hour's drive from Paris under optimum conditions, and he wanted to make sure he'd arrive well before the start of the workday and be the first supplicant to step foot in the door.

The next item on his ever-evolving agenda was to schedule an informal chat with The Louvre curator who'd assembled the Eugene Delacroix retrospective in 2018. He emailed the curator, requesting a get-together on Thursday, April 16, at whatever hour convenient. As with his email to the mayor, he included an apology for the short notice.

Having no more immediate issues to deal with, he decided, with some lingering reluctance, to call it a day. He showered, threw on a pair of jockey shorts and T-shirt, set his cell phone alarm for 6:00 a.m., turned down the bed and flopped onto it. His last thought before sleep overtook him: *What have I forgotten to do—must be something I left undone.*

Chapter 11

Harrison was wide awake an hour before the alarm was set to go off. He reached for his cell phone on the night table and canceled the alarm, then rose from the bed. He spritzed his face with water, ran his fingers through his hair and brushed his teeth. From the sparse array of clothing he'd hung in the closet after he'd returned from Madame D's, he chose a pair of khaki pants, white buttoned shirt and brown tweed blazer as acceptable attire for a mayoral visit. Socks and loafers completed the outfit.

He checked himself in the full-length mirror on the back side of the closet door and found himself judging his appearance through Erika's eyes. *When the hell had* that *started?* He smiled, tickled by the idea of being in her power. It made her feel present. He imagined her cocking her head and pretending to have reservations, but in the end approving. Satisfied, he shut the closet door, grabbed the apartment key from the dresser top and headed for the exit.

The Rodin Inn, he had learned from the manager's assistant, Justine, offered a self-serve continental breakfast in the lounge off the main lobby from five to nine every morning. He could smell the rich aroma of coffee from the top of the staircase leading to the main floor, and his nostrils flared in anticipation.

Just outside the lounge, a small pedestal table containing a neat stack of *Le Monde* newspapers stood against the wall. Harrison guessed he was the first guest to lay hands on a newspaper that morning, and indeed he was right. The lounge, he discovered on entering, was empty, waiting with open arms, it seemed, for visitors. Each of its five round tables was cloaked with a spotless white tablecloth and meticulously laid with four porcelain settings of cups, saucers and dinner plates and perfectly aligned napkins and utensils. In the center of each table, a small glass vase containing a sprig of wildflowers added a welcome touch of color. He chose a table closest to the coffee urns, placed his newspaper on one of its accompanying straight-back chairs upholstered in beige velour and, with cup in hand, headed to the table containing the assortment of coffees, teas and embellishments. He poured himself as full a cup as safely transportable of the coffee labeled "Italian - Dark Roast," and carefully delivered it to its awaiting saucer. Unwilling to postpone his first sip a moment longer, he stood over the table and lifted the cup to his lips. The coffee was strong, with perhaps a hint of hazelnut, and bitingly—welcomingly—hot. He took another few sips and returned the cup to its saucer. Already anticipating a second cup, he carried his dinner plate to the serving table against the wall at right angles to the hot beverages and scanned its contents of baked goods, cold cereals and juices. He plucked a croissant from its serving plate with silver tongs lying parallel to its upper rim, then claimed an irresistibly plump corn muffin from the adjacent dish. He added two pats of butter and a one-serving jar of blackberry jam to his plate and ambled back to his table. Still no one in sight. It was as if the array of offerings had materialized out of thin air.

By the time he was polishing off his baked items and draining his second cup of coffee, it was six-thirty. As yet, he'd been the only guest to have graced the lounge, although Louis Corsair had stuck his head in and out of the doorway like a clock's cuckoo, retreating the second he spotted Harrison. What the hell was up with this guy?

Waving off his discomfit as unwarranted, he spent the next forty-five minutes in his apartment distractedly leafing through the newspaper, before returning to his notes from the previous day with the hopes that an unexamined research angle could be nursed into being or spontaneously reveal itself. Neither occurred, and at seven-fifteen, he stowed his note pad and pen in his jacket pocket and returned to the main floor to wait for his driver just outside the inn's entrance, on the way out making sure to avoid eye contact with Louis, back at the front desk. He was on the move now; no time to be weirded out.

It was promising to be another glorious day, taunting and tempting with its languorous beauty, setting the city aglow in the dawning of the light. Harrison was touched by it, but only in passing, as his thoughts gained momentum on the possibilities of what lay ahead.

His driver, a middle-aged woman in a rakishly cocked chauffeur's hat, pulled up to the curb in a black town car at seven twenty-nine, one minute earlier than scheduled. "Allow me!" she commanded more than offered, as she jumped out of the car to fling open the rear door. She was wearing a black suit and tie; very dapper. "You're Harrison Wheatley, I take it?"

He acknowledged the fact and slid into the back seat. He hoped she wasn't going to turn out to be a talker.

"Betsy Ross, no relation to the flag-maker," she said brusquely, in a distinctly New York accent. "So, we're going to Auvers-sur-Oise, are we?" Her French was mellifluous in stark contrast to her English. "Route A115 is looking great. Should get you there in record time."

"Excellent," Harrison said coolly, hoping to establish an environment of mutual reticence. It would have been more like him to ask her about her origins, how she'd come to live in Paris. But on this day, he wanted to be alone with his thoughts.

Betsy caught on at once. "You'll notice there's bottled water in the door sleeves. Mixed nuts, too. You let me know if you need anything, you hear?" She turned around in her seat to grant him a "Roger, and Out" smile along with a decisive nod and turned back to face the windshield. She buckled her seatbelt, waited to hear the click of Harrison's—he knew it was the law in France—and without another word, pulled away from the curb.

During the uneventful drive north to Auvers-sur-Oise, he hardly looked out the window, and when he happened to, his gaze was unfocused. His mind was elsewhere, circling the figures of Alekhine, Hans, the Eisenbergs, Bloom, trying to herd them together with some binding element, alternately thinking *It's out there somewhere!* and *Am I being fucking naïve?*

It seemed hardly any time had passed since they'd set forth, when Betsy announced, "Here we are!"

The car was still in motion, but was slowing down. Harrison looked up from his cell phone, where he'd just begun checking for incoming emails and text messages. "Oh?" He looked out the window and saw that he'd been transported to what appeared to be a quaint rural town, whose homes were constructed in a variety of architectural styles, each with a texture and character of its own. It was only when Betsy turned a corner onto its main street and he spotted the historic landmark of which he'd seen numerous photographs, that he realized they'd arrived at Auvers-sur-Oise, specifically the rue du General de Gaulle. He'd meant to visit the building during his teaching stint in Paris, but had never gotten around to it. "Auberge Ravoux," he said reverently, more to himself than his driver.

"The Maison de van Gogh, as it's more commonly called," Betsy answered, as if on cue, pulling up to the curb in front of it for a quick survey. "This is the inn where Vincent van Gogh spent the last seventy days of his life," she said, as if reading from a script. "While in Auvers, he produced eighty paintings and sixty-four sketches."

He wondered if he should interrupt her tour-guide presentation, and decided it would be rude to do so. "Aha," he said instead.

"On July the twenty-seventh 1890," she continued, "he shot himself in the chest in an attempt at suicide. He died two days later at age thirty-seven. According to Vincent's beloved brother, Theo, his last words were 'the sadness will last forever.' Theo died six months later at age thirty-three. They're both buried in the public cemetery here in Auvers. You might want to stop by if time permits."

"Thank you, I'll try to," Harrison said cordially, though with budding impatience.

Betsy must have picked up on it because she immediately proceeded to move down the street along the curb before stopping again. Shifting into idle, she announced, "You're now in front of the address requested, number 38 rue du General de Gaulle." She unlocked the doors.

"Thank you, Betsy." He looked at his watch. It read "8:31." None of the potential delays he had taken into account when determining his pick-up time had occurred, and the building that housed the mayor's and tourist offices did not open until nine-thirty. Nevertheless, he was eager to start the day in earnest. He would walk the town, immerse himself in the environment that was, for a critical period, home to Madeline Paquard and her lover (possibly her husband), Hans. *Who knows*, he reflected, *I might run into her son without knowing it.* The thought energized him, and he undid his seatbelt and scooted out of the car before Betsy had a chance to react in a timely manner. She shrugged and rolled down her window as he appeared at her door.

"You're a fast one," she said. "Do you have any idea of how long you'll be here?"

Harrison whipped the notepad and pen from his pocket. "I can't say, but give me your number and I'll call or text when I know more. I assume the company gave you mine."

She dictated her number and confirmed that she had his. They exchanged palm-up salutes and he stepped out of the way to allow her to pull away from the curb. As he did so, he realized a car was parked behind them. Since Betsy had just scooted curbside along the avenue, the driver must have pulled up seconds ago. Had anyone gotten out of the car? Intending to steal a look inside, he started to walk toward the passenger window, but pulled up short. What was he doing, trying to get himself arrested? With a bemused grin, he brushed aside his meddlesome paranoia and reclaimed his prior mood.

As if his steps had been choreographed, he began walking toward the end of the street and toward the less built-up part of town. It was only when he'd come to a place where he could take in the vista of green fields dotted with homes and in the near distance, rugged cliffs, that he realized he'd been seeking such an encounter. The landscape bore a wonderful similarity to his parents' horse ranch in South Dakota, a ten-thousand acre spread with a backdrop of rolling plains and, yes, with the same glorious light that had inspired painters like van Gogh, Daubigny, Cezanne, Pissarro to change the way they viewed the world. He took a deep, rejuvenating breath and raised his arms to the sky—anyone seeing him would have imagined it was to God in heaven, but it was nature he extolled, not the fictive brain behind it. He stood there for some moments, hands back at his sides, and for that span of time his investigative drive receded into the sea of unstructured thought.

He took a divergent path until the River Oise came into view, and it was here he imagined himself setting up with all the accouterments of a painter—easel, canvas, palette, brushes, oils—to create a wash of bright and muted blues with floral yellows and reds reflected in its mirrored surface. He smiled to himself. An art history professor with no artistic talent. At the apex of his smile, a tanned laborer carrying a hoe, dressed in overalls and rolled-up denim shirt and looking as if he'd just stepped out of a Jean-Francois Millet painting, passed him on the path and smiled back at him. Harrison nodded in return, transforming his contemplative smile into a greeting. As he watched the man walk away, he tried to see him purely as a retinal translation of reflected light, whose weight was undetermined, perhaps non-existent.

He was absorbed in his attempted interface with impressionism, when his cell phone summoned him—raucously, it seemed—to the world of hard facts. He pulled the device from his jacket pocket and checked the screen before accepting the call. He recognized neither the name, "R. Guillaume," nor the number, but maybe because of the ambient light or the man who smiled or the infusion of pleasant memories, he anticipated good news. He tapped the green circle. "Hello…Monsieur—or Madame Guillaume?"

"Madame. Mademoiselle, actually, although that's become an obsolete form of address. Have I reached Professor Wheatley? Harrison Wheatley?"

The woman's English was perfect. "You have. May I ask—"

"I'm Raquel Guillaume," she returned abruptly. "Assistant to Mayor Meziere. Unfortunately, the mayor will be out of the office this week, and from the tenor of your email it looks as though you'll be in the area only briefly. Perhaps I can help you."

Harrison looked at his watch. The mayor's office would be opening in forty minutes. "I'm actually here in Auvers. Shall I drop by the office at nine-thirty?"

Ms. Guillaume expressed her surprise, then, without answering his question, went straight to one of her own: "Exactly what information are you looking for, Professor?"

Harrison began with the spiel that had worked on Francois at Chez Aristede, then added the story he'd concocted on the drive to Auvers, when he'd realized, with a start, that he'd overlooked the need for one: "In order to do a laudable history of Paris's art galleries," he said, wincing at the archness prompted by her brusqueness, "I must try to make contact with individuals with first-hand knowledge of the standards, the styles, the fads, in the galleries' heyday. The Paquard family of Paris, I've been told, were avid art collectors in the 1920s and '30s, and I'd set my mind on interviewing them, only to learn that they were deceased. Their daughter, Madeline, I've since discovered, relocated to Auvers-sur-Oise around 1941 with her then lover, and around a year later bore him a son. Madeline died about twenty-five years ago, but I believe her son still resides here in Auvers. If I'm lucky, he'll have memorabilia of the Paquard family to share, from which I hope to glean a few personal insights of the era that will bear fruit, so to speak."

"I see," Ms. Guillaume responded after a pause, during which Harrison hoped she was deliberating where best to begin her research on the Paquards. "This is interesting. What specifically do you want to find out? Are you concerned only in learning Madeline Paquard's son's address? That would be easy enough to check out."

"That's the essential thing," Harrison declared, "but I would also be interested in attaining any vital records on file that would give my study more heft, as it were. For instance, I don't know the name of Madeline's lover, nor do I know if the two ever married."

"I would imagine you could find this out from their son," Ms. Guillaume suggested, a quizzical note in her voice.

"Of course," Harrison agreed, with more assuredness than he felt, "but as an historian, I'm rather obsessive about verifying data, whenever possible."

After what sounded like a drawer opening and closing followed by an interval of paper shuffling, Ms. Guillaume spoke: "I'm not a scholar myself, so I'm not going to question the relevancy of these records to your research, but I must tell you, the time it would take me to obtain them depends entirely on their accessibility. In any event, for me to release them, I would need to see proof of your identity and, most importantly, sufficient proof of your credentials. Did you bring such documentation with you today?"

"Yes. Shall I stop by at nine-thirty, or would later this morning be more convenient for you?"

Harrison heard what sounded like furniture being moved. He took a wild guess at Ms. Guillaume's desk chair. "I'm on a tight schedule myself today, Professor," she said. "I'm attending a meeting at the primary school at nine forty-five. The board is reviewing blueprints for an annex, and they must be advised on building restrictions and zoning regulations. I dropped by my office to gather my materials and was planning to grab a coffee at the Café de la Paix, right down the street from us. We're number thirty-eight; the cafe, eleven. Do you know where the mayor's office is, by the way?"

"I do," Harrison said. "I can be there in five, ten minutes."

"No, that would waste time. If you know where we are, you can find the café. Here's the plan. I'm going to see if I can find the information you're after. If it's been entered in the computer database, it won't be difficult. If it's among our unprocessed documents, we'll have to search for it another day. In any case, I can probably get you Monsieur Paquard's address and phone number. How about we meet at the café in fifteen minutes—nine o'clock. I'll either have something for you or not."

"That would be great," Harrison said. "Either way, thank you."

"Please have your credentials at the ready."

"I will, yes. Absolutely."

"I'm wearing a navy blue pant suit," she clipped, before terminating the call.

* * *

Harrison knew he'd arrived at the rustic pub-like cafe before Ms. Guillaume because the only patrons there were either in pairs or threesomes. He started for one of the available centrally located tables while directing an is-this-permissible? look at the only staff member in sight, a young waitress bearing a tray of steam-emanating mugs to an occupied table. She gave him a pleasant confirmatory nod, and he took a seat, making sure to face the entrance.

The first person to stride through the door was an impeccably dressed gentleman in a gray herringbone suit, white shirt and paisley tie. He looked like he might have just rolled off the *GQ* conveyer belt, were it not for his one distinguishing feature: an angry crescent-shaped scar running from the corner of his mouth to his scalp. His raven hair was gelled back off his forehead, displaying the scar in full, like a badge of honor, as if the man wished to spare the onlooker the effort of not staring. Look all you want. Try not to be jealous. He pulled up a chair at a nearby table and immersed himself in a magazine he'd had tucked under his arm. Interesting character. Harrison imagined a van Gogh portrait of him. For the second time this morning, he wished he were an artist.

From Ms. Guillaume's officious phone presence, he expected a matron with a hardball chignon to march through the door in navy blue pant suit and matching orthopedic shoes. For that reason, he assumed that the shapely young woman who within minutes strode through the door, red mane bouncing, stiletto heels clicking, was attired in a form-fitting blue pant suit by sheer coincidence.

"Professor Wheatley?" the woman inquired in the business-like tone he recognized, as she approached.

"Yes," he answered, politely half-standing as she took a seat opposite him. Close up, he noticed her freckles, further confounding his preconception of her. He extended his hand. "Madame Guillaume, I hope I haven't upset your schedule."

"Call me Raquel, it'll save time. Have you ordered?" She placed her leather portfolio bag on her lap and waved at the waitress who scurried over to the table. *"Bonjour, Vivienne. Pour moi, café noir, s'il vous plait."* She eyed Harrison with a touch of impatience.

"Le meme," he said, both curious and amused by the discrepancy between the visual and aural impressions of the woman, as if they were of two distinct personae.

The waitress, Vivienne, suggested that the raspberry tarts were especially popular this morning. Raquel demurred. Harrison could not resist ordering one, despite the fact that Raquel's sigh of resigned tolerance made him feel like a greedy schoolboy. Nevertheless, his ego's diminution did not override his eagerness to get to the point: "Were you able to find any pertinent information?" he posed, leaning forward in his captain's chair, realizing, as he did so, that he had not seen the gentleman with the magazine turn a single page. *Slow reader?*

"I was about to get to the data," Raquel said, patting her portfolio. "Not much to offer, I'm afraid, but all the same, I need to check your credentials."

Harrison was prepared. He fetched his wallet from his pants pocket and whipped out the cards he'd slipped into one of its empty slots: his TSA-compliant driver's license and his New York University Institute of Fine Art's photo ID. "The star in the upper right section of my driver's license indicates that its security level is equivalent to a passport's," he explained, handing over the cards for her perusal.

"I'm aware of that," Raquel said, turning over each card in turn. She looked from the photo on his driver's license to his face, then repeated the act, squinting as she did so, as if she were deciding if he were a clone or an extra-terrestrial.

"You can also check out my book on Amazon," he suggested. "And if you need to speak with an associate of mine at NYU, I can give you the number of my department head." He shrugged. "Of course, it's only about three in the morning in New York, so—"

"This is fine," Raquel interrupted, reaching out to hand him back his cards.

Their fingers brushed as he retrieved his cards, and he could have sworn the beginnings of a wistful—no, sorcerous—smile had touched her lips, surprising him anew. He tucked his cards back into their slot and returned his wallet to his pocket.

Their coffees and Harrison's tart arrived as Raquel was unzipping her portfolio. She took a sip of her coffee and slid the mug aside.

Deferring beverage and accompaniment, Harrison waited. She seemed to take forever extracting an envelope from her bag, opening it and withdrawing the folded paper within. He thought that this is what it must feel like to be nominated for an Oscar. She handed him both the envelope and paper. "Take a look and see if you have any questions. I made a copy of the page where the data had been entered. The black patches indicate information extraneous to your research that I've redacted for security purposes."

"I see, thanks." He scanned the sheet:

PAQUARD, HENRI ne: 12 Novembre 1942

Nom de la mère: MADELINE PAQUARD nee: 09 Septembre 1920

décédée: 23 Janvier 1996

Nom du père: INCONNU

He was not expecting much more than this, if *even* this, but he was a bit disappointed, nonetheless. Below the printed copy Raquel had neatly penned: **Henri Paquard's address: 28 Rue Victor Hugo; landline: +33 130 37 77 23.**

"Sorry there isn't more, but I assume this will be of help," Raquel said, before taking a few more sips of her coffee.

"It surely is," Harrison said, setting the material aside to cut into his tart. "This *alone* is worth the trip," he reviewed after sampling a forkful. He couldn't help noticing the man with the magazine had hooked his finger through the mug handle, but was not picking up the mug.

"I take it you'll be attempting to arrange an interview with Henri Paquard today," Raquel remarked, bypassing the small talk. "If so, I should call him first and vouch for you." She took a heartier swig of her coffee and, anticipating his reply, retrieved her cell phone from her portfolio.

"That would be kind of you, Raquel."

Reading the number from the sheet Harrison had set aside, Raquel punched in Monsieur Paquard's landline. "I'd put the call on speakerphone," she said, "but it would be rude in a public place." Without acknowledging Harrison's nod, she drummed the fingers of her free hand on the table as she waited for Paquard to pick up. After about ten seconds, she began what was clearly a canned directive to leave a message. Harrison had no problem understanding her French, which was fast-paced but beautifully enunciated, perhaps for his benefit. She was in the middle of itemizing his academic credentials, when her monologue was abruptly interrupted by a live person coming on the line. She mimed a message to Harrison indicating Paquard had picked up, then began her monologue anew. Hearing only one side of the conversation, Harrison understood that Paquard was willing to see him, but not exactly when. The fact that Raquel ended the exchange with "*Il sera la!*"—he'll be there!—was a good sign.

"Henri was coming in from gardening, when he heard his phone ring," Raquel explained after the call ended. "He seemed genuinely interested in meeting you and expects to see you at his home within the hour." She quickly relayed what appeared to be easy walking directions to the address on Rue Victor Hugo, then in one continuous motion, dropped her cell phone into her portfolio and retrieved her wallet.

"That's great!—are you joking, put that away!" Harrison replied respectively to her spoken and unspoken communications.

"Thanks," Raquel acknowledged, forgoing demureness as she promptly dumped her wallet back into her bag and zipped it up. She gulped down the remainder of her coffee, which Harrison understood as the precursor to her departure, but instead of rising from her chair, she sat forward in it. "How would you like to come unwind at my place this evening?" she proposed, taking Harrison by surprise. "Nothing elaborate—wine and pasta, most likely. I can offer you an insider's view of Auvers that should give your work-in-progress an air of authenticity. Does eight, eight-thirty work for you?"

It was impossible to miss the twinkle in her eye toying with the bluntness of her invitation. He thought it best to go with the least circuitous response: "That's kind of you, but I'm married."

Mugging confusion, Raquel looked about, as if for the stalking wife. "And?"

He shrugged. "There's nothing to add."

She smiled in disbelief. "How about life is short?"

"Exactly. There's no time to lose, perfecting a relationship. Call me a pompous prude—"

"You're a pompous prude."

"—but that's how it is," he completed, both of them smiling.

She rose to go. He would stay to finish his coffee and tart, but stood to bid her good day. She gave his hand an unmistakably fraternal pump, perhaps to make clear her capitulation. "I hope I find myself just such a pompous prude someday," she added, brusque as ever, before turning on her stiletto heel to head for the door.

Harrison sat back down, smiling inwardly as he watched her go, her officious and free-spirited selves at last merging in his mind to form one delightful individual he would not regret having met.

Without his having earned it, the man with the magazine became the vibe's collateral beneficiary as he followed in Raquel's footsteps. For no good reason Harrison nodded good-day to him as he passed by his table. The man either didn't notice or pretended not to, but no matter. It was turning out to be a good day.

* * *

As Harrison strolled due north to Rue Victor Hugo, as directed by Raquel, the sun's rays became more intense and clarifying, and he peeled off his jacket and slung it over his shoulder. Perhaps it was the ease of the gesture combined with his unbroken stride that affected his take on himself, but for a passing moment he felt like the subject of a painting, a local field hand, like the man he'd seen earlier, and that just around the bend, turning onto Rue Victor Hugo, he would come upon a budding van Gogh, waiting for just such a man as he to step into his line of vision and be captured for all time in the ripeness of manhood. The corniness of the image did not escape him, but did not lessen its impact. He was obliquely aware that he might soon be closing in on facts pivotal to his investigation, and for that reason he should be turning fiercer with each step transporting him nearer his quarry. But instead, charged by van Gogh's abundance of light and by his own luminous virility (he saw in his mind's eye how confidently he strode; how his left hand clutched the draped jacket in the posture of Michelangelo's David: holding the sling's pouch over his left shoulder), he could not help but feel, at least for this voluptuous instant in time, hungrier for life than knowledge.

Moments later, the resurgent man on a mission stood facing number 28 Rue Victor Hugo, his ascendant greed for knowledge making his temples pulse. He tried to imagine the German he'd painted in his mind—goose-stepping Olympian with deep-set haunting eyes—waking up every morning in this rustic wood-frame cottage with a projecting shingled entrance bay that appeared to be an afterthought, but well-intentioned. He knew nothing about what building materials were available in the area—what trees were hewn to construct houses, that sort of thing—but the structure looked home-grown to him, in the vernacular style, as his colleagues in Architecture would say. It had been painted white, a few times over judging from the blurred delineations of the entrance bay's shingles, and approaching the need for a refresher coat. The weathered look added a stalwart dimension to its character, he thought, and perhaps its being set further back from the street than its neighbors and on slightly elevated ground contributed to the perception.

He donned his sports jacket before knocking on the front door—who knew why, except he felt like a schoolboy called to the principal's office—and waited for the German officer's son to make his appearance.

The door opened almost at once and the figure occupying the space before Harrison, despite what he believed was his readiness to come face to face with a Gestapo knock-off, took him by surprise. Aside from being at least six inches taller than Harrison, who was himself 6'1", the man's sinuous form, sharply chiseled features and mop of ashy blond hair made his real age of—what was it, seventy-eight, -nine, who could calculate at this moment?—meaningless. The man was a cross between Clint Eastwood and Mount Rushmore. "*Salut, je m'appelle* Harrison Wheatley," Harrison said, thrusting out his hand. "Monsieur Paquard?"

"*Oui, bienvenu*—welcome," the man greeted, his voice softer than Harrison had anticipated. In blue jeans with pressed creases, spotless white T-shirt and just-out-of-the-box sneakers, he had obviously changed since gardening. The two shook hands, and Harrison was ushered in. "Would you like to speak in English, Professor Wheatley?" Henri asked, as he shut the door.

"Please, it's Harrison. And yes, if it's okay with you," Harrison replied, grateful for the offer to once again converse in the language with which he felt most at ease.

His host smiled. "I'm Henri."

"Thank you—but I haven't yet thanked you for seeing me, and at such short notice at that."

"This is my pleasure." Henri gave a little shrug. "But I don't know if I can be of help with your project. Madame Guillaume gave me only a general idea of the topic. You'll have to explain more fully." He motioned toward a faded brown upholstered couch and two side chairs on one side of what was clearly the central room of the house where most of the living was done. Two walls were lined with bookcases stuffed with upright and horizontally laid books of all sizes along with stacks of file folders and loose papers. The remaining wall space was filled with a mélange of oils and watercolors in styles as diverse and yet harmonious as a bustling city. At the far end of the sprawling space, two matching oak desks stood facing each other; one strewn with papers and writing materials, the other bare except for a small potted plant and two writing instruments lying side by side in perfect alignment. Harrison was intrigued. "Have a seat," Henri said. "Would you care for a cup of tea or coffee? A cold drink, perhaps? I have scones and blueberry muffins. What will it be?"

Harrison had maxed out on carbs for the morning. "Actually, just water would be great. Thanks." As Henri headed for the door leading to what Harrison presumed was the kitchen, he wandered over to the seating arrangement. The middle cushion of the couch looked the least sinkable of the five available, including those nested in the side chairs. He took out his pad and pen from his jacket pocket, laid them on the sea chest serving as coffee table and took his chosen place.

There were two black-and-white photographs framed in knotted wood sitting on the sea chest. One was of a beautiful young woman standing beside a tree and posing like a model, one knee bent coyly against the other; the other, a strong-featured young man standing rather stiffly in front of the cottage on Rue Victor Hugo and looking very serious, his hair combed to one side and slicked down. Harrison had his opening.

"Are these your parents?" he asked Henri, on his return with two glasses of water along with two ceramic coasters.

Henri carefully placed the items on the sea chest before answering. "The woman is my mother," he said, as he sank into one of the side chairs. "In her youth. As I like to remember her. The other is of my life partner, Julien, taken shortly after we met. Both are gone now," he added, with an evenness that could have been mistaken for coldness, were it not for the downturn twitch at the corners of his mouth. He reached for his glass, took a sip of water, then neatly set it back on its coaster.

"I'm sorry to hear that," Harrison said, as his only option.

Henri nodded. "They both died of cancer—my mother in 1996; Julien, just two years ago. My mother was gone within eight weeks of being given a diagnosis. Julien suffered for many years, but with intermittent remissions. We lived our fullest during those remissions. We were together for twenty-three years. Not long enough."

Harrison could not help but glance at the room's face-to-face desks, then, wordlessly, back at Henri.

"Yes," Henri said, answering the unspoken question. "The neat one is Julien's. We used to work opposite each other, sometimes on the same project. We were both freelance translators, you see. Well, I still am. Actually, we met at a publishing house, in the waiting room of an editor seeking a translator for an up-an-coming French novelist looking to make a name for himself in America. We were competing for the same job. Fortunately, the editor was late getting back from lunch and Julien and I had a chance to talk to each other at length."

"Which one of you got the assignment?" Harrison asked, sensing an elevation of mood and wanting to encourage it. He took a swig of his water.

Henri sat back in his chair. "Neither of us. The job went to a professor from the University of Pennsylvania."

Harrison relaxed into a guffaw, and Henri could not help but follow suit, his sudden expulsion of energy causing one of his long legs to shoot out, the spasm terminating with a resounding thud as his foot struck the base of the sea chest, prompting another round of shared laughter. "Life is absurdly tragic," Henri observed, recovering his equilibrium. "Tell me about your project."

Harrison was not by nature a liar, but by now his fictive pitch had become second nature to him. This was disturbing. *I will have to write an article about the history of Paris art galleries*, he decided mid-stream, to ease his rising guilt. The decision authenticated his custom-made add-on regarding the senior Paquards and their connection to the local art galleries. Wrapping up, he remarked, "I was hoping among your mother's personal effects there would be some items relating to her parents' art-collecting activities—journals, photographs, documents, primary sources of any kind." Harrison did not feel safe divulging the true goal of his probing. Judging from Henri's life style and temperament, it was unlikely he was a chip off the old block, but who could be sure what lay behind the clear blue eyes of this agreeable giant? Only time would tell—maybe. His mouth felt dry. He downed the remainder of his water.

"I do have a collection of my mother's—Madeline's—memorabilia," Henri offered. "It's not very extensive and it might be of no use to you, but I'll get it now." He rose to his feet. "It's in my bedroom; I'll be right down." He started for the stairs; stopped and turned back. "It might be easier to examine the items if you're sitting at a desk. Why don't you sit at Julien's, and I'll bring the collection to you?" He pointed toward Harrison's glass. "Would you like more water—or anything else—before moving to the desk? I don't think you should bring any spill-able items with you."

"Good idea—and nothing more, thanks," Harrison said, grabbing his pad and pen and rising from the couch. As Henri trotted upstairs, he headed for the desk. On the way, he took a cursory glance at the artwork adorning the walls and made a mental note to take a closer look later on. Erika, he realized with a tick of longing, was in spirit seconding him on the thought. The quintessential editor, she believed it an oversight if one failed to examine any available artifacts that had a chance, however remote, of deepening one's insight into the subject under investigation.

Before lowering himself into the solid oak desk chair, whose seat was polished with wear, he moved to the side the two aligned writing instruments, a black lacquer Waterman fountain pen and its matching mechanical pencil. Only after the fact was he aware of the reverence in his movement.

As Harrison took occupancy of the chair, Henri reappeared, a bulging carpetbag suspended from his right hand. "I'll leave this with you," he said, setting the bag on the floor beside the desk chair. "I'll be right here if you have any questions." He raised the hard cover book he was holding in his left hand. "Reading," he added somberly.

"Thank you for sharing this with me," Harrison replied, as resolutely as both the occasion and Henri's demeanor seemed to demand. Despite his eagerness to view the contents of the carpetbag, he was drawn to studying Henri's retreat. He watched him hover for one or two seconds over the same chair he'd occupied earlier, then opt for its mate on the other side of the couch. He sank down into it and sat motionless for another brief span. When he moved again, it was to give the armrest a few quick but delicate strokes before opening his book. The chair, Harrison realized, could only have been by tradition, Julian's. He looked away, embarrassed by his having intruded on Henri's private moment.

Snatching the leather handle in line with his knee, he hoisted the carpetbag to his lap. It was made of tapestry fabric patterned with flowers in muted tones and put him in mind of Mary Poppins. Heart racing, he undid its brass buckle, pulled open its sides and peered inside. His first impression was that the contents consisted mainly of loose papers and photographs. He reached inside the bag and carefully scooped out a handful of items, making sure not to brush them against the opening's hard rim. After gently placing them on the desktop, he repeated the action two more times, then set the half-empty bag on the floor beside him.

His first impression proved to be correct. Looking down at the miscellaneous papers and photographs of all dimensions and states of wear, he reflected on how he might proceed. He did not want to disturb Henri repeatedly, so he decided the best idea would be to set aside any items with which he had problems and present them at a single session of Q and A. He needed to get Henri's approval of this strategy, and there was another issue he had to bring up as well.

Harrison politely cleared his throat as a prologue to his query, and Henri looked up from his book with raised eyebrows and an accommodating smile. The upshot was that he would be happy to go along with the plan. "And might I have your permission to photograph on my cell phone any items I find of interest?" Harrison cautiously posed.

On this point Henri was ambivalent. "I suppose so, yes, only I would not want you to publish these images either in print or on social media. Not without my permission, that is. Can I trust you on this? I don't mean to sound mean-spirited, but my mother was a very private person, and I am as well, only perhaps to a lesser degree."

"I wouldn't think of publicizing a single photo without your unqualified permission," Harrison declared. "The same stipulation would apply to anything I write about your family. I'd be happy to sign a formal agreement if you like."

Henri waved off the suggestion. "That won't be necessary. There are enough signed agreements in the world. Whatever became of the spoken promise?" With a shrug, he returned to his book.

The sprawl of papers and photographs—with one or two greeting cards spotted between the layers—flaunted itself as a researcher's dream. Harrison reminded himself that he had a primary objective here, and that was to ferret out information on the German officer. All material should be viewed with that in mind. Any references to the Eisenberg Gallery would be of great help in his double-pronged investigation of murder and looted art, but there were other sources from which he could glean information about the gallery. He must remember that only here, in this home, was he ever likely to find a clue leading to the identity and machinations of the elusive German.

He began poring over the material, examining each item before setting it in one of two piles: review and discard. Most of the photographs he relegated to the discard file with agitated regret. They were mostly shots of Henri as a child and young adult, neatly identified and dated in black ink on the back of each photograph. Harrison was curious to know more about this individual—was he scorned as a child? Bullied by his peers for his origins? In a few of the photos he was standing beside his dog—"Leo," according to the printed notes. The dog had the general appearance of a German Shepherd, but the rounded snout and moony gaze of a Labrador. Harrison wondered if it was a mixed breed; wanted to ask Henri about that, and about what had become of the animal, and if there was a replacement dog somewhere on the premises—in the garden, perhaps? What book was he reading, anyway? Harrison was ignited by curiosity.

In the interest of efficiency, he managed to limit at least the breadth of his curiosity, and when he was done sifting through the first half of the carpetbag's contents, there were only two photographs in the review pile: one of Madeline holding the infant, Henri, in her arms; the other of her standing by a park fountain with an adult male, the explanation on the back, a tantalizing: *"Nous voila. Mai* 1940." The remainder of the photographs, those destined to the discard heap, were either of Madeline's parents, in portraiture and visiting a number of European landmarks, and those of her grandparents, aunts and uncles at various stages of their lives and undertakings.

He thought that reviewing the documents—letters mostly—would be more challenging. They were in French and his initial assumption was that those contemporaneous with Madeline's association with the German, or later, should be gone over carefully for references to the couple. What he discovered was that the bulk of written material were Christmas notices from friends of the Paquards senior, monologues detailing the year's comings and goings: babies' first steps, career changes, wisdom acquired. He carefully read the few letters penned during the critical time period, clearing hurdles of idiom and penmanship, but no useful information could be coaxed from them. The greeting cards, though colorful, were equally unforthcoming.

Harrison sighed, pushed the discard pile to the back of the desktop, the two precious photographs for review off to the side, and reached into the carpetbag to withdraw first one handful of material yet be examined, then another. The bag appeared to be empty, but to make sure he swept his hand over its interior. To his surprise, the tips of his fingers hit upon an object lodged in a corner. He drew forth a small pink velvet pouch closed with a drawstring. With bated breath, he tugged apart its pleating and carefully poured its contents onto the desktop. Three items were displayed before him: a silver cuff bracelet, a hinged gold locket on a knotted fine chain, and a thick silver ring with an Iron Cross—*Eisernes Kreuz*—motif running around its shank. He checked the ring's inner shank for an inscription and beheld: *"H.L. 1914."* He whipped out his cell phone and snapped photos of the ring from all angles. Who was "H.L."? Hans's father? Uncle? He felt as if he'd been racing and paused to catch his breath.

Next, he picked up the cuff bracelet and examined it from every angle, but found no revelatory markings. The locket moved into center focus. He studied its exterior: its rounded topside was engraved with a simple *fleur-de-lis* embellished with intricate scrollwork; its flat underside, blank. He snapped open the locket, unreasonably hoping to come upon a photograph of his missing person, complete with name, rank and serial number. Instead, he only found, coiled within, a lock of flaxen hair. His heart leapt, just the same. He hastened to capture images of his find on his cell phone and was about to close the locket and restore all three objects to their protective pouch and probable obscurity, when he stopped to consider an alternative action. *I should ask permission,* he warned himself. *What if permission is not granted?* he countered. Except for a Snickers bar when he was six—seven, at the outside—he had never stolen a thing in his life. *Fuck it, this is too important to debate.* He remembered the slim pack of tissues he'd stuck in his pants pocket, and with as little hip movement as possible, reached for it. He plucked out a tissue, laid it flat on the desktop, then dropped the pack into the pocket of his jacket to avoid a repeated hip action. He could not resist taking a furtive glance at Henri. Thankfully, his host appeared immersed in his book.

With the precision of a surgeon, he pinched several of the outermost strands of hair of the coiled lock between the fingernails of his thumb and third finger. Gently, he tugged his prize free, enfolded it in the tissue and slipped the parcel inside his jacket pocket. *Guilty as charged,* he railed at himself, though with unexpected swagger. He snapped shut the locket and returned it, along with its mates, to the pouch. He drew shut the pouch and placed it alongside the items intended for review.

There was still a fairly daunting amount of material to go through. His next two finds were at the top of the heap, and although they did nothing to advance his real investigation, they did add an air of authenticity to the one he'd fabricated and since earlier this morning felt obliged to undertake. The first was a letter written in 1918 by Monsieur Paquard senior to his future wife. In it he is clearly trying to impress his betrothed with his knowledge of art as well as his clique of gainful connections. He drops the names of several famous art collectors in and around Paris and mentions others he claims to be of lesser note but of greater *sensibilities artistique.* The second was a 1931 inventory of the Paquard art collection. It listed not only details of the artworks themselves, but the names of the local galleries from which they were purchased. Harrison set the two items aside and continued his hunt for greater rewards.

As he was placing a lovely but irrelevant photograph of a seascape into the discard pile, his hand brushed the mound of unexamined artifacts, changing its configuration and exposing a segment of a brightly colored greeting card. He pulled the card from its mooring and viewed its entire front cover, a riot of red, purple and yellow flowers with a birthday greeting superimposed in ornate black script: *Bon Anniversaire.* He unfolded the card and felt his eyebrows shoot up like a cartoon character's. The hand-printed text appearing on the card's interior was in German! With quickened breath, he scanned the series of dark blue letters. His knowledge of the language was limited, but the message before him did not require mastery.

Liebling,

Du bist meine sonne, mein mond, meine sterne.

Du erleuchtest mein leben

Von deinem Adler

He recited the translation silently, aware his lips were moving. *Darling, you are my sun, my moon, my stars. You light up my life. From your eagle.* He felt a kind of awe, uneasy, cynical, as if he had unearthed an ancient relic that could have come from either a poet or a demon. He set the card aside, hastily, he realized, as if there was a danger he'd be led astray by its professed sentiment. Wishing he had accepted Henri's offer for more water but reluctant to disturb him just yet, he went on with his search.

From the material left to be gone over, he was able to find only one article that piqued his interest. It was a typewritten bill of sale, made all the more alluring by a series of large, thickly inked exclamation points running along the bottom of a sheet that had been crumpled and imperfectly re-smoothed.

PAUL ROSENBERG ART GALLERY

21 Rue la Boetie

PARIS

27 Septembre 1928

Pieter de Hooch 1629-1683 L'ecole de Delft

Huile sur toile 50.8cm x 60.96 cm (1658)

"femme donnant du pain a un garcon"

Prix: 990 Fr

Paul Rosenburg - Roger Paquard

!!!!!!!!!!!!!!!!!!

Harrison had completed his examination. Bit by bit, he painstakingly returned to the carpetbag all the material he had discarded. Those destined for review he arranged in the center of the desk. There was one more task he had to accomplish before submitting his questions to Henri. So far he had photographed only the objects found in the velvet pouch. All the rest needed to be recorded for future reference. He set about photographing each of his finds, afterward checking the results for clarity. When he was satisfied all was in order, he turned in his seat to address Henri. To his surprise, Henri's book lay closed in his lap, and he was studying him, or seemed to be.

Harrison opened with a tentative smile. "You haven't been having second thoughts, I hope."

Henri laughed. "Not at all. I've been contemplating lunch."

"And I've been holding you up," Harrison replied, inadvertently glancing at his watch.

"I realize it's before noon," Henri said, noticing. "But at five this morning I was already cracking my poached egg and planning my gardening chores—How did it go?" he added abruptly. "Find anything useful?" He lay his book on the sea chest and rose to his feet.

"I did, yes," Harrison said, feeling an inexplicable distance spring between them. "In one of your grandfather's letters, he refers by name to a number of contemporary art collectors. It gives me a lot to follow up on."

"I say we have a light lunch before discussing the details," he said, amiably but firmly, closing the distance without ceding leadership. "A fresh salad will do nicely."

"I'm really not—"

"The tomatoes are from my garden. You can't possibly turn them down. They'd be terribly hurt."

Harrison laughed. "Now that you put it that way, how can I refuse?"

"*Exactement.* Come along."

Harrison followed him to the kitchen. It was a modest space furnished with what must be its original rough-hewn oak cabinetry, table and chairs along with a display of high-end modern appliances.

"Julien loved to cook," Henri said, in response to Harrison's surveyal. "He was not so good at it, but that made his passion all the more endearing. Would you like to chop the carrots?"

"I'd be honored," Harrison said, and waited for Henri to provide him with the needed items.

* * *

Harrison set down his empty water glass gently but with a definitive click to mark the end of their lunch break. They must have been sitting at the kitchen table for over half an hour—he hadn't dared glance at his watch a second time—and although the salad had been remarkably fresh, the conversation on the curative nature of gardening, instructive, he was anxious to get down to business. "So," he pronounced, gracing the meaningless syllable with a cordial smile.

Henri pushed back his chair and rose to his feet. "Time to have a look at your discoveries," he said, with forced levity, as if pumping himself up for the task. "No, no, leave that!" he commanded, as Harrison, on the rise, was reaching for their plates. "That can wait! To be honest, I didn't expect to feel this way, but I'm not looking forward to an up-close-and-personal encounter with the memorabilia. If we don't get started right now, I might bail out."

Harrison's hands shot up from the plates like they were hot coals.

"Figured that would get you," Henri said, with a wry grin. "Let's go." He headed for the living room, straight to the desks, Harrison following at his heels. "Take a seat," he said, nodding toward Julien's chair. When Harrison had done so, Henri brought his own desk chair around to what had been Julien's workspace and placed it at an angle so that he and Harrison would be sitting catty-corner to each other.

When they were settled in, Henri waved at the compilation of items in the center of the desk. "Is this the extent of your find?" Without waiting for an answer, he punched, "Frankly, I was expecting more of a haul. I'm relieved."

Harrison did not think Henri looked relieved. Almost apologetically, he passed him the letter written by Monsier Paquard to his betrothed. "Do you perhaps recognize any of the collectors' names cited by your grandfather?" he asked, overly solicitous. "Did you meet any of these people, or know any family members? I'll do my best to track them down for interviews, but people are generally more approachable if you come armed with a personal reference."

Henri scanned the letter. "No, I don't recognize any of these names," he said at last. He handed the letter back to Harrison. "My grandparents moved to Spain when I was very young—six or seven—and I didn't see them much. Certainly not any of their friends or art collector buddies."

"I see," Harrison said pensively, as if he were hearing of the Paquards' emigration to Spain for the first time. He placed the letter aside, setting it apart from the items still to be reviewed. "No problem. It was an outside chance at best. What about your paternal grandparents?" he ventured in attempted off-handedness. "Were they at all involved in the art world?"

"I wouldn't know," Henri clipped. "I never met them."

"Ah, that's unfortunate," Harrison replied, feeling more deceitful by the minute.

"I'm not so sure," Henri shot back. "What's next?"

Harrison showed him the 1931 inventory of the Paquard art collection. As expected, Henri failed to recognize any of its references. Next—getting closer to his real mission, but holding the most targeted items in abeyance—he presented Henri with the photographs. "I have to admit," he said, "I was drawn to these out of sheer curiosity." Pointing to the one taken in May of 1940 of Madeline with an unidentified adult male, he asked, "Can you identify the man standing beside your mother?" It was difficult not to hold his breath as he awaited the answer.

Henri shrugged. "An uncle or a cousin, I suppose. This was taken before I was born. Maybe whoever it was moved away or died."

Harrison let out his breath. "And this one?" he asked, trying to conceal his disappointment. "I'm wondering who took this photograph of you and your mother?" He tried to project the answer to Henri's brain: *Oh, that'd be my dad.*

"I can't help you there, either," Henri stated bluntly.

Time to shake things up. "This, too, piqued my interest," Harrison began, reaching for the birthday card. "Although it probably bears no relevance to my project." He lay the card in front of Henri and waited for a reaction.

Henri heaved a sigh of what might have passed as boredom, had Harrison not noticed his hands trembling as he opened the card. "This has to have come from my *father*," he fairly spat. "My mother used to call him her *Adler*—her eagle. I thought it was his name until she told me otherwise—after he'd gone. His name was Hans. That's all I know. Nothing else. She was closemouthed about him, and I was close-minded. It worked for both of us."

"He was a...?" The word was coming, but a millisecond too late.

"Nazi, yes." With a quizzical look, Henri sat up straight—surprised, it seemed, by his utterance of the word, or by the ease of it. "I had a hard time after the war," he said, addressing Harrison, but looking through him. "The kids called me Heinz, what did I know? They bullied me relentlessly."

"You must have felt…ambivalent about your parents," Harrison suggested. "Still do, I would imagine."

"My middle name, Ambivalence." He leaned forward. "So, what else have you got to salt the old wounds?"

It was a miracle Henri hadn't by this time guessed that he was being interviewed under false pretenses, Harrison reflected. Was he too busy marveling at his ability to objectify his past to notice that he was being grilled about matters unrelated to the history of Parisian art galleries?

He was wishing he had something to exhibit that would reestablish, at least temporarily, his staged legitimacy, when he noticed a corner of the sales slip from the Rosenberg Art Gallery peeking out from beneath Paquard's letter to his future wife. He must have mistakenly picked it up along with the letter and then set them both aside.

He drew forth the sales slip and handed it to Henri for his perusal. "I found this interesting for two reasons," he said, as Henri stared at the document. "First, it's the only sales slip from an art gallery in your mother's collection of memorabilia. Second, it's bordered by strident-looking exclamation points, which must signify *something*! Was your grandfather, Roger, angry with the dealer, Paul Rosenberg, for charging him nine-hundred francs for the de Hooch painting? Was it the condition of the painting itself that troubled him? Did your mother ever discuss this transaction with you?"

Henri lay the bill of sale on the desk and ironed down the corners with his right forefinger. He pushed back his chair and rose to his feet. "Come with me," he announced. "I want to show you something."

"Will it be appropriate for me to bring along my cell phone?" Harrison thought to ask, as he, too, rose. "Will I be allowed to photograph what I'm about to see?"

"Yes, of course."

Harrison pocketed his cell phone and followed Henri to the front of the room. then up a flight of a creaky wood stairs to a narrow hallway. "This way," Henri said, turning right. "My mother's room is at the end of the hall." When he arrived at the open door, he stepped aside to allow Harrison to stand alone at the doorsill. "Notice anything odd?"

The room was small and square, with a single bare window into which the sunlight streamed in unfiltered. The wood floor had abraded to yellow in patches where it had seen the most traction. The only furniture in the room was a plain four-poster bed covered in a thin quilted coverlet and a dresser of similar, but not matching, style. "My first thought is *American Gothic*," Harrison said, turning toward Henri with a smile. "You consider that odd?"

Henri shook his head. "Simplicity is universal. Step into the room. Look around."

Harrison did so. Other than the standing oblong mirror tucked beside the dresser, the only thing that piqued his interest was that there was only one framed work of art in the room. It hung on the wall opposite the foot of the bed, but because of the angle of the sun, he could not make out its subject. He shielded his eyes and walked up to it and found himself staring at an empty frame.

"Yes," Henri said, acknowledging Harrison's jaw drop. "It calls our attention to the bill of sale we just examined, bordered with those strident exclamation points, as you put it."

The frame, like an exiled royal, was the only ornate object in this modest cell. It was fashioned from some dark wood, probably mahogany or walnut, fancifully carved, and with its outer perimeter coated with gold leaf. "It held the Pieter de Hooch?" Harrison asked, knowing the answer.

Henri nodded. "It was a gift from my mother's parents." He snorted. "To their *daughter*."

As opposed to whom? Harrison silently asked, heart racing. He waited for Henri to elaborate.

Instead, head-cocked, Henri fixed his gaze on Harrison. "What are you thinking?"

"I'm thinking your father stole the damn painting," he said boldly—and why the hell not? After getting a glimpse of Henri's sentiments about his father, he was hardly throwing caution to the wind by expressing this opinion.

"Exactly what my mother believed," Henri replied without losing a beat.

"The painting went missing the day my father vanished."

"I'm assuming he fled the country. Do you know where he relocated?"

"Harrison, you must remember I was a small child when this occurred, and hardly a word was spoken about it until years later, when my mother shared with me what little information she was willing to impart. The only thing I knew up to that point was that my mother's affection for my father turned around the day he disappeared, and that her animus was bonded to the empty frame from that day forward." Again, he cocked his head and scrutinized Harrison. "You don't hide your feelings very well, do you, my boy?"

"I guess it wouldn't make sense for me to answer, 'Whatever do you mean by that?', would it?" His grin was irrepressible.

Henri's was deliberative. "No. The spike in interest is revealed by your expression—your eyes, especially—every time the subject of my father comes up. Would you care to explain?"

Harrison's cover had been blown—again. As with Madame D, his exposure had fortunately taken place after he'd surmised where his interviewee's sympathies lay. "Don't get me wrong," he crudely began, "I'm interested in the history of Parisian art galleries, and I intend to write an article about the subject. However..."

"However, the *looting* of art galleries is your primary interest. Hence, your interest in my father, a German occupier who was in close contact with at least one major art collector. I'm guessing you heard about him through the grapevine, including his disappearance without notice."

"Jewish," Harrison amended.

"Excuse me?"

"My interest is the looting of *Jewish*-owned galleries. One in particular." Without revealing his informant's name, Harrison outlined Madame D's story regarding the murders and looting associated with the Jules Eisenberg Gallery and her suspicions regarding the individual responsible for it.

From his stony expression, it was hard to tell if Henri was speechless or just holding his tongue.

Harrison waited.

"No wonder your eyes lit up at the discovery of the empty frame," Henri finally uttered. "It was a step toward validating the rumors."

"You don't believe them, then."

"What? Of course I do," Henri shot back. "It wouldn't surprise me in the least to hear he'd run off with a truck-load of stolen art. I wish I could offer you some useful information, but I'm as much in the dark as you are, and in truth that's where I prefer to remain. I have no wish to find out what became of him, or if he's dead or alive. My mother's reason for silencing the past was different from mine. She feared reprisals from both the foreigner who abandoned her and her fellow countrymen who first shamed, then shunned her. Although its source may be more complex, my reason is simpler. Disgust."

"I'm sorry."

"For what?"

"For causing you discomfort."

"Nonsense. I'm not as fragile as you think—or as I *myself* thought, for that matter. Our session has taken the witchcraft out of it, somehow. Isn't that peculiar?"

"Not really. I think silence may bestow a long-held secret with unwarranted power," Harrison suggested. More brazenly, he posed, "Didn't you talk about this with Julien?"

"Barely. At the beginning, I was afraid of losing him over the slightest negativity. It was all so new to me, the magic of it. And when he became ill, nothing but his happiness, and finally his comfort, meant anything to me. Can you understand that?"

"I can, yes."

"All right, then. Do you have anything else you want to show me? I noticed a small pouch on the desk."

"Yes, that's the last of the items, and then I'll be out of your hair."

"I was never a fan of that expression," Henri said, in an obvious attempt to lighten the mood. "Though it improves with translation. *Je vais sortir de tes cheveux.* You agree?"

Harrison smiled. "Dare I not?" He paused. "Henri?"

"Yes?"

"I have a question."

"No surprise. What is it, Harrison?"

"There are numerous paintings hanging on the walls in the room below. Why do you suppose your father would abscond with just the one painting? Was it perhaps the only one of great value?"

"No, but there's an easy explanation. The works hanging on the walls of the main room post-date my father's disappearance. They were either acquired by my mother, myself, or Julien, who brought a few wonderful pieces from his home when he moved in with me. And now let's complete our job, shall we?" He strode out of the room and headed for the staircase. As he was about to plant his foot on the first step, he suddenly changed his mind and turned to face Harrison. "Wait. There *is* one."

"I'm not following you."

"One painting that pre-dates my father's disappearance. An oil painting, signed and dated June the twelfth, 1942. Five months before I was born. It won't affect your research, but it might be of interest. Have a look." He resumed his descent.

As Henri ushered him to the far end of the main room, where the painting in question reportedly hung, Harrison thought it his duty to review the wall display en route, although any art not in a league with Rembrandt or Picasso that did not have the potential of bringing him closer to tracking down Hans, pre- or post-demise, was not about to grab his interest.

"Here it is," Henri announced, a yard or two ahead of his guest. He pointed to an oil painting hanging almost at the walls' juncture. "I'll turn on the light so you can see it better." He switched on the table lamp a foot from the painting and got out of the way so Harrison could freely position himself.

The painting was about sixteen by eighteen inches, mounted in a narrow cherry wood frame. Its near neighbors were a pair of fine watercolor depictions of rural life that on any other occasion Harrison would have been eager to pause over and critique. But not now. Not when he was confronted with a portrait that set his mind off on a riff of tantalizing scenarios. Here, in a rendering consisting almost entirely of gradations of yellow, green and rose, was a portrait of a young woman seated at a table. Her head is turned. She is looking out, a pensive expression on her face, and seems to be returning the viewer's gaze. Her blond hair is pushed to the side and cascades down one shoulder, fanning across the bodice of her satiny green dress. Her right hand lies in her lap in a fold of material. Her left forearm rests on the table; the hand dangles from its edge.

Harrison was duly impressed by the beauty of the young woman and the artist's confident brushstrokes. What captivated his imagination, however, were two facts outside the realm of art. The young woman bore a remarkable resemblance to the photograph he'd seen of Madeline Paquard, and, more intriguingly, her elbow was in direct contact with the corner of a chess board.

No, Harrison derided himself, *it's not possible that Alexander Alekhine could have met this woman, no less her lover. Then again, isn't anything possible in a world where contemporaries are no more than six degrees of separation from each other?* He steadied his thoughts and turned toward Henri, who had returned to Julien's desk, ready to wrap up the session.

"Is this a portrait of your mother?" he asked. "It's lovely."

"It is," Henri replied, pulling open the silk pouch. "She was an amateur chess player in those days. A pretty good one, apparently. I didn't know this until after her death, when I was clearing out her drawers and discovered her gold ribbons from local and city-wide competitions."

"Any newspaper clippings to go along with them?" Harrison asked, as he imagined an accompanying snapshot of Alekhine presenting the young devotee an award.

"No, nothing like that." Henri was turning the locket over, studying it. "She taught me how to play, but never mentioned her past triumphs. I suspect she was ostracized from the chess clubs after the war." He opened the locket and touched the exposed lock of hair. "At least they didn't shave her head, as far as I know."

Harrison's primal reaction to that demoralizing practice was complicated, so he did not comment on it. He would have liked to have pursued the chess connection, but there was no way he would let slip the name 'Alekhine.' He was certain it had caused the death of his student, and he was not about to jeopardize Henri with it, or through him, the chance of leaking it into circulation. He and Erika would discuss a way to follow up on the chess association—a just-above-feeble lead—and in the meantime, he'd put it on record with a photo.

He snapped a couple of shots of the portrait from different angles and distances and checked them out, zooming in on each to test for clarity. As he enlarged the last of the lot, he centered on the signature and date in the bottom right-hand corner, and realized he'd overlooked this notation when taking in the painting directly. He pocketed his cell phone and gazed at the real thing.

The artist's signature was finely scripted in broken strokes of black paint: G. Wishaar.

The name was familiar. Where had he come across it?

"Are you ready to finish up?" Henri inquired. He was slipping the ring with the Iron Cross motif on and off his third and fourth fingers of his left hand, as if through this method he could determine the heft of the man who originally wore it.

"I am, yes—oh!"

Henri swung around in his chair. "What is it?"

"I forgot to call my publisher!" Harrison ad-libbed—brilliantly, given his state of mind. "I was supposed to have called him yesterday. Oh, well, nothing I can do about it now. It's before dawn on the east coast. I'll call him this afternoon." The artist's name was tugging at him for attention like an unruly child.

"Is there a deadline involved? I've been delinquent myself on more than one occasion."

"No, no, I'm just obsessive compulsive when it comes to sticking to the plan." *G. Wishaar—Grace Wishaar*—his ears were ringing with the name. Thank goodness he had done his homework. Grace Wishaar was Alexander Alekhine's wife! He had come across her name when he was boning up on the life and times of the master chess player. It came back to him in a rush. The couple had met at a chess exhibition in Tokyo in 1933, where she'd won a copy of his book. In 1944, she won the Ladies Chess Championship in Paris. And, as luck would have it, she was a painter, too; had painted the portraits of Jack London's daughters, in fact.

This was as close to a deus ex machina as Harrison could have hoped for. The degrees of separation between Alekhine and Hans, the man who Madame D was certain had been responsible for, or at least cognizant of, the looting and murders at the Eisenberg Gallery, had, in an instant, been reduced to one!

With as casual a gait as he could muster, Harrison traveled across the room to join Henri at Julien's desk.

Henri was shuffling the articles he'd taken from the pouch into different positions on the desktop as if they were game pieces.

"Do you know whose hair clipping was placed in the locket?" Harrison asked, drawing up his chair.

"I don't. It could have been any one of us. We were all blonds. Why do you ask?"

"If need be, for DNA evidence down the line."

"You mean, in the eventuality you track down my father, or think you have."

"Yes. Henri?"

"What?"

It was inevitable, his coming clean. "I removed a few strands of hair from the locket."

"And?"

"I should have asked your permission. I'm sorry."

"Nonsense. It's fine. I wish you better luck than I've had in that department."

"I don't understand. You've attempted to find your father?"

"Heavens, no."

"Because there's a good possibility he fled to Brazil."

"If you find him or the whereabouts of his remains, I might be curious to know, but certainly not for the purpose of making contact with him in person, dead or alive. My guess is that wherever he resettled, Brazil or elsewhere, he created a new identity for himself, one that he would protect by any means necessary." He uttered a sardonic laugh, as if the joke was on him. "Can you imagine this man putting his DNA on record?"

"You mean on one of the ancestry dot com sites? No, I can't. Not ever."

"Exactly. On the other hand, I felt free to put *my* DNA out there. I wanted—not desperately, but keenly to…how shall I put it? Normalize myself. Purify, may be the better word, although that sounds sanctimonious. Let's just say I wanted to discover I'm a second cousin to Albert Schweitzer and leave it at that. The point is, my cheek swab did nothing for my morale."

"I hear the gathering of data can take some time," Harrison offered.

"It's been a year."

"Ah. Which is why you wished me better luck with *my* genetic pipe dream."

Henri smiled. "Tracking down Hans. Yes." He scooped up the items he'd been idly moving about and dropped them into the pouch. He tugged on the drawstring. The movement had an air of finality. "I know nothing more about these items than what can be seen with the naked eye." He slid the pouch in front of Harrison. "You take them. Maybe they'll be of use to you."

The gesture seemed more like an act of emancipation than goodwill, which is why Harrison was so deeply touched by it. *You're defined by what you make of yourself*, he wanted to say, *and not by your parental fuck-ups.* Instead, he gushed, "You're too kind! I couldn't possibly accept your offer, but thank you all the same!"

Henri grabbed Harrison's arm. "But I insist. Anything that promises even the remotest possibility that some good will come from our meeting gives me hope. Take these things. They are no longer mine!"

Harrison had no choice but to concede. He ceremoniously placed the velvet pouch inside his jacket pocket. "I'll return the items after I complete the project," he said, overturning what had just come out of Henri's mouth.

"No, you will not," Henri countermanded. "You will keep them or give them away. The only thing I ask you to do is to allow me to see beforehand any printed or aural material you plan to disseminate."

"I've already promised that, Henri. I would have done so even if you hadn't requested it." He rose from the chair and collected his cell phone, notepad, and ballpoint pen. As he found relatively unoccupied pockets into which to stow them, he said, "I've truly enjoyed talking with you, and I sincerely hope I haven't overstayed my visit." His lips curled into a sly grin. "Although you'd never let me know if I had."

"That you'll never know," Henri replied, rising to his feet, his impish smile a beguiling grace note to his lofty stature. "Shall we exchange cards?" He drew one from the back pocket of his pressed jeans.

"I was about to make the same suggestion," Harrison said, taking the card from Henri. He glanced at it. It was a business card that listed Henri's certifications as a translator and the professional associations of which he was a member. He drew his wallet from his pants pocket and carefully inserted the card behind his driver's license and credit card, then plucked one of his own business cards from the bottom of the same pocket. "Say, I wonder if you'd care to translate a monograph of Eugene Delacroix I've been working on. I'm quite sure the publisher will accept the idea. Have you ever worked on an art book?"

"Four or five, mostly on the contemporaries, Jeff Koons, David Hockney, a compendium…but yes. I'm qualified. It's a lovely idea, and I'd be flattered."

"Excellent. I'll give you a definite answer after I touch base with the publisher—Phaidon—and again, when I've got a final draft."

They headed for the door simultaneously, Harrison, for once, in the lead.

* * *

Betsy Ross arrived in front of the Maison de van Gogh on the main street in town within five minutes of Harrison's call. "I had myself an invigorating walk," she announced, as Harrison resignedly allowed her to usher him into the rear seat as if he were the lord of the manor. "How did *your* morning go?"

"I accomplished what I set out to do," Harrison replied, attempting once again to create the impression that he was a man of few words, take no offence. He adjusted himself in the seat and retrieved his cell phone.

Reminded of her passenger's reticence, Betsy chirped a friendly but clipped "Terrific!" and made her way to the driver's seat. "Are we headed straight back to the Rodin Inn, Professor?" she found it necessary to inquire.

"Sorry, yes," Harrison replied, looking up from his emails, in which he was already immersed. Inadvertently, he glanced out the window and caught sight of a retreating figure. The gentleman would not have piqued his interest were it not for the unmistakable gray herringbone suit. What was up here? First, the peculiar behavior of the inn manager, then the car nuzzling up to Betsy's too close for comfort, and now this questionable figure showing up again—*had the man consumed even a drop of coffee?* Harrison wondered if he'd been in the man's sights earlier, when he himself had been in a contemplative haze, absorbed in the play of color and light and his own sense of wellbeing. He grasped onto a past experience, forcing it into a consoling analogy. When he'd been working on his Delacroix monograph, he'd run across a couple of discrete artifacts that formed a compelling argument for the painter's having engaged in a *menage a trois* with George Sand and Mozart. Only after much time examining sources was he able to conclude that the argument, though seductive, was at best, inconclusive. This time he would not allow a team of coincidences to lead him off course.

He was diverted from his tortured reasoning when, as they exited the town and were on their way to the main thoroughfare leading to Paris, he was alerted to an incoming text from Erika. *Tell me you haven't left Auvers-sur-Oise yet!* it read. Harrison had to smile at her unabridged English. Even with a message that seemed to require an immediate response, she was a stickler for proper usage—as was he. He answered, *We've left. What's up? Shall we head back?*

'We'? she replied.

What?

You said 'we.' Who's your traveling companion?

My driver. Betsy Ross. He shook his head; laughed—almost.

Can you call me, or isn't that permissible?

Good idea. Give me a minute. They were nearing an exit ramp. "Excuse me, Betsy," he called. "Could you turn off here? We may have to double back."

"Sure thing." Without questioning his instructions, Betsy did as she was told. By the time she had pulled off onto the shoulder of the exit ramp, engine idling, Harrison was reconnected to Erika via phone. "Hold on," he told her, feeling the aftershock of her unwarranted—*attack*, had it been? "Betsy," he called out. "Would you raise the divider? Thanks!" Back to Erika, he asked, "Is everything okay?"

"Of course!" she answered, jovial almost. "I was reading all about Auvers-sur-Oise. In particular, about Dr. Paul Gachet. You've heard of him?"

"Yes, he tended to van Gogh in the end." *Why the sudden mood change?* The answer struck him like a blow: she had heard him call out to Betsy; it proved he wasn't sitting alongside her. "The doctor knew a number of contemporary painters—Cezanne, Pissarro and the like. He swapped remedies for paintings; was an avid collector. Why am I sitting by the side of the road, sweetheart?"

"Just listen. After the good doctor died in 1909, his kids kept his art collection safely hidden away for forty years. Every source I looked into reports a different hiding place. A tunnel leading to the cliffs, a cave, an underground shelter in their garden. The point is—"

"I never even thought to ask!"

"If there's a suitable hiding place at the Paquard's, you mean?"

"Yes!"

"I can't imagine Hans stowing a bunch of paintings under Madeline's nose, can you, Harrison? Especially if he intended to ditch her in the end. There's probably less than a one percent chance he left any scraps of evidence behind, but wouldn't it add credence to our theoretical crime if we could establish the element of opportunity for its commission?"

"You're brilliant."

"That said, are you going back to have a look?" she asked, her voice quivering on the verge of a laugh.

"What do you think?"

"That you are. Call me with the results ASAP."

"Of course. Love you."

"Love you, too."

* * *

"My wife Erika leaves no stone unturned," Harrison informed Henri, who appeared surprised, but not unpleasantly, to see his guest back on his doorstep.

"Smart woman," Henri commented, after Harrison had more fully elaborated. "Let me show you something."

Again, Harrison found himself trailing after Henri, this time to the rear of the house.

"This is my garden," Henri lovingly pointed out on their arrival.

The word "garden" hardly did the site justice. About half of what Harrison estimated to be an acre of land was dedicated to growing vegetables and herbs: a farm. The other portion, nearer the house, was a glorious quilt-work of flowers that looked like a painting by Renoir tailored to fit a geometric pattern conceived by Mondrian. "Ordered chaos," Henri said, responding to Harrison's open-mouthed wonder.

"It's beautiful—the colors!" Harrison marveled. "I probably can't name more than two of the flowers."

"I'd give you a guided tour, but that's not what you came for." He gestured for Harrison to follow him to the far end of the house. There, half hidden by the overgrowth of a flowering shrub Harrison was actually able to identify as a Hydrangea, were the double-doors of an exterior basement, held shut by a standard combination lock. "I find the steel trap an eye-sore," Henri said, so I don't trim the shrub. "I never use the storage area, anyway. There's a story behind it. Are you curious?" He smiled, knowing the answer.

"Of course!" Harrison already pictured himself exploring its dark interior like a spelunker.

"First, I should tell you that before Julien entered my life, I had never seen these doors opened. There had always been a heavy-duty lock securing them, and as far as I knew, the lock had never been changed. However, when Julien made this his permanent residence, we had the entire place thoroughly checked out for hazardous substances. Julien was by nature eco-conscious, but on top of that, chemo-therapy had compromised his immune system, making him super-sensitive to antigens. The upshot was that the professionals found no trace of asbestos in the interior of the house, but when they sawed off the lock on these doors they discovered asbestos to be one of the components of the insulating material lining all four sides of the underground compartment. In fact, the galvanized steel doors were not only weather-stripped, they, too, were insulated. The insulating material is called rock-wool."

"I've never heard of it. Has it been outlawed?"

Henri shook his head. "No, but it no longer contains asbestos. Here's the interesting part. The experts told us that rock-wool itself has been around since 1800, but after analyzing the material found in our basement they determined that the particular ratio of its components—fiberglass, mineral wool and asbestos—placed its manufacture to around the 1940s, latest 50s."

"From what you've said," Harrison pronounced slowly, as his thoughts raced ahead with its ramifications, "it couldn't have been the 1950s."

"No, it couldn't have. The cellar was locked during that period. The experts suggested that the people who owned the house prior to my parents added the cellar to the property, and it seemed like the logical explanation. But..."

"Are you thinking what I'm thinking?"

"That your wife will be pissed I didn't bring this up earlier?"

Harrison laughed. "Now that you mention it..."

"Seriously, this is the first time I'm seeing an alternate explanation."

"That your father insulated the existing basement to protect his stolen canvases from moisture and other harmful elements."

"You're suggesting he did this in front of my mother's nose?"

"No. Before he asked your mother to move in with him."

For a moment Henri was speechless. "How could I have not thought of that?" he finally questioned. "How could I have been so blind?"

"It was a subject you were not exactly keen on focusing on."

"I'll accept that. Thank you."

"Besides," Harrison added, "it's just a possibility."

"A possibility that dovetails perfectly with your theoretical narrative."

"It does," Harrison agreed. "And I'll thank you for *that.*"

Henri placed a hand on Harrison's shoulder. "We had the rock-wool removed and relined the walls and ceiling with concrete; the underside of the doors coated with rust-resistant paint. The place is clean as a whistle, as they say, but I know you'll never forgive yourself if you don't take a look for yourself. Am I right?"

"You are."

"You'd have to answer to your wife."

"I would."

Henri got down on his hands and knees, pushed aside an infringing Hydrangea growth and manipulated the combination lock. "I keep the doors locked to avoid any mishaps involving overly curious children from the neighborhood," he explained. "The combination is Julien's birthdate." He executed a final twist and snapped open the lock. Careful not to mall the shrub's overhanging globes of Monet blue, he slowly swung open the steel doors and stepped aside. "Watch yourself," he cautioned Harrison. "The stairway's steep and the steps are far apart."

Harrison climbed down the steps and looked around. He guessed the space was about the size of a prison cell. He knew straightaway there wasn't a shred of foreign matter to be found in this tomb-like structure, but he turned on his cell phone's flashlight to scour the entire area. Only when he'd confirmed what he objectively knew to be true did he realize he'd harbored a hope of discovery. He took a few photographs for his records and headed back to the staircase.

"I can see you're disappointed," Henri said as Harrison stepped back onto the grassy turf.

"Despite myself, yes."

Henri shut the doors and clicked on the lock. "That was to be expected," he said, rising from his knees. "Still, knowing that this convenient niche exists must give you some comfort."

"It does." Harrison snapped a shot of the cellar doors and stowed his cell phone. "Thanks for bearing with me."

"We'll have none of that," Henri chided, brushing off the dirt from his jeans.

A moment later they were shaking hands by the side of Harrison's hired limo parked in front of the house. Betsy had remained in the driver's seat, knowing better than to flurry about the rear door.

"So, I'll be seeing you," Harrison pronounced, withdrawing his hand.

"Yes," Henri returned, his tone more questioning than declarative.

"At the book launch?"

"Ah, your book on Delacroix. You're that certain I'll be assigned the translation?"

"Yes, I'm that certain," Harrison assured him. Mentally he was punching in Erika's cell phone number and trying to predict her mood. "I'll get back to you with the details within the week. Phaidon will email you a contract, and after you iron out any problems, you can sign it online. Will that be suitable?"

"*Vraiment!*" Henri replied, clearly pleased.

* * *

In a continuous motion Harrison's hand went from waving goodbye to Henri through the car window to fetching his cell phone.

Erika answered his call in a flash. "Well?" she opened, wasting no time.

Harrison expounded on demand, concluding, "No tangible proof of our hypothesis, but an exterior basement insulated during the critical time period definitely bolsters it."

She agreed. "What are your plans for tonight?" she side-stepped.

"Nothing much. Organizing my notes, having a bite to eat at the inn." *Changing my flight to an earlier one!* "You feeling okay?"

"I'm fine. What do you mean?"

He imagined her stiffening. "You seemed a bit out of sorts last time we spoke."

"I suppose I was over-tired. I can't sleep on command when the opportunity arises. My biological clock has a mind of its own. It needs to be retrained, is all."

"Maybe there's a med you can take to normalize things. Don't you have a doctor's appointment coming up? You can ask—"

"Out of the question. I'm not putting a poisonous substance into my bloodstream, especially while I'm breastfeeding!"

"Not poisonous, darling. Something that's approved for nursing women."

"Harrison. *Darling.*"

"Yes?"

"I know you have the best intentions, but I'd rather you let me sort out the transition on my own, okay?"

"I worry about you."

"Don't. It makes me anxious."

"I'll try." *I have been trying!*

He heard the baby whimper in the background. It didn't sound urgent.

"I've got to go," Erika said. "Luc is crying. Time to feed him. Talk tomorrow. Love you."

"Love you, too, sweetheart," he said, a beat before the line went dead. He felt the tiniest nip of resentment, his very first. *Luc couldn't have waited another damn second?*

* * *

Back at the Rodin Inn, the first thing he did was move his early morning flight home from Friday to Thursday—tomorrow. The estimated time of arrival at JFK was 10:00 a.m. Next, he called Bill to alert him to his pickup time change. Bill was fine with it.

He grabbed an apple from the dining room and ate it on his walk to the Père Lachaise Cemetery, where he wended his way through the multitude of tombs—it looked to him like a crowded town of gnomes, each with a compulsion to publicize his uniqueness in a domicile like none other—until he came to the bronze edifice of Theodore Gericault. Odd he had written a comprehensive monograph on Gericault, but he had never visited the artist's final resting place. He wondered if his perspective of the man would have been altered, to however small a degree, if he had. Gericault's recumbent figure lay atop the tomb a la an Etruscan funerary effigy, one hand balancing an easel, the other idly bearing a paintbrush. Dressed in a loose-fitting garment with casual folds, giving him a romantic air, Gericault appeared to be looking off into the distance—or perhaps at a work-in-progress. The front of the tomb was a low-relief version of Gericault's painting "Raft of Medusa" by the tomb's sculptor, Antoine Etex. Harrison had seen a high-quality photograph of the tomb, but being in its presence—no, in the presence of the artist himself, of his *bones*—was a different, more intimate, experience.

The need to be in Erika's presence suddenly overtook him. He must be near her, face-to-face, touch her, to understand the subtle, albeit intermittent, change in her behavior. There was nothing he could do about getting home any faster than he had planned, but he could at least ease his restlessness by hurrying back to the inn and throwing his things together in preparation for the trip. His plan to visit the Louvre to meet with the curator of the museum's 2018 Delacroix retrospective would have to be scrapped. He'd make arrangements for a long-distance chat when he got home. As his thoughts flew ahead of himself, edging out time, he heard the welcome sound of the plane's landing gear snapping into place.

Chapter 12

Erika wasn't quite sure why Harrison was returning a day earlier than planned, but she was happy he was. She glanced up at the wall clock in her study. It was nine o'clock. Factoring in a delay or two, she calculated he'd be home by noon.

At the moment Kate was feeding Lucas a bottle of formula milk in accordance with Erika's plan to diversify Lucas's diet, primarily to afford Harrison a less restrictive paternity leave, but also to introduce a modicum of freedom in the family's day-to-day lives. It being an especially warm and sunny mid-April morning, Kate was going to take Lucas for a neighborhood stroll in his carriage after feeding time. Grace, being the over-protective and discreetly competitive nanny-once-removed, would likely invent a polite excuse to tag along, barely concealing her true motivation, which would be to check up on Kate's out-of-door caretaking performance. As an overly cautious mother, Erika hoped the double guardianship would prevail, but repressed the urge to promote it outright.

Showered, breakfasted, and clad in a white cotton blouse tucked into a pair of fitted jeans in lieu of her usual sweatpants option, Erika was as formally attired as she'd been in well over a month. She was ready for a ball, no less her husband's return from Paris, and therefore had approximately three free-and-clear hours to spend any way she wished. On the floor next to her desk sat the unopened box FedEx had delivered an hour ago. In it were the *Gazette des Beaux-Arts* issues from 1928 to 1940 that she'd had overnighted from the rare books store in Brooklyn. She was as eager as a child on Christmas morning to open the box and delve into its contents, but Harrison's anticipated arrival was prioritizing her emotions, and she wanted to be deliciously unencumbered when she immersed herself in the task. Late at night, when all others were asleep, she would tip-toe to her study, break open the box and begin her treasure hunt for references to the Eisenberg Gallery.

She remembered she hadn't yet contacted John Mitchell with the provenance history of Chuck's flipped house. Here was something she could get done that didn't require an uncluttered swath of time and mental absorption. She reached for her cell phone, intending to either call or text him. In the pause of indecision, she was alerted to an email just in.

Hi Erika,

Apologies for unloading on you and thanks for bearing up. I hope my presumptiveness hasn't jeopardized our working relationship. Aside from our call two days ago—from my perspective, restorative—the enthusiasm with which you approach your assignments, professional and self-initiated, has always been a pick-me-up in and of itself. I've been a fan, from the first article I read of yours—on Mother Fucker's graffiti, what a blast!—to the piece on Benday dots—and the list goes on. Had to get this off my chest.

Looking forward to hearing from you regarding any matters for which I can be of some use.

Luv,

Greg

Luv? What was *that* all about? She never would have expected such a banality from Greg—aside from the overblown content of the missive itself! As she was inwardly sniping at the man, she realized her testiness was a pathetically disguised pretense. She enjoyed the admiration from an esteemed outside source, and the awkward sexual undertone was gratifying as well, taking her back to her Puritanism-exempt days. She was relieved, at least, with her honesty. She dashed off a response in record time in an attempt to give the matter short shrift.

Greg: Nothing to apologize for. Thanks for the positive review of my work. It means a lot coming from you. Back shortly with the results of my sifting through a heap of pre-war issues of Gazette-des-Beaux-Arts. Hugs, Erika

God almighty. *Hugs?* She quickly punched in John's number to dispel the cloying aftertaste. He answered after one ring, saving her. "What's up?"

She relayed the information Bonnie had given her on the flipped house; asked if he could fill in the gaps. Were there any renters during the time period in question, for instance? Was there any personal data on the owners or renters accessible to him? Wishfully thinking, she recited, "Employment history, arrests, political affiliation, personality disorders, you name it." He surprised her by assuring her that if there was any dirt to be dug up, he was in possession of just the right shovel. Adding, without her having to ask, "Not to worry, nothing illegal. Almost everything about everybody is on public record, only it takes a mastermind to nose it out." He would shoot her an email after he'd done the research.

Short and sweet. She still had over two hours to kill. She'd grab the opportunity to polish up her article on Performance Arts. It had had time enough to marinate. She needed to fact-check a couple of dates, and she also wanted to beef up her reference to Yoko Ono's *Cut Piece*. Ono was a pioneer in the genre, and this work, in which she has members of the audience take turns cutting up the clothes she's wearing, had debuted in Kyoto in 1964 and had influenced many artists since. Ono's iconic quote "I thought art was a verb rather than a noun" must be added to the article.

After a reasonable amount of tweaking, she deemed the piece was fit to be published and emailed the PDF version to Sara Madsen. Feeling the urge to recognize her professional persona more collaboratively, perhaps to verify that it was still intact, she followed up the email transmission with a direct call. Without losing a beat, Sara solicited her opinion on several problems needing immediate attention: the format of a two-page spread; a "ticklish" grammatical issue; a disagreement over fonts. The validation was heartwarming.

After the call, she thought she'd pop down to the kitchen and prepare a couple of sandwiches for whoever wanted them. She herself was ravenous, not unusual for her these days. Luckily, her metabolism had kindly kept pace with her appetite.

She had descended the stairs to the second floor and was walking along the balustrade toward the kitchen, when she looked below and spotted Harrison shutting the front door. His back was toward her and for a second she thought—*wanted* to think—he was a stranger, so that she would be doubly thrilled to discover it was Harrison, after all.

He turned. Looked up. Let go of the suitcase handle and walked toward the staircase.

She waited for him at the top of the stairs. "Hi," they said in unison as he approached.

They fell into each other's arms with all the homecoming relief lovers experience after a journey incurring a degree of risk. It was only when they drew apart that a ripple of tension disturbed the air. "I've missed you," he said. "How have you *been*, darling?"

Her throat tightened at the stressed word. "I've been good. Is that why you came home early? You were worried about me?"

"Of course not," he said, too airily. "I'd done all there was to do." He tried a carefree smile. "Why? Would you rather I'd stayed?"

"Don't be absurd!" she protested grandly. "Go get comfortable and join me in the kitchen. I'm famished." She threw her arms around him. "In more ways than one, I might add," an archness to her delivery, though achingly true.

He held her face in his hands and gazed at her until the tension fell away.

"I've missed you, too," she said at last, before their lips met.

* * *

"Lucas's siesta will be longer than usual," Erika predicted, as she passed another roast beef sandwich to Harrison. "He was out like a light after his walk in the park with Kate and Grace. They were surprised he didn't sleep through it, but apparently he was alert the whole time."

"I was tempted to wake him up," Harrison said, greedily eyeing his sandwich. Whether because he hadn't eaten much on the plane or out of sheer relief to be home, once the food was on the table, he'd discovered he was every bit as famished as Erika; more so. "It reminds me of a song my parents used to sing to my baby sister, Nell. A bouncy tune about keeping a baby awake by the Talking Heads. "Baby, baby, please let me hold her," he crooned off key. He took a hearty bite out of the sandwich.

"Him," Erika corrected.

"My parents changed the lyric?" he asked. He smiled, despite the full mouth. "What *else* don't I know about them? I thought they were an open book." He reached for his glass of water. "Where are our baby minders, anyway?"

"Kate's off on a lunch-and-study date and Grace is out shopping for the ingredients for her prodigal's homecoming feast. We have time for a debriefing. Except for the news of Henri Paquard's exterior basement, I know nothing of what occurred on your visit with him. Were there any other discoveries?"

"Groundbreaking ones, actually." He took a gulp of water and firmly set down his glass. "I was going to tell you about them, but you cut short our call, remember? Lucas was demanding your immediate assistance."

She decided it would serve no purpose to bring attention to his show of pique. Instead, she took a bite of her ham sandwich and asked, "Why don't you fill me in now?"

"Let me unpack, shower and put on some clean clothes first."

"By that time, we won't be alone, and anyway, I don't want to wait that long."

"How selfish," he said, grinning.

She smiled to herself. *He's glad I didn't call him out on his little show of jealousy.* She turned toward him and studied his profile. He was so rarely childish. It was endearing, really.

He turned to face her, and they kissed. "Mm, I got a taste of your roast beef," she said.

* * *

Erika snapped shut the locket containing the blond curl and placed it on Harrison's desktop, alongside the other items he'd retrieved from the pink velvet pouch. It intrigued her, but not as much as the ring with its *Eisernes Kreuz* motif and *"H.L. 1914"* inscription. The ring was a single cell from which she cloned an image of the Great War. If she could only twist its meaning in on itself by using it for the good.

"There's that pensive frown," Harrison said, sitting across from her at his desk. "What plans are afoot?"

"You think you can read my mind, you tell *me*."

"I'm afraid to look."

"Worried I'm up for a bit of derring-do?"

"Yes. And we haven't even touched on those groundbreaking discoveries." From beneath the desk came a dream-state bark from Jake, asleep at his master's feet. "See? Even Jake's on tenterhooks." He put the items Henri had given him back in their velvet pouch and stowed them in the bottom left drawer of his desk; the one that locked.

"I'm waiting," Erika said, as Harrison placed the key to the drawer back in the secret compartment built into the desk's top drawer.

"Be patient." From the desktop, he grabbed the beaten-up pad he'd carried with him in Paris. "It's all in here," he said. "You can review what I'm about to tell you if you can decipher my scribble. Take a look at it while I'm in the shower." Earlier they'd compromised on the agenda. He'd been allowed to unpack his suitcase and throw on a T-shirt and sweatpants from its contents, but was obliged to postpone his shower until after his debriefing. He handed the pad to Erika across the desk and leaned back in his chair. He was about to disclose the most critical facts garnered from his trip to Paris.

* * *

"Let me get this straight," she said, after he'd laid it all out for her as if he were pitching an idea for a Sherlock Holmes episode. "All the players in our story are now connected. If you want, we can draw a diagram with interconnecting lines."

Harrison nodded. "Right."

"Your previous account of Madame Denise's experiences established Hans's knowledge of the Eisenberg Gallery. And now, with what you learned from your extended visit with Henri Paquard, it looks like Alexander Alekhine's association with Madeline Paquard and her lover, Hans, has been added to the equation. This is quite remarkable. You've found the missing link."

"Exactly!" Harrison agreed, his excitement devoid of pride. "Alekhine's wife, Grace Wishaar's portrait of Madeline, concurrent with her cohabitation with Hans, seals the deal. The fact that Madeline was a chess player herself reinforces it."

"You realize, of course, that lacking first-hand evidence of the looting and without a clue to either the fate of our primary suspect or the lost art, our theory remains plausible, but stagnant; our group of interconnected players—"

"A closed circuit."

She gave a resigned shrug. "In any case, I've got to send Greg your photo of the Pieter de Hooch painting." She averted her eyes without meaning to.

"What?"

"What *what?*" she asked, feeling herself flush as she redirected focus back to him.

"It looked as though you just thought of something."

She uttered a laugh not quite her own. "Is it so unusual, my *thinking* of something?"

"Hardly. I only meant…never mind." If he only knew which of her nerves were raw, he'd know where not to touch.

"Actually, I was thinking about the *Gazette des Beaux-Arts,*" she said, skidding back on course with an ad lib. "I don't think I told you that the issues I ordered were delivered this morning. I was planning on digging into them tonight."

"Without me?"

Eyes front! she warned herself. "I thought I'd let you sleep off your jet lag."

"Jet lag is best overcome by ignoring it."

"Good," she said, unexpectedly relieved. She realized her plan to study the *Gazettes* on her own had taken on the aura of secrecy—and she did love working with him; she always had. *Guilt is best overcome by ignoring it*, she counseled herself, plagiarizing him.

* * *

Bending over in her chair, Erika placed the June 1931 *Gazette-des-Beaux-Arts* on the rising stack of scanned issues by the foot of her desk. "On its own merits, leafing through the pages is fascinating," she said, straightening up. "But for our purposes, it's an exercise in futility. What were we thinking?"

"This doesn't sound like you," Harrison declared from the chair alongside her. Using his thumb to hold his place in the issue he'd been surveying, he reached for another one from the carton. "Here you go." He slapped the issue onto her lap. "Let's see that positive attitude of yours!" he fairly barked, as if he were her football coach.

She smiled. It was impossible not to be encouraged by his fortitude. "I'm on it," she said, picking up the issue he'd assigned her, dated May 1937.

They'd been at the task for over an hour, and their ritual had become more streamlined, if a bit less thorough. They'd started out scanning for a reference to "Eisenberg" in every article, but after a while they'd eliminated those in which the chance of the Jules Eisenberg Gallery being mentioned was less than negligible. Scholarly excursions on the subjects of numismatics and philately were the first to go. Archeology followed close behind. They'd also cut down on wandering off course reading articles that spoke to their more particular spheres of interest. Harrison, after being caught up in one entitled *"Une Exposition Posthume des Ouvres d'Eugene Delacroix,"* deprived himself of an equally inviting detour, *"La Critique d'Art en Italie a l'Epoque de la Renassance.* Erika had become similarly sidetracked by *"Renoir et Les Origines d'Impressionnisme"* and another, *"Leonard et Michel-Ange."* She had put a stop to her wanderlust midway through the latter, especially since she was compelled to call upon Harrison's superior translation skills every five out of ten sentences, further bogging them down. Moments ago her optimism had taken a hit when her hopes had soared and crashed in rapid sequence. She had been scanning the text of an essay covering the art of emerging cities, when her eyes lit upon an entry that appeared like a diamond in the sand: "J. Eisenberg." She uttered a high-pitched squeal a nano-second before realizing that the miraculous assemblage of letters referred to the ceramic artist Jacob Eisenberg, designer of Tel Aviv's first street signs, created just after the city's founding in 1919.

As she flipped open the cover of the issue on her lap, a sigh escaped her lips.

Harrison shook his head without looking up. "Courage. For every jackpot there's a winner."

Erika chuckled. "Thanks. Not that that makes any sense."

"Who said sense was a component of success?" he asked, as the edge of his palm slowly swept down the page before him.

She skipped the first article, a short study on the coins of ancient Rome, and smoothed the opening two-page spread of the second article which detailed the provenance of several art collections currently on display at the Musée de Montpellier. She had just begun her line-by-line scan, the tips of her fingers gliding from left to right and back again in a continual motion, when a strident "Ho!" caused her to jump in her seat. The *Gazette* slipped off her lap, falling to the floor. "What *is* it?" she shot at Harrison.

"Our reference!" he cried. "*Paragraphs*, it looks like!"

"Come on." She picked up the fallen gazette. "You can't mean the Eisenberg Gallery."

"That's *exactly* what I mean."

She rose from her chair, dropped the *Gazette* onto it and stepped behind Harrison so she could peer over his shoulder. "Where?" she asked, bending over him so that their cheeks were touching. "I think you're pulling my leg."

He pointed to a spot on the page. "This look like your leg?"

She read the line. "Oh!" She wrapped her arms around him and aimed a kiss at his cheek, landing it on the side of his nose.

"So, *now* you love me?" he gibed. "Sit next to me. Let's look at this together." His eyes were glued to the text.

She drew her chair up against his. "You've been reading, so give me a head start," she said, settling in.

He moved the periodical closer to her so it rested on both their thighs, his left, her right. "Let me begin with a word on historical setting."

"Not too long. I'm impatient." Her elementary French was already hung up on the first sentence she'd set her eyes on. "Go, go!"

He grinned, delighting in her eagerness. "I promise, no *Moby Dick* digressions. First off, the issue is dated November 1938. This is a month after Paris's annual *Salon d'Automne* art exhibition, established in 1903 to counter the conservative policies of the official Paris Salon, run by the *Société des Artistes Français*. It displays innovative art, beginning with the likes of Renoir, Cezanne, Matisse, Gauguin, Duchamp."

"'Degenerate' art," she couldn't help interjecting. "Hitler's 1937 exhibition of it must have been simultaneous with Paris's *Salon d'Automne* that year. There must have been Parisian critics who sided with Hitler's denigration of the art. Ironic. Sorry, go on."

Harrison sat back. "I hadn't visualized it that way." He slowly shook his head. "Two distinct groups of onlookers, at the same moment in time, ambling by the paintings and sculptures, pausing in front of them, cocking their heads, making up their minds. How did opinions vary in Munich and Paris? How true to the heart? How pressured?"

"Let's hope individuals can rise above the dictates of autocrats," she said, not so much answering his question as underlining it. "You were saying…?"

"Right. Getting back to the article which is a review of the 1938 *Salon d'Automne*—that is, with a very pertinent aside for our benefit. The author starts off with a general description of the artwork on display. He says that the exhibit is entitled '*Albert Gleizes et ses amis*' and that it's heavily weighted with Gleizes's works. From the text I've already skimmed through, I gather he's no great fan of Gleizes. He throws in a couple of barbs about him, mainly over the artist's claim to have founded the Cubist movement, when, in fact, the credit belongs to Braque, Picasso and Metzinger. He goes on to say—and here's where I caused you to pop out of your chair—that he considers the Jules Eisenberg Art Gallery's concurrent exhibit to be the superior one, despite its lack of fanfare."

Erika zig-zagged her finger up and down the text, searching for the reference. "Where?"

Harrison guided her finger to it. "I read a little further than this, but let's begin here."

At a glance, she spotted a number of artists' names and instinctively felt the need for pad and pen; vetoed it. She read a few sentences to get the gist. The reviewer was claiming that the Eisenberg exhibit included seminal artists in the Cubist movement that were overlooked by the *Salon*—Jean Metzinger for one—and that, in general, far more thought had gone into its mounting. He goes on to admit—sarcastically, Erika believes, in her imperfect French—that the *Salon* exhibit is all about Gleizes and his friends, so it's understandably limited in scope; the Eisenbergs, he supposes, may simply have a larger circle of friends. "'*Au Velodrome*,'" she read aloud. It was the name of a painting by Metzinger, the study for which, the critic pointed out, was being displayed at the Eisenberg Gallery. "*Au* what?" she asked.

"'At the Cycle-Race Track,'" Harrison translated. "Shall we turn the page?" Its corner was pinched between his fingers, ready to go.

"Not yet. This is fascinating. The author refers to works at the Eisenberg exhibit that are spin-offs or studies related to works on display by the *Salon*. For instance. Robert Delauney's 'Rhythm number two' and 'Rhythm number three' are on exhibit at the *Salon*'s site, but number *one* is being shown at the Eisenberg Gallery. There are other artists mentioned in the same vein, but their works related to those at the *Salon* are not specified. Sorry, you've already read all this. Go ahead, turn the page—wait!"

"What is it?"

"The word '*catalogue*.' Here." She pointed to it. It was on the last line of the right-hand page, at the start of a sentence to be continued. "What does it refer to? Okay, turn the page."

When he did so, their gazes converged and paused on the same disclosure. "I can't believe I skimmed right by this," Harrison said.

She waved off the put-down. "So, there's an illustrated catalog of the 1938 *Salon d'Automne*." Look at the footnote! The reviewer notes that the illustrations in the catalog depict counterparts to works exhibited at the Eisenberg Gallery! We only have to match the names he cited with the illustrations! We've got to get our hands on one of these catalogs!"

"Absolutely. There's a good chance it would get us more of a handle on the Eisenberg inventory—*partial* inventory."

She grasped his wrist. "My gut tells me that all we need to do is track down a single art work from the Eisenberg collection, and we'll know how the entire collection was dispersed, as well as…" Her hesitation was palpable.

"As well as who would go to any lengths to stop us in our tracks?" Harrison suggested, with a sidewise glance.

"My concern was baseless," she said, waving off his ESP. "Let's not exaggerate our importance. We're peripheral characters. We're not regarded as threats—if we're regarded at all!"

Harrison thought of the suspicious-looking man in the beret, the inn manager's odd behavior. Perhaps Erika was the only one of them who had remained *un*-regarded. If so, he would do whatever it took to keep it that way.

"Besides," she went on, "I thought you were determined to go all out."

"Not if it puts you in harm's way."

"We've had our dose of paranoia, and I propose we get back to reality," she pronounced, as if a conclusive tone could forestall danger. "Let's try to pick up one of those catalogs." She slid the *Gazette* further onto his lap. "You check to see if there are any more surprises. I'm going to search the internet."

"Why not try Charlene first?"

"Maybe not," she said, drawing her chair back to her desk. "I actually thought about asking her to track down the *Gazette*s we were after, but I didn't want to tell her about Chuck's murder and stir up memories. I know she does enough of that on her own." Charlene Miller, owner of The Book Den, a used and rare bookshop in lower Manhattan, had suffered a tragic loss barely a year ago during the course of Erika and Harrison's investigation of master art forger, Eric Hebborn. Although their friendship with Charlene had deepened in the months that followed, the only time the subject of its origin arose was when Charlene herself brought it up. "I didn't want to lie by omission either," Erika added.

"I see your point," Harrison said, returning to the previous page in the *Gazette*, "and I agree." He began reading the relevant passage in the article, this time more carefully. "Will you hand me a legal-size pad and a pen? I want to make a list of all references to works at the Eisenberg exhibit, both specific and oblique."

She withdrew the items from her desk drawer and passed them to him. "Good idea," she said, awakening her computer with a random tap on its keyboard.

Almost instantly she discovered that the bookseller in Brooklyn who'd sold her the gazettes was in possession of a copy of the 1938 *Salon* catalog. Within minutes she was able to arrange for the publication's overnight delivery. It was all too easy. Against her decidedly unsuperstitious nature, she wondered what was destined to go wrong.

Chapter 13

Henri Paquard exited the Federal Express International Building at 63 Boulevard Haussmann, Paris, feeling good about himself for once. *I've performed a good deed, maybe even a service for humanity,* he thought in his native tongue, immediately backtracking with a reproachful *Let's not go overboard, fucker*—an epithet he did not use lightly.

He stood in front of the neighboring optician's storefront and pretended to be studying the display of eyeglasses as he reviewed his actions thus far. Had he removed the envelope from the inner pocket of his jacket and passed it to the agent behind the counter in a manner that was surreptitious without being histrionic? He believed so. Was the agent's quizzical expression projected to the far corners of the lobby when he declined to accept the receipt slip for the parcel? He wasn't sure, but there was no sense beating himself up over something out of his control. He could hardly have told the woman that he wanted there to be no trace of the transaction, either on his person or anywhere else. He must focus, rather, on his cleverness in asking for a supply of express envelopes and airbill forms for the purpose of sending manuscripts to the United States. *"Je suis traductrice, tu vois,"* he had added chummily, revealing the nature of his work to validate his request. He had employed this tactic so that he'd be walking out of the building with a plastic bag containing items he'd purportedly come here for, should anyone wonder. *Why should anyone wonder?*

He had no reason to believe he was being followed, yet he felt he was being followed. The young man lurking by the motorcycle legally parked opposite the storefront exactly where it should be, along with two other bikes similarly poised—why wasn't he mounting it or walking away? The woman who was just now emerging from the Federal Express building—why was she looking at him while making a point of *not* looking at him?

Perhaps he had *always* been on the lookout for individuals or groups who were after him, meaning to expose him for the outsider that he was—the outcast that his father, and by association his mother, had *cast* him as. Perhaps today's mission was finally bringing to light something he had known all along, only innately, so that he had never been fully cognizant of it. Except for the brief respite he'd enjoyed with Julien, hadn't he always been essentially alone, avoiding being *found out*? He had been branded with his father's sins, hadn't he? Out of the somber recesses of his childhood, when Sunday School was having a go at his redemption, came a passage from the Bible proclaiming that "the son shall not bear the iniquity of the father." *Think again, Ezekiel.*

He must get on with his self-imposed assignment. If anyone should be on his tail, they would certainly not believe his trip to Paris was solely to pick up a couple of FedEx envelopes and forms, hence he had planned a visit to the Musée Jacquemart-Andre, situated right down the Boulevard Haussmann—number 158—a ten-minute staged saunter away.

En route to the museum, he thought of the painting he was making a point to see, Rembrandt's *"Les Pelerins d'Emmaus."* The museum had recently announced that after a lengthy absence, the painting would once again be on exhibit beginning in April, and here it was, April 17th. He remembered years ago, standing with Julien before the painting and silently marveling at the close bond they had formed—so quickly, so ineffably. Setting aside his current mission, he studied the painting imprinted in memory. Focusing on the foreground, he wondered, as he had in Julien's company, what was on the minds of the pilgrim and the impromptu visitor, Jesus Christ, sitting across from each other at the table. They are leaning away from each other, the pilgrim in stupefaction, Christ, in a less readable form of surprise. Is Christ confounded by the pilgrim's awe, or more by the fact that he himself inspired it? Henri wondered if he wasn't reading his own thoughts into the mind of Christ, because that's what he himself had thought when first he'd been the subject of Julien's adoring gaze. Not that he seriously compared himself to Christ, but because of his unusual height, he was a commanding figure who often prompted a kind of guarded respect when walking through a crowd or buying groceries. Never love, though. Not until Julien. It had amazed him. It still did.

Was anyone following him? He hardly cared.

* * *

He was home before nightfall and—how mundane it seemed after so momentous an afternoon—hungry as hell. He tossed the plastic bag of FedEx supplies on the couch and headed straight for the kitchen. He was reaching for the meat patty defrosting since morning on the second shelf of the refrigerator, when he heard a knock at the front door. It did not seem particularly aggressive. The second notice, a trio of solid raps, was more so. His paranoia kicked in, but with a surprisingly higher dose of curiosity than fear. He shut the refrigerator door and went to see who had come for an unannounced visit.

"*Qui est la?*" he inquired through the closed door, pleased with the projected strength of his voice.

"General Directorate for Internal Security," a baritone responded in affectedly mellifluous French. "Jacques Fabron and Daphne Moliere."

"Counter-intelligence—what does that have to do with me?" he asked, playing along. "Let me see your credentials!" He snapped the chain-lock in place and opened the door a crack. A laminated ID card gripped by a set of stubby fingers was inserted into the opening and withdrawn in a flash. Impossible to read it. No matter.

"We have a few questions," the alleged Daphne advised, her tone as cloying as her partner's. "The interview will take five minutes at most."

On the level or not, these two would gain access, one way or the other. Henri's stomach was growling. He was in no mood for wasting time on preliminaries before the inevitable face-to-face encounter. He opened the door.

The appearance of the pair threw him off guard. The man, dressed in a three-piece suit and tie, resembled a company executive who'd been struck in the face by a scythe, leaving him with a nasty scar. The woman, looking more like a construction worker, was his sartorial opposite, in jeans, lace-up work boots and plaid flannel jacket.

"May we come in?" the man asked, the melody gone from his voice. It was a rhetorical question, Henri realized, as the two pressed past him.

In one continuous movement, the man shoved Henri aside and kicked shut the door. At the same time, his mate drew a pistol from her pocket and pointed it at Henri's mid-section. Henri was composed enough to admire the pistol's plum-colored grip. "Give us the letter," the woman said, her dulcet tones vanished, like her comrade's. "That's all we want, and we'll be out of your hair."

"Provided you keep our visit to yourself," the man qualified.

"What are you *talking* about?" Henri asked, feigning utter confusion. Under no circumstances would he allow them to suspect that he was onto them.

"The letter you received from abroad," the woman said. "In the last day or so."

Henri presented a furrowed brow, then walked to Julien's desk, on whose polished top he had strategically placed the original envelope. It contained the letter in what could pass for its pristine state, since he had been especially careful handling it. A wry grin bloomed inwardly, as he mused *If one's paranoia proves to be justified, does that mean that one's paranoia is non-existent?"*

"Don't open any drawers," Daphne warned.

Henri picked up the envelope. "This is the only letter from abroad I've received recently. It's of a personal nature, and I don't know how it could be of any interest to you."

"It's government business," Jacques replied solemnly, plucking the envelope from Henri's fingers. "This is all you need to know. "He removed the letter from the envelope, delicately unfolded it, and briefly reviewed its content. "Good." He refolded the letter, placed it back in its envelope and tucked it into the inner pocket of his trench coat. "Have you contacted anyone about the letter?" he asked, with unconcealed menace.

"I haven't, no. Why?"

"What were you doing at the Federal Express Building?"

"Picking up mailing supplies. I'm a freelance translator. I work with publishers all over the world."

"There was another transaction at the counter."

Damn, I was too slow. Now *be quick!* "Yes. I sent a sample of my work to Phaidon Press. I'm looking to translate a monograph for them on the artist, Delacroix." He started for the bookcase. "I can show you a copy of the article I sent them."

"Never mind. Did you contact anyone about the letter from abroad via email, text, phone or by any other means?"

"I haven't, no. Why?"

"Because a person of interest has visited you lately. I'd like to see your phones, cell and landline, and any computers and laptops you have on the premises. Can I trust you to bring them to me, or are we going to have to tear the place apart?"

"All my devices are on this floor. There's a landline extension upstairs, but it only duplicates what the phone in the kitchen has on visual display or on voice mail. My computer is on my desk—the far one—and in the top drawer you'll find my laptop. I'd still like to know what the clandestine business is all about."

"For your own safety, it's best you don't," Jacques advised, heading for the desk indicated, while the woman stood silently in place, keeping the pistol trained on Henri.

The fact that they weren't curious about the existence of a second desk probably meant that they'd done their research on him. It didn't faze him. He'd prepared for any number of versions of what was presently taking place. These people would not find a trace of the letter's reference anywhere, even if they decided to tear the place apart, after all. Since he'd mentally rehearsed multiple variations of the scene, he felt in control of everything but its outcome. This was causing him trepidations but they were, not surprising to him, mild in nature and concerned exclusively with the possibility of his having to suffer pain.

Chapter 14

Erika lay Lucas on his back in the bassinet and switched on the overhead mobile. As the Brahms lullaby tinkled into being, she re-hooked her nursing bra and buttoned her shirt. "I'll be downstairs in the study," she told Kate, who'd been standing by, waiting for instructions. "You think you can take Jake for a walk? Grace is out shopping and—"

"Sure," Kate said, cutting to the chase and unknowingly provoking a resentful wince, invisible to the naked eye. (What did *she* know about quirky hormones?)

Compensating, Erika gave Kate a friendly pat on the shoulder. "Thanks. See you in a bit." She bent over the bassinet and kissed her baby on his forehead and breathed in his summer-fresh scent, a balm for all ills.

Harrison was hunched over his desk, editing the list he'd begun yesterday, before this morning's express delivery of the 1938 *Salon d'Automne*. He had a class to teach at 11:30 and was already dressed to go in his ivy league ensemble, in stark contrast to her hausfrau get-up: sweatpants and wrinkled shirt.

His briefcase sat in the chair across from him. She set the brazen object on the floor and took her rightful place opposite her husband. "How's it going?" She'd flipped through the catalog before seeing to Lucas, but had left the in-depth examination to Harrison. Basically, all she'd had time to discover was that all the photographs of paintings were black-and-white, except the Gleizes cover.

"I'm just about done." He passed her the legal pad and the catalog. "I may have omitted something. Tell me if you think Greg can work with this."

She scanned his notes. It was obvious he'd made an effort to make them legible. "Looks perfectly clear, but I'll double-check. Have you taken photographs of the paintings we want Greg to reference?"

"I was hoping you'd do that. I'd like to get in early, drop by my office before class."

"A meeting?" she asked, all innocence.

"No. Seeing if I've gotten any mail, papers to grade while I've been away."

"Oh, okay."

Thanks for the permission, he kept to himself. He rose from the chair, feeling guilty for the passing thought. "Back by three," he said, making up for it. He kissed her cheek as he bent to grab his briefcase. She turned her face to receive another on her lips, but he was already on the rise and didn't notice.

After he left, she took the material to her study, the domain where she felt most at ease with herself. She turned on her computer and clicked onto her email. After confirming that Greg had been communicating to her from his secure address, she tapped "reply" at the end of his last message and typed her opening.

Hi Greg,

Harrison and I have put together a list of artists and their works that we'd be grateful if you could research for us. The first is an oil by Pieter de Hooch, *femme donnant du pain a un garcin* (1658), sold to Roger Paquard by the Paul Rosenberg Gallery, Paris, 9/27/28. It went missing around 1940. We don't have a photo of the painting, but you're familiar with Hooch's interior scenes of domestic life and the specificity of the title will aid in its recognition.

Having aligned herself with Harrison to thwart any temptations at coquettishness, her own or Greg's, she felt comfortable moving on. She reviewed and edited Harrison's notes, then took photos of the paintings illustrated in the *Salon* catalog that applied to them, giving each image a reference number. She transcribed the summary into her neater hand.

Six painters whose works were looted from the Jules Eisenberg Gallery, Paris, circa 1940. Their missing works closely resemble the following:

Albert Gleizes "Terre et Ciel" (see image # 1)

Robert Delauney "Rythme no. 3" (see image # 2) NB: the title of the missing work is specified as "Rythme no. 1"

Sonia Delauney "Rythme et Couleur" (see image #3)

Leopold Survage "Composition" (see image #4)

Serge Ferat "Nature Morte" (see image #5)

Andre Lhote "Le Rugby" (see image #6)

Seven paintings looted from the Jules Eisenberg Gallery; images unavailable:

Jean Metzinger "Les Trois Arlequins" 1925

Jean Metzinger "Joueur de banjo" 1931

Georges Braque "Clarinette et Piano" 1915

Fernand Leger study for "Le Grand Dejeuner" 1921

Francis Picabia "The Dance" 1913

Henri Le Fauconnier "Figure au Bord du Lac 1913

Pablo Picasso preparatory drawing for "Les Demoiselle d"Avignon" 1907

Three artists whose works were looted from the gallery; titles, images unavailable: Auguste Herbin, Alfred Reth, Anne Dangar

Continuing her email to Greg, she typed a brief exposition of the art recovery mission, the sources for the list to follow, and then the list itself. She deliberated for a full minute—*idiot!*—before opting for a sign-off that would neither alienate Greg nor encourage his flirtations:

Thanks so much for any information you are able to come up with. We appreciate every tidbit, however seemingly insignificant. As always, it's great working with you! All best, Erika

Without allowing herself to mull a second longer on her parting words, she came down on "send" like a gavel.

Minutes later, as she was stowing the source material in her desk drawer, she received an email response from Greg:

Erika, this looks interesting, and I'll do my best to work with your clues. It may take a little longer than a straightforward search, but I'll let you know how I'm progressing within the next couple of days. Btw, much to my surprise, my ex-partner—ex temporalis, it appears—returned to my domicile this morning, hat in hand, convinced that our problems can be sorted out. Clearly, my knowledge of women is sorely deficient. Regards, Greg

Erika was irked by the reply, or rather her response to it. Here was a perfect expression of leonine pride camouflaged by feigned self-deprecation from a man who meant nothing to her, and what was her gut reaction? To feel rejected. She recognized the fictitious slap to her ego as a self-generated con job, but that didn't stop it from smarting:

Again, thanks for your efforts, Greg. Glad to hear you're working it out with your significant other. Best of luck, you two! Erika

* * *

"What's up?" Harrison asked, walking in on Kate as she was Velcroing Lucas into his quilted outer gear. He squirted a dab of Purell from the dispenser on the night table onto a palm and rubbed his hands together. "Mountain climbing this afternoon, are we?"

"We're going for a walk on this beautiful day!" Kate chirped directly at Lucas, patting him down like a TSA agent. "Aren't we, sweetie?"

Harrison scooped Lucas into his arms. "Hi, my boy." He kissed his fingers, then his cheeks. How good he smelled. Popcorn and apple, was it? No, not quite. He could not find an adequate comparison. Perhaps there was none. He wrapped him closer. Was that an actual coo whispered in his ear? He melted at the thought of it.

The sound of a flush followed by running water came from the en-suite bathroom. The door opened. "Oh, what a picture," Erika crooned. "Come for a walk with us. Jake is due for one, too." To Kate, she asked, declaratively, "You won't mind sitting it out, will you."

"Of course not," Kate replied, displaying her perfect smile. "I'll put through a wash, catch up on my course work." She kissed the top of Lucas's head, perilously close to Harrison's. "Have fun, you guys."

* * *

Strolling up Madison Avenue with her family in perfect synchronization was, as Erika experienced it in that uncompromised moment, the epitome of contentment. Harrison, lightly gripping the carriage handlebar in a boyish display of helmsmanship. She, with one arm comfortably looped through his, while the other dangled at her side, her hand loosely clasping the leash. Jake, padding along at the end of it, setting his pace to coordinate with theirs. Lucas, fast asleep on his back, Erika envisioning his chest rising and falling in harmony with hers. Even the weather, stereotypically balmy, a light breeze stirring the air without calling attention to itself, seemed ideally suited for their outing, in empathy with it.

Without warning, her lovely—*too* lovely?—tableau slipped from an alliance of unique individuals moving through space to a Facebook troop of goody-two-shoed avatars sauntering through the matrix, her concoction of the ideal revealed to her as a bloodless abstract, floating away like a hot-air balloon come untethered.

In the altered silence, Jake, whose favorite tree was coming up fast, tugged at his leash to get to it at once, snapping Erika off balance. In reaction, Harrison grabbed hold of her forearm. It was as if her companions had resolved to re-tether her to their singular and preciously flawed union.

She held onto the leash as if her life depended on it.

* * *

Erika set the wood coaster and mug of tea on Harrison's desk, out of elbow's range.

He grabbed the mug's handle. "How'd you guess?"

"Tarot cards." She smiled. "Is it too strong?"

He took a sip. "Perfect."

"I'm going to bed now."

"I'll be up soon. Just a couple more papers to grade. I left the bulk undone before Paris."

She slipped her arms around him from behind, careful not to bump the hand holding the mug. "I missed you, you know."

"Me too. Wait up for me."

"Hmm, I'll think about it." She let him go and turned toward the door.

"Wait," he said, stopping her in her tracks. "I'd like to shoot Henri an email about the contract Phaidon's preparing for him. His card's in my wallet—in my pants, hanging on the chair in the bedroom. No need to come back down. Just text the email to me."

"Sure."

After checking up on Lucas—dreamily dreaming; *when do secrets begin?* she wondered—she fetched the leather wallet from Harrison's pants pocket. Plucked a bunch of cards—credit, health insurance, business, from what appeared to be the main holding compartment—and shuffled through them. Paquard's was among the first to catch her eye. Taking precedence was another, a pink one, so feminine she imagined it was perfumed. She sniffed at it, feeling stupid but helpless. It smelled of leather, Harrison's leather. Just what was it about Celeste that had prompted him to record her cell phone number? She imagined her voice sounded like miniature church bells, like the celeste itself.

A noble wife would have tucked the card, along with the others, back into the wallet, but nobility was not one of her defining traits. She shoved the card into the pocket of her sweatpants and texted Harrison the requested email.

* * *

"Who's Celeste?" she whispered, before Harrison had found his groove beside her.

He pulled the cover over his nakedness and shifted closer to her. "What did you say?"

"Shh, don't wake Lucas. Celeste. Who is she?" The card was on her night table, ready to be presented as evidence.

"Celeste?"

"Yes." She scanned for signs of betrayal. Missing, or too subtle for detection.

"Ah, yes, Celeste Marin. How did you…of course, my wallet. Damn, I wanted to surprise you." He laid a hand on her shoulder. "I guess that's not possible, given your emotional state, am I right?"

"Episodic."

"Huh?"

His confusion was pristine, devoid of guilt. "It's not an emotional state," she said, down-playing her paranoia with a trace of a smile. "I have episodic flights of madness. There's a difference."

"That mean every other Friday you trust me?" He stroked her shoulder.

She shrugged, taking the question seriously, as he meant her to. "I never know. I'm sorry. Really."

"You're seeing the doctor. You won't cancel, will you?"

"No."

"You'll tell her everything that's bugging you?"

"I won't hold back. What's the surprise?"

He slipped his hand beneath her sweatpants. "You can't be distracted?"

"Not yet," she said, while allowing his hand to explore. "What is it?"

He told her about his purchase of a garment for her at *Chez Aristede.* "Don't ask for details."

"I'm sorry," she said again, stoking her guilt to purge its cause.

"Enough of that. Shall we go to the Blue Room?"

"As long as we're quiet, we don't need to. Turn off your light."

He rolled over to reach for the switch at the base of his lamp. When he turned back, her thumbs were hooked on the waistband of her sweatpants, tugging at it. "Let me." He laid her hands to her sides and pulled off her pants, then helped her out of her blouse and nursing bra.

She tossed her clothes to the foot of the bed and opened her legs. "Here we are," she said, giddy with her unexpected mood reversal, as if it had been visited upon her rather than come from within. She pulled the covers up around them. "Slow, deep," she whispered, pressing him down on her. She raised her hips, and he swept his hand under her and held her still as he entered her, heedlessly letting go a grunt of satisfaction.

"No sound," she murmured, sliding her fingers between his buttocks to test his self-restraint.

Slow and soundless, she decided without thinking, would afford them optimal control. Instead, their stealth gave them space to marvel and torture over every rise and fall, every sensory delay, until the tension could no longer be endured. In the final instant of mind over matter, each of them clamped a hand over the mouth inches away to muffle whatever groan or cry was about to break free.

Afterward each lay motionless under the cover, in a silence glutted by the presence of the other.

How could I have ever doubted him?

How could she have ever doubted me?

Chapter 15

Four days after PI John Mitchell had been given the provenance info on the flipped house, he called Erika's cell to reveal what he'd come up with. It was Monday night, 8:00 p.m. He figured she'd be home. The background noise indicated otherwise. "Where are you?" he asked, competing with the cacophony of voices and classy canned music.

"We're at dinner. Capital Grille." She clicked wine glasses with Harrison and had a sip. It must be the fourth time they'd toasted; no words needed. "Any news for us, John?" she asked, identifying the caller for Harrison's benefit.

"It can wait. I'll call later. You should shut off your phone."

"With a baby at home? You kidding?"

"Of course, sorry. When's a good time?"

She glanced at her watch. "Ten, ten-thirty too late for you?"

"Done. Say hi to Harrison for me."

The call ended, and she set the phone on the table, off to the side. "John says hi."

"You look beautiful," Harrison returned, as the busboy swooped down on them to remove their empty appetizer plates. The busboy smiled. "Not you," Harrison said, smiling back. The busboy bore an uncanny resemblance to Brad Pitt, so no harm done.

"Thanks," Erika said, after the busboy had gone off with their plates. It wasn't the first time Harrison had remarked on her beauty that evening; the first, before they'd left the house, as she was descending the stairs to meet him in the lobby. The black satin jumpsuit had arrived from *Chez Aristede* earlier in the day, but he hadn't laid eyes on it until what by chance had turned out to be her grand entrance. She felt quite daring and at the same time shy in the costume: the halter-top covered her breasts except for two lateral crescents of flesh never before seen in public. It was thrilling, really, imagining Harrison here and now leaning toward her and slipping a hand into one of the halter's side entrances. She flushed.

He noticed. "Wine getting to you?"

She shook her head. "It's this outfit. It's making me feel…"

The waitress arrived with their main courses—salmon for her, T-bone for him. They chorused their thanks and she retreated.

Harrison cocked his head. "I'm waiting."

"Naked, if you must know."

"Due to the unusual exposure?"

She reached across the table and ran her fingers across his lips. "Nice though, yes?"

He captured her hand and kissed her fingertips one by one.

In her imagination, her crescent moons emerged from the shadows, waxing to gibbous, to full. She shot him a wicked grin. "What do you say we get doggie bags?" she suggested, only half in jest.

* * *

In the end, entrees were consumed; desserts forgone. Whether due to the wine, the peekaboo halter or the fact that it had been their first legitimate date in quite some time, it was inevitable that a celebratory romp in the Blue Room would ensue. Afterward, they showered together, threw on sweat suits and flip-flops, and headed for Erika's study to await John's call. Kate was tasked with the preparation and delivery of Lucas's upcoming feeding, one of the interspersed formula meals.

At exactly ten-thirty, John's call came through on Erika's cell phone. "We got to have a face to face," he started, waiving the small talk. "I have information from a source who says it's confidential and will not permit it to be posted in any way, shape or form. I think the guy's an over-cautious prick, but I've got to respect him. If you've got some time—shouldn't take long—I can pop over. Otherwise it can wait. What do you think?"

No private consultation needed. "Come over now," Erika said, close to demanding. "As long as it's okay with you," she added, for form's sake.

Twenty minutes later the three were ensconced in Erika's study sampling their first sip of tea. "Very fancy," John commented. "What the hell is it?" He laid his mug on her desk.

She grinned. "Genmaicha. A Japanese blend of green tea and roasted rice. Sorry you went with 'whatever'?"

"It's fine—great!" He was sitting in Erika's desk chair. He bent to pick up the manila envelope at his feet. "I know you're anxious to get to it."

Erika was sitting on the vanity chair; Harrison was beside her, on the club chair's ottoman. They each took another swig of their tea and deposited their mugs on the vanity top.

John drew his chair closer to them, undid the envelope's string closure and pulled out a number of loose sheets of paper. "Let's review. Your mission is to learn of any and all occupants of a flipped house in Westchester County who, time-wise, would have had the opportunity to hide a box of artifacts under said domicile's attic boards. What narrows down the field is the year 1946, which appears on an important document found in the box. Therefore, occupants permanently exiting the premises prior to 1946 were ruled out. I'm being long-winded."

"Never," Erika objected.

"I'm concerned about time. I'm keeping you up."

"The reverse is true," Harrison reasoned. "You went out of your way to trek over here despite the inconvenience to you."

"No inconvenience. I'm happy to be of service. Anyway, the good news is there's only one party in the mix that fits the bill. If this was a movie with off-the-wall twists, not an absolute certainty, but in real life, pretty damn close. I'm talking about"—he glanced down at the top sheet—"Brigada Limas. Brigada rented the house in the suburbs from—"

"Wait," Erika interrupted, rising from her chair. "Let me grab a pad and pen."

"Sit. I'm leaving you my notes."

"Ah, great." She sat back down.

"So, Brigada Limas rented the house in Westchester from one Edward Ainsworth. Remember, you told me Ainsworth bought the house in 1940 and sold it in 1952? Researching the county records, I found that Brigada was the sole tenant from 1945 to 1946, when her three-year lease terminated upon her death. Next, I looked up her obituary, which appeared in the *Herald Tribune*. Date of death, April fifteen. Dual citizenship, US and Brazil. No family members mentioned. Praise, regrets, thanks-for-your-service from staff and friends of the diplomatic mission of Brazil to the United States of America." He observed their reaction: dropped jaws, and continued. "The obit says her nine-year tenure as administrative assistant at the Embassy in Washington, D.C. ended in December 1945, when she moved to New York to serve as deputy director of communications for Brazil's Consulate General."

It was an effort for Erika to remain silent; forever the smart-ass schoolgirl flailing her hand in the air. "How did Brigada get her hands on the letter Alekhine mailed to Ambassador Martins? He directed that letter to the Embassy in Washington, D.C., *after* Brigada had moved to a suburb of New York City!"

"The woman died a month after Alekhine's death," Harrison segued. "Do you know the circumstances? Were they as controversial as the chess master's?"

John raised a hand as a call to order. "Save your questions. I'm getting to phase two." He took a sip of his tea; winced a little. "Still weird." He riffled through his papers; extracted one.

"Here's where we are. My initial research went without a hitch—I got the data on the house, came up with the obituary. The next step was to gather any filed or anecdotal information on Brigada from Brazil's Consulate General's office over on Forty-first Street, Murray Hill area.

There, I ran into a roadblock with the aforementioned priss in charge of records—guy looked like he was born wearing a tux. Only after I handed him a signed and notarized statement from my buddy in the New York art theft division of the FBI saying that I was acting on his behalf, did the bastard give me the time of day. Only then was I given authorization to rummage through the sad little box stored in the agency's basement, along with the other orphans of history with no known relatives to take them in. For three-quarters of an hour I sat on a folding chair at a bridge table, sifting through what looked like the contents of Brigada's desk from which all sensitive matter had been removed, all the while watched over like a hawk by the upstairs-downstairs butler sitting opposite me. I was not allowed to take photos. In fact, my watcher confiscated my phone for the duration, I guess in case he dozed off on the job.

"My notes describe in detail every item I came across, down to a pearl hatpin. For instance, I copied verbatim what looked like a to-do list, leaving it to you to translate from the original Portuguese. Same for a couple of postcards. There was a wedding invitation with a note scrawled across it. 'Obrigado, casamenteira,' exclamation point. Pithy enough to Google a translation: 'Thanks, matchmaker!'" John handed over the papers to the nearest host, Erika. "Take a look, you guys. See if you've got a problem making any of it out. Not much there, I'm afraid."

Erika slowly flipped through the papers at an angle comfortable for Harrison. "Any questions?" she asked him.

"Not right now—about the presentation, that is. Meticulous, by the way, John. Thanks."

John nodded acknowledgment. "But you still want to know about the circumstances of Brigada's death, Harrison. I haven't forgotten."

"Yes, I find it curious that it took place so soon after Alekhine's. Since it seems likely she's the one who intercepted the chess player's letter to Ambassador Martins and brought it with her to New York, where she hid the damn thing, I can't help thinking the deaths are related. The way I see it, some person or persons wanted to get their hands on that letter to obtain the information it held and or to stop it from going public. As the primary source of the information, Alekhine was eliminated. You agree, Erika?"

"I do, yes." She lay the papers on the vanity table. "Anyway, whatever motivated the violence back then, it remained unfinished business."

John ticked a nod of agreement. "Right you are. Charles Bloom's death was linked to the unearthed letter."

"It had to be. It was the only artifact Chuck specifically referred to in his presentation announcements. So, John, do you have an answer to Harrison's question?"

"Yes, I do. Brigada Limas was hit by a car and died at the scene."

Erika and Harrison sat forward, anticipating an Aha moment.

John shook his head. "This was no hit and run, if that's what you're thinking. The driver was a teen-ager, who not only stuck around, but gave the victim mouth-to-mouth until the rescue team arrived. Not everything rises to the status of missing puzzle piece, guys."

Erika nodded. "You're right. Still, her death, accidental or not, put the problem to rest—or on hold—until recently, when Chuck unwittingly revived it."

"Sleeping Beauty with a twist," John commented, on the rise.

"I meant to ask," Harrison said, as he and Erika rose in unison, "do you know where the cops are in their investigation? The detective still fixated on Gary Kessler?"

"Sure is. Word's out there'll be an indictment any day now. You're Kessler's only hope, looks like." He gave a resigned shrug. "We're good, then? You won't hesitate to call if you need me?"

"Can you recollect us ever hesitating to call on you?" Erika asked.

John looked up at the ceiling in mock contemplation. "Not really. But now I must get back to my wife." He started for the exit, the Wheatleys following his cue. A foot from the doorsill he turned and cocked his head in the direction of his barely-touched cup of tea. "I'm a simple man," he declared. "Next time make mine a Lipton. Hold the rice."

After he'd closed and locked the front door behind John, Harrison turned to Erika. "He never lets us down, does he?"

"He's a good friend." She shook her head.

"He isn't?"

"No, no, I was thinking how incredibly frustrating it is—to be so near and yet so far. I mean, it's pretty much a sure thing we've got the identity of the person who somehow got her hands on the Ambassador's—her *ex-boss's*—letter, right? So, we add her to our group of interconnected individuals, and *still* we can't get to the guy we're looking for, dead or alive!"

"Hans."

"It's like these people are a cluster of islands just off the mainland, only with no route *to* it!"

He put his arm around her shoulder. "Tomorrow we'll get to work building a raft. Now let's get some rest."

"I want to take a closer look at the material John gave us." She slipped out from under his arm. "You go to bed. I'll be there soon."

He knew by the set curve of her brow there would be no dissuading her. "You want me to help?"

"It's fine. Ten minutes. I'll time myself."

* * *

She'd meant it when she'd said ten minutes, but that was before she'd come across John's replication of a letter to Brigada, temptingly short enough to make a stab at translation. On the top of the page there was a message from John, painstakingly printed, each letter standing rigidly alone: Best I could do with this handwritten note from "C.M.," whose handwriting is worse than mine, and in Portuguese, yet.

True to his word, John had copied each letter of the note as best he could, replacing letters he couldn't make out either with question marks or slashes separating guessed alternatives. Words omitted in their entirety were indicated by three consecutive x's.

Erika booted up her computer and logged into WordReference, then onto "Portuguese-to-English." She entered one unambiguous aggregate of letters at a time, writing down the meaning of each, or, in cases of clear divergence, meanings. When she had completed her hard-won sequence of words, she read it aloud, retaining the definitions that in context made more sense and, a la the gestalt theory, filling in the omitted words with words that best rounded out the thought under scrutiny. She then typed out the letter as she imagined it had been written, more or less.

March 5, 1946

My dear Brig,

As discussed, here is the heap of unopened letters that flooded the mailroom following the much-publicized embassy party at which my wife chose to unveil her latest sculpture. I anticipate the correspondents will be evenly divided between those who praise me for being forward-thinking and those who wish to see my head on a platter.

Your replacement, Clara, is an eager and pleasant young woman, but I have neither the heart nor patience to initiate her with such a colossal task. Thank you for acceding to my request by responding to these letters as you have so admirably done in the past, and alerting me to those missives where you deem it absolutely necessary.

I have enclosed stationery, postage, seal embosser, along with a check for the hours estimated. Please advise me if more hours are required to complete the task, and I will see to it that further remuneration is made to you.

Much gratitude, my dear. We sincerely hope you are enjoying your new position, but, alas, we do miss you!

Yours truly,

C.M.

The task Erika had taken on had been more wearing and time-consuming than anticipated. She was exhausted but exhilarated; couldn't wait to tell Harrison that the mystery of how Brigada had gotten her hands on Alekhine's letter to Carlos Martins had been solved. Less altruistically, she was looking forward to him heaping some praise on her for her diligence. She shut down the computer, stowed her worksheets and John's papers in a desk drawer and hurried off to the master bedroom.

Lucas was lying peacefully on his back, one arm flung up alongside his head as if he had fallen asleep swimming backstroke. Holding back her hair so it wouldn't fall in his face, she leaned over the basinet and kissed him on his forehead.

Harrison was also lying on his back in quiet repose, looking about as untroubled as his son. A rogue thought—*he should have waited up for me!*—was shamed into retreat as Erika climbed into bed beside him. His body twitched in response to the disturbance and rolled onto its side, away from her.

***

The last frame of a dream or the first on awakening: *where am I?* The digital clock was facing away from her. Was it very late or very early or outside of time? Harrison was turned toward her yet in a space apart. She wanted to touch his shoulder, nudge him awake, but was afraid of what uncensored expression would stamp his features as he was torn from the musings of his deeper self. A castaway on the island of gloom, she waited for the light to come.

Chapter 16

Harrison jumped up from the couch as Erika opened the front door, reaching her before she'd stepped foot into the lobby. "How did it go?"

His anxiety level was way higher than a routine GYN appointment warranted. "What's wrong, Harrison? Why are you home at this hour? Don't you have a class?"

"I cancelled. What did Dr. Robin have to say?"

Erika noticed a FedEx envelope lying on the couch; tops of papers fanning out from inside it. "Anything important?" she asked, nodding at them.

"Yes—later. First tell me how it went."

"I told her everything, as I said I would. Even my weird experience from the other night; my isolation episode, or whatever you want to call it."

"And?"

"Dr. Robin was not overly concerned. Especially after I told her my anxiety relates only to you." She offered a wry grin.

He was not buying the humor. "What course of action did she suggest?"

Erika shook her head. "She says I should ride it out. She said fretting—fretting, that was the word she used—will only create a self-fulfilling prophesy."

"That's it? No diagnosis?"

"Sorry to disappoint you. No post-partum depression, no baby blues. Apparently, my fear of losing my sex appeal—and losing you in the process—is at the root of it. I told her how my father's abandonment all but destroyed my faith in men, and how meeting you had restored it, and she suggested that a flux of hormonal activity may have caused it to falter."

"Back up. You're afraid of losing your sex appeal? What the hell, Erika. Are you seeing yourself through the eyes of a pimp? Don't you get it? You're not a desirable object, you're the object of my desire!"

"Tell that to my amygdala. It's got a mind of its own." He looked like he was about to snap. "I'm joking. I need to joke. Just give me a hug and never let go."

He wrapped her in his arms; held her without moving.

"Okay, you can let go now," she said, still needing to make light of things, he seemed so deadly serious. "What's in the envelope?" she asked, certain it must be contributing to his high level of tension. She watched his jaws clench. "What *is* it?"

Without answering, he grabbed the envelope from the couch and pushed the papers more securely into it. "Let's take this to my study. Come." He headed for the steps.

Only after they were seated opposite each other at his desk, and Jake had received some—never his fill—tactile love from them and had resettled himself under the desk, did Harrison pull out the papers from the FedEx envelope. "There are two letters. They need no explanation. Read this one first." He handed her a single sheet—of stationery, Erika saw mid-transit; with Henri Paquard's letterhead, she realized, once it was in her possession.

The letter, she noticed immediately, had been typed on a manual type-writer rather than on a computer. She assumed this was to avoid leaving any traces of it on the cloud or elsewhere. It was dated "Friday, April 17," and opened with "My dear Harrison."

Will wonders never cease. A letter I thought would never come arrived yesterday, the day of your departure. In fact, you and it may have crossed paths. It is a letter written in Portuguese with a heading in French I took as an apology: Je suis pas linguiste. I have enclosed my translation of his letter. I will be express-mailing the parcel to you today. You should receive it in three business days.

I believe I may be in some danger. I say this not to alarm you, but to urge you to take the following precautions: Under no circumstances are you to call, text or communicate with me in any way. If you have already done so, I do hope it is solely in regard to the Delacroix project. If my suspicions are unfounded, you will hear from me soon. If my worst fears are realized, I implore you to make no inquiries into the matter. For your own safety, you are not to respond in any way to news of my disappearance or demise.

The only way you will be able to make use of the information provided in the enclosed letter is to remain off the grid. My only wish—my dying wish, if it comes to that—is that through you I may in some way make restitution for the sins of my father.

With deepest gratitude,

Henri

Erika's glance leapt from the text to Harrison's face. "Is he dead?" Stupid question; she knew the answer.

"I don't know."

"What about contacting him—you haven't, have you?" She suddenly felt out of breath.

"I did send him an email yesterday, but—"

"Oh, no!"

"—but only to reference the Delacroix monograph and the contract Phaidon was offering."

"If Paquard's in danger, it must mean that by association you are, too."

"No, not at all."

"You're holding back. I can tell."

"Really?" He tried to scatter his thoughts of the man in the beret and the oddball inn manager, as if this were a game of hide-and-seek and Erika was It. "What's the telltale sign? Is my left eyelid twitching or something?"

"Now you're deflecting."

He thrust two sheets of paper in her direction. "Games later. Read this."

"Fine." She took the sheets. "Doesn't mean you're off the hook."

Henri had headed his translation with the sender's address in Sao Paulo along with his phone number and the date recorded on the original: April 12. Hampered by disbelief, Erika needed a second to register the full impact of the letter's salutation: "To my half-brother, Henri Paquard."

Her focus shifted to Harrison. "Have we found Hans? Could this be true?"

"Read on," he said, and she knew by his set features that was all she'd get from him.

She returned her gaze to the letter.

To my half-brother, Henri Paquard,

I received notice of our kinship through the DNA service we both employed. I will come right to the point. My knowledge of our family history is scanty. When I was a boy our father, Theodor Andersson, informed me that he had emigrated from Sweden in 1940 after having been "persecuted by the liberal mob running the country." His words ring in my ears to this day.

Once settled in Sao Paulo, he opened a small jewelry shop, which he later expanded, in the Jardins district. It is called Andersson's Joalheria. Early on he joined the only white nationalist organization in town. In 1946 he married a like-minded woman, Ladonna Sanchez, and in 1947 I was born of their union; their sole issue.

I know nothing of the grandparents on our father's side, and I will not bore you with relatives on my mother's. Our father died of cardiovascular disease in September of 2015 and my mother died seven months later.

I have always harbored suspicions that our father's story was invented, and that our history is rooted in an even more ignoble past. He may have shared his secrets with my mother, but she remained closemouthed until her dying day. I am hoping (and dreading) that any secrets withheld will be revealed by your story.

My wife, now deceased, bore our son, Sandro, in 1972. He has been a great disappointment to me. Despite my efforts to set him on the right course, his "Poppa Theo," a more magnetic and hence more persuasive individual than I, succeeded in brainwashing him. Your half-nephew belongs to the organization that our father joined many years ago, but is a more active member than he ever was. After working alongside Theodor throughout his adult life, Sandro is now the sole owner of Andersson's Joalheria as well as the balance of our father's estate. You should be aware that although I am loath to inform Sandro that I have corresponded with you, I feel obligated to do so, and shall.

All my life I have fought to lessen the harm our father's malignant views have caused, and to erase those institutions that aspire to perpetuate them. When I was in law school, I served as an intern for a year with CERD, the Committee on the Education of Racial Discrimination, and even now, I try to attend their twice-yearly conventions at the United Nations headquarters in Geneva. It is at least a comfort to know that Brazil is a ratified member of that organization and fully in tune with its noble mission. I also work pro bono for clients in need when their cases involve matters of racial and social injustice. I tell you these things not to promote myself, but to let you know exactly where I stand. For a long while I hesitated to reach out to you, I suppose out of inertia and fear, but curiosity got the better of me and quite frankly, I have become a lonely, solitary man—though if your sympathies are opposed to mine, I will happily remain so.

Sincerely yours,

Miguel Rodrigo Andersson

Erika looked up. Harrison was studying her, waiting for a reaction. For a moment they stared at each other without saying a word.

"We found him," she said, breaking the silence. "Hans—Theodor."

He nodded. "Too bad he's dead."

"Because he got off scot free? Most of them did. She placed the letter on the desktop and rose to her feet. "Don't move. I'll be right back."

Moments later she returned with John's notes plus her own. "Here's my translation of Ambassador Carlos Martins' letter of instruction to Brigada Limas," she said, reclaiming her seat opposite Harrison. She handed it to him."

"Yes, love, you showed it to me after you'd stayed up all night working on it. It's a brilliant recreation, especially considering what you had to work with." He set it aside.

"I thought maybe you'd want to have another look, since I thrust it in your face after you'd barely opened your eyes."

"I didn't mind. No, I read it thoroughly. It answered the question of how Brigada got her hands on the sealed envelope containing Alekhine's letter to the ambassador. Correct?"

"Yes. Just checking we're on the same page. So, now we're agreed we've got our hard evidence proving *opportunity*"—she passed him another sheet of paper—"have a look at this. Then let's talk *motive*."

Harrison glanced down at the line-up of rudimentary letters. "This is John's reproduction of the wedding invitation he spoke of. Along with the scrawled notation '*Obrigado, casamenteira*,' translated, 'thanks, matchmaker.'" He did a long take on the text before him, as Erika did a long take on *him*.

When his eyes widened, she knew he'd put it together.

"It's uncanny," he stated at last. "This is an invitation to the wedding of Ladonna Sanchez and Theodor Andersson—that is, Hans and his 'like-minded' wife, as Henri's half-brother referred to her. The personal note scrawled across it thanks Brigada for her role in getting the pair together. And just look at the date of the wedding, December 23, 1946. We've got ourselves a sequence of events that can't have lined up by chance."

"Let's see them in black and white. Pad? Pen?"

He pushed them toward her. "You're the calligrapher around here."

She headed the page boldly: 1946. "It was a busy year," she said. "Where do we begin?"

"Alexander Alekhine's letter to Ambassador Carlos Martins. Mid-February."

She jotted it down.

Within minutes the critical events were before them.

mid-February—Alekhine writes letter to Ambassador Martins. Indicates he knows the details of a major art heist and the whereabouts of the thief.

March 5—Martins includes Alekhine's unopened letter in a stack of mail he sends to Brigada, instructing her to respond, as was her custom while in his employ.

Late March—Alekhine dies. To this day, a cold case.

Dec. 23—Ladonna marries Hans aka Theodor. Brigada the acknowledged matchmaker.

They processed their thoughts independently. Erika was the first to speak. "Now that it's in front of us, it's hard to miss."

"Brigada Limas's complicity, start to finish."

"Exactly. The moment she opened Alekhine's letter, she knew she had the key to information that could make her a fortune."

"Blackmail or black market? Which do you think?"

"Either way, her motivation was self-serving. She did hide the letter, after all. Here's another unanswered question. What exactly took place between the time the letter was read and the time its secrets were prodded from the man who wrote it? Did Brigada murder Alekhine, or orchestrate it? Who knows? From the timeline, though, it looks as though she made immediate use of the information by manipulating the pairing of Ladonna—I'm assuming a friend of hers—with Hans." With a shrug Erika added, "Maybe all she wanted was a finder's fee."

Harrison shook his head. "It hardly matters at this point. We've got our raft. Let's not get lost in the reeds."

"Agreed," she said, smiling at his reference to an earlier conversation of theirs.

"Harrison smacked his palm down on the revelatory wedding invitation. "What I don't understand is why the hell Brigada didn't destroy this, when it damn well serves as circumstantial evidence?"

"Speaking for myself, I clean out my desk drawers once in a blue moon. Did you see the list of stuff John recorded? The pearl hatpin wasn't the only stray item among Brigada's effects."

Harrison grinned. "Guess you're right, darling. So, where do we go from here?"

"To Brazil," Erika replied without losing a beat. "Where else?"

Harrison's grin expired on impact.

* * *

"Are you sure you want to get yourselves directly involved?" Greg asked via his secure phone line, after he'd been briefed on the Wheatleys' latest findings. "You must be aware of the risk factor."

"We can handle it," Erika assured him. She was planning to bar Harrison from traveling to Brazil with her, but a conference call was not the setting in which to enlighten him.

"Ideas, Harrison?" Greg warily inquired.

"Not five minutes ago Erika and I were taking notes on Brigada Limas's culpatory time line," Harrison answered emphatically, with a glare in her direction. "We haven't fully processed it yet."

"Let's just suppose we had," Erika blithely countered. "Greg, would you have any ideas on how to set up a…*recovery* operation for want of a better word?"

"I'll give it some thought, but only if both of you are interested."

"I know when I'm overruled," Harrison muttered. "When will you be in New York? I'd prefer we speak face to face."

"I'm in town now, and will be for at least a week. Give me a few days to make a couple of inquiries."

"Let's meet here, at our home," Erika suggested. "Saturday good?"

"Fine—actually no. Saturday is the day of rest for someone I may want to tune into our brainstorming. How about Sunday, say eight a.m.?"

"Sure—okay with you, Harrison?"

"Why not?" Harrison replied, a cynical bite to his yielding. "Any reason for the early hour, Greg?"

"It'll be three p.m. in Tel Aviv; best time to catch our guy."

Chapter 17

Harrison and Greg were huddled over in conference, heads close to butting, when Erika walked in on them. For a moment she imagined they were talking about her, in particular about her foolish reaction to Greg's review of his love life. *Stupid thought.* Her foolishness had been strictly internal, therefore unobserved. Still, disquieted by the look inward, she double-checked that the buttons of her blouse she'd just been nursing in were properly secured before approaching the men.

"What did I miss?" she asked, as Jake scrunched out from under the desk to greet her. "Hi, boy."

"Not a thing, darling," Harrison assured her. "I've just been showing Greg all our artifacts in person."

Erika took note of his cheerful tone. She and Harrison hadn't touched on the subject of going off on an investigative hunt to Brazil since their phone call with Greg, so Harrison probably assumed—or chose to assume—that the subject was defunct. Poor man. She gave Jake a loving caress, and he trotted off to find a more private nook in the house. Four's a crowd, she anthropomorphized.

The men rose to their feet. "Erika!" Greg exclaimed, opening his arms as he strutted into her space. "You're looking grand!" He gave her a hug, too bearish for her liking, and nudged her toward the chair he'd been occupying—her usual, opposite Harrison. Redirecting his attention to Harrison, he gestured toward a nearby straight-back chair, piled high with loose papers topped with five-by-seven inch cards.

"On the floor's fine," Harrison said, anticipating the question.

Greg cleared the chair, drew it up alongside Erika's, and the three settled into place.

"Before we discuss a course of action, let's hear what Greg's got for us," Erika declared, jumping in as moderator.

Greg pulled a notepad from the inside pocket of his sports jacket and placed it on the desk without bothering to open it. "Not much," he said. "But, as we'll see in a bit, this might be a good thing."

His hosts' quizzical looks were accompanied by a knock on the door.

"That'll be Grace," Erika said. "I had her fix us a breakfast tray, if anyone's interested. Come in, Grace!"

Clad in her usual starched uniform, Grace wheeled in a bar cart containing a thermal coffee carafe, an assortment of buns and tarts and, on the lower shelf, the necessary serving items. "Good morning," she said with a tiny nod, refined yet unobtrusive.

Her presentation was greeted with a round of thank-yous, and she retired with a formal Victorian-like bend at the waist.

"Adorable," Greg remarked on her parting. He glanced at his watch. "Eight-twenty. Can we skip the coffee break for the moment? If we're planning on calling my Israeli friend, it best be within the next ten minutes. As I said, there's not much to tell. I found no leads to anything resembling the Pieter de Hooch painting. No leads to the Hans Arp and Max Ernst paintings mentioned in the chess player's letter to the Brazilian ambassador. And lastly, not a sign of the works described in your email to me, Erika. That is, apropos of the 1938 *Salon d'Automne* exhibit. From the Albert Gleizes and Robert Delauney look-alikes to the named works of Leger, Picasso and the rest. Nothing. Nada. And not for want of probing, I hasten to add."

"You said this might be a good thing?" Harrison asked, somewhat crestfallen.

Greg sat up straight, looking more the Olympian as he did so. "As I see it, there are two possible explanations for this curious state of affairs." He raised a cupped hand, as if he were about to catch a baseball. "Correction. *Cogent* explanations. The first scenario would be that this Hans fellow of yours unloaded all his stolen artworks on the black market early on, and that his clients were fully advised of the dire consequences should they attempt to resell them on the open market."

"I find this hard to accept," Harrison suggested. "If the works are invulnerable, and the thief is dead and therefore beyond retribution, why the hell are people being murdered over this? Chuck was killed because of a letter claiming knowledge of the thief's identity and whereabouts, and I'm pretty sure that Henri Paquard's discovery of his father's extended history has gotten him murdered as well!"

Erika suddenly lit up. "What if they're stockpiled?" she asked, her voice up an octave.

"Spoiler alert," Greg declared. "I was getting to that."

"You mind telling me…" Harrison began, before the answer dawned on him. "Ah, yes. If at least a portion—if not the *bulk*—of the plundered art has not yet been sold, there's ample motivation to shut down at all costs any investigation that threatens to expose it."

Greg nodded. "What I was getting at. The good bit. Discounting the murders, that is."

Erika sat forward. "Let's think about the rationale behind this. After the war, there was a major reaction to the old world regimes and their allegiance to traditional art. There was a rise in individualism and experimentation, and those artists who best embodied the movement rose in fame as their works rose in value, and continue to do so. Who wouldn't want to hold on to a van Gogh, for instance? His portrait of his landlord, Dr. Gachet, handed over to him in lieu of rent, was sold in 1990 for over eighty-two million dollars to a gallery in Tokyo. Am I right, Harrison…Greg?"

The men bobbled their heads in unison.

She went on. "I'm guessing Hans was not an art connoisseur, although if he was, it would only serve to make the argument even stronger." She waited for takers; did not want to hog the show.

Harrison took up the thread. "If Hans had no foresight, there were people around him who did. As you know, I discovered on my visit with his son, Henri Paquard, that Hans was on occasion in the company of the chess master, Alexander Alekhine and his artist wife, Grace Wishaar, and therefore, by association or hearsay, familiar with Marcel Duchamp and his mistress, the flamboyant avant-garde artist, Maria Alvez. Point in fact, in the early 1940s Alvez bought Piet Mondrian's 'Boogie Woogie' for eight-hundred dollars, and later, when his fame was on the rise, donated it the Museum of Modern Art. Then, of course, there's Duchamp himself. Not only was he an innovative artist and thinker, he was a promoter, a spokesperson for the new art. He curated any number of exhibitions, his most famous probably the 1938 Exhibition of Surrealism in Paris. Hans might very well have been influenced by these people." Harrison looked to Erika for a response.

Greg was about to speak, when Erika grabbed the baton from Harrison. "Yes, and let's not forget that Roger Paquard, father of Hans's lover, Madeline, was an art collector; another influence right there."

Harrison, fuguing: "Not to mention Roger's close ties to the brilliant art dealers, Paul Rosenberg and Georges Wildenstein!"

Greg whipped out his cell phone from his breast pocket. "My friends, are we going to call Tel Aviv or not?"

"I'm beginning to warm up to the idea of traveling to Brazil," Harrison admitted, speaking over him.

It's now or never. Erika took a deep breath. "Harrison, I'm going to Brazil without you," she declared, muscles tensing for the reaction.

"What?" the men chorused, Harrison's release the more vehement.

"You're compromised, sweetheart, you know that," Erika fairly cooed, realizing her attempt at gentleness made her sound like she was talking to Lucas.

Greg waited. Harrison, fuming, held his tongue.

"Hear me out. In Paris you were seen in the company of people associated with our investigation. One of them. Henri, is presumably dead. I think he was being stalked, and I think you were, too. Whenever we came close to the topic, you failed to look me in the eye."

He looked away, even now.

"After Chuck's death you went all out, took off to Paris without a second thought. Despite my trepidations, you had my blessings. Now give me yours." She was surprised to find herself close to tears. "Please. I need to do this."

To feel whole *again?* he stabbed silently, not having the heart to utter the words. He was angry, but facing her fiery sincerity: helpless. "I only want you to be safe. You do get that, don't you? I'm terrified for you."

"Easy on the drama," Greg urged, growing impatient. "My contact is more dependable than anyone I know."

"Who the hell *is* this Israeli, anyway!" Harrison belted.

"A seasoned member of Mossad, the foreign intelligence arm of the Israeli intelligence community, and a perfect candidate for this mission. He's worked on the recovery of stolen art, but behind the scenes. No chance of his being exposed. I've given him the basics of the case and after today's meeting, I'll be able to fully brief him. His preconditions are first, that I not divulge his name and second, that you're fully committed. If he detects a rift between you two, he'll back out." Greg held up his cell phone. "Well? Are you okay with Erika's venturing into the field for a couple of days?" He refocused on Erika. "You're okay with leaving your infant for that span of time?"

Her body cried a primal *No,* as she said, "I've had ample opportunity to watch Kate and Grace in action, and I'm sure they can handle the situation. And I know Harrison will be a big help in his free time."

Harrison rose to his feet. "Harrison will not be having 'free time.' Harrison will be home!"

Erika's body slumped with a relief she could not have anticipated. "You'd take time off? Before your leave of absence?"

"What do you think? I'll shave the time off my paternity leave."

Good enough commitment for Greg to punch in the Israeli's number. Harrison began pacing the room. As Greg waited for the Israeli to answer, he silently implored Harrison to stop. His fixated stare had no effect. Only when the connection was confirmed with Greg's brightly forced "Shalom!" did Harrison stop dead in his tracks to demand the call be put on speaker phone. "Press it!"

Greg shook his head.

"Another precondition?" he fumed.

Greg gave a helpless shrug in the affirmative and carried on with his exchange, which divulged nothing other than the news that Erika was going to be advancing the project on her own. "He'll speak to you now," he advised Erika, after a bit. He handed his cell phone to her. "It's a secure line."

As if she hadn't guessed. "Hello?"

"This is so damn cloak-and-dagger," Harrison balked, hovering over her.

"Am I speaking to Erika Shawn?" a voice lustrous as a cello's inquired.

"Shawn-Wheatley," Erika felt obligated to inform.

"Do not respond to what I'm about to say. If you work with me, you will become another person. Now you may respond, but only with a yes or a no. Are you willing to forego all connections and communications to your present life for the duration of our mission? Think before you answer."

"Yes."

"You will trust me absolutely? Yes or no."

"Yes."

"I will need some time to work out the details. If I call you on your cell phone within four to six days, will you be ready to go?"

"Yes."

"Greg has told me the length and color of your hair, but there is one unanswered question. Is it virgin—natural, unprocessed?"

"Yes." There was a question inherent in her tone. It went unanswered.

"Think carefully, now. Are you willing to keep this as well as all other of our talks and activities confidential? Wait before you answer. This includes your husband."

"Yes."

"And are you absolutely sure you're *capable* of doing so?"

"Yes."

"You did great. You'll be hearing from me." The line went dead.

Harrison had barely been able to contain himself. "What the hell was *that* all about? Let me guess. You're not at liberty to say."

"For your benefit as well as mine," Erika said, the answer she believed her handler would have prescribed. She turned to Greg. "One more thing. I don't care what you—what *any* of you—think, I'm insisting that my family be provided with full-time security. Bodyguards—the works!" She handed him back his cell phone.

"Well, of course," Greg replied without pause. "That's been our understanding from the start." He pocketed the device and rose to his feet. "So, mates, you think the coffee's still hot?"

Chapter 18

Harrison knew nothing of what had transpired on Erika's call with the Israeli, but he'd guessed that whatever plans were in the works, the opening gambit was imminent. That night, five days after the call, he and Erika had made love with all the tortured urgency of soldiers going off to war. One hour later, at midnight, the Israeli had contacted Erika on her cell phone. The call was brief; instructions, varied but concise. Overwhelmed with regret for not having offered greater resistance when Erika had pitched her solo flight, Harrison had sat on the edge of the bed and watched her spring into action. A woman with a cause. She was glorious. He was miserable.

It was now 2:30 a.m. A limo was coming for her at 4:00 a.m. They were sitting at the dining room table in sneakers and sweats and sipping coffee, pretending it was an ordinary day. "I've just emailed Sara Masden," Erika said. "Along with a couple of editors who may try to reach me during the next few days. I said I'm visiting a close friend I've known since childhood with stage four cancer."

"Ghoulish."

"Yes, but a good excuse to be giving such short notice, and that's what I was told to do." She handed him her cell phone. Greg will be picking it up some time this afternoon to deliver it to a woman in Connecticut, purportedly my gravely ill friend. Don't ask questions, Harrison, just hand him my phone. You're to periodically text my number and ask how my friend and I are doing. My surrogate will text you back. It's a precaution."

"Better be an unnecessary one. No creeps trying to track you down."

"There won't be." She ran her index finger around the rim of her coffee cup. "I want you to tell Grace this story, and Kate. Unless I see either of them before I go."

"This is all you're allowed to tell me? I have no way of reaching you? Your phantom self in Connecticut is all I've got?" He grasped the edge of the table as if to steady himself. The kaffeeklatch pretense was wearing thin.

She covered his hand with hers and gently pried it free. "Only a few days." She kissed his hand and held onto it.

Shifting to less worrisome ground, he asked, "Did you freeze any of your milk?"

"Some, yes. My production has tapered off some since we've been alternating with formula. Lucas isn't fussy, though. He chugalugs both with equal gusto." She took a bite of her English muffin, grown cold. As she prepared to wash it down with a swig of coffee, she suddenly remembered something. Repressing the impulse to jump from her seat and provoke another inquiry, she lifted the cup to her lips and savored a sip or two, then slowly rose from her chair. "Don't go anywhere, I'm just going to look in on Lucas."

Not a lie; an omission. Before checking in on Lucas, she scurried downstairs to Harrison's study, where she headed straight for his desk. From the secret compartment in the top drawer she withdrew the key to the bottom left drawer. It took less than a minute to fetch the object she was after from the velvet pouch, bury it in her pants pocket, return the pouch to the drawer, the key, to its secret compartment.

Lucas had begun to gurgle and stir by the time she entered the master bedroom. She scooped him up and cradled him in her arms. Squiggling and cooing, he bumped and buried his face in the crook of her neck. *My delicious beautiful baby.* Her tears came suddenly and without warning, like a summer storm.

Kate entered the room at the height of it. "Is anything wrong? I heard Luc on my monitor, but he didn't sound at all stressed." She wrapped her flowered silk robe more securely around her hourglass figure and retied the belt.

"No, no, Lucas is fine," Erika managed, wiping her tears with the cuff of her sweat jacket. "I'm only thinking the next time I see him, my friend will be gone," she explained, using a true emotion to authenticate a lie, following it up with the more complete story. "Will you take extra special care of him?" she pleaded, tumbling out of the fabrication. "I'll only be gone a few days."

"Of course, of course! Do you want to get ready to go? Do you want me to take him now?"

"Yes, would you?" Another minute and she would be unable to part from him.

Hurrying back downstairs to be with Harrison, Erika felt as if she were playing out her last hours on earth. As she came upon him, sitting motionless at the table as if time had stopped, she realized in a sense it was true.

Chapter 19

The lobby window was Erika's vantage point as she waited for her ride to—well, wherever; she had to trust her handler. Harrison was glued to her side, no longer asking unanswered questions—Why are you still wearing a sweat suit? Why no luggage? No handbag, no watch?—and appeared to be resigned to the mission in progress, as if fate, and not Erika herself, had visited it upon them. She heard him suck in his breath as the black stretch limo pulled up at 4:00 a.m. in front of their home, and still, he said nothing, managing a ragged "I love you, be safe" only when she was in the doorway. She answered in kind and gave him a quick hug, before heading for the limo.

Because its windows were tinted black, all she could see in the glow of the streetlamp when she tried to look inside was her gawk-eyed reflection.

The passenger window rolled down and the driver, a middle-aged man in a black suit, produced a confidence-inducing smile. "Four-seven-three-one-eight," he recited, matching the number the agent had told her to listen for. "Apologies for not assisting you. Please step into the rear of the vehicle." The window slid shut.

Before Erika shut the door, she looked back at the house. Harrison was standing at the window, his raised palm flat against the pane, signaling either *goodbye* or *stay,* and she raised her palm to him, first touching it to her lips.

The partition separating her from the driver was curtained in black opaque fabric. A device identified as "audio communication" was mounted on a panel of temperature and entertainment controls below the partition. On the floor of her commodious quarters lay a large black plastic bag pinched closed with a twist-tie. She had been told in advance the general nature of its contents, but the details would be a surprise.

"We are not far from our destination," the driver said, startling her with his amplified voice. "I will park around the corner to allow you to prepare yourself in a leisurely fashion. We are in no rush. Are you seated? I am about to start moving."

"I'm ready." His accent was identical to Netanyahu's. "Are you Israeli?" she asked as he pulled away from the curb.

"You have a good ear, miss."

She wondered if she had broken some undisclosed protocol, or by responding, *he* had. "Thank you." There would be no further inquiry.

She tried the window; it was locked. Cut off from the visible world, she knew only from the listing of her body that the driver had made an immediate right turn onto 78th Street, heading east. The car moved slowly along the street until what she guessed was midway between Madison and Park, where it came to a halt. "I will double-park here unless I am forced to move," the driver informed her. "I will warn you beforehand."

"Thank you," she said again, more stiffly, as she began unzipping her jacket. Once removed, she tossed it onto the floor, kicked off her sneakers and peeled off her sweatpants, forcefully expunging the embarrassing image of a striptease. Next, she lifted off her T-shirt and added it to the pile at her feet. She had thought to purchase a lightly padded bra to absorb any potential leakage, but looking down at it now, she felt a wave of guilt for her level-headedness. *I'm brave, not cold-hearted*, she countered inwardly, re-engaging with renewed dedication.

Quickly, she removed the tie from the black bag and pulled out its contents, arranging them beside her on the gray leather bench seat. She approached the task systematically. First, she stepped into the white tank body suit and snapped shut its crotch. The navy suit came next—the skirt, then the jacket. The fit was perfect. Sheer luck, since not all size eights are cut the same. In a half-crouch, she adjusted the skirt's alignment and smoothed its front. The hem hit just below the knee. She buttoned the jacket and cinched her waist with the blue snakeskin belt provided. The blue and white spectator heels—snug, but endurable—finished the outfit.

The wig was a surprise, although thinking back to her conversation with the Israeli, not a complete one. Removing it from its mini hatbox, along with a mesh object she assumed was a wig cap, she uttered a muted "oh."

From the front, "Are you all right?"

"I'm fine."

"The street is quiet. I don't think we'll have to move. Take your time."

Their exchange threatened to turn conversational. Uncomfortable, given the circumstances. She declined to answer, focusing instead on dealing with the wig, a bright auburn creation, straight, short, with bangs flipped to the side. She pulled the mesh cap snuggly into place and forced her chestnut hair beneath it, making sure to capture the strands straggling outside its rim. A hand mirror had been included in her provisions, and she checked herself in it before donning the wig itself.

Embracing her skull, the generic headpiece came to life. She rotated her head, studying her reflection from every angle, fascinated by the change in her appearance.

From the remaining pouch of unknowns spilled a vial of Chanel no. 5, a pair of pearl stud earrings, a small jar of ivory foundation, a dark brown eye-liner and a tube of deep red lipstick. She utilized all items. After her transformation was complete, she threw whatever was not attached to her person—sneakers, clothing, cosmetics, all of it—into the black plastic bag. She was about to close it off, when she realized she'd forgotten something. With bated breath, she dug her sweatpants from the bag and plunged her hand into its pocket. Empty! The recollection of a second pocket impacted like a godsend. There, in its depths, she found what she was after: the ring with the *Eisernes Kreuz* motif. The agent had cautioned her against traveling with any of her possessions except her wedding ring, but she had countermanded him on this sole point, believing that she'd find a use for the ring somewhere along the way. She placed the stowaway inside the flap pocket on the right side of her suit jacket. "I'm ready," she announced, tossing her sweatpants into the bag of discards.

* * *

In her isolation chamber, Erika waited for the click of the lock. *There.* The car door opened. She took the proffered hand and, like a butterfly emerging from its chrysalis, the new version of herself stepped into the world.

"Welcome to the Plaza," the doorman intoned, releasing her hand. The gold braiding on his cap glistened in the light radiating from the hotel's entrance, the bulbs studding its eaves like a tennis necklace. In a few hours the hotel's porte cochère would be bustling with taxis and limos, but in the dark before dawn, it was quiet; Erika was the premier guest.

The driver popped open the trunk and removed a small suitcase, stood it on its end and released its retractable handle. Erika noticed the Louis Vuitton logo pattern covering the surface of the luggage and suppressed a wince. By choice, she was opposed to the flaunt-your-designer approach to fashion; her repurposed persona apparently was not. The doorman hastened to retrieve the suitcase from the driver who in turn swung shut the lid of the trunk. "Have a pleasant stay, miss," he stated without inflection, before heading for the driver's side.

"Thank you," Erika replied flatly, taking his delivery as her cue to reply in like manner.

The doorman escorted her up the red-carpeted staircase and through the entryway into an opulent expanse of white and Breccia marble. The lobby's west end opened onto the iconic Palm Court, where she had once been treated to high tea by her boss. Sara, she remembered, had been thoroughly amused at her expression of horror on reading the prices embossed on the menu.

At the lobby's center a magnificent chandelier overhung a stalwart table supporting a massive array of flowers. There, the doorman transferred his charge to a uniformed bellhop. Grabbing the handle of the suitcase, the attendant proceeded to lead Erika to the check-in counter at the lobby's north wall.

The lone star at this early hour, Erika was addressed at once by the sole receptionist on duty. "Good morning, may I help you?" the young woman cheerfully asked, her words striking Erika's chest with the force of Emergency Room paddles. Lights! Camera! Action!

"Good morning. I believe my husband has already checked in." *Does she see my hand is shaking?* "Noah Richtman." The words sounded jabberwocky. *Repeat.* "Noah Richtman. I'm Sofie, spelled with an 'f.' Sofie Richtman." Out of nowhere, she realized her lipstick was an even deeper red than the receptionist's.

"Here we are. Yes. Room 429. I have your key." The receptionist—'Olivia Green,' if one could trust a lapel pin in this alternate universe—slid the computer card into a little white envelope and set it aside.

Is she having second thoughts?

Olivia slid a card and ballpoint pen toward Erika. "We just need you to sign in."

Erika gripped the pen tightly to stop her hand from quivering.

"Bottom line," Olivia prompted.

Deep breath. On the line indicated, Erika signed her new name in a simple variation of her old handwriting, deciding on the spot to reverse its slant and convert the dots over her 'i's to cocky little circles. Her inventiveness, never mind how meager its display, gave her confidence a modest boost. "Here you go, Olivia." She slid the card and pen back to the receptionist and was rewarded with the envelope containing the room key.

With a spring to her step, as authentic as a scripted cue, she followed the bellhop out of the lobby and through the corridor leading to the bank of elevators, all the while fiercely girding herself against another attack of nerves.

When the elevator doors slid open and she stepped foot onto the fourth floor, her singular focus shattered into a kaleidoscope of emotions: dread, excitement, terror, suspense.

The bellhop turned right, suitcase in tow. "This way, miss."

She trailed after him, the tapered heels of her spectators sinking into the carpet—familiar beige-with-floral-pattern in the palest hues, nudging thoughts of home.

"Here we are. Do you want to use your card?"

Erika paused, between worlds.

The bellhop took it as a no and knocked, and the door sprang open—or maybe only appeared to.

"Darling, at last!"

She heard the words before she'd processed the visual image, and then it was too late. She stiffened within his embrace, barely managing to curb the impulse to land a knee to his groin. Once freed, she froze in place, like a mannequin in a store window, surprisingly with a human voice. "Hello, Noah," it said.

"Must have been a pain, the flight delay."

"Yes, it was." He had come into focus. Tall, well-built, thick peppery gray hair just beginning to recede. Strong features, stubble beard. Sean Connery on steroids came to mind. The mannequin could think.

She was positioned just outside the doorway, facing the room's interior. He sidled past her.

"Thank you," she heard the bellhop say, signaling a tip had been received.

"Sofie, love, you must be *exhausted*," her newly acquired husband declared, purportedly for the benefit of the departing bellhop. "Come."

The Taser-touch of his hand on her shoulder set her in motion, and she darted into the room to get out of its range.

He tapped the door shut with the heel of his sneaker. "Damn, I hope you're a fast learner." In the sitting room of the suite a couch upholstered in a nubby beige fabric was set against the far wall. He dropped into it and flung his arms across its back. "Sit down. We've got precious little time to learn our lines."

"*What?*"

"Figuratively. Relax." He tapped the cushion next to him.

"Please. I need a minute."

Finally, a smile. Much more open and friendly than she would have predicted. "Trainees were never my thing. I only work with seasoned agents. I don't mean to be brusque."

"I think you do."

"Good line. There's hope for you yet." He raised a hand to ward off her counter. "Just kidding. You want a drink? Soft drink. Tonight, we'll test our skills at the Champagne Bar."

Alarms were going off. The king-size bed, visible from where she stood, added to the cacophony. "I assume you reserved a room for me. This"—sweeping hand gesture—"marital arrangement is just for show, yes?"

"Yes and no. The setup is dual-purposed. It's the easiest story for our Brazilian target to swallow, but mainly it allows me to keep you in my line of sight twenty-four-seven." As if prompted by the thought, he gave her a candid once-over. "You look the part. It's a head start. Beauty is an asset when you're trying to put something over on someone. Distracts the hell out of them, plus they want to please you."

"This is awkward for me."

"Of course it is. Sit down. I'll explain why it shouldn't be."

If he'd remove the arm still sprawled on the back of the couch, she'd join him. Eagle-eyed, he caught her glance flit to his outstretched arm and knew to tuck it at his side.

She positioned herself as far from him as possible; started to cross her legs; thought better of it.

He tugged at a cuff of his black crew neck sweater. "It's unwise to dwell on our identities outside our mission, but for this to work certain things must be understood. You should know that in one capacity or another I've teamed up with various women during the course of my long career. Some of them were just as lovely as you, but I've never had sex with any of them, and I have no intention of starting now. I'm a faithful husband. Simple as that. I've been married thirty years. We share everything except state secrets. I will not be risking that relationship on any account. From this moment on, there will be no worries on your part. Understood? My function is to act as your bodyguard and co-planner, nothing more." He frowned. "Why are you smiling?"

Am I? "I suppose because you remind me of my husband."

"Why? He work for the CIA?" Again, that unbridled smile.

"Because he's a rare breed, like you seem to be."

"What are we, endangered species? I think I'm insulted."

"Don't be. I've got trust issues. I'm working on them. Your earnestness helps, actually."

He raised a hand. "Enough soul-searching. First order of business: define the mission. Give me your version."

Taken aback by his abruptness, she had to admit it was wise to move on. "Our goal is to unearth the art looted from the Jules Eisenberg Gallery, or whatever remains of it," she began. "The consensus is that the works were stockpiled, to sell off at a later date, when their value would presumably skyrocket." Her shoes were making her toes throb. Would she ever feel comfortable enough to kick them off? "Our focus will be Sandro Andersson."

"Why?" Testing her.

"Because Sandro is the beloved grandson of Hans aka Theodor Andersson and his acknowledged heir. Odds are, whatever remained of Hans's cache of stolen art was also passed on to Sandro, if surreptitiously. But you've been briefed on all this."

He nodded. "I wanted to hear it from you to be sure we're on the same page." He crossed his legs; grabbed hold of his ankle. "Next on the agenda: strategy. Ideas?"

"I'm sure you've got a plan."

"It's not set in stone. Greg tells me you've got a creative mind, and I'm always open to suggestion. Why are you rubbing your foot? Do the shoes hurt? Take the damn things off."

She took his advice. It seemed absurd not to.

"At least five, six pairs to choose from in one of the suitcases in the bedroom, along with a sizeable wardrobe. The rules governing baggage weight are more flexible when you're traveling private jet." He gestured toward the small case she'd come in with, still standing by the door like a tentative guest. "That one's got loungewear—*gym* wear more accurate," he corrected, catching her raised brow. "Also, toiletries, make-up, that kind of thing."

"Who's *paying* for all this?"

"Later. We're getting side-tracked. Tell me how you think we should approach our man Sandro."

"It's likely you've cast me as a private art collector. A rich one, from the looks of it—slick suit, monogrammed suitcase. I can't imagine a more appropriate role."

"You got it."

"I suppose you should play something along the lines of a shipping magnate or oil baron. One who can't say no to his acquisitive wife."

Noah grinned. "We agree on the dynamic, but for purposes of flexibility, I'm a freelance investor. Besides, it's part of the ready-made bio I've taken out of the mothballs."

"What I'm unclear about is how we're going to come up with our *in*. I wish we had the name of an underworld collector or dealer who we can say recommended Sandro to us."

"We do. Greg's provided us with one. Dealer picked up last year who turned state's evidence in exchange for a spot in the witness protection program. Nothing to do with this case, but a name well known on the dark web. I prefer not to reference specific individuals—always a risk of being off base—but there may be no other option. Can you think of one?"

"I haven't been able to."

"Table it. Let's move on."

"Noah—do I call you Noah?—I want to know why I'm in disguise. Why, for instance, the wig?"

"Yes, call me Noah. As far as you're concerned, that's my given name. As for disguise, disguise is used to bump up security, but more important, it makes it easier to switch out of character. The less Sofie looks like Erika, the easier it is for her to be her own woman. After we go over your credentials and order up breakfast, you're going to dye your hair red, same shade as the wig. The product is in the bathroom."

Her expression was question enough.

"An observant individual, especially if he questions your authenticity, can detect that's a wig. He asks himself, what's under there? If she's got a decent head of hair, what's she doing covering it up? You see where I'm going with this?"

"He'll suspect I'm in disguise. Why auburn?"

"To me it says rich and snooty. No other reason. Platinum blond would have been more so, but it would have been more difficult to accomplish. Are you offended?"

"Why would I be?"

"Because I'm stereotyping." He rose from the couch. "I'll be right back. Don't run away." He started for the bedroom area.

She heard a closet door open then shut. Seconds later he returned with a woman's shoulder bag—standard Louis-Vuitton-brown, bucket-style, with drawstring cinched opening. Another of the designer's products paw-printed with his monogram. Noah sat back down and pulled open the leather drawstring. "Here we are." He laid the contents of the bag on the long cherry wood coffee table. "Take a look."

From the slots of the slim wallet—Vuitton's, of course—Erika plucked three cards. The first, an American Express gold credit card in her new name, Sofie Richtman. "You're the associate member," Noah commented. "I'm the primary. Mine's platinum. Easy all around to piggy-back you onto my revived alias. By the way, we were married two-and-a-half years ago. Christmas Eve. Easy to remember. On the beach in Maui. Just us and a local witness. No relatives for you to memorize. Carry on."

The second, a health insurance card. "Do we have vision and dental coverage?" Erika asked facetiously.

He grinned. "Too plebeian."

The third, a Real ID driver's license, which would allow her to board a plane. The placid-looking woman in the photograph stared up at her. She stared back in disbelief. Her first thought: *a doppelganger*.

"The wonders of computer generated imagery," Noah explained, demystifying her take. "The photo is from your college yearbook. We rotated it slightly from three-quarter to full frontal and dyed your hair. Painted your lips, too, of course. Can't have you looking like an ingénue."

"Where'd you get the photo, the registrar's office?"

He smiled. "I pegged you as savvier than that. No, not NYU. From the all-knowing internet."

"I am."

"Pardon?"

"Savvier than that. I was taken off guard."

His face fell. "Of course, you were. I warned you I wasn't good with trainees."

She nodded; slipped the cards back into the slots; noticed there were a few bills of varying denominations in the billfold. "Reals?" she asked, coming back at him with her knowledge of Brazil's currency.

"Yes. Mainly twos, tens, fifties. Couple of centavos in the purse compartment." Back to business; remorse short-lived.

She put aside the wallet; picked up the passport and turned to the first page. Same photo as the one on the driver's license. "Where have I been, I wonder?" she asked, flipping through the pages. There was only one entry, back-dated two months. "Only Germany? I picture us as jet-setters. Wait. This must be counterfeited as recently issued." She checked the date on the first page. "Yes," she confirmed and looked up. "Again, not much to remember, should my memory be called into question. Very clever. Really."

"I'm an old hand. Take a look at the cell phone, Sofie. Is the case too drab for you? I can change it if it is."

"It goes with my Louis Vuitton ensemble."

"I detect a note of sarcasm. Try to keep your distance, Erika. Observe, don't hover."

"Understood." She began placing the strewn items back in the bag. They included, along with the ones discussed, a tortoiseshell comb, a travel-size bottle of hand sanitizer, a packet of tissues and a little pad-and-pen unit, the pad cover and mini-pen both sterling silver. The initials "*S R*" were engraved on the pad cover. "You are thorough," she said, cinching shut the bag.

He rose to his feet. "Breakfast," he announced, without segue. "What it'll be, Continental or the works?"

* * *

They'd each settled on Continental, double-down on the coffee. Noah had wheeled the serving cart out into the hallway, leaving behind their cups and saucers and a three-quarters-full carafe for later reinforcement. He had returned to the couch to continue reading his Kindle version of *War and Peace*, purchased on his flight from Jerusalem. Scratch one off the bucket list. "Let me know if you need any help!" he called out to Erika, before clicking on the e-book.

"I'm good, thanks!" she called back from behind the locked door of the bathroom, at the junction of the bedroom and sitting room, where she was going over the instructions on how to dye her hair. Recklessly ignoring the advisory to perform an overnight skin-patch test for allergies, she divided her hair into sections with the clips Noah had provided, donned the latex gloves included in the kit, then moved on to the serious business of preparing the mixture of developer and color. She didn't much care if the product stained the tank top she'd scooped out of the small suitcase that had been moved to the luggage stand at the foot of the bed, but Noah had provided her with a store-bought bath towel for the occasion, so she wrapped it around her shoulders and secured it with one of the extra hair clips. Well along on the meticulous-to-OCD spectrum, Noah had surely planned to dispose of all signs of her transformation.

She could have used his assistance brushing the product onto the back section of her hair, but there was no way she was going to instigate such a domestic scene. She made do with her beginner's skill and a hand-held mirror. An hour later, shampooed, conditioned and blown-dry, she emerged from the bathroom, tentative but not totally displeased.

Noah looked up from his Kindle.

"You're frowning," she said.

"You would be, too, if you were on page 93 of 1,407. You did a good job. It looks great."

"It feels garish."

"It's striking. More so, since you combed it back off your face. Classy. With the dark lipstick and any outfit besides a stained bath towel and sweats, you'll knock his socks off."

"Sandro's?"

"Who else? Listen, make yourself comfortable and come back out here. I've got some reading material for you."

"The tutorial continues." A pullover shirt and sneakers later, she was again tucked into the far corner of the couch. This time the offering atop the coffee table included a bunch of newspaper and magazine articles, a book by Alfred Montero entitled *Brazil: Reversal of Fortune*, and a list of numbers and codes hand-printed on a 3"x5" index card.

"Commit them to memory," Noah instructed. "Most important, you must remember that the password to our joint account is a password in name only. It has another use we need not discuss now, as it would serve only as an academic exercise. What *is* essential if ever you're called upon to punch in that series of characters and symbols, is that you must allow at least a one-second interval between each of them. Don't ever forget that. The reading material is meant to brief you on the zeitgeist. When it comes to the matter of ingratiating yourself, you never know when an item of local interest can come in handy."

As Noah plodded on with *War and Peace*, Erika delved into the closest article within reach, one dated January 17, 2020, from the AP Morning Wire. It covered a televised speech delivered by Brazil's Culture Secretary Roberto Alvim, which promoted an arts initiative designed to focus on nationalism and religion. The AP report excerpted a portion of his speech that had been obviously hijacked from one delivered in 1933 by Nazi propagandist Joseph Goebbels. Alvim's anti-Semitic innuendos had caused quite a stir, and despite his claim that the duplication of words had been a case of "rhetorical coincidence," he was relieved of his post by Brazil's President Jair Bolsonaro. Erika wondered what Hans's neo-Nazi grandson, Sandro, had made of all this, and if bringing up the subject in conversation might be at all useful to her.

Next under scrutiny, an article from *The Rio Times* dated November 20, 2019, reporting a Brazilian research study focusing on the rising number of Nazi-oriented groups currently operating on the internet. Taking second place in the count was Santa Catarina, home of sixty-nine active cells (groups of three to forty members); outdone by Sao Paulo, with no less than ninety-nine. Was Sandro a member of one of them? Erika pictured him and his cohorts getting together on Zoom. If only she could crash their party!

Noah threw aside his Kindle and rose to his feet. "I need a shot of coffee. You?"

"Yes, sure." She retrieved another article from the supply. "This material may come in handy. As you pointed out, a means to ingratiate ourselves."

"Read a little more and we'll brainstorm." He strode to the desk where the coffee carafe, cups and saucers had been placed earlier. No additives had been kept in reserve, since they both took their coffee black. He poured two cups and returned to his post. "Still steaming," he said, placing them on the table. "What are you looking at now?"

"An article from the *Wall Street Journal* dated March 4, 2020. The headline announces the slowdown in Brazil's economic growth."

"For a more comprehensive picture, you might want to thumb through Montero's book on the history of Brazil's economy, although it's not required reading. To be honest, I brought it along for my own edification, nothing more."

She smiled. "That's a relief. Economy is not my favorite subject." She took a swig of her coffee. "Are you going to want lunch?"

"Myself, I'd rather have an early dinner, catch up on the news and get some shut-eye. We'll be checking out before dawn tomorrow. If you want, we can have a meal sent up for you."

"No, thanks. I can only think about getting on with this. I'll read a few more articles and then let's have that brainstorming session. I'm worried about not being *prepared*, somehow."

"No worries. Just memorize that list of numbers, you'll be fine."

* * *

"And you, miss?" the young waiter asked, blushing with the helplessness of love at first sight.

"I'll share the split of Dom Perignon, thanks. What do you think, Noah, shall we add a cheese board to our order?" Sofie was coming out of her shell.

Aiding the emergence was the bright red hair, rakishly clipped back on one side, exposing one of the diamond stud earrings her appointed husband had given her at the last minute, just before they'd exited their suite. The dramatic eye liner, the fair skin made-up fairer, the pop of red lip color, all contrived to captivate the observer and had, in fact, gone a long way to captivating Erika herself. Her outfit, the navy form-fitting suit worn earlier in the day, now accented by a bodysuit in bright coral, a color alien to Erika's wardrobe, further added to Sofie's budding confidence.

"Good idea, the cheese board," Noah replied, clearly pleased with his cohort's demeanor. "The caviar tray would not have sufficed. Matter of fact, add a tuna tartare." His nod to the waiter served as both a confirmation of the order and a dismissal.

The Champagne Bar, just off the lobby, was an elegant venue with a variety of seating arrangements—bar, cocktail tables, couches. Noah and Erika had chosen a curved couch at a window overlooking the Pulitzer Fountain topped by the freshly gilded bronze statue of Pomona, goddess of abundance. A round table at knee level trapped them in fellowship. Except for a couple seated at a cocktail table at the other end of the room, they were the establishment's sole patrons.

Noah, following Erika's example, spread his linen dinner napkin across his lap. "How are the shoes? More comfortable than the spectators?"

"Much." She wiggled her toes inside the black leather pumps to reassure herself. "You were going to tell me who's financing this project," she said, wasting no time to get down to business.

"There's Israel, for obvious reasons," Noah replied flatly, his narrowing eyes the only feature betraying his resolution. "France, too, as the country of origin," he went on, delivery returned to normal. "I considered approaching Brazil, as it's France's main partner in Latin America for cultural, technical and scientific endeavors, but I was worried about news of our operation leaking to Sandro Andersson. Too close for comfort." Spotting the waiter walking toward them, he abruptly changed the dynamic of their exchange by nudging closer to her, and with an air of intimacy declaring, "Here comes our champagne, babe."

She jerked away, prompting a look of concern—or perhaps hope—from the besotted waiter, just arriving. To compensate for her character-role misstep, she turned to Noah and tremolo-ed, "Yes, dear!" cringing at the fraudulence of it.

"And you were doing so well!" Noah complained, though not without the hint of a smile, after the waiter had poured them each a glass from their bottle and departed. "This is a dress rehearsal, remember."

"I'm sorry. You took me by surprise."

"Don't let it happen again." The smile had vanished. "Did you see the look on the waiter's face? We don't want to see that look in Brazil."

"It won't happen again."

"Think of it this way. The actress never quite loses herself in the character she plays. She just doesn't allow anyone to see her."

"I told you, I get it. Please don't patronize."

"I'll try not to. Now, tell me your revised social security number."

She reeled it off like a miffed robot; followed it up, unprompted, with a recitation of her new cell phone number, e-mail address, physical address in Arizona and password for their co-owned account with an international investment firm fabricated, for the occasion, by the Mossad. She raised her glass. "Cheers," she sniped.

"To our detente," he answered without rancor. "May it continue."

Their glasses faced off, and as she clinked hers against his just shy of shattering, the caviar tray was delivered along with the tuna tartare. The cheese board would be along in a moment, they were told. The dapple of black and orange roe, chopped scallions and onions and diced hard-boiled eggs put Erika in mind of a Pointillist painting, but she was in no mood to share the thought.

* * *

Noah reached for the spare blanket and pillow on the closet shelf of the suite's bedroom. "You'll at least agree our dry run was useful?"

"I'll give you that. Yes." Admittedly, despite their minor falling-out, or maybe because of it, their dinner date had served its purpose. As the meal had progressed, so had Erika's ability to sustain her part as Sofie.

"Good. Subject closed." He snapped shut the closet door to punctuate the matter. "How about I use the bathroom first, then you can have it as long as you like?"

Another point of agreement. They were on a roll.

An hour later, they were tucked away in their respective quarters. As luck would have it, there was a television set in each of their sleeping areas, which allowed them to limit the duration of shared time and space. Enough was enough with this warped rom-com, Erika thought. From her plush king-size bed (feeling not one iota of guilt for Noah's having to make do with the pull-out sofa-bed), she could hear the evening news droning from his television set. She had tried to concentrate on a news program herself, but after a few minutes of fidgeting had given up the effort. Surfing channels had not helped to lessen the unease. Neither had the new car smell that clung to her bedtime gym suit. One thought had taken charge ever since she'd crawled under the covers, and that was the urgent need to call home. Against the rules, according to her handler, but she wasn't about to allow that to dissuade her. Trouble was, she couldn't make the call on the hotel phone for fear of being overheard, and the Vuitton handbag that contained her new cell phone, with which she could hide out in the bathroom, was in Noah's part of the suite.

The night table lamp worked on rheostat control. She reduced the ambient light to a birthday-cake candle's worth, then waited for him to fall asleep.

A half hour later, his television went silent—off or muted. Another eternal span of time—on earth, fifteen minutes—and his room turned almost completely dark. There remained only the faint flickering of lambent light that Erika figured could only be coming from the television screen. Was this to be the status quo for the night?

Apparently so, she decided, when after another half hour had trickled by without change.

Time to see for herself. Noiselessly she slid out from under the covers and rose from the bed. As she tip-toed to what she thought would be a protected vantage point from which to observe a reclining form on the sofa-bed, she heard a low whooshing sound coming at short intervals from the general area. Expulsions of air, that's what it was. Noah's, it must be. An odd variation of snoring? It was imperative she verify he was asleep. The need to make contact with Harrison and through him, Lucas, was beginning to feel like the writhing discomfort accompanying the flu.

Holding her breath, she peered out from behind the arched opening in the wall dividing the sections of the suite for a better view. The sofa-bed came into sight, or enough of it to determine that it was unoccupied. Yet the rhythmic huffs continued—but from where? The urge to holler "Noah!" and be done with her damn vigil was countermanded by the need to call Harrison without Noah preventing her from doing so. She had to explore further. If something was amiss, she was bound to find out sooner or later, anyway.

She stepped into the main room and the hitherto unseen edge of the sofa-bed came into view, along with the floor space beside it, where Noah was performing pushups, the soles of his feet facing her. Clad in tank top and gym shorts, the well-defined musculature that had been suggested by his fully clothed body was confirmed, and judging from the vigor of his performance, his endurance was top-notch as well. All very reassuring, given that he was to serve as her bodyguard, but she wondered if his show of prowess meant that he might be up all night; that his having expressed a need for some "shut-eye" earlier was merely to disarm her. She'd give him an hour to nod off. After that, she'd have it out with him. As long as it wasn't by means of hand-to-hand combat, she stood a fair chance of winning.

Moments after she was back under the covers, Noah was poised outside the bathroom door. Pretending to be asleep, with half-lidded eyes she watched him place his hand on the doorknob then glance toward the bed as fleetingly as a hummingbird, most likely to verify he needn't knock on the door. Another small, but curative, sign of trustworthiness.

After ten minutes or so listening to the sound of running water, she watched him leave the bathroom, shut the door quietly, then without a glance in her direction, head back to his quarters.

No way could she hold out for the full hour. Fifteen minutes later, she slithered out of bed and crept straightaway into Noah's territory, caution be damned. First thing she noticed is that he was sleeping or faking the part as she had. Didn't matter to her anymore, as long as she wasn't intercepted. Second thing she noticed was that the armchair that had been next to the sofa had been moved to the door of the suite, blocking it. The man was certainly keen on security.

The designer bag was perched like a princess on the straight-back desk chair. She snatched it from its throne and made her getaway to the bathroom. She set the bag on the lid of the toilet seat, and, in slow-motion to remain as close to soundless as possible, shut and locked the door.

Switching places with the bag, she planted herself on the seat and dug for the cell phone. Better be charged! She placed the bag at her feet and threw the cell's snooty-beige case into it.

She pressed the home button and the screen lit up with the entry format, ready for her to punch in the pattern of digits with which to unlock the device. What was it? With a humiliating jolt, she realized that Noah had divulged every sequence of numbers in the book but that one! *Bastard!* she mutely raged, less at his failure to impart the number than on her failure to pick up on the fact. She had half a mind to throw the damn device to the floor, but like the reasonable little girl she was, placed it back into its case and returned the unit to the bag.

Plan B: call out on the hotel phone. She exited the bathroom with the caution she'd used on entry, stowed the bag in the bedroom closet shared with Noah and, heart racing, went for the phone receiver and pressed it to her ear. No dial tone. She drummed on the cradle buttons, but it was just as futile as in movies, as she knew it would be. The scene regressed to slapstick when she discovered that there was no telephone wire attached to the base of the phone. In his effort to acclimate her to her new role, Noah had apparently left no stone unturned.

Back to his quarters she stealthily marched. Surely *his* landline was functional! If she was lucky, he was a deep sleeper, and she and Harrison would be able to exchange a few words of mutual support while Noah soldiered on in Rambo dreamland.

Plan C was scrapped before it had begun when she discovered that his landline had disappeared from the end table abutting the arm of the couch. Its wire led to the edge of the cover draped over Noah and disappeared beneath it, plainly leading to the bulge against his hip.

There was only one option left: the hotel lobby. She retreated to the bedroom, where she slipped on the pair of designer sneakers earlier spotted in her carryon suitcase and zipped the gym jacket up to her chin. Finding the image in the closet door full-length mirror to be acceptable for public display, she was about to head for the exit, when she realized she was not in possession of the key to the suite to provide reentry and had no idea where Noah had stowed it. No point in looking for it. She would have to knock on the door afterward; put up with his lecture. Time to make her move.

It was not that she'd forgotten about the armchair blocking the door, she'd just not taken its bulk or the carpet's resistance into account. As she tried to heave it away from the door, its arm bumped against the door's metal surface.

"Hey!"

Not a deep sleeper, after all. "Don't shoot," she declared, only half in jest.

He threw off the cover; rose from the mattress. "What are you doing?" One of the hotel's terrycloth robes was heaped at the foot of the bed. She watched him put it on and secure the belt. Their movie had digressed to the 1940s.

"I must call home. Since you've made it impossible to do so up here, I thought I'd go down to the lobby." As she spoke the words, it dawned on her that the chair had been placed at the door not to prevent someone from breaking in, but to prevent her from breaking out. "You don't understand, I know. You're thinking it's been less than twenty-four hours, why's she so desperate to make contact? Well, for one thing I've never been apart from my baby!" The tears would flow if she let them. She would not give him the satisfaction. "End it. Give me a phone."

Noah shook his head. "No, I won't. But you're wrong, I do understand." He approached her. She cringed. "God help us, I'm only going to move the chair back to where it was!" In one effortless movement, he hefted the chair and lay it down in its original spot. With an usher's hand flourish, he requested that she sit in it. "Let me explain."

There was no choice but to hear him out. She was committed to the mission. She planted herself in the armchair. "I'm listening."

He sat on the edge of the sofa-bed, the edge nearest her, and leaned toward her, elbows on his knees, hands folded. "My precautions are stringent, yes, but in no way are they gratuitous. They are meant to keep your family safe. Your husband is the individual most at risk, you recognize that, I know. It's why you didn't want him accompanying you on this trip, isn't that right?"

"Yes."

"So, let's think. His cell phone is not secure. Your home landline is not secure. Which means they can be hacked at any time. If we're not obsessive about our rules, your husband's true motives will be confirmed and as a bonus, our cover blown." He held up his hand as she was about to speak. "I believe your primary reason to connect with your husband is to make sure that he and your child are safe and sound. Sure, you want to hear his voice, but knowing for certain that your family's doing fine isn't a bad second-best option, agreed?"

"I don't know. Maybe. How can you know *for certain?*"

Bolstered by her softening, he let slip a small sigh of relief. "Three days ago, security measures were begun with the installment of rotating security guards outside your home."

"I wasn't aware."

"That's why we call them undercover. By now, your husband has been informed. Then, this morning, after you left for the hotel, a bodyguard was posted *inside* the house. This job will also be performed in shifts to provide twenty-four-seven coverage."

She shook her head. "I'm afraid Harrison will dismiss them."

"I've heard otherwise. He's actually been very accommodating. He's doing it for you and the baby, he says."

"How do you know this?"

"I'm in touch with both the exterior and interior guards. We all have secure phones, and I don't mean the security you can buy in the app store. I spoke to the parties in place when you were en route to the hotel. Would you like me to check in now?"

"Of course. Yes!"

He stretched back to fetch the cell phone under his pillow. Concealing the screen from her, he punched in a series of digits to unlock the phone. "Don't ask to speak with your husband, please. If you understand that direct communication will not be a possibility for the duration of the trip, you will not be distracted by the thought of it and can more fully immerse yourself in the task at hand. I know this from experience." He waited for her acquiescence, which came in the form a nod, then punched in the number to reach the guard stationed inside the home. Anticipating her demand, he tapped on the speakerphone.

Erika strained forward to make sure she'd hear properly. A stranger's voice struck the air with a recitation of numbers; his ID, she assumed. "Make sure to ask about Lucas!" she cried, almost falling over onto Noah's lap.

In the end, she was reassured by the exchange between Noah and the guard. Harrison had accepted the security precautions and Lucas was doing great. Harrison's only source of worry was his wife's safety. Noah's report of her wellbeing should ease his mind.

"Are you okay?" Noah asked after the call. "I know this has got to be hard for you, but *are* you?"

She would have to be. "Yes, I'm okay." She rose to her feet. "But we'll have to make some changes."

He stood to face her; tightened the belt of his robe. "What?"

"We have to establish a partnership of complete trust. Put the phone back on my night table. Put the phone back on yours. Give me the password to my cell phone."

He smiled. "I agree to your conditions." He extended his right hand. As she took it, he lay his left hand over their clasped two. It was only fitting she place her left hand over his to complete the union. "To comrades," he said.

"With a shared mission."

His "Amen!" was not so much a solemn ratification as a call to arms.

Chapter 20

Six-twenty a.m. and the sky was as blue as Erika's Versace slim jeans. "You picked a great day for flying," the square-jawed pilot, who'd just introduced himself as Captain Tom Monroe, assured the attractive couple standing beside the private jet poised on the Tarmac. "Our transport today will be a Beechjet 400A. It's forty-three feet long and propelled by a twinjet turbofan engine. Its cabin is configured for seven passengers, but I believe there will be three of you flying with us, am I correct?"

"Yes," Noah confirmed. "My wife and I will be joined by our driver"—he glanced at his watch—"who should be here shortly."

Erika gave a peremptory nod to indicate her knowledge of this, although it was news to her, like everything else this morning. She had never heard of Teterboro Airport, or in fact of the existence of *any* airport in Bergen County, New Jersey, a mere twelve miles from midtown Manhattan. She'd never flown on a private airplane or even seen one up close. The only way she'd ever boarded a plane was from a pathway inside a terminal.

"Our time of departure is set for seven, and our estimated travel time is eight hours. Our time of arrival in Sao Paulo, Guarulhos International Airport, will be approximately four in the afternoon. I suggest you set your watches one hour ahead before we leave. Besides myself, our crew will include my co-pilot and one flight attendant, both of whom are already on board. A varied food and beverage menu will be provided, and you can select from it any time."

Erika's grip tightened around the shoulder strap of her Louis Vuitton bag as every word tolled the impending flight, the absolute parting. Beneath her tailored white blouse her breasts ached for the touch of her sweet baby—*be happy, don't cry for me!*

"Your suitcases have been stowed," Captain Monroe nattered on, "and if you'd like to relax and have a drink—champagne, a mimosa, if you'd prefer—why don't you climb aboard yourselves?"

Thoughts elsewhere, she looked to Noah for guidance. He nodded, giving her a ladies-first gesture, and she preceded him up the rollaway staircase.

"Ari, the fellow who drove you to the Plaza," Noah began, once they were settled in their white leather lounge chairs with their drinks and left to themselves by their unobtrusive male attendant. "Ari's on our team. We've worked together many times and I can vouch for him without reservation." He took a healthy swig of his mimosa and dug a couple more cashews from his cup of warm nuts.

"Why didn't you tell me beforehand?"

"I didn't want to burden you with more than you needed to process. Are you okay with this?"

She raised her champagne glass to her lips and took another swallow. Two had taken the cutting edge off her longing for home. One more blurred the desire to call out Noah on his demeaning response. "I'm okay. Yes."

On cue, it seemed, the clatter of footfalls on metal stairs signaled Ari's arrival.

"Sorry I'm late, guys," he announced, in a far more companionable manner than he'd exhibited as Erika's chauffeur. He gave Noah a bear hug and Erika, a warm handshake, introducing himself, first name only. Bending down toward her, he whispered in her ear, "I know the story, Erika, and I'm here to support you." On the rise, he said aloud, "So, Mr. and Mrs. Richtman, are we ready for our second honeymoon?"

* * *

The travelers, bags in tow, entered Guarulhos International's ultra-modern terminal 3 at 4:40 p.m. Ari had rented a sedan two days prior, and while he shuttled to the rental agency to fetch it, Erika and Noah found their way to the pick-up area just outside the terminal to wait for him. Despite her having polished off a glass of champagne, Erika, whose alcohol threshold was below sea level, had not slept more than ten minutes during the flight. "Think there's time to stop by Sandro Andersson's jewelry store today?" she asked, shifting her weight like a race horse at the starting gate.

"The place closes at seven," Noah answered. "It'll take us about a half hour to get to the Jardin District, which is where our hotel and *Andersson's Joalheria* are located." He looked up, calculating. "If we take no more than fifteen minutes to freshen up, we can make it to the store by six-fifteen, six-thirty. You don't want to waste a minute, do you? Good."

A couple of wasted moments later, a run-of-the-mill black luxury sedan pulled up curbside behind a tan SUV. A horn tooted, trunk door popped open, and Ari jumped out from the driver's seat to scurry the ten yards or so to meet Erika and Noah to help with the luggage, eyes widening as he witnessed Erika moving with the urgency of a bank robber fleeing the scene of a crime.

Chapter 21

Harrison sat Kate and Grace down at the dining room table. It seemed as good a place as any to unload his pack of lies. The bodyguard was hunkered down in the living room reading, or pretending to read, a book he'd plucked off one of the shelves. Out of hearing range, Harrison liked to think, but who knew, he may have an earpiece that could pick up a cat's meow three blocks away. "You must be wondering," he started before Kate interrupted.

"About Jeffrey Crow, the man who slept on the couch last night," she said curtly, revealing a side he'd never seen. "You introduced him as a *friend*?"

Harrison cleared his throat. "That wasn't quite accurate."

"To be honest, he gives me the creeps, Dr. Wheatley," Kate admitted, revising her tone at the prompting of Grace's laser-look.

"I didn't want to make you feel uncomfortable by explaining the situation," Harrison went on, "but I've decided in all fairness that I must. You see, there's been an incident, I should say a crime, associated with NYU School of Fine Arts. A member of the faculty, a professor of Early European Art, in fact, was attacked in her home three days ago. She suffered a serious gunshot wound, but she's in stable condition at a local hospital—we weren't told which one. It's all very hush-hush because the individual who assaulted her hasn't been caught yet. The thing is, all we know is that her home office was stripped of her files and computer. Cash and valuables were untouched. The assumption is that the offender was looking for information. What, specifically, nobody knows. To be on the safe side, the Board of Trustees has decided to assign bodyguards to all art history staff members for a limited amount of time. I believe they're being overly cautious, but that's the way it is."

"And I believe it was a sensible decision," Grace declared, repositioning the cut glass bowl dead center on the table. "Will Mr. Crow be joining us for dinner? I'll be picking up some groceries later and—"

"No, you won't, Grace," Harrison interrupted. "For at least the next few days we'll be under, well, I guess you could call it protective house arrest. Food will be ordered in. Jake will be walked by Jeff. And, of course, Lucas will not be taking his daily constitutional." He smiled, hoping to lighten the mood. Grace cracked a smile to show her support. No visible reaction from Kate, until she rose from the table.

"I'm afraid I can't work under these conditions, Dr. Wheatley," she said, grasping the back of the chair. "I mean, I'm afraid, period."

"I'm sorry you feel that way, Kate, but it's not my place to try to persuade you to stay if you're truly anxious about it. How about we give you a paid vacation until all this blows over? It shouldn't be long. What do you say?"

Kate lifted a hand from the chair and gave her flaxen pony tail a twist. "Are you serious?"

"Of course."

"It's okay if I pack right now and call my boyfriend to pick me up? You'll be okay, I mean you and Grace, with Lucas? You know when he's due for his next feeding? You know how to give him a bath in his little tub and everything?"

Again, that laser-look from her baby-care competitor, Grace.

"We can handle it," Harrison said.

Kate was on the move. She turned back. "I gave Mrs. Wheatley my home address—it's my mother's place. You know, it's where I'll be staying?" The real question was hidden, but not that well.

"I've got your address, sure," Harrison said. "I'll post your checks there."

"Great. Thank you so much." She continued on her way.

When Kate was out of sight, Harrison turned to Grace. "So, Grace, looks like we're on our own. How do you feel about that?"

"Suits me just fine!" Grace said, with an enthusiasm that encompassed more than her dear boy, Harry, could begin to guess.

Chapter 22

"All set?" Ari asked, as Noah opened the door to the suite. "Wow," he commented on entering. "I guess you have to be a couple to rate the royal treatment."

Indeed, Erika and Noah's accommodations at the red-brick boutique hotel, the Fasano, were as commodious and elegant as they'd been at the Plaza. The furnishings, here, too, were an amalgam of Modern and nineteenth century Traditional. Noah frowned. "You're not unhappy with your room, are you, Ari?"

"Of course not." Seeing Erika emerge from the bedroom area, he declared, "Lovely!"

"Your room?" Erika asked, rather than acknowledge a compliment. There was no time for irrelevancies. "Let's go," she added without pause, indicating she had no wish for him to answer. It was already 6:10. *Andersson's Joalheria* would be closing in fifty minutes.

Noah looked pleased with her attitude. "The car ready?" he asked his cohort, as he shut the door behind them.

"Right out front. Valet let me leave it there as long as it would be for less than a half hour."

"We're well ahead. You got Sandro's license plate number?"

"Of course."

Turning to Erika, Noah said, "First chance we get, we'll be putting a tracker on his car."

"Why?"

"Because we can."

"How did you get the number?"

"Ari has his sources."

Their rooms were on the third floor. By mutual agreement, they opted for the staircase as the no-wait route to the ground floor. As Ari had assured them, their car was waiting for them right outside the hotel. The valet handed the keys over to Ari, and in turn Ari slipped him a tip.

The drive from Rua Vittorio Fasano to Rua Oscar Freire took no more than six minutes, although Erika thought they might have made better time. Once disembarked, however, the stark reality of standing face-to-face with a stranger she was supposed to call her husband hit her full on, and she felt the rush of intention suddenly diffuse, like a racer who's lost sight of the finish line.

Noah caught the moment of dissociation in her eyes, her stillness. "Stage fright," he whispered. "It'll pass." He knew not to touch her.

Ari was already striding across the street, putting distance between himself and the pair. He would be a window-shopping tourist until they'd entered the jewelry store, then he'd actively search among the parked cars for Sandro's license plate. The tracking device was tucked inside his pocket. He was a seasoned pro at getting the job done swiftly and without drawing undue attention.

Erika focused on her immediate surroundings to ground herself. In front of her, an upscale Gucci shop; beside it, Lacoste. Across the street, an inviting café and alongside it another isle of fashion, Cris Barres—Brazilian designer? The sheltered tree-lined street had the feel of a Greenwich Village enclave studded with Madison Avenue chic. As an integral part of the landscape, she took herself in. She'd chosen to wear the blue suit, her favorite, along with a black crewneck bodysuit with a sheer nylon panel, which revealed a good deal of her cleavage, a style she deemed pragmatically alluring for the occasion. As was the striking hair color and style, she thought, recalling the most recent image of herself captured in the bathroom mirror. She turned her back on Noah to perform a quick check of the ringed finger she'd skillfully kept shielded from view with the help of her designer bag.

Having a one-up on Noah, the old pro, gave her the boost that tipped the scale. When she turned to meet his look of expectation, she felt, for the first time, that they were on equal footing.

"Back in business?" he asked. He knew the answer from her expression. "From the way the numbers are running, the store's a few doors down. "Here we go, Sofie. Remember, lean in when I do."

She hooked her arm through his and gave him an unsolicited lean-in, just to cause his backlash. "That will never do, Noah. Try to keep up."

"Consider me chastened," he said, breaking into a grin, as they arrived at the display window of *Andersson's Joalheria*.

"Stand and admire for a minute," she suggested, pointing with staged eagerness at a pair of chandelier diamond earrings. "The man behind the counter—he's looking at us. Please let it be Sandro."

"It is. I've seen his photo. Ready to wing it?"

From their vantage point, they could see several paintings hanging on the wall behind the counter. "I already have a plan," she said, noticing only the barest hint of surprise leak into his expression. "Doing better," she praised, giving him a gentle tug toward the door.

"You're not about to close, are you?" Noah greeted Sandro. "My wife has her eye on those magnificent chandelier earrings."

"Darling," Erika scolded, "the man may not speak English." Aiming a look at Sandro that crossed Queen Elizabeth with Marilyn Monroe, she asked, "*Do* you speak English?"

Sandro smiled, exposing a set of conspicuously capped teeth. "Yes, of course I speak English, and no, I am not about to close." He rubbed his hands together, putting Erika in mind of Dickens's Uriah Heep, only Sandro looked more like the Devil's disciple than an obsequious clerk. The gelled-back dyed black hair against pale skin, the black suit…but perhaps her observation was informed by what she knew of him rather than what actually met her eyes. "Sandro Andersson," the man announced, with an air of bravura. "As proprietor, I can close shop however early or late I choose. How may I help you? You wish to see the chandelier earrings?" He started toward the end of the counter in order to step from behind it.

Erika raised her hand. "No, no, wait."

"Oh, but you must try them on!" Noah objected.

"Later. I'd like to look at the bracelets first. Please, Mr. Andersson."

"*Sandro*," he corrected, retracing his steps. Looking from one to the other, he queried, "And you are...?"

As Noah introduced himself and his lovely wife, Erika decided it was a good time to begin throwing curious glances at the painting behind Sandro. Let him wonder.

If Sandro noticed her eyes wander, he did not show it. "What kind of bracelet are you looking for? Any stone in particular?"

"You'll laugh," she said, "but I have an exact picture in my mind of what I want. Diamonds encircling the wrist, with a bold flat-leafed flower like a daisy as a center-piece, encrusted with diamonds, but with a cluster of rubies at its center."

Noah morphed his look of surprise into one of loving forbearance. "But darling!"

"I understand perfectly," Sandro directed at Erika. "You're a woman who knows herself. If you don't find what you want, we can always have the piece custom-made."

"Excellent." She swiped another look at the painting on display behind him. "Let's see." She began side-stepping along the counter, gliding by the dazzling smorgasbord of bijoux without conspicuous interest, until she deemed it appropriate to produce a little gasp of delight and plant her right palm on the countertop, fingers fanned, as she leaned over the counter to focus more acutely at—well, she'd choose *something*.

She waited for the men to fully take in the presence of the wide band silver ring on the third finger of her splayed hand before she spoke. "There!" She pointed at a group of items on the far side of the display case, closer to Sandro.

"The diamond and sapphire choker?" he asked, his focus flitting from the contents of the case to her ring.

"No, the diamond and ruby band. It'll be a lovely complement to my diamond wedding band." She turned to Noah. "Don't you think, sweetheart?"

"I agree, absolutely. As long as you consider the chandelier earrings. We're not leaving until you do." He kissed her forehead. "Go ahead, try on the ring."

Sandro had already removed it from the case. She let him slide the ring onto the fourth finger of her left hand until it touched her own diamond wedding band, the one item Noah hadn't outlawed. "Stunning," she assessed. She removed the ring and handed it back to him. Can you resize it to a five?"

"Of course," Sandro said, unable to tear his gaze away from the silver ring that Erika continued to flaunt. "Mr. Richtman?"

Noah produced a laugh perfectly modulated for the occasion. "My wife knows her own mind, and I love her for it. What's the price?"

Sandro checked the tiny tag suspended from the ring. "Thirty-two thousand dollars, less fifteen percent when stones are removed sizing down. Of course, I'll give you a substantial discount if other items are purchased."

Another, more muted—disparaging—chuckle from Noah, clearly indicating that the practice of haggling was beneath him. "How long will it take to resize?"

"About a week, perhaps less."

"We won't be here a week. You can ship it to us if it's not ready."

Erika grinned as she fidgeted with the silver ring, twisting it on her finger.

"That's an unusual ring," Sandro remarked. "I'd like to have a look at it, if I may."

At Last! "You may." She closed her eyes and softly recited her invented prayer: *"Lobe Gott und land und seine leute."* Opening her eyes, she informed her rapt—although Noah was pretending not to be—audience, "It's a prayer I learned from my grandmother. She used to say it every time she put on the ring or took it off, and so now I do, too." She slipped off the ring and passed it to Sandro.

"Praise God and country and its people," Sandro translated for good measure, with more reverence than Erika had mustered. He ran his finger over the iron cross—*Eisernes Kreuz*—motif running around the ring's shank, then checked for an engraving on its underside. "H. L. 1914," he read aloud. He looked across at Erika, who forced herself to lock gazes with him. To make her eyes water, she thought of him cramming Jews into cattle cars, wouldn't he have enjoyed it, the babies crying, clinging to their mothers, riding to their deaths. She might have felt guilty—maybe she should have—for using their suffering to produce glistening eyeballs, but she didn't. She needed to use her tears to make her lies ring true.

"The initials stand for Helmutt Lange," she explained. "He was my great-grandfather. I never met him, but he makes me think of my grandmother, whom I miss terribly. She was so proud of her father, who was awarded this ring for his heroism during the Battle of Tannenberg in August 1914, the first month of World War I. He was only eighteen years old. Can you imagine? Russia's second army was almost completely destroyed during that battle, did you know that?" She was looking past him, spilling out her words as if they'd been bottled up forever. Noah must have caught on by now. *Say something!*

"Sofie, dear, Sandro may not agree with your ideas," Noah gently suggested.

Good prompt, only you should have said our *ideas, not* your *ideas!* "When did Brazil pass a law preventing a person from speaking her mind?" she admonished. "I keep my ideas to myself most of the time, or debate them on social media, mostly with idiots. Sometimes I feel like I'm about to explode." Whisking back to Sandro, she stated, "Please give me back my ring." He did so, and she mumbled her fake prayer and slipped the ring back on her finger. "I'm sorry I snapped, darling," she offered Noah. She rested her head on his shoulder. "You understand, I know you do."

Noah dabbed his palm against her cheek. "I do, yes."

"I hope I haven't offended your political sensibilities," she clipped, back to her Sandro ploy. "You're not a Jew, are you?"

"Respectively, no, and *God* no," he replied. "I'm actually further right than you'll ever be."

"Don't count on it," she lightly retorted. It was time to move on. Dispensing with a segue, she gawked at the painting behind him. "I haven't run across an Albert Gleizes in years," she said, cocking her head. "I don't know what draws me to him. I think it's the unexpected juxtaposition of shapes, along with the muted colors. I feel a darkness even in his bright tones. Do you agree? There's a contemplative quality about his paintings you don't often see in purely abstract paintings." Her staged look, when she returned her attention back to Sandro, was expectant, eager. His, on the other hand, was one centimeter shy of agape. "Is the painting for sale?" she barreled on. "I'm a collector—an amateur, mind you, but avid all the same."

Noah slid his arm around her shoulder and pulled her close. "You're incorrigible, darling," he whispered *sotto voce*. "I thought we were planning a visit to Sotheby's Sao Paulo tomorrow. We scheduled a private showing weeks ago. Got all our ducks in a row, obtained pre-authorized transfer of funds up to…well, *you* know. Do we really need to snatch this gentleman's art right from under his nose?"

She laughed. "Yes, I think we do!"

"No, no!" Sandro suddenly cried, flailing his arms over his head while he took off to the front of the store crying "Closed! *Fechadas*!" as a young woman was in the act of opening the door. In Portuguese he sputtered what Erika guessed were his apologies to the woman, who reacted by marching off in a huff. Upon her departure, the door to the shop was locked, the closed sign turned to face the street, and Sandro was back to the counter. This time he didn't scoot behind it.

"You're really interested in purchasing the Gleizes?"

Erika raised a brow. "I thought I made myself clear. Do you have any others?"

"Others?"

"I'm looking to expand my collection of that era. Robert Delaunay, Serge Fèrat, Georges Braque—I'm *dying* to get my hands on a Braque!" A wave of her hand took in his entire wall space. "I see you have a penchant for the abstract. That Survage piece—she pointed to a painting two canvases from the Gleizes. "That caught my eye as well. Not that I'm opposed to representational panting." She uttered a token laugh. "Mind you, I wouldn't turn up my nose at a da Vinci."

Sandro caught her laugh and expanded on it. Noah merely grinned, the touch of ennui communicating *that's my wife, doing her thing*.

"Amazing, how white nationalists have a tendency to go too far," Erika mused. "All that nonsense about abstract art being degenerate. And all that fuss over the Jews. What were they afraid of? Why couldn't they recognize the Jews' marvelous sense of color? Marc Chagall, Mark Rothko, Chaim Soutine. All they had to do was keep those people from getting their hands on the national purse strings. That could have been done without all the unnecessary slaughter, which, while they were at it, alienated a good part of the world." Sandro appeared to be engrossed in what she was saying, so why stop now? "Your very own ousted Culture Secretary, what's his name, Roberto Alvim—there's another example of heavy-handedness from the far right. What was *that* all about, funding an arts initiative to focus on nationalism and religion—and plagiarizing from Goebbels's 1933 speech to boot? Don't these people know that white supremacy, like cream, will rise to the top without the suppression of artistic freedom?" *Shut up before Sandro starts to flag*. "Do you agree? Do I have a friend here?"

"I agree with your ideas about art," he replied. "Although I do believe your rather lax ideas regarding the containment of the Jews may be somewhat naïve."

"Our dentist is a Jew," Noah said. "Let's give him special dispensation, at least until he finishes my root canal."

Sandro let loose his first full-bodied laugh. "Will do!"

Erika threw up her hands. "I've taken us off course. What about the painting? Will you part with the Gleizes?"

"I think so, but I'd have to consult my art expert for an update on its estimated value."

"Your 'art expert'? I knew it! I knew you were a connoisseur the moment I walked through the door and saw these paintings—these *particular* paintings—on display." She turned to Noah. "Didn't you feel it, darling?"

Noah gave a good-natured shrug. "You're the collector, Sofie. I'm merely the enabler." To Sandro, he posed, "Do you have any more paintings up your sleeve, Sandro? Save us a trip to Sotheby's altogether?"

Sandro knit his fingers together. "As a matter of fact, I do. I've been a collector myself for a good many years." He cleared his throat. "Although if I'm to sell you any of my works, you have to understand that unlike Sotheby's…"

"There'll be no red tape, no taxes," Erika finished. She gave him a friendly elbow bump. "This isn't my first rodeo, Sandro."

Sandro nodded. "You won't mind if I take a look at your papers, do you? With transactions of this nature—there's no delicate way of saying this—I like to do a quick check."

"Sure." Both she and Noah went for their wallets. From the breast pocket of his suit jacket, Noah also produced their passports. Sandro brought the items to the end of the counter where he made copies of what he deemed necessary on the printer housed on the shelf below the cash register and credit card processor.

"What about those chandelier earrings?" Noah questioned Erika as they put away their IDs. "I hate to sound like a broken record, but I'd really like you to try them on."

"I will, but not tonight. Before we leave town. I promise." She grabbed Sandro's wrist. "When may we see the paintings?"

"Tomorrow night. I'll pick you up at—where are you staying?"

The information was given; arrangements made.

"Before we overstay our welcome…" Noah began.

"Never," Sandro protested.

"…let me prepay for the ring you're re-sizing," Noah finished, fishing for his wallet again.

"Put it away," Sandro insisted. "We'll take care of that later."

As they parted at the door, Erika thought to give Sandro a symbolic cheek-to-cheek kiss. "I'm so excited for tomorrow!" she whispered in his ear before breaking away, making sure to deliver a puff of hot breath in the process. Give him something to think about tonight besides the legitimacy of his new clients.

* * *

"Did what just happen just happen?" she asked Noah as they slid into the back seat of the car.

"Indeed, it did, thanks to you."

Erika smiled. "And you, Ari? How did it go with you?"

"Mission accomplished," Ari said, before pulling away from the curb.

Chapter 23

"We did good tonight," Harrison said, praising himself and Grace for their first baby-care stint without Kate's help. "Went without a hitch, wouldn't you say?"

"It did," Grace acknowledged, placing the cup of tea he'd requested on his desktop.

Lucas had gone to sleep without a whimper of resistance. "What do you think, Grace? Beginner's luck?"

"Speak for yourself, Mr. Harry," Grace replied, cracking her first joke in what must be ten years. "Don't forget, you were in my charge more often than not back in the old days, young man. Will that be all for tonight?"

"Thanks, yes. By the way, I'll take care of Lucas when he wakes up. You stay put, okay?"

Grace reluctantly agreed. As she was leaving his study, she nearly bumped into Jeffrey Crow, who was about to rap on the open door.

"Am I interrupting anything?" the bodyguard asked, foregoing the rap.

Yes, I'm trying not to lose my mind worrying about my wife. "No, not at all," Harrison said, waving at the galley proof of his Delacroix monograph. "Busy-work."

"I thought I'd take the dog for his walk," Jeffrey said, leash in hand.

"*Jake,*" Harrison gently corrected.

At the sound of his name, the old pup stirred.

"There you are. Want to go for a walk?" Jeff asked, bending his bulky form to get closer to his potential charge.

"It's okay, boy," Harrison urged. "Come on out."

Jake slunk out from under the desk and stood at attention, as if remembering he had to pee. He looked from his beloved master to the stranger holding the leash and took his place by the latter's sneakered heel.

* * *

A tic of his, Jeff double-patted the gun in its holster before committing to exiting the premises. House keys in the right pocket of his Windbreaker? Check. Plastic sandwich bags for poop collection—he'd grabbed a bunch the day before, first day on the job—left pocket. Check. "About to walk dog," he texted the external guard, strategically parked a couple of car lengths south of the Wheatley entrance. "Roger," appeared the near simultaneous response. Jeff shoved his cell phone into the pocket containing the keys. "Let's go, pal. Try and make it quick."

Some people exude Alpha-ness. Jake knew to stick to this one's side; make a good impression.

Jeff jiggled the latch to make sure the heavy oak door was locked, then proceeded to the wrought-iron gate. The gate could be opened from inside of the property, but to gain access on his return, the combination code to the alarm pad needed to be punched in or, in the event of a sudden bout of amnesia, Harrison could let him in by releasing the lock from inside the house.

On both dog-walking occasions the day before, Jake had led Jeff to his favorite maple tree, the one with the sod base laden with the familiar smells of dogs he knew but had never met. The tree was a half-block north, between 78th and 79th Streets, and Jake, sensing the man was not out for an amble, headed straight for it.

"Good boy," Jeff commended, as Jake got right to it. He retrieved one of the plastic bags from his pocket and pulled it over his left hand, intending to pick up the poop, then turn the bag inside out to entrap it. The last step would be to dispose of the package in the receptacle at the corner. He knew the drill, but was still not at home with it. To free up his right hand to aid in the task, he slipped the leash handle onto his wrist. "You laugh, you're dead," he muttered to Jake, as he crouched to grab the load.

"Goes for you, too," a voice behind him answered, at the same time pressing against the back of his neck what Jeff had been trained not to second guess: the butt of a gun.

One hand trapped in a plastic bag, the other hampered by Jake's tension on the leash. Social awkwardness was something Jeff had struggled with, physical awkwardness, never! *Fuck.*

"Spread your arms like Christ on the cross—open!"

No choice—not yet. He spread his arms. Jake pulled on the leash. He could feel the leash handle was about to slip off his wrist. *Yes!*

As if the man had heard the thought, he pulled on the leash, drawing Jake closer. Having created a slack, he twisted it around Jeff's wrist, almost cutting off its blood supply. "Now, stand up slowly."

Jeff obeyed, as plans for making a move auditioned without success. Where had this guy come from, and what the hell did he want?

"Good. Now start walking, nice and easy, nobody'll get hurt, back to the house."

"What house?"

The butt jammed harder. "No games. Wheatley house."

Shit! exploded in his brain—by chance, just as a young woman emerged from the apartment building yards from him and his assailant. She stood out of range of the street lamp, but Jeff imagined he caught her eye. *Get the hell away!* he telepathed, but she was in the prime of life and immortal, and so she pulled out her cell phone.

The shot rang out, and the woman's hand swung upward, the cell phone flying out of her hand like a freed bird. Like a bird shot out of the sky, she herself crumpled to the ground without a whimper.

Yet the butt of the gun had never moved from Jeff's neck. A second weapon had been fired; he'd seen it flash in the corner of his eye and heard the rustle of clothing as it was returned to its housing. The incident had taken no more than three seconds. The man was a goddamn pro.

"Hands at your sides now. Walk!"

Nobody near enough to witness what had just happened. Had anybody heard the shot? In this neighborhood, probably think it was a car back-firing. Girl was moving. *Got to get my hands on a phone, call 9-1-1.* Jeff drew his hands to his sides, pulling Jake even closer to ease the pressure on his wrist. He tried to shake the plastic bag off his hand, but it stuck to him. He began walking at a fast clip, the man keeping up, encouraging him, even, to pick up the pace, the gun butt remaining in contact every step of the way. He might have tried a maneuver he'd picked up in kick-boxing, but thought better of it. Better chance of overcoming the guy with backup. The external guard—George on tonight, tough as nails—he and the perp'll be in George's sights as soon as they approached the house—like now! *Where the hell is he?*

"Open the gate!" the assailant ordered. "Put in the damn code!"

"Shut the fuck up. I'm trying to think." They were facing the house, their backs to the street. Jake, relatively calm until now, was beginning to fuss, taking little jumps with his front legs to show his eagerness to return to his family. To buy time, Jeff tapped in a sequence of wrong numbers.

"Blast your head off, you don't get it right!" Cocky-tough, not knowing what was coming from behind, as the trajectory of George's salute—rigid as an axe-edge—headed for its terminus.

Crying "Aach!" as the chop to his forearm whacked the limb off to the side, George seizing the opportunity to take possession of the weapon dangling from the end of it.

Jeff spun on his heels despite Jake's unintentional hindering, and with all the force of his burgeoning rage, kicked the perp's legs out from under him. "He's got another gun!" he warned George, as the man, even as he was sent sprawling, was reaching for his pocket or belt—*something* at his left side.

George fired the confiscated gun at the man's left thigh. That done, he felt for the second weapon, snatching it from the pant waist. "Quick, get him off the street!" He pocketed the second gun and, with his free hand, punched in the code. The gate swung open.

Jeff tore off the plastic bag clinging to his sweaty hand, stuffed it into his jacket pocket and unwrapped the leash cutting into his wrist. After having uttered a single yap of pain, the wounded man had settled into a steady groan. "Shut the hell up," Jeff ordered. "Help me move him," he directed at George.

Together the bodyguards hoisted the man to his feet. Jeff kicked shut the gate, and George gave it a yank to check that the lock had reset. As they dragged the upright figure to the front door, Jake trailing along beside them, a passerby hailed them from the sidewalk. "You okay?" he asked, pausing by the gate.

The wounded man was facing the house, so his blood-soaked pant leg was not visible to the concerned senior citizen.

"A little too much to drink!" Jeff replied jovially. "Thanks, anyway."

"You say a word, it'll be your last," George whispered into the slouched figure's ear.

"No chance of that," Jeff assured his cohort as the elderly gentleman continued on his way. "He just shot a woman. I think he'd rather take his chances with us rather than the cops. Plus, I'm guessing he'd rather not have to answer to his boss why he failed to complete his assignment." He nudged the guy. "Am I right?" As he turned the key in the lock, he heard the sound of a siren in the distance.

"Not a word," George reminded their charge.

No one to greet them. Jeff unsnapped the leash and tossed it on the lobby floor. "Go fetch your master, Jake," he ordered, with no real hope the dog would obey. Jake took off, probably just to get the hell away from them. "No point staining the couch. Let's lie him on the floor. At least the carpet's red. I've got to call 9-1-1; should have done it by now."

"To report a woman's been shot?" George asked, as they lay the man down.

"What else?"

"I heard a siren. There's a chance it's for her. Where'd she drop? On the sidewalk?"

"Between 78th and 79th, yes."

"I'll take a look. First let's get this creep tied up. Hand me the leash."

"I'll do it. Keep the gun trained on him." With a few sleight-of-hand maneuvers, Jeff secured the wounded man's wrists with his dependable Handcuff knot. "Looks like he's passing out on us. We should be applying pressure to the wound; getting some antibiotics into him." Without waiting for confirmation, he pressed his hands, one on top of the other, over the site of the wound, indicated by the hole in the pant leg. "Go check out the scene, George, but get back to your post PDQ. Text me what you see. I'll take it from there."

Harrison appeared in the lobby, Jake in the lead, as George was closing the door behind him. "What the *fuck*?"

"No worries," Jeff said, as the ring of a cell phone sounded from the wounded man's pant pocket. "You want to grab that, please?"

Dumbfounded, Harrison did as he was told.

"Don't answer it. Whoever it is will call back, take my word. Hopefully the guy will be awake for it. Put it right there, next to me. Thanks. You want to feel for a wallet while you're at it?"

Chapter 24

"I wish we didn't have to wait until tomorrow night to see Sandro's collection," Erika said, throwing herself into the easy chair then jumping out of it. "I don't think I can bear it."

Noah grabbed a diet cola from the suite's mini-bar. "You've come through with flying colors so far. Keep it together." He popped open the can and took a swig.

"What's Ari doing tonight?"

"Staking out Sandro's digs in Alto de Pinheiros, west end of Sao Paulo. Following him if he goes anywhere. Why?"

"I don't know. I thought maybe we could join him, make ourselves useful."

Noah laughed. *"Relaxing* is how we can make ourselves useful. Think about it. If *we're* being monitored, shouldn't we appear to be as laid back as possible?"

"I suppose so."

"In fact, we should distance ourselves from Ari here on in."

"I suppose you're right about that, too. Doesn't stop me from feeling strung out."

"What you need is a leisurely dinner accompanied by a glass or two of wine. I've done the research and decided the hotel restaurant—the Fasano—is our best bet. I've already made reservations. Quit pacing and let's go."

* * *

It helped that Erika's threshold was well below average. One glass of wine had taken the edge off her fluttery impatience. If it hadn't been for Ari's call to Noah immediately after they'd gotten back to their suite, she would have been ready to pack it in on the spot. But Ari had gotten her wound up again. Reportedly, after Sandro had closed shop, Ari had followed him home and had parked within eyeshot of the entrance to Sandro's apartment building. After approximately a half hour, he spotted him exiting the building, where he waited in the porte cochère for his car to be delivered by the house valet. "I followed him through the city streets and into the sticks," Ari said, as Erika listened in on the amplified call. "But I couldn't tail him after that without him noticing. The surroundings turned desolate. Totally barren. Dirt road leading God knows where. It was enough, I thought, to get the coordinates of the spot where I stopped tailing him. He returned from the wilds forty-five minutes later and now we're back at his residence, where I'll sit it out. Figured the mystery environs could be explored more freely in the daylight. That is, if you think I should."

Erika shook her head.

Noah agreed. "Stay away. You get spotted, it'll blow our operation. Text me the coordinates and delete." The call was terminated.

Ari complied. Noah copied the coordinates on a page torn from his note pad and deleted Ari's text. "May come in handy," he said, placing the paper in his pocket.

"Shouldn't you dispose of that before we meet Sandro tomorrow night?"

"Of course. You're really on your toes, aren't you?"

"Just keyed up. Where did Sandro go, do you think? To visit his art stash?"

Noah shrugged. "Or his drug dealer. Or his mistress. Or his boyfriend. We may never know—or need to."

* * *

Erika's dreams led her up narrow alleys that opened onto barren terrains, silent and forbidding; no place to hide, but someone was hiding...*somewhere*. When, in the early morning, she awakened to the silence of her room, it took a moment or two for the ominous mood to dissipate. She crept out of bed and slipped the hotel robe over her tank top and sweatpants, hoping her movements would not disturb Noah, asleep in the adjoining room. Surprisingly, she was famished, and wondered if she could trespass onto Noah's sanctuary to grab some snack or other from the mini-bar—potato chips, manna from heaven!—without waking him up.

"Good morning," Noah greeted, standing at the window as she tiptoed across the border. He was wearing jeans and a white shirt, open at the collar, and sneakers. The sofa-bed had already been stowed. "Looks like it's going to be a beautiful day."

He did not seem particularly uplifted by the thought. "Morning," she said, wondering about his tentativeness, or if she was imagining it. She fiddled with the belt of her bathrobe, as if that would put things right. "How long have you been up?"

"About an hour. Since three."

"And I thought *I* was restless. I'm going to get something from the mini-bar." Walking toward it, she asked, "You want something?"

"No, thanks. Room service is available at this hour. Let's order something."

"Good idea, but first, I'm craving a bag of potato chips." She removed one from its niche on the bottom shelf; tore it open and dug in.

He gave her an avuncular smile, a bit forced. "Sweet. How was your night? You sleep well?"

Crunching: "Not great. I had dreams. Must have been inspired by Ari's account of his activity last night. You?" There was definitely something up with him. Something worrisome.

"Oh, fine."

"I don't think so," she said.

"What?"

"Not fine. I overestimated your acting ability, Noah. What's on your mind?"

After a pause, he said, very quietly, as if he didn't want her to overhear, "I can't say. Your husband made me swear."

The potato chip bag fell to the floor. "Is Harrison okay? The baby?"

"Yes, yes, everybody's okay."

"I don't care if you swore on a stack of Bibles. Tell me what's going on!"

"There was an incident. It did not take place on the premises. There was a confrontation with one of the bodyguards when he was taking the dog out for a walk."

"Jake—is he, all right?"

"Jake is fine. The situation is well in hand. The assailant was subdued and is in the process of being…interrogated. This may lead to a breakthrough, Erika. A *good* thing."

Extracting the full story from a security-obsessed agent would be impossible, she knew, but what was the harm in trying? "'A *good* thing'?" she parroted. "So why the long face?"

"I'm afraid you'll be distracted from our job tonight," Noah admitted. "Worrying about the incident, and, might I say, screwing up?"

"No, you might *not* say!" she fumed. She whisked up the potato chip bag as if it were a blight on the earth. "On the contrary, this will fire me up to do the best damn job anyone could possibly imagine, you included!" She slammed the potato chip bag into the trash basket. "So? Where's the menu?"

* * *

If she had been raring to go last night, after this morning's provocatively scanty account of the Manhattan incident, Erika had been more like a caged animal. Pacing the room until breakfast had been delivered. Scarfing it down as if acting in haste could speed up the passage of time. It was only after she'd thrown on her street clothes and was staring into the bathroom's magnifying mirror, about to pin back her bright red hair over one ear with a tortoiseshell clip, did she pause to consider her behavior. Noah had been right, hadn't he, to insist that she forfeit her identity in order to pull off her role as Sofie? It was well and good, allowing the Manhattan incident to stoke her motivation, but she must not let it devour her. *You've got the whole damn day to go*, she'd cautioned the bug-eyed redhead staring back at her in alarming 10x magnification. *Get it together!*

In the end it had been their afternoon in Sao Paulo's Ibirapuera Park that had set her back on track. It had been the perfect place to play a happily married pair of tourists, who just might be under surveillance. Such a variety of attractions to amble through and pause by in this seemingly endless green space—gardens and trails, lakes and playgrounds, monuments and museums. The Museum of Modern Art, ultra-sleek yet inviting, had been her favorite. In their tour of the galleries, they'd discovered a Brazilian artist new to them both: Anita Malfatti. Malfatti had flourished in the early twentieth century, the exhibit's accompanying pamphlet instructed, characterizing her style as "controversial expressionist." From Erika's perspective, Malfatti's style could not be so glibly pinpointed. One canvas seemed to reference Gauguin; another, Cezanne; still another; Rousseau. Yet all her paintings were singular creations, both in concept and execution. Erika planned to study the artist further—when she got *home*. Interesting, how she could wear the guise of Sofie, take Noah's arm with staged intimacy, yet at the same time, murmur beneath the surface as her truth self.

Later, right before they'd left the park to return to the hotel to have a bite to eat and talk over the scenarios Sandro might come up with that night, and what negotiations they themselves might propose, they'd sat on a bench overlooking a lake surrounded by a glorious variety of flowers, none of which Erika could name.

"I trust you completely," she'd said, out of the blue. "It's a good feeling. I trust myself with you, too, which is even better."

"Ah," Noah had answered, raising a brow. "How nice for you."

"It substantiates my faith in human nature, to be honest. Does that sound arch?"

"Absolutely," he'd replied, poker-faced.

Surely, if any of Sandro's henchmen had been spying on them at that moment, the couple's laughter would have erased all doubts concerning their authenticity.

Now, at 8:10 p.m., ten minutes past the appointed hour, they sat stiffly on the couch, each in his own world, waiting to hear from Sandro that he'd arrived at the hotel. "Maybe we should go down and meet him—what if he doesn't show up?" Erika finally voiced, hardly expecting Noah to respond to her divergent thoughts.

"He asked us to wait for his call," he answered, looking straight ahead. "Do you remember the password to our investment account and the steps required to transfer funds?"

"Yes. Why?"

"Going over my mental checklist. Your phone charged?"

"Yes, and I've got my charger." She patted her bag on the cushion between them. An instant later, a strident ring sounded from the hotel room landline.

Noah, nearer to the side table displaying the phone, grabbed the receiver. "Yes?" After a pause: "They're coming up? Oh, okay. Fine." He hung up; rose to his feet, Erika joining him, a beat, behind.

"Who's 'they'?" she asked, reaching for her bag and looping the strap over her shoulder.

"Sandro and his *assistants.* I don't like it."

"It's fine. Maybe one of them has to pee. At least we weren't stood up."

He shook his head. "I was afraid they'd take off if I said no."

"Their faces have been seen at the reception desk. They wouldn't dare try to bump us off."

"Not funny. I should have said no."

The debate ended at the sound of the doorbell.

Sandro and his escorts were formally dressed in black suits and ties. In contrast, Erika was casually attired in sneakers, jeans, white silk shirt and bomber-style denim jacket, and her partner was comparably clad in jeans and Lacoste polo. For the play's sake, Erika chose to interpret the fashion disparity as a means of identifying herself and Noah as upscale clients with no need to impress, while the Sandro sales team was, on the contrary, obligated to do so.

One of the escorts was bursting out of his suit, in the last stage of his transformation to The Incredible Hulk. The less burly one was marked with a disfiguring scar on one side of his face, fully—boldly?—displayed by his slicked-back hair style.

"We're not late, are we?" Sandro asked on entering. Without waiting for an answer, he introduced his maxi-me as Bruno Rizzo; the other, simply as "Jacques." He shifted his weight. "And this is Mr. and Mrs. Richtman. You two don't mind if we search you for weapons, do you? I assure you we'll be quite respectful."

There was no choice but to submit to Bruno's surprisingly genteel pat-down.

"Shall we go?" Noah prompted afterward, containing his impatience. "My wife and I have had a long day and—"

"Ibirapuera Park was glorious," Erika interjected. "We discovered an artist today, your Anita Malfatti. Do you have any of her works in your collection, Sandro?"

"Darling, I thought we'd narrowed the field to three or four artists this go-round. We mustn't spread ourselves thin. Shall we, gentlemen?" He took hold of Erika's elbow, intending to usher her out the door.

Sandro planted himself in front of the door, barring their way. "There's been a change of plans, I'm afraid. I've been advised by my insurance agent that for security reasons I must from now on allow only one client on the premises per visit. Either that, or engage more security guards, which I think my clients would find, well, inhospitable."

"I'm accompanying my wife and that's the end of it," Noah stated firmly. "I'm not having her going off with a couple of strangers, in some foreign country, no less."

Sandro gave a helpless shrug. "I'm told my insurance policy will not cover any damage or loss—any *attendant* damage or loss was the exact phrase—if more than one client is in attendance. These are the facts. I hope you can accept them."

"I can't." Noah turned to Erika. "I'm sorry to disappoint you, darling, but we'll have to make do with Sotheby's—not such a shabby choice, after all. Yes?"

"But I have my heart set on this...*darling*," Erika insisted, eyes narrowing. No way was this opportunity going to get away from her. Her adrenaline gland had pulled out all the stops; she could conquer the world.

"Bruce will keep you company," Sandro cajoled, "and we'll call you before any final decisions are made. How's that, Noah?"

"Unacceptable. I will not be kept hostage by some glorified bouncer—what is he, moonlighting?"

"Rudeness is uncalled for, Noah. Bruno is a trusted colleague. It goes without saying you're a passionate man. You'd take off after us like a bat out of hell if left to your own devices. Go have a drink at the bar lounge with Bruno."

"The hell I will. Besides, Sofie needs my assistance transferring funds."

"You may regret taking a pass on the bar lounge. They've booked a great bossa nova group tonight.

There was no doubt in Erika's mind—she suspected, in Noah's, too—that the looted artworks in Sandro's possession were uninsured. Sandro just wanted her to himself; figured he could best manipulate a spendthrift, politically compatible little woman without the interference of her art-indifferent husband. So be it. The mission had become her calling. She was not going to bail on it just because her chaperone was forced to. "I have the authority and capability of transferring funds out of our joint account, Noah. This is a once in a lifetime opportunity. I'm not going to miss it." She planted a kiss squarely on his lips to prevent him from answering. In the instant it took him to gather his wits, she bounded for the door. Sandro and Jacques stood aside as she flung it open, then they scooted out behind her. The door was slammed shut by Bruno, Noah, or a force of nature. What followed within was of secondary concern to her. She was on her way to making history. The crimes against the Eisenbergs were about to be brought to light, one way or another.

Chapter 25

J eff shoved his plastic-encased ID card in front of the perp's face, letting him catch the FBI reference, but concealing his name and serial number. "I can do whatever the fuck I want, but the gentleman who put a bullet in your leg? I'm a softie compared to him. The man wouldn't hesitate aiming a little higher, know what I mean? In self-defense, of course; he'd say you'd been waving a weapon at him; can't have that now, can we?" He returned the card to his pocket. "Up to now you've given us empty chatter. You ready to try again? Nod, if yes."

Harrison sat in his desk's side chair, which he'd turned to face the interrogation scene as if it were being played out on stage. At the sound of a ringtone, his first reaction was to feel embarrassed at having interrupted the performance; his second, to jump from his seat and slide the cell phone from his pocket as he headed for the door. Caller ID read "John Mitchell."

* * *

"Where'd you end up putting him?" John asked, with rising concern.

Harrison, out of hearing in the first-floor bathroom, nevertheless pressed the cellphone against his cheek, lips brushing the screen. "In my study," he said, his earlier deer-in-the-headlights monotone gone from his voice, although incredulity still hung about him like a swollen rain cloud. "Sitting in my easy chair. Tied up. Duct tape over his mouth, except to drink or when he's willing to talk. Jeffrey's bound up his thigh and has started him on antibiotics. He was going to get a scrip for them, but I had a batch of Keflex on hand from six months ago. Why I didn't throw them out when I discovered I was allergic, I don't know. How's his victim? You find out where they transported her?"

"Yeah, I called precinct headquarters and was told EMTs took her over to Presbyterian at 8:30 p.m.—what's that, about an hour and a half ago? Lucky girl. Bullet glanced off her shoulder causing a surface abrasion that required minor plastic surgery. They're keeping her a while longer to settle her nerves before sending her home. They thought she'd cracked her skull when they picked her up because she was out cold, but she'd only fainted. As I said, lucky."

"Thanks, John. You haven't said a word to anyone about the circumstances, right? Jeff's been drumming that into my head."

"Not a word said. I heard there was a shooting over on Madison and 78th. That's it. How's Erika's friend—in Connecticut, is it?"

Harrison felt the heat rise to his cheeks. "Not so good. Having a really bad reaction to the last chemo round. Erika says she's refusing further treatment."

"Sad. But at least you must be grateful Erika's missing all this. How's the baby and the rest of your household bearing up?"

"The nanny left before the incident, and Lucas and Grace have slept through it."

Mitchell grunted. "Nap can't last forever. When are your boys planning to get their captive the hell out of your house?"

"I don't know."

"You need me for anything, you call any time day or night, you hear?"

"Thanks," Harrison replied, feeling another pang of guilt at having to deceive John, the detective's expression of loyalty rubbing salt in the wound.

* * *

Jeff pulled Harrison aside the second he returned to the study. "I'm guessing that was your detective friend," he said, once he'd backed him out of the room. "What have you got for me?"

Harrison reported the condition of the shooting victim. Jeff made him swear to keep it to himself, and they returned to their places in the study.

"Got some bad news for you," Jeff advised his detainee with mock empathy. "The lady you shot is dead."

Harrison kept his surprise in check. "You piece of shit!" he muttered to back up Jeff's claim.

The man's body language was restricted; mouth taped. No reaction was visible in the eyes.

Jeff drew his folding chair closer so that their knees were touching. One bump to the wounded leg and there'd be pain. "You have a choice, Ronny—you don't mind if I call you Ronny, do you? Ronaldo's the name on your fake driver's license, after all. Oh and did I tell you the building's security camera got you on tape? Are you listening, Ronny?" He jabbed his knees against the man's.

A muffled howl detonated from behind taped lips.

"So, as I was saying, Ron, you have a choice. You can tell me everything, and I'll do my darndest to see that you get transported to a safe place. Or you can talk shit and I'll turn you over to the cops, unless your boss gets to your sorry ass first and dumps you off a bridge. You're already on record for one homicide. A couple more won't add to your problems. Be smart. If a tell-all will garner you some kindness, isn't it worth it?" Another knee-bump; another muffled protest. "Eh?"

Finally, a nod.

"Good boy." Jeff ripped off the tape. "You want some water? Soda?" He turned to Harrison. "You got rolls or something?"

"Croissants," Harrison replied, cringing at the elitism.

"Water," the man said. "You got a couple of aspirins?"

Jeff raised a hand. "First, let's test your good intentions. Why were you asked to come after my client? No beating around the bush, Ron. Spill."

"We got ahold of a computer—real estate broker's. You know, Charles Bloom?"

"No, I don't know."

Harrison shot up, ready to throw himself at the man.

"Sit down, Harrison. Go on, Ron."

"We checked out Bloom's computer, found an email to this guy right here—Wheatley." He cocked his head toward Harrison. "Bloom let on that he found a letter from some chess player, can't remember his name. Nothing much, but my boss thought it was important enough to get a fix on Wheatley. Sounded to him like Bloom looked up to the guy. Had him tracked to Paris and tailed him himself while Wheatley was there. Seemed to lose interest in him, so I was surprised when I got the call to pay him a visit."

"Back up, Ron. Your boss have a name?"

"No way. I'm done 'til I get my water and pills."

Screw the bodyguard: Harrison sprang to his feet. "Did you kill Charles Bloom?" he seethed, trying not to raise his voice and wake up Lucas and Grace.

"Fuck you, man. Pain killer first."

Chapter 26

Sandro ushered Erika into the back seat of a sedan parked just outside the hotel's entrance area and slid in after her. His sidekick took his place behind the wheel. "My car's in the shop," Sandro explained, "but Jacque's been kind enough to take us over to the site in his own vehicle." He shut the door.

Jacques waved a hand without turning around. "My pleasure, Mrs. Richtman." He started up the car.

"We can dispense with the formality. Sofie's good." What had Sandro just removed from his jacket pocket?

"Pull over for a moment," Sandro requested, once they'd left the hotel grounds. He shifted in his seat to face Erika after Jacques had done his bidding. "You understand the need for security," he politely suggested.

"Absolutely," she bravely acknowledged, even as she identified the object in his hand.

"May I?" he asked.

"Of course." She swiveled in her seat to make it easier for him to fit her with the blindfold. She could see it had a Velcro closure.

"There. Is it comfortable? Too tight? I can adjust it."

"It's fine."

"It won't be long." He patted her knee, lingering just long enough to cause a frisson of alarm, but not enough to demand they turn back.

* * *

The car pulled to a stop after what Erika estimated to be about forty minutes, the last fifteen of which had been over unpaved roads. She reached for the closure of the blindfold.

"Patience," Sandro cautioned, stopping her hands with his. "Only a moment or two to go." He opened the car door and slid out. "Here, let me help you. Watch your head."

She allowed him to guide her out the door onto solid ground—gravel, it felt like through the soles of her sneakers. She listened for sounds of life other than theirs. There were none.

With Sandro at one elbow, Jacques at the other, they walked straight ahead—thirty-two paces, Erika counted, clutching for clues, however senseless—before coming to a stop. Sandro let go of her elbow and after some shuffling about, he—she assumed it was he; who else?—produced a series of clinking and snapping sounds she interpreted as the release of multiple locks. A labored grunt followed, along with the groan of what could only be a massive door straining against its hinges. "Come now," Sandro bade, his hand on Erika's back, urging her forward. "Watch yourself; small step ahead." Jacque's vise-like grip tightened as she traversed it. "Good," Sandro praised. Another grunt of effort, and the door slowly swung shut. Erika's breath caught at the sound of the door's resounding thud, followed by the click of a deadbolt. *I'm at their mercy now.* She went for the blindfold to dispel the thought.

Again, Sandro stopped her. "A few more steps to achieve the optimal effect."

Another door was reached, not as eerily Gothic as the first, but close enough. It, too, was unlocked then shut with a resonant thump of finality.

"Lights on," Sandro announced. "Ah!" He undid the blindfold.

Speechless.

"Unhand the poor woman, Jacques."

First thought in her head: "I wish my husband could see this!" The enthusiasm acutely genuine because of course it was Harrison she imagined beside her. "What time is lift-off?" she asked, more in tune with her alias.

Sandro grinned. "It does indeed resemble a spaceship. I hadn't thought of that."

How could he not have? Erika wondered. They stood in an enormous, windowless cylinder; diameter maybe twenty feet. A spiral staircase led to a level—levels?—above, making it impossible to calculate the height of the structure. All surfaces and furnishings were uniformly white, from the continuous wall to the Thassos marble tile floor to the swivel armchairs circling its midpoint. The dozens of paintings were the only source of color in the sterile enclosure, yet it was not for that reason alone that made them come so thrillingly *alive.* They were mounted in such a way that made them appear to be floating in space, creating an effect all the more striking. Only on the double-take did she realize how it was achieved. Each canvas was framed in clearer-than-glass acrylic and suspended six inches or so from the wall by an acrylic bracket fitted with clamps gripping each of the canvas frame's sides. Against the clear frames, the clamps of the same material were practically invisible.

She stepped toward the center of the circle and turned one way, then another, surrounded by the spectacular exhibit. She could see where Sandro had devoted an area of the wall to painters she'd mentioned in his shop. There was the Gleizes, of course, the painting she'd originally emoted over. And look, there was a Robert Delaunay, with those fractured concentric circles she remembered from her study of the *Salon d'Automne* 1938 catalog. Could this possibly be the canvas entitled *Rythme no. 1*, mentioned by the *Gazette* reviewer as part of the Eisenberg exhibit he'd admired? Ah, there was a Georges Braque—had to be, with those familiar intersections of shapes and guitar motif! She would have to make a big play for that one, really get his entrepreneurial juices flowing! And beside it, a painting by Serge Ferat, reminiscent of another illustration in the catalog: Ferat's *Nature Morte.* The *Gazette* reviewer had noted seeing a similar work at the Eisenberg Gallery. The pitcher and glass were missing from this iteration, but the fruit, the free-floating leaves and most noticeably the open-mouthed fish in the foreground were in evidence. Her heart raced in anticipation—of discovery, of gratification.

Her knees buckled with the shame of it. Dazzled by the display, she had beheld it purely as art, when she should have been struck dumb by the fact that it was a bewitching presentation of *hostage* art. And when the concept of looted art finally seeped into consciousness, not to have thought of reparation, but of acclaim!

"I have more from that era in storage," Sandro said, stepping up beside her.

Like whores in the back room, waiting for you to sell them off? she railed inwardly, remorse energized to rage.

"Are you okay?"

"I'm fine," she said, recalibrating. "Overcome by it all." She shook her head in feigned awe. "And you say there's more in storage?"

"Tip of the iceberg," Sandro boasted, with a sweep of his hand.

Son-of-a-bitch, your stash includes more than the Eisenberg collection! Erika realized, kicking herself for not guessing, or at least hypothesizing about this, from the start. "Let's begin with the group on display," she suggested airily, managing to hang onto her Sofie demeanor despite the static from within. She pointed to the Gleizes, Delaunay, and Ferat canvases that had first caught her eye. "Can you remove them from the wall so I can take a closer—oh there, higher up, there's my Braque!"

"I have several more of his works in storage, but I did not want to overwhelm you. And I believe this is the most impressive of the lot."

"Please, take it down!"

"Of course—Jacques, would you?"

Jacque nodded, and, as Erika looked on in grudged fascination, seated himself in a specially designed chair and motored to the area under scrutiny with the aid of a hand device mounted on an armrest. Before proceeding further, he reviewed with Sandro and Erika the paintings to be retrieved. Using the hand control, he then raised the chair to the desired height by expanding the folding gate-like mechanism compressed beneath it. In this manner he was able to maneuver himself directly in front of each framed canvas, deftly free it from its perch and gently insert it into one of the padded compartments attached to the sides of the chair. "Four is the chair's maximum load," Sandro informed Erika. "I'm looking into an upgrade."

"Watch how you handle my Braque!" Erika cautioned, as Jacques was placing the precious painting into the last empty compartment.

"No worries, ma'am," Jacques replied. "Georges is safe with me."

About half a circumference away, a bank of acrylic easels stood waiting to receive the precious cargo. With all the selected paintings on board, Jacques motored to the site and placed each of them on an easel, while Erika and Sandro stood by, watching him like hawks.

"Why don't you sit and study them for a while," Sandro suggested to Erika, pointing to the swivel chair perfectly positioned for that enterprise.

"No, I'll never be able to sit still," Erika said, rooted in front of the Braque.

"Would you like me to fetch another of Braque's paintings?"

She shook her head. "It'll only cause confusion. I'll take your word that this is your most impressive example. Another time, perhaps. Picasso is on my bucket list as well. I have a pen- and-ink of his, but I don't consider it a major piece."

"I have several Picassos if you'd care to—"

"Sandro, don't make me nervous. Any more than what is before me, and I'll be overwhelmed." She sighed. "Maybe I will sit down, after all. Come sit beside me. I have a question."

Sandro happily obliged.

"I want to know if my Braque and his companions have been living in a suitable environment. That goes for the ones in storage. How are they maintained?"

"Excellent question. It shows you care. I have a sophisticated Heating Ventilation and Air Conditioning system that takes care of the environment throughout. The temperature is kept at seventy degrees; the humidity, at fifty percent. The system can be controlled on the premises as well as remotely, off-site. If a problem occurs—no system is perfect—alerts will be tripped both here and on my mobile device. I have a reliable service team to call on if any repairs over my pay grade are required." He reached over and laid his hand on her forearm. "Have I answered your question?"

"More than adequately." She felt, or imagined she felt, the heat of his hand through the sleeve of her denim jacket. Rather than swat it away and spoil their rapport, she rose to her feet. "Let's get down to business, Sandro. What is the asking price on each of these four paintings? Have you consulted with your expert? Obviously, my Braque will be the one we might come to blows over." She smiled amiably, both to invite him to smile along with her and to make up for the dismissive treatment she'd given his wayward hand.

He rose to stand beside her. Smiling, he said, "I've consulted with him, yes, and he's of the opinion that I needn't revise his most recent appraisals. When we're done here, we can discuss prices and terms in my office. How's that?"

"Good." For a few minutes she said nothing more, slowly, pacing back and forth in front of the displayed paintings, stopping multiple times before each, tarrying the longest before the Braque. "I'm undecided about the Ferat," she said at last. "My husband's not a great fan of fish, and this one has its mouth open, which he might find particularly offensive. May I text him a photo of the painting?"

"Unfortunately, not. I'm sure you understand."

"Then let's call him. I can describe the subject of the painting and also let him know how I'm doing. You know he was worried about my going off with strangers!"

They chuckled, sharing a moment of disingenuous amusement.

"That'll be fine," Sandro said. "We did say we'd keep in touch, after all." He took his cell phone out of his jacket pocket. "I'll call Bruno; have him put your husband on the line."

"When are you getting back here?" Noah barked the second Bruno handed him his phone. "I'm worried like hell about you!"

"We'll be wrapping up very soon, darling. What have you been doing? Did you go down to the bar?"

"Hell, no. What's happening there?"

"Noah, please. Don't treat me like a child. I wanted to ask if you'd mind my purchasing a Serge Ferat painting. It's—"

"A *what*?"

"A—never mind. It's a painting with a fish in the foreground, sweetheart. I wondered if you'd have objections."

"I don't know. If you love it, get it. If not, don't. If it were up to me, I'd take a pass. Just get back here. How are they treating you?"

"Just fine. I'll see you soon. Love you." She handed Sandro's phone back to him as Noah's undoubtedly clench-jawed "Love you, too" trailed off.

* * *

"I knew we'd come to loggerheads over the Braque," Erika declared, coming on strong as the cool business bitch she wasn't. "*Le Violon* went for over $8,000,000 at Sotheby's about five years ago, and the one on offer is close to its dimensions and vintage. Granted, the work has risen in value, but, come on, not by sixty percent." She and Sandro were holed up in his inner sanctum of an office, about a half city-block's walk through an underground tunnel from the main showroom. By all rights, she should have been feeling like the walls were closing in on her, trapping her for all time with a contemptible captor, but the synergy of her real and stage personae was lifting her to new heights of Derring-Do.

Sandro smiled, apparently enjoying the game of price-sparring, a form of foreplay, perhaps. He had just poured them each a fluted glass of Dom Perignon, and he took a sip from his. "As a matter of fact, my dear, the comparable *Paysage a la Ciotat* was sold for $15,845,000 at Sotheby's two years prior." He toasted the air and took another sip.

Erika pretended to take a sip of her own bubbly, but had no intention of clouding her mind with so much as a drop. "Ah, my friend, but you must consider the fact that Sotheby's transfers- of-ownership do not come with the restrictions that you impose, yes? To begin with, you've told me I must agree not to sell the paintings before 2045—not that I'm about to, but still! I do hope our celebration has not been premature," she impishly warned. "Are you willing to drop the price from $13,000,000?" They were sitting across from each other at his high-gloss white executive desk in a relatively small enclosure, room enough for the desk, a file cabinet and three chairs, including the two they occupied. Erika crossed her legs and waited for a reply.

Sandro punched in a series of numbers on his cell phone's calculator app. "I can drop to $11,400,000," he concluded.

She shook her head. "For the Gleizes and Delaunay—I've eliminated the Ferat—plus the Braque..." she paused for effect, only because the moment seemed to demand it. "... $9,500,000."

Sandro also opted for the dramatic pause. "9,750,000," he stated at last.

This time without losing a beat, Erika countered, "9,600,000. My final offer."

Sandro uttered a sigh of resignation, though the upward curve at the corners of his lips transmitted otherwise. "You drive a hard bargain, Sofie Richtman." He extended his hand. "Done."

They shook hands with the firmness reserved for momentous occasions and clinked glasses to memorialize it further.

Erika advanced right to the execution of the deal. "Before I transfer payment to the entity of your choice, I'd like to finalize the documents you'll be providing me with—authentication papers, provenance, proof of purchase, et cetera—and those I'll be required to sign. Shipping won't be an issue, since we'll be flying the paintings home by private jet. I trust they'll be packed with extreme care." With a wily grin she added, "You know I'll be back for my Picasso ...well, we'll see...so you'll want to stay in my good graces!"

"Trust me, your paintings will be handled with the utmost care, and we'll time their transferal with your departure."

"We'll make arrangements when we pick up my re-sized ring," Erika suggested. "And when I finally try on those chandelier earrings my husband seems to have developed a fixation on."

After a brief exchange of spousal humor at Noah's expense, the documents relating to their agreement were dealt with. The papers were in order—signed, witnessed (by Jacques), and delivered—in under forty-five minutes. Erika wondered if any of the names appearing on them—authenticator: Nathan Meredith, seller: Virtual Gallery, previous owner: Oliver Berman—were by any manner of means traceable. Greg Smith, the FBI, ICE and the like would have their work cut out for them, of that she was certain.

She stowed the manila envelope containing her share of the documents in her shoulder bag, and while she was there, removed her cell phone. The most critical stage of the mission was about to be launched.

Sandro, taking her lead, snapped up his cell phone from his desktop, where it had been sitting since he'd performed his calculations. "Do you need to charge your cell?" he thought to ask.

Her throat had started to pulse. She wondered if he'd noticed. "No, I'm good."

"You didn't drink more than a sip of your champagne, if that," he said, suddenly wary.

"I was too excited—more so, now. Weird?"

"I guess not really," he said, softening. "Let's get on with it then. Tell me exactly what you're about to do."

She willed the pulsing to stop. *Let him wait. Almost there.* "Well," she began, relative calm restored, "I'm about to call the number of our investment firm, preferred clients, line. I'll be instructed to punch in my username and password. That done, I'll ask to be connected to an agent for the purpose of wiring funds to an outside account. The agent will transmit a verification code to my cell phone and—"

"Wait," Sandro interrupted. "What you're describing is an ordinary wire transfer. It may take three hours, maybe *longer*, for me to see the funds in my account."

"Not so. When we were in your shop, we told you that we'd set up a potential transaction in advance. We were prepared to make a purchase at Sotheby's Sao Paulo, remember? There was a cap set on the withdrawal amount, understandably, but it was a generous one. Any amount higher, and the express option would have been negated. You'll see the funds in your account within minutes, I assure you."

Sandro's shoulders relaxed. "Thank you. I'm relieved. Go on, then."

"So, after I parrot back the verification code, I'll tell the agent the dollar amount I wish to transfer, and that I'm about to hand over the phone to one Sandro Andersson. You will then recite the routing number of…whatever terminus you choose, and the account number." She took a breath. "How does that sound?" *Pretty damn good!* she silently replied, pumping herself up.

"Fine, but would you be offended if I left the room for a moment while I recite my numbers?"

"Not at all. I'll begin, then." She punched in the Richmans' dummy investment firm's number. Her hand was trembling, not enough for a bystander to notice, but enough to make her proceed slowly and with deliberation. Just as well, since Noah had in no uncertain terms directed her to enter the password with at least a one-second interval between each letter and symbol.

When the steps leading up to Sandro's participation had been smoothly traversed, she handed her cell phone to him. He gave her a quick finger-in-the-air sign as if he were hailing a cab and left the office, closing the door behind him.

Being left in the room alone gave rise to a new stratagem. For it to be set in motion, the transference of funds must be completed. Not for the event in and of itself, but for the bonhomie it would bring Sandro.

"We wait," he said on reentry. He handed Erika her cell phone while continuing to gaze down at his own. "It's been a good two minutes," he grumbled, pushing shut the door with his free hand.

"Be patient," Erika advised, wondering what to do if the transfer should fail. Had she entered a wrong symbol, or the right one in the wrong place?

Another minute went by.

Grasping for straws, she suggested, "Why don't you try refreshing the page?"

"What?" he asked, distracted. His face suddenly lit up. "Never mind. The funds have been delivered!" He stared reverently at the screen a moment longer, like a groom at his new bride, then punched off the device. "Well, then."

"Excellent," Erika said, then waited a bit before mugging a regretful look. "I hope you won't be irritated with me, but…"

"Irritated? Whatever for?"

"Because I'm regretting not having added a Sonia Delaunay painting to my purchases. It would have paired so well with the one by her husband, Robert. Stupid!"

"Nonsense. I have two paintings by Sonia. Would you like to see them both?"

"Just one—to go with the new one by Robert. I trust you have impeccable taste. You choose the more substantial of the two for me. Are you sure it's not inconvenient? If the price is at all comparable to that of Robert's, I could easily get the amount authorized by American Express."

"No problem."

"Could you fetch it for me? It would give me a chance to at last unwind"—she raised her glass—"with my nice little glass of champagne."

Sandro laughed. "It must be flatter than water. Let me get another bottle."

She shook her head. "As long as the alcohol content has remained intact." She took a dainty sip. "It has."

"You're an amazing woman, you know that?"

"So, my husband tells me, but who can believe one's husband? Always an ulterior motive there." She shot him a winsome smile and took another token sip. *Go boldly and think happy thoughts of me!* she messaged.

After he shut the door behind him, she waited ten seconds without making her move; just in case he changed his mind and came charging back. Then she went at it, starting with the middle drawer of his desk. Here she found pens, printer ink cartridges, paper clips and other nonsense. Next, she tried the top right-side drawer, only to discover a heap of blank forms, mostly purchase and supply orders. The drawer below was more promising, or appeared to be. From beneath a stack of blank copy paper, she withdrew a worn leather-bound journal she naively expected to disclose the secrets of the realm, complete with names, dates and zip codes. Instead, she was nonplussed by multiple pages of numerical entities arranged in four distinct columns. Leafing through the pages, she made several perplexing but tantalizing observations: the number combinations in the first column were in declining order; in the second, they were repeated over and over—must have been ten to fifteen combinations in all. The third column also contained repetitions, but there were more of them. The last column was all over the place; no use mulling it over. Perhaps there was a key in the back of the journal. She checked—to no avail. She thought about whipping out her cell phone and snapping pics of random pages, but there would be no talking her way out of *that* definitive a misdeed if she were caught in flagrante. No, she would simply continue her manual search.

But first she must give credence to her wish to stay behind. Taking care not to spill a drop, she emptied her glass into the half-filled champagne bottle.

A cursory look into the remaining desk drawers revealed nothing of interest. She shoved the journal back where it came from and proceeded to the file cabinet. All but the top drawer was locked, but this did not discourage her. Even the most *un*-classified scrap of information could lead to a body of information that *was*. She pulled out the top drawer more fully and discovered it was filled with folders with unmarked tabs. She plucked out the first in the line-up and was about to have a look, when she heard the ominous click of the door handle.

How could this be? Sandro had been gone no more than three minutes!

"What the hell!" Jacques shouted, angry as the scar branding his face. He rushed at her, snatched the folder from her hand and flung it onto the desk. "What do you think you're doing?" He grabbed her by her shoulders, backed her against the nearest chair and threw her into it.

Terrified, the words would not come. She was prepared for a friendly kerfuffle with Sandro, whom she thought she'd won over, but not for an attack by his volatile assistant.

"Where is Mr. Andersson?" he growled. *What have you* done *with him?* implied in the utterance.

"He went..."

"*Yes?*" His hands clamped onto the arms of her chair, trapping her in it.

"...to get me a painting," she sputtered as he hovered over her, relishing her fear.

"He left you alone?" Leaning in; forehead touching hers; foul breath violating.

In reflexive defense, she thrust her palms against his chest and pushed with all her strength. "Get off me!"

"Bitch!" he seethed, punching her shoulder. He took a step back and pulled a gun from his belt.

"What are you going to do, shoot me?" she cried, her recklessness exploding along with her fear. Her shoulder throbbed with the pain from his blow. She refused to rub it; wouldn't give him the satisfaction.

"Put that gun away!" Sandro barked from the doorway, shifting the position of the plastic-encased painting tucked under his arm. "This woman is a valued client!"

"But she—"

"Put the damn thing away!"

Grumbling, Jacques did as he was told.

Sandro propped the painting against the desk and approached Erika.

"Thank you!" she fairly wept, wincing and rubbing her shoulder, now that it was the opportune time to do so.

"What went on here? Did Jacques hurt you?"

"I caught her rifling through your things!" Jacques protested.

Sandro's eyes widened. "*Sofie?*"

Erika gave a helpless shrug. "I admit it. I'm an incorrigible snoop."

"*Really?*"

"I was feeling daring, on a high from the sale and after the champagne, well, I couldn't help myself." She sighed. "Let's put it behind us. May I see the Delaunay, please?"

"You're kidding," Jacques scoffed. "That's it? Sandro, you haven't even heard what I came to tell you. Are you even interested?"

"Don't play games, Jacques. What is it?"

"The garage called us. The mechanic had your car on a lift and discovered someone had attached a tracking device to its underside. My money's on this bitch or her husband."

"Watch your mouth. This woman has just transferred close to ten million dollars into my account." He turned to Erika, expecting her to react.

"I'm speechless," she replied grandly, managing to hold on to her character role by a hair. "I've never been so insulted in my life."

"Your husband," Sandro pronounced. "To be honest, I had bad vibes about him from the start. He didn't seem to be—how do I put it?—one of *us*." Without waiting for her response, he turned back to Jacques. "Call Bruno. See what's going on at the Fasano."

"I tried reaching him. He's not answering."

"Why didn't you tell me this?"

"I'm telling you now."

"Get your ass over there and check it out. I'll stay here with Sofie." He glanced at Erika, not quite as benignly as before.

Jacques headed for the door.

"Wait," Sandro said, stopping Jacques in his tracks. "Before you go, hand me one of your guns."

Chapter 27

"Enough pampering," Jeff snapped. "You've had your water and aspirins. "Talk!"

Alias-Ron squirmed in his chair, as if the name he was being forced to give up was working its way up his intestines. Just as it looked like he was about to spit it out, his cell phone rang.

Jeff had already prepped Ron on how to handle an incoming call, but to be on the safe side, he snarled a reminder, "You give us away, you're dead." He grabbed the phone from his pants pocket, where he'd stowed it, swiped the call through, tapped on the speakerphone and held the device up to Ron's ear.

"Yeah," Ron opened.

"Done?" the caller answered, equally terse.

"Yeah, boss."

"Mess the place up?"

"Made it look like a robbery, yeah."

"Where are you now?"

"Headed for the airport," Ron recited, as per Jeff's instructions.

"I may have a problem here. Going to see to it now. You probably won't be needed, but don't lose touch. You hear me?"

"Yeah, boss."

The connection was terminated.

Jeff attempted to ID the caller, but to no avail, as expected. "Who was that?"

"My boss."

"That I got, smartass. What's his name and where's he at?"

"I know him as Jock. No last name. He may be in Brazil. I can't be sure."

"*Brazil?*" Harrison cried from his observation point, leaping from his chair. "*Where* in Brazil?"

Jeff shot a squint-eyed warning at him, but it was ignored. "*Where* in Brazil?" Harrison repeated, approaching the pair.

"I got this, buddy," Jeff cautioned, tight-lipped. He rose, placing himself between Harrison and the stoolie, just opening up.

"*Where?*" Harrison repeated, pressing against Jeff, trying to get at the guy.

"Come with me," Jeff ordered, like a bull, breathing hard, nostrils flaring.

Harrison could see the man meant business; must be for a good reason. He followed him out of the room, though every fiber in his body protested.

Jeff shut the door. "Listen carefully," he began, taking hold of Harrison's wrist. "To ensure your wife's safety, folks went to great lengths to see that she can in no way be connected to you. Don't screw it up now."

"But she *is* in danger!" Harrison came back, his anger compressed to a hoarse whisper.

"Maybe, maybe not. Either way, blowing her cover isn't going to help her situation."

Harrison wrenched his arm free. "Cold son-of-a-bitch!"

"Want me to crack up like you? Sorry, man, didn't mean that. Look, you're jumping to conclusions. Your wife's probably doing great, and we're wasting time. You want to come back in with me? Think you can control yourself?"

"Wait a second. Let me text my wife's number; see if the surrogate knows anything."

"Now we're talking. Go ahead."

Harrison made it quick: How are you doing? Friend okay? Love you. Answer came back with barely a pause: Friend a real trooper. I'm good, but miss you. Love back.

"All's well," Jeff unequivocally affirmed. "Let's head back."

Harrison followed him. By no means calm, his raging, fist-swinging fear had at least for the moment been tamed by Jeff's authoritative manner.

First question after recess: "Any idea, Ron, just *where* in Brazil this Jock fella of yours might be?"

The subject shrugged. "I dunno. Maybe Sao Paulo."

Harrison kept himself in check. Barely.

"Address?" Jeff continued.

"No. Some things he tells me, some things he doesn't."

"Uh-huh. And can you think of any distinguishing features of this guy—tattoos, scars, missing limbs?"

"Oh, yeah. Big scar one side of his face; think the left. Ear to mouth. No idea who did it to him."

An unearthly sound, low and gravelly, issued from Harrison's throat, as he remembered the man with just such a scar in Auvers-sur-Oise, first at the café reading a magazine—*pretending* to read, he now knew for sure—and then again, when he appeared at the scene of Harrison's departure from town. "Into the hall—now!" he commanded, impaling Jeff with a look that could kill before tearing out of the room.

"The man with the scar, he was in France!" he rasped, as Jeff shut the door behind him. "This is the man who tailed me! This is the man who may have killed Henri Pacquard, and for all I know, Charles Bloom! And now he's getting things done in Sao Paulo! I want to speak to Erika!" Choking from the effort to keep his voice down, he was forced to take a breath.

Jeff put his arm around Harrison's shoulders. "Don't lose it on me, okay? I'm going to call our contact now. The man who's watching over her. Believe me, he's the best."

I *should be there seeing she's okay—me!* he silently howled, the restraint it required constricting his throat even more than the words he'd spoken.

From his untraceable cell phone number, Jeff punched in Noah's equivalent, then waited with ever-heightening concern—Harrison could read it in his face—until the call went to voice message. He recited his code number followed by the words: "Call. Urgent."

"Be more specific!" Harrison angrily demanded. "Try the number again and say *why* it's urgent!"

"I'll try again, and I'll keep trying until I get through," Jeff promised.

Adding, more solemnly, "But I'm afraid I can't give anything away in a voice message."

Harrison's rage swooned into misery. "In case his phone has fallen into the wrong hands, you mean," he said, in wonder almost, the feeling so new to him. Their darling boy sleeping so near, yet he had never felt so alone in his life.

Chapter 28

Like a father to his beloved little trouble-maker, Sandro asked, "What am I going to do with you, Sofie?"

"How about no television for a week?" Erika glibly suggested over the roar of her terror. "Seriously, to say that I'm irritated would be putting it mildly."

Sandro shook his head. "I think you can understand the position I've been placed in, my dear."

"*What* position? I've just delivered $9,600,000 to your account. Are you uncomfortable with that amount? What portion would you like to refund?"

"Come now. You were poking around my things; caught in the act. I was willing to give you the benefit of the doubt, but then, to find on top of that, that a tracker had been attached to my car, I mean, really."

"Who decided that the tracker was attached yesterday? Why not last week? Last month? When was the last time you checked the underside of your car? Besides, what would have been our motivation? Think we were planning a heist?" *I'm sounding manic. Am I sounding manic?* Sandro's office space was closing in on her. Poe's cask of Amontillado came to mind. "Why are we sitting in this cramped space? Can we at least go back to the showroom while we're waiting to hear from Jacques?"

No vocal response from Sandro. Judging from the pensive frown, something had just occurred to him. The frown blossomed into an expression of concern; escalated to alarm. "What if the funds were not actually transferred?" He roved Erika's face like a mine detector, searching for signs of admission. "You can do almost anything with a computer these days, you hire the right hack."

There was only one way to dispel Sandro's growing suspicions, and that was to throw caution to the wind. "Isn't there some trusted individual you can call? Some real, flesh and blood person at the receiving end?" *The funds are there, please let them be there.*

"You mean…of *course!*" He whipped the cell phone from his pants pocket, briefly exposing Jacque's spare gun sticking out of his waistband. Within seconds he had punched in three series of characters, which, to all appearances, connected him to a voice, real or robotic. "Yes, I do," he responded to it, and waited. "Sandro Andersson," he stated after a finger-thrumming pause. He bit his lip in suppressed impatience. "I'm *fine*, thank you. May I have your name and agent ID number? Yes, I recognize your voice, I'm just being…my wife's good, and yours? *Good.* I'd like you to verify a deposit made to…yes, *there*…in the amount of $9,600,000…" A ring indicated a second caller was attempting connection. Sandro's tension ratcheted up a notch. "Emergency. Got to take this call. Be right back. You check the deposit. I need to be absolutely certain that the funds were delivered…what?"—forcing a laugh, "On your life, yes." He switched to the call waiting. "Well? What's going on? Slow down, I can't make out…" His jaw dropped. "Don't fucking move! Stay on the line, I'll be right back. Hear me? Do not hang up!" He glared at Erika and reconnected to the first caller. "Hello? Hello? I thought I lost you. What'd you find?"

The funds are there, please let them be there.

Sandro's demeanor improved, but from Erika's point of view, not nearly enough. "I'm relieved, yes," he said. "Thank you. Sorry to cut you off, but… you take care, too." He punched back to the line still open. "Jacques? Now talk—*clearly!*"

Erika tried to make out the gist of the exchange from Sandro's squawked exclamations and severed thoughts, but her picture was as disjointed as what came out of his mouth. She was thoroughly confused when the call was ended, and his dumbfounded expression offered no clues.

"What's happening?" she ventured, counting on the wire confirmation to stand her in good stead.

Her question set him in motion: the laptop sitting on his desk was skidded around to face him; its lid popped open. Its screen was in Erika's view, but he either didn't realize this or was too agitated to care. He tapped in a series of letters in rapid succession and the screen came to life. Another tapped-in command and a panel of six black squares filled the screen. One more play on the keys and the squares lit up, revealing the zones surveilled by security cameras, each with place, date and time of day printed in its top left corner. "They're fucking *here!*" Sandro shouted, either to the universe or in answer to Erika's question.

In the square marked "southeast perimeter," a van and three official-looking vehicles were parked, no individuals within view. Erika was torn between this image and the one staring at her from the zone marked "storage," where an unknown quantity of what appeared to be framed canvases were stacked in tiered cubbyholes of varying dimensions.

"What's your husband up to?" Sandro snarled. "You must know!"

On screen, the doors of all vehicles simultaneously opened.

"My husband?" Erika cried, mustering indignity. "Whatever is going on here, why do you assume Noah is the instigator?"

From the front of the van two uniformed officers emerged.

"Why do I *assume?* Sandro mimicked. "The hotel valet told Jacques that he saw your husband and another man—got to be Bruno—climb into the back of a van. For sure, that wasn't *Bruno's* idea!" He eyed her narrowly and pulled out his weapon; without pointing it at her, allowed her to reflect on the possibility.

Appearing on the screen: a grainy image of Noah assisting Bruno, in handcuffs, step from the back of the van, followed by a trio of rifle-bearing officers. From each of the accompanying vehicles, two more armed officers.

Erika considered the most logical sequence of events: Noah confronts Bruno, overpowering him; forces him to divulge Sandro's location; calls in the troops to aid in her rescue. Bottom line, Noah was in command of his situation; he would agree she should try to gain a foothold in hers. "Is it possible Noah could have been planning something?" she asked, opting for a wide-eyed look of bafflement. "I mean, he *has* been acting strange lately, so over-the-top doting. I thought he might be having an affair, but… "—imploring look—"do you *think*…?"

On screen, the group slowly moved forward.

Sandro sprang from his chair as if into action, then froze. "What have they got on me? Not a damn thing!" Looking Erika in the eye, he stated evenly, "I'm going with my gut about this. I think your husband's trying to pull something over on us. There's nothing to hide. A sale was made; papers in order." He stuffed the gun back in his waistband. "We're going to stay level-headed. Otherwise, we give them an excuse to restrain us, or worse." He cocked his head toward the door. "Now, let's go greet the bastards."

Tricking herself into a state of intrepidness, she followed him out of the office.

* * *

Bruno, looking like an overfed saint, cuffed hands outstretched, beseeching. "I had no choice, boss. If I didn't unlock the door, they were going to blow it up."

Sandro, in the process of being patted down by one of the officers—authoritatively introduced as "Federal Police!"—paid him no attention. "It was legally acquired," he griped, as the officer relieved him of the weapon.

Noah had begun to snap photos of the showroom's spectacular display with his cell phone camera. The discolored swelling under his right eye supported the scenario Erika had come up with in a moment of desperation.

"Boss, do you know where Jacques went?" Bruno asked, still with that air of supplication.

"No. Keep your mouth shut." Addressing the officer nearest at hand, Sandro pontificated, "There is absolutely no earthly justification for your presence here, sir. Mrs. Richtman and I"—delicate tap on her arm—"have just been conducting business and—"

"Sandro Andersson," the officer recited, as if his "on" button had been punched, "You are under arrest for the possession of stolen property." He went on to mechanically read Sandro his rights, including the right to remain silent, which went unheeded.

As were Sandro's protestations. Sandro, along with his cohort, were dispatched to the awaiting van with hardly a sign of resistance other than Sandro's bellowed promise to bring the scourge of his lawyers upon all his enemies. Erika, whose knowledge of such rifle-toting scenes had come only from action movies, was more than grateful to have been spared the horror of having had a gun held to her head at some point in the proceedings.

"Where *are* we, anyway?" she asked Noah, after the skirmish was over, and all who remained on site were the two of them plus three of the federal officers. "As you probably guessed, I was blindfolded."

Noah snapped another photo and turned to her. "Sorry not to have filled you in. By the looks of it, the complex includes an abandoned cement factory and lime quarries. Domes, silos, sheds, structures of all sizes and shapes, all linked in some way or other. Looks like a Rube Goldberg setup. Don't know who owns the property, but guaranteed, we will."

"Of *course—la fabrica!*" Erika exclaimed.

"Who?"

"A run-down World War cement factory, purchased in the 1970s by a Spanish architect, Ricardo Bofill, who repurposed the site as his home-office. A magnificent place. I should have thought of it!" She spread her arms in an all-inclusive embrace. "The silo, here, contained the limestone. The tunnels—'galleries,' they called them—where they stockpiled gravel, crushed stone and the like—'aggregates,' the fancy name."

"*Tunnels?*"

"Yes! Come with me, I'll show you!" With one of the officers tagging along, the other two remaining on guard in the showroom, Erika led the way through the tunnel passageway to Sandro's office, undisturbed since she and Sandro had occupied it.

* * *

"Where's all this going to be carted off to?" Erika asked Noah, as their accompanying officer documented the contents of Sandro's office, corroborating his notes with photographs taken with his cell phone. "All the papers—and the artworks! To what *country*?"

Noah, snapping photos himself, presently of the journal of inscrutable codes Erika had earlier puzzled over, switched focus to her. "Maybe it all remains on site, for the time being," he said. "The HVAC system seems to be in good working order, so why not catalog the art right here? Same for the office material. Forensic art experts, art authenticators, tech teams—they can do their research on the premises. What'll be challenging is searching the stolen art database for possible matches and facilitating restoration. Who'll coordinate the project? The three countries who invested in it: Brazil, France, Israel. A committee with representatives from all three will thrash it out. Unraveling the criminal activity and rounding up the suspects, that'll take another village altogether."

"But who'll *watch* over all this precious art?" Erika persisted, her maternal instincts agitating on their behalf.

"Don't worry, they'll be safe," Noah assured her, handing the journal to the officer. "See that nothing happens to this," he cautioned in an aside. To Erika: "The Brazilian officers will be reinforced by military agents assigned by the Israeli and French embassies located in Sao Paulo. They're on their way as we speak. With locksmiths to re-secure the site; you can count on it."

Did he just flash her an avuncular grin? No matter. "Let me show you something," she said, going for Sandro's computer.

"Don't touch!" the officer warned.

"It's okay," Noah interceded, patting the air in an "easy, boy" gesture. "My *wife's* not going to delete anything." He gave Erika a knowing nod, which she took to be a reminder to stick with her alias. She supposed that he'd called for help from Brazil's feds only because the need for them had outweighed the risk, but that he still worried there may be a bad apple among them.

Undeterred by the guard, Erika punched a random letter on the computer's keyboard and prayed the device hadn't automatically shut down after Sandro had abandoned it. "There!" she cried, as the screen awakened to the panel of areas under surveillance. "You see that? The room marked 'storage'?"

The men gawked at it. "Where the hell *are* you?" Noah asked the image, stepping back, as if distance would bring it into perspective.

No answer forthcoming, Erika grabbed her bag and she and the men exited the office.

Barely ten yards farther down the tunnel—"gallery," as Erika had explained—a second portal had been hacked out of the concrete wall. A keypad door-latch required the entry of a passcode. "If this leads to the storage area, it's where Sandro went to fetch my Sonia Delaunay," Erika informed her companions. "He left on his computer; maybe he left this door unlocked, expecting I'd be wanting to see more."

"No more suspense," Noah said, pressing down on the latch.

As it released, an audible sigh issued from each of them.

Another inarticulate, but more stunning response when Noah, after fumbling for a wall switch, flipped it on.

A moment of silences, each in their own.

More cavernous than its appearance on screen, the windowless space was lined with multiple tiers of partitioned quadrangles of assorted dimensions. The units contained art works framed in acrylic, like those on display in the showroom. Here and there, in the less crowded chambers, a canvas was partially visible. It was impossible to estimate how many creations were held captive in this unholy place, and for Erika, too soon to try.

Approaching one of the sectioned walls, she discovered that at the base of each unit, a series of numbers divided by slashes was printed on what appeared to be a dry-erase magnetic strip. Somewhere, she knew, there was an inventory spreadsheet that deciphered it all, but right now their amassed *presence* was all that mattered.

She slid an arbitrary canvas from a unit within reach. It was a relatively small piece, no more than eight by ten inches: a cluster of poppies in thickly laid vibrant red oil paint. In the bottom right corner, printed in black paint that had been applied with a very thin brush, it read: "M. Nussbaum 1902."

Who was this artist? Did he or she survive the Holocaust? Was there a husband or wife? Children? She thought of the little girl in the red dress from the film *Schindler's List*. The painting, like the anonymous little girl, was one in a crowd of singularities.

Erika wanted to say aloud to this lovely outcropping of M's soul, *you're free now*, but when she played it in her head it sounded corny, because, of course, it *was* corny, so she kept it to herself.

Chapter 29

Harrison activated the speakerphone so Madame D could connect the group gathered in his den. "I've been wanting to reach out to you, Denise, but for safety's sake—*your* safety—I was advised not to. Someone was on my tail in Paris, you see, and—"

"I figured as much," Madame D cut in. "An unsavory couple came by to interrogate me about you."

"Oh, no! They didn't hurt you, did they?"

"Not after I told them to be brief, I had a lunch date with General de Gaulle at noon—who's that laughing?"

Harrison introduced Denise to her audience: Erika, John Mitchell, Greg Smith and Sandro's father, Miguel Andersson, "who's flown all the way from Sao Paulo to be with us." Each thanked her for the major role she'd played in unearthing the lost art works, which turned out to have included a lot more than what remained of the Jules Eisenberg collection.

"It's only been a week since Erika returned from Brazil," Harrison informed Madame D, "and the consensus is, it's too early to risk exposure on video conferencing. I predict it won't be long, though, when we can get together on Zoom."

"Count me out," Madame D replied. "At my age the *word* zoom gives me palpitations. Tell me, what do you people mean when you say your find included a lot more than the Eisenberg collection?"

"It's a many-layered story," Greg, as principal cataloguer felt it his place to explain. "Briefly, the find represents a conglomerate of nine individuals or entities in possession of stolen art. All with the same political persuasion."

"A consortium," Madame D suggested.

"Exactly. I can tell you how it's structured, if you like."

"Save the details. I can guess its mission—to disseminate hate. That's all I care to hear. Perhaps another time…Harrison, I want to hang up now. Let me know when the thugs are behind bars."

"You're upset," Harrison said, kicking himself for stating the obvious. "I want to thank you again, Denise, for leading the way, despite how painful it was for you. We'll speak soon, yes? Erika and I will be collaborating on an article for *Art News*, and of course we won't allow it to go to print without your approval."

"Fine, fine. Will you and your family be visiting me as you promised?"

"Yes, we will, Denise!" Erika chimed in. "We hope to see you in Paris sometime this fall."

"With your little one? I have no family, you know. Perhaps I can be his doting great-godmother, if you'll allow it."

Erika's heart went out to this woman she'd never met. "We'd love that," she replied without hesitation, glancing at Harrison for the confirmation she knew was guaranteed.

"We'd be honored," he assured Denise, before letting her go.

The group returned to their huddle, without a word pulling their chairs into a tighter circle, like troops closing ranks. Earlier, Grace had wheeled in a cart-load of brunch fare, but nothing had been touched, nothing requested. Greg and Miguel were catching flights in a couple of hours, and John had taken on a stakeout job requiring his presence even sooner. Time was precious. Any rambling unrelated to the Sao Paulo operation, a waste of it. Without having to be asked, Greg launched into his recap.

"First, I want to apologize for"—air quotes—"'Noah's' absence. He shows his face only when necessary." He turned to Erika. "You must have sensed how closely he guards his anonymity. He wanted me to make it clear, though, how much he valued your input. He knows he treated you like a subordinate at the start, but by the end of the operation, he felt quite the turnabout." Addressing the group, he continued, "Please understand, everything Noah's learned about this case, he's relayed to me. Let me begin by fleshing out the description of what Harrison's friend, Madame D, aptly dubbed a consortium. This is the brainchild of Sandro Andersson and"—waving off Miguel's recoil—"was begun shortly after his grandfather's death in 2015. It started small, with a loose partnership between Sandro and one of his neo-Nazi friends from the local cell. With his talent for salesmanship and his wife's meticulous bookkeeping, Sandro assumed the role of CEO, or the equivalent. Through networking and word-of-mouth, the group gradually added new members; its reach became international.

"This is how it works. The members pay Sandro a fee for storage in his ideal facility, the abandoned cement factory, purchased in 2003 by his father for the purpose of housing the balance of his Eisenberg loot, and upgraded in 2015 by Sandro himself. Each time a sale is made, Sandro receives a modest commission and a more generous tithing is distributed to White Nationalist groups for a variety of propaganda services, from recruitment to political media storms, campaign ads to military training. Questions?"

"What became of the nearly $10,000,000 I helped wire to Sandro's account?" Erika asked. The process was never fully explained to me."

A smile accompanied Greg's helpless shrug. "Well, Noah *fully explained* the process to me, but I'm still at a loss, except for the end result: the recovery of the funds. Apparently, the set of symbols posing as your password provided our master hacker transit to a bird's-eye view of the account Sandro would subsequently access."

"Like a sort of wormhole?" Erika asked, on shaky ground.

"Yes, I guess that's it exactly!" Greg marveled.

"Good, because I have no idea what I'm talking about. The funds were recovered, you said."

Greg nodded. "The account's in a bank in Malta. Malta is looking to enhance its standing in the world. Freezing the account and citing legal justification for distributing the funds to the countries of origin is a step in that direction." He scanned the circle. "Any other questions?"

John raised his hand and without waiting for a nod from the self-appointed moderator, asked, "Was all the hoarded art confiscated from the Jews?"

"All but two of the consortium members were in possession of art looted from the Jews during the 1930s and 40s. The two exceptions are Nazi sympathizers whose heists were of private collectors in recent times. The committee in charge of the find is in the process of restoring works to their original owners or heirs. As for the Eisenberg collection, the works that the Anderssons had not already sold will be released to the Louvre, with the exception of the Hans Arp and Max Ernst paintings"—to Erika:—"matching the descriptions you sent me, from that chess master of yours. Those two will be going to the Tel Aviv Museum of Art. By the way, I should tell you, Erika, that the lookalikes you referenced from the 1938 *Salon d'Automne* catalog helped pinpoint at least a couple of Eisenberg pieces, namely a Leopold Survage and one by Andre Lhote. As for the little domestic scene by Pieter de Hooch? It was found hanging in Sandro's living room; its new home: the Rijksmuseum in Amsterdam.

"Among those organizations trying to track down the art already sold by the consortium and those works still in its inventory are the Art Loss Register, of which I'm a board member, the International Committee of the Red Cross and the World Jewish Restitution Organization." To Erika, again: "You know, the journal you found in Sandro's office. the one with the columns of puzzling codes? Well, the committee was given the *key* to those codes. The columns represent a record of sales transactions: dates of sales, works of art, sellers, buyers. What a godsend!"

The more Greg elaborated, the more questions he provoked. "You said 'the committee was given the key to the codes,'" Erika quoted. "Just *who* gave it up? Sandro didn't exactly strike me as the accommodating type."

Another squirm from Miguel. What was up with him? Erika wondered. She had heard that he had been the prime mover in breaking open the case and rounding up the felons—including the vanished Jacques. Why was he so uncomfortable about it?

"Kudos to Miguel for his indispensable help!" Greg praised, lifting an imaginary glass in the gesture of a toast.

"Please!" Miguel objected, shifting around his compact figure, as if there was something on the seat he was trying to avoid.

Greg wagged his finger at him. "Modesty is not in order here," he chided, missing the anguish in Miguel's voice. "You're right, Erika, Sandro was not at all cooperative. He gave nothing away. A kind of loyalty, I suppose. No, it was his wife, Alena, the consortium's bookkeeper-accountant and on the side, treasurer of the local neo-Nazi cell, who became our informer. And why? Because of her father-in-law, Miguel." He paused to reap the full effect of audience anticipation—only Miguel, reacting in reverse, shaking his head with the regularity of a metronome: no, no, no, no.

Greg leaned forward in his seat to deliver his punchline. "It was Miguel who *turned* her."

"I'm not getting the dynamic here," John said. "What are you saying?"

Greg surveyed Miguel as a doctor views his patient. "It's not that Miguel *preached* at Alena," he said. "It was hearing him go on about his clients, the injustices they'd suffered, sometimes watching him in court, pleading a case. It was through example, she said—his everyday life, not sermonizing, that transformed her. The final—*lesson,* she called it—was overhearing her husband on the phone asking Jacques if he'd eliminated the problem. The problem, it became clear, was called Henri Pacquard."

"Henri is dead because of *me*!" Miguel cried. "If I hadn't told Sandro I'd found my half-brother through that genetic service, he would be alive!"

Erika glanced across at Harrison, sitting opposite her, knowing what he was thinking. Until they were alone, she could only address the issue indirectly. "Miguel," she said, "you couldn't have guessed that the exposure of your family history would be a threat to your son's business. How could you have known that the business was founded on art seized by your father, a Nazi officer? I wouldn't be surprised to learn that your father had in fact shared with your son the secret of his identity, along with his bloody storming of the Eisenberg Gallery. Please. Don't blame yourself!"

"I suspected," Miguel said, almost inaudibly. "I suspected my father wasn't who he said he was. I should have kept my mouth shut."

Greg shook his head. "There must be a Confucius saying on the perils of second-guessing oneself. Really, Miguel. Stick to what's real. Your redeemed daughter-in-law gave up the company books and all the dirt she had on its associates. She choreographed a sting to draw Jacques and his partner, Daphne out of hiding, ostensibly to hand over the balance of cash owed them by Sandro. Were it not for Alena, that twosome might have been gone for good."

"Miguel, why are you here?" John suddenly put forth. "I don't mean to be blunt, but if this is so painful for you…"

Outcry from Erika: "John!"

Miguel raised his hand. "It's all right. The question is a good one. I've asked it myself. I don't know. I wanted to—*had* to—be in your company. Yours, Erika. And Harrison's, and Greg's, and yours, too, John. I had to hear you talk about what happened. I had to hear firsthand what crimes were committed by my father and after him, my son. I had to hear you talk about the victims of those crimes, about all that was suffered. I had to…had to…"

"Bear witness?" Erika gently suggested.

"Yes," he said.

John, maybe because he was pressed for time, was more abrupt than usual. "Where are these bandits going to be tried?" he asked, without waiting for the ambient emotion to subside. "France?"

Greg shook his head. "Noah said he doubted the extradition treaty would be implemented. He spoke to an aide to Brazil's President Jair Bolsonaro. The aide thought the visibility of such a trial—*trials*—would be good for the president's image; garner some support from the liberals, which has been slipping lately."

"You're forgetting Charles Bloom!" Harrison bristled. His murderer will stand trial in the United States!"

"That's a given," Greg assured him, taken aback. "That man, alias Ronaldo, will not be leaving the country."

"I've spoken to the detective in charge," John offered, his tone suddenly placating. "You remember, Tim Riley?"

"What do you think?" Harrison grumbled. "I haven't forgotten a second of that day."

"So, he explained how your bodyguard, Jeffrey Crow, hauled the bum's ass over to headquarters kicking and screaming—well, not so much kicking, what with his leg wound—insisting he hadn't meant to kill Bloom, only put him out of commission so he couldn't give chase. No sympathy from the detective or the judge. Ron's being held without bail."

"Thank you," Harrison replied grudgingly; John's attitude too damn lighthearted for him. "At least Gary Kessler's been let off the hook," he added sardonically.

"For Charles's murder, yes. Not for the assault on his wife, Jodie."

"No, of course not," Harrison quietly agreed, all at once contrite. Why was he lashing out at others, when the only one in the room he should be railing at was himself?

"Anyone care to have something to eat, or at least to drink?" Erika inquired, desperate to break Harrison's train of thought.

Still, there were no takers.

* * *

"I know what you're thinking," Harrison said as he sank into the couch beside Erika in their lobby, guests just now departed. They adjusted themselves to sit face to face. "You don't have to say it."

"What? That I hate seeing you beat yourself up?"

A wan smile. "Yes, that."

"I thought you'd gotten over feeling guilty about Chuck's death."

"Miguel awakened it."

"But you saw that Miguel's guilt over his half-brother's murder was unfounded. Surely you saw that."

"Guilt doesn't respond to logic."

"Put that in a fortune cookie," she said, throwing up her hands in frustration.

"But it might respond to nonsense," he returned more cheerfully, lacing his finger with hers and guiding their hands down to waist level. After a pause, he asked, "Do you miss it—the adventurous life?"

"You mean the stirring experience of playing undercover agent?"

"I mean the adventure in general."

"I'm glad it ended with a success, and for that reason, I wouldn't have missed it for the world. But do I *miss* it?"

Was that actually an expectant look? "Oh, Harrison, are you serious?" She drew their connected hands out to the sides, stretching their arms to encompass everything here and now. *"This* is my adventure!"

* * *

The baby carriage stood in the hallway, waiting to receive its passenger. Just inside the kitchen, Erika was holding Lucas, his head resting on her shoulder. Harrison had Jake by the leash: not tugging, but given the snorts, wanting to.

Grace was at the counter, cutting up carrots. When she turned to them, she broke out into a grin, less reserved than her usual. "Every time I see you, Miss Erika, there's a little shock," she said. "It looks really pretty, the red hair, it's only that I'm not used to it."

"I've got an appointment with the hairdresser tomorrow morning," Erika said. "I'll be my old self by lunchtime. By the way, Kate will be coming back tomorrow from her time away. Mid-day was my understanding."

Grace acknowledged the information with a hard-fought smile. "Aha."

"We'll be out for a while," Erika said. "Taking a walk in the park." Her mind raced ahead, imagining the sun, the breeze, her family close; Jake part of it.

"With renewed warmth, Grace answered, "Have a good one!" and returned to her carrots. Her gray hair was tucked up in a little bun, and as she lowered her eyes to attend to the task, a few strands came loose and fell in front of her face. She brushed them away with the back of the hand that held the knife, and whether it was the angle formed by the knife and her forearm, the starched white collar of her uniform against the delicate lines of her neck, or some other element in Erika's frame of vision, the image proclaimed itself a portrait, a precious work of art to be gone in a flash. On the brink of action, Erika shut her eyes and traced the portrait in memory so it would live a while longer.

A Note From the Author

While I was looking to jump-start the third book in the series, I came across a quote by painter and chess enthusiast, Marcel Duchamp: "Not all artists are chess players, but all chess players are artists." I thought about conjuring up a brain-teaser centered on one of his chess-board paintings, but decided instead to search for a contemporaneous chess player to see if I could find or invent a connection between them to get the ball rolling.

I didn't have to look far before finding an apt quote from World Chess Champion Alexander Alekhine: "Chess for me is not a game, but an art." When I discovered first, that he had played on team France with Duchamp in the 1933 Chess Olympiad and second, that his death in 1946 remains a cold case to this day, I realized I had found my inspiration for weaving another mystery prompted, but not dominated, by history.

Among numerous magazine and newspaper articles on World Ward II, research included: Pablo Moran's A. Alekhine: Agony of a Chess Genius (McFarland and Co., Inc., 1989); Catalog of the Salon d'Automne, 1938: Albert Gleizes et ses amis; The Circle of Montparnasse: Jewish Artists in Paris 1905-1945 by Kenneth E. Silver and Romy Golan (Universe Books, 1985); The Apparently Marginal Activities of Marcel Duchamp by Elena Filipovic (The MIT Press, 2016).

My gratitude to Jeanne Thornton for her helpful initial read. For their astute and meticulous edits, many thanks to Verena Rose and Shawn Reilly Simmons of Level Best Books. They are a joy to work with. Together with Harriette Sackler, they form the mainstay of a publishing company that doubles as extended family. Thanks to Marcia Rosen for her skills in public relations.

Eternal thanks to my father for his incisive intellect and earthy humor, and for telling me bedtime stories—endless, but never enough. And to my mother, for bravely countering her prudish heart with liberated pronouncements, unwittingly teaching me the conflicts of feminism. You two are entwined forever in living memory.

About the Author

Claudia Riess, a Vassar graduate, has worked in the editorial departments of *The New Yorker* and Holt, Rinehart and Winston, and has edited several art history monographs.

You can connect with me on:
- https://claudiariessbooks.com
- https://twitter.com/ClaudiaRiess
- https://www.facebook.com/ClaudiaRiessBooks

Also by Claudia Riess

The Art History Mysteries

False Light

Scholarly sleuths Erika Shawn, art magazine editor, and Harrison Wheatley, art history professor, tackle another brain teaser. This time they aim to crack the long-undeciphered code of prankish art forger, Eric Hebborn (Drawn to Trouble, Edinburgh 1991), and reveal the whereabouts of a number of his brilliant counterfeits.

Stolen Light

STOLEN LIGHT is a suspense novel set in the art world and involving murder, the Italian Renaissance, and the Cuban Revolution, as well as a love story.

In 1958 in Cuba, the main house of sugar plantation owner, American-born WILLIAM DELANEY is vandalized by a band of Castro's rebels, who seize Delaney's art collection to raise money for weapons. Delaney is killed during the incident, and his pregnant wife, fearing for her safety and that of her unborn child, flees Cuba, never to look back.

Now, over fifty years later, Delaney's wife dies, and his daughter, motivated by the desire to "know" the father whose life was kept shrouded in secrecy by his wife, is determined to restore what she can of his legacy.